A DECLARATION OF LOVE

Madeline scanned the garden in case any of the children had followed them. But no one was there. "Harry."

She turned so she was facing him, gazed up into his eyes, and took his hands in hers. "I have something to ask you." This was much harder than she thought it would be. Should she kiss him first? Yet, if he did not love her, what would he think? "I love you. Do you—"

"Desperately."

Suddenly she was in his arms, and he was kissing her.

Madeline quickly overcame her surprise, threw her arms around his neck, and kissed him back. His tongue touched her lips, she opened them, allowing him to explore her mouth. This was as good as she had been told it would be. She copied what he was doing and melted against him. And to think there was more to come . . .

The HUSBAND LIST

ELLA QUINN

ZEBRA BOOKS
Kensington Publishing Corp.
www.kensingtonbooks.com

ZEBRA BOOKS are published by

Kensington Publishing Corp.
119 West 40th Street
New York, NY 10018

All Kensington titles, imprints, and distributed lines are available at special quantity discounts for bulk purchases for sales promotion, premiums, fund-raising, and educational or institutional use.

Special book excerpts or customized printings can also be created to fit specific needs. For details, write or phone the office of the Kensington Sales Manager: Kensington Publishing Corp., 119 West 40th Street, New York, NY 10018. Attn. Sales Department. Phone: 1-800-221-2647.

First printing: July 2023
ISBN-13: 978-1-4201-5448-1
ISBN-13: 978-1-4201-5449-8 (eBook)

10 9 8 7 6 5 4 3 2 1

Printed in the United States of America

To my granddaughters Josephine and Vivienne.
May you find your purpose in life and the happiness
you are seeking.

ACKNOWLEDGMENTS

Carina Chachacha and Eileen Dreyer for Wilhelm and for Eileen's idea of adding the Irish name. And Aletta We for Comet. Thanks to my mother-in-law Margaret Baker for helping me with Bobby's story. I think he'll be back.

CHAPTER ONE

Lady Madeline Vivers stared at the list of requirements for husbands she and her sisters-by-marriage, Lady Alice Carpenter and Lady Eleanor Carpenter, had written and, remembering her mother's pointed remarks about expecting her next daughter to marry appropriately, sighed. As tempted as she was, Madeline would not add her mother's demand that the gentleman be a peer or an heir to a peer. If either of her sisters saw it, there would be a conversation she did not wish to have. If she did not marry "appropriately," what Mama could and would do was engage in strong hysterics. And after witnessing what her second eldest sister, Augusta, had gone through, Madeline would be happy to keep the peace, as it were. Aside from that, the chances she would be introduced to anyone her mother thought unsuitable were unlikely. All the gentlemen presented to her and her sisters had met Mama's requirements. What Madeline really must do was be clear, at least in her own mind, what she wanted from a marriage. Charlotte, Madeline's sister by marriage, and Louisa, Madeline's eldest sister, were as involved in politics as their husbands. Augusta and her husband had no interest in politics but were involved in academic studies. Grace, Madeline's brother Matt's wife (ergo Madeline's sister-in-law), were the linchpins of the family. They kept all the members, both by marriage and by new births, and her husband and their dependents together and moving forward. To Madeline's mind, that was just as important as politics. Then again, the combined Vivers-Carpenter family was quite large and, at times, took up a great deal of time and energy. The only problem was that she must first *meet* a gentleman who was interested in her and vice versa to be able to do anything. And there she went, off on a tangent again, before she even addressed what she wanted personally from marriage.

A knock sounded on the door, and Madeline sighed again. Her question would not be answered today. "Come."

Roberts, the footman assigned to her, stepped into the room. "My ladies, I have been sent to tell you that Lady Merton and her brother, Mr. Henry Stern, are in the morning room."

Well, that was much more interesting than what Madeline was currently doing. She knew Dotty well, but her older brother was almost a stranger. "Thank you, Roberts."

Alice suddenly looked up from her book. "We will be there directly."

The footman bowed. "Yes, my lady."

Madeline followed her sister out of the room trying to remember what Harry Stern looked like. She had a vague memory of a gentleman a few years older than Dotty, but that was all.

"I wonder what he is doing in Town?" Alice asked.

Now that she mentioned it, Madeline thought it was odd as well. He was a barrister in Bristol. "Especially because he did not even go to Dotty's house for Easter."

Ignoring any sense of decorum, they rushed out of the door and down the stairs, and almost literally ran into Eleanor.

She moved quickly out of their way. "What is going on?"

"Dotty is here, and she brought her brother Henry," Alice said. "We have not seen him in years."

Eleanor frowned. "Was he not home for Christmas last year?"

"Only for a day, and *we* did not see him," Alice huffed.

Eleanor joined them as they went to the morning room. "What is he doing in Town?"

"*That* is what we are going to find out." Madeline almost rolled her eyes. That was the question they all had. "I think I have only met him once, and for a very short time."

Eleanor glanced into the parlors they were passing. "Where are they?"

"In the morning room," Alice said over her shoulder.

Madeline took Eleanor's hand and hurried after Alice. Until they were twelve, when Matt married Grace, Eleanor and Alice's elder sister, the twins had grown up not far from Dotty and her family.

They reached the morning room, and a gentleman rose. One could immediately see the resemblance to his sister. Both had black curls and green eyes, but while Dotty was feminine, he was decidedly masculine. His nose was straighter, and his jaw was almost square, with a dent in it.

When he smiled, his eyes smiled too. "You grew up."

Alice gave him her haughty look. "And, apparently, you did not."

"She has you there." Dotty's lips twitched. "This is the problem with knowing someone since he or she was a child."

"Or from birth." Harry bowed. "Please forgive me, my lady."

Alice inclined her head and dipped a shallow curtsey. "It is good to see you again."

"It is good to see you too." He glanced at Eleanor. "How have you been?"

Eleanor stepped forward and hugged him. "We are all

fine." She waved her hand for Madeline to come forward. "Do you remember our sister, Lady Madeline Vivers?"

She met his gaze as he obviously tried to place her, then shook his head and smiled slightly. "I remember seeing a dark-haired girl who was always sheltered between you and Alice." Harry bowed. "My lady, it is a pleasure to meet you again."

It was such an accurate description, Madeline had to laugh. "I am pleased to meet you again as well."

She, Alice, and Eleanor hugged Dotty. The twins sat on the sofa across from Dotty and her brother, but Madeline took a chair closer to Harry.

Eleanor turned her attention to him. "What are you doing in Town? As I recall, you were always too busy to bother coming."

His eyes started to sparkle, and he grinned widely. "Meet the newest Member of Parliament for Bittleborough."

An MP! Madeline waited for the twins to discover how that had been accomplished.

"Excellent!" Eleanor clapped her hands together. "How did it happen?"

"Grandmamma spoke with my uncle and convinced him that even if he had not liked Mama and Papa's marriage, he should not hold me back. She reminded him of the success I've had as a barrister." Harry slid a look at his sister. "Dotty also spoke with him." He grinned again. "She, you know, is in his good graces for having married to fit her station." Harry shrugged. "When the seat came open, he supported me for it."

His grandmother was the Dowager Duchess of Bristol, and his uncle was the duke.

"Papa, as you are aware, does not support the idea of peers selecting candidates for Parliament," Dotty said. "But he did believe that Harry was the best man for the position, and was prepared to campaign for him if our uncle had not supported him."

Papa was Sir Henry Stern. He supported the Radical Party, which believed in the abolishment of the peerage and universal suffrage, among other things. Would that put Harry at odds with his father? "Will you do as the duke tells you to do?"

Harry's smile dimmed slightly. "Naturally, when I believe it is the right thing to do. Merton has invited me to his circle's next luncheon so that I may discuss with them which ideas that group has been supporting."

It was a good thing that the Duke of Bristol could not replace Harry when he did not agree with him. Although, Madeline supposed, he could make reelection more difficult.

"But until then," Dotty said, "he has come to ask you three to stand up with him at Almack's."

"Excellent." Eleanor glanced at Alice and Madeline. "That makes three sets for which we have partners."

Now, at least, Madeline would have a partner for one set that did not include her sisters' suitors. Then another thought occurred to her. If he was attending Almack's, did that mean he was also looking for a wife? That thought prompted her next one. She had just met a gentleman who did not meet her mother's requirements. Madeline gave herself a mental shake. He was handsome and obviously intelligent, but that did not mean she was attracted to him.

The tea tray arrived, and Eleanor poured. "Have you attended any of the sessions yet?"

Harry took a cup from Eleanor and handed Lady Madeline one as well. Keeping busy was the only thing that was stopping him from staring at her. Even the word "beautiful" did not seem to be sufficient. And how should he address her? Should he call her Lady Madeline? After all, he had not been raised around her, as he had been with the twins and the rest of the Carpenter family. On the other hand, the

Viverses and Carpenters had made themselves into one family and expected to be treated as such. "Yes. I've been fortunate that I didn't have to immediately look for lodgings and could start attending directly." He grimaced slightly. "I will have to find a place soon, though. As much as I enjoy staying with Merton and Dotty, it is only temporary."

Madeline tilted her head, and her nicely shaped brows wrinkled. "I must suppose that you have the freedom to come and go as you wish."

"Oh, yes. But that is not the issue. I do not feel as if I should take over their house by inviting colleagues to meet there." Should he tell her he was also looking for a wife? His grandmother had explained how helpful it would be for him to have one. Then again, that might make things awkward. He didn't know her as well as he did the twins, and he was almost certain he didn't want to know her in the same manner. The twins were like younger sisters to him.

"I understand." She took a sip of tea. "Hopefully, you will soon find something to your taste."

"I share your wish. Merton has his secretary helping me." As she bit into a lemon biscuit, and when her tongue peeked out to catch a crumb, Harry became distracted by the deep pink of her lips. "Have you done anything interesting yet?"

Madeline shook her head. "The Season is just starting. We have developed the habit of riding early in the morning. It is the only time we can get in a good gallop."

That was interesting. "What time do you go?"

She swallowed the last of her biscuit and delicately wiped her hands on the serviette. "As it is just getting light."

That would give him enough time to ride and arrive on time at Parliament. And to get to know her. He glanced at the twins and Dotty. They were involved in their own conversation and not paying any attention at all to him and Lady Madeline. When she'd first entered the parlor, he was stunned at how lovely she was. Chestnut curls framed her perfectly oval face, and those eyes. They shone like polished lapis. Then he'd reminded himself that she was the same age as the twins, and for the life of him, he could not think of them as of an age to wed. Still, he was attracted to Madeline in a way he hadn't been to another lady, and he'd met plenty of them in Bristol. Riding would be a perfect way to learn more about her.

Nothing ventured, nothing gained. "Would you mind if I joined you?"

Her brows rose slightly. "Not at all. Two other gentlemen ride with us when they can rise in time." That last part was said in a rather disgusted tone. "You are welcome to join us."

Harry could see there would be no shirkers for Lady Madeline. "Thank you." Dotty was putting on her gloves. "Should I call you Lady Madeline or Madeline?"

His question seemed to surprise her. "You do not use rank when you address Alice and Eleanor. We are sisters. Therefore, there is no reason to use rank with me."

Except, perhaps, in a formal setting such as a ball or Almack's. Still, the lack of formality would make his interactions with her easier. "Thank you." Dotty rose and he stood. "I shall see you in the morning."

Madeline gave him a curious look. "I look forward to it."

His sister hugged the twins and Madeline. "Thank you for tea. We are making the rounds today." Dotty gave them a conspiratorial look. "Grandmamma has ordered me to marry him off."

Eleanor and Alice grinned wickedly, and Alice said, "You are welcome to join us in making your come out."

Harry almost groaned. Leave it to Alice to make that comparison, and for his sister to tell everyone he was looking for a wife.

"Were you not on the Town before?" Eleanor frowned, as if she was trying to remember.

"For a short time after university." Harry remembered his

father saying that he'd not sponsor him to run wild and gamble in Town. "I was here for a month or so." Just long enough to understand what his father meant. "But I already had an offer with a prestigious firm of barristers in Bristol and had to take up my position."

"I am sure you will be fine," Madeline said. "Dotty and Merton will be able to advise you."

He bowed to her. "You are correct, of course. I am relying on them."

"Come along." His sister looped her arm though his. "We have a great many people to see today."

The girls—he stopped himself; they were not girls any longer—the *ladies* accompanied them to the door, and he bowed to the three of them, but he found his gaze lingering on Madeline. "I enjoyed tea and spending some time with you."

"I am sure we will see you soon," Alice said.

"You will." Harry wasn't going to mention riding with them. "We'll see you later."

He helped Dotty into her high-perch phaeton and went around to the other side to climb in. "Is there any reason you decided to announce I was seeking a spouse?"

She patted his hand. "My dear brother, I rarely do anything without a reason."

It was starting to occur to him that he didn't know his sister as well as he thought he did. "Would you mind telling me what it was?"

She nodded to the groom to release the horses, and they started down the street and turned out of Berkeley Square. "You are not a peer and will probably never be one. You do not have a significant fortune, and you are a Member of Parliament." That explained his situation succinctly. "Ergo, you must find a lady who is willing to accept you, not your status." She glanced at him. "Your assets are that you are very good-looking, you are the grandson and nephew of a duke, and you are personable. You also have expectations."

He nodded, more to himself than to her, as she was paying attention to her horses. "I can afford some of the elegancies of life, but not all of them."

"Precisely," Dotty said in a tone of approval. "That also means you do not have to marry an heiress."

He hadn't thought of that. "Thus making me more acceptable than not."

She flashed him a quick smile. "It is better to separate the wheat from the chaff early on. The young ladies and their parents will know what they can expect from you."

"In other words, I am eligible, but not highly eligible." He shouldn't feel disgruntled about that, but he did. "At least I won't have to wonder if a lady is interested in me or my status."

Dotty pulled up to a house in Green Street. "I hope not. Although you might have to deal with parents who want their daughter to make a more advantageous marriage."

Such as what his parents had suffered. His mother's stubbornness and his father's steadiness were the only reason they were able to wed at all. Well, his grandmother had helped, but without those traits, they would have married others. He needed to find a lady as stubborn as his mother. "Where are we?"

"We are visiting Lady Turley." Dotty waited while a footman went to the pair's heads. "She is a friend of Henrietta. I am hoping Lady Exeter will be present as well."

Another footman came out and helped Dotty descend, and Harry jumped down and offered her his arm. "How many times will we do this?"

She gave him a slight smile. "As many times as I think necessary. Dom will introduce you to the gentlemen. You need friends and connections."

They were ushered into the morning room, containing four ladies and several small children.

"Harry!" His sister Henrietta jumped up from the floor, where she'd been helping an older baby stack blocks. "Dotty, why did you not tell me you were showing him around?"

"I just got into Town late yesterday," Harry said, not wanting any conflict between his sisters.

Dotty kissed Henrietta's cheek. "I sent a note around this morning, but you probably have not got to your correspondence. Did Grandmamma tell you he must wed?"

"Yes." Henrietta nodded. "I am enlisting Dorie and Adeline's help." She turned to glance at the fourth lady in the room. "Augusta will not be any help at all. She and Phinn do not care about most entertainments."

A lady who looked a great deal like Madeline shrugged her shoulders. "Phinn and I are scholars. That leaves us only enough time to spend with our families and friends."

Another lady laughed. "Which is exactly the way they like it."

The ends of Augusta's lips curled up. It wasn't until then that he made the connection. "You're Matt Worthington's sister?"

Rising from the floor, she held out her hand. "I am. Otherwise known as Augusta Carter-Woods, or Lady Phinn. I think you are the only member of your family I have not at least seen before."

"Good Lord," Henrietta said. "My manners have deserted me. Dorie, Adeline, allow me to present my eldest brother, Mr. Henry Stern. Harry, Dorie is the Marchioness of Exeter and Adeline is Viscountess Turley."

Lady Exeter and Lady Turley had each inclined their heads when introduced. "Ladies, it is a pleasure to meet you."

"We have heard a great deal about you," Lady Exeter said. "Congratulations on your seat in the Commons."

"Yes, indeed." Lady Turley smiled. "Congratulations. We look forward to helping you this Season."

"Thank you." This Season was going to be much busier than he'd thought. He'd need morning rides just to keep his head clear, and, hopefully, find a wife.

CHAPTER TWO

The sky was just beginning to lighten when Madeline opened her eyes. Would Harry Stern join them, or had he simply been making conversation? She would soon know.

Harper, her lady's maid, had already laid out Madeline's riding habit. She scrambled out of bed and went behind the screen to make her ablutions. By the time she was finished, her maid had a piece of toast and a cup of chocolate waiting.

"Your sisters are up as well," Harper said. "The horses will be waiting by the time you are ready."

"Perfect." A year ago, Grace had hired maids for Madeline and her sisters in preparation for their come out. She could not have been happier with Harper. The woman always knew exactly what to do. Madeline dressed and finished her toast and chocolate as her maid put her hair up in a knot and affixed a small hat.

She went into the corridor, where Alice and Eleanor joined her as she made her way to the hall and outside to their horses. "What a pretty day this will be."

Their grooms helped them mount their horses, but only one groom would accompany them on their ride. Today it was Madeline's groom, Finnigan. Like many of their male servants, he had been in the army. He walked with a limp, but the damage to his leg did not stop him from riding.

She and her sisters rode out of Berkeley Square and onto Mount Street. They turned onto Park Street, and Harry Stern hailed them. "Good morning. It looks to be a fine day."

He had an excellent seat and really was handsome, as was his dark bay horse. She glanced down and noticed the stallion had matching white socks.

Alice peered past him down the street. "It looks like Lord Montagu and Lord St. Albans could not rise in time to join us."

Harry brought his horse up beside Madeline, which required Alice to move to ride next to Eleanor. For years Madeline had ridden between them. "Their loss."

She grinned. "Not everyone finds it easy to get up early."

They rode through the gate, and he glanced at her. "My whole family are early risers. I don't think I'd know how to sleep in if I wanted to."

"Everyone in our house is up before times as well." It probably had to do with younger children and animals. "We usually ride either to the large oak tree or the Serpentine."

"Lead on, my lady." He grinned.

Rose, Madeline's Cleveland Bay mare, was ready for a gallop, and took off at her signal. Despite her slight lead, Harry reached the tree at the same time she did. "Your stallion is fast."

He patted the horse's neck. "He likes to run."

She tried to place the breed but could not. "What is he?"

"A Trakehner." Harry stroked the stallion's neck. "My brother-in-law, Nate Fotherby, has one. His was the second one I'd seen. When I had to retire my old horse, I bought Willy. His formal name is Wilhelm Cóiméad, to show his Irish and Prussian heritage." His gaze shifted to her horse. "Your mare is quick as well. Is she a Cleveland?"

"She is." She smiled just thinking about her mare. "Her name is Rose." Madeline glanced at her sisters. "Eleanor and Alice decided to use classical names, but Rose just seemed to fit her."

"It's a pretty name for a pretty lady." Harry scanned the Park. "Where do we go from here? Another gallop?"

"Yes. To the Serpentine." He had the same energy his sisters Dotty and Henrietta had. Even when he was sitting still, he seemed to be in motion. "Are you ready?"

"Always." He grinned.

Madeline liked his ready smile. As they urged their horses into a canter, she had the feeling he could have ridden ahead but chose to keep pace with her. Once again, she admired his seat. Yet, his horsemanship was to be expected. His sisters rode well too.

When they reached the spot at the Serpentine they used, her sisters were already there, and they were joined by Henrietta, Dorie Exeter, and Georgiana Turley. They all exchanged greetings.

"Harry," his sister said, "Nate sent a note to you regarding an early meeting today of the committee discussing bankruptcy. He found out about it quite by accident and believes it was set at a time when most of the younger MPs on the committee would not be able to attend."

Harry's brows drew together as he frowned. "What time is the meeting being held?"

"At eight o'clock."

"Two hours before the session begins. I was told meetings are normally held after the sessions."

Madeline looked at her brooch watch. "It is six thirty. If you are to dress and break your fast, you should leave now."

"Thank you." He flashed her a smile. "Will you ride with me in the Park at five?"

"Yes. I would be happy to." She was glad to see him taking his duties seriously, but had she really expected anything different from a member of his family?

"I will see you then." He raced his horse toward the gate. He really did have a superb seat.

She glanced at the others. "Does anyone else want another gallop before we leave?"

By unanimous consent, they spread out and gave their horses their heads to the old oak tree. Alice got there just ahead of the rest of them, and they turned their horses toward the gate.

Madeline was about to take her traditional place between the twins when Henrietta came up beside her. "It is wonderful having Harry in Town. Ever since he moved to Bristol, we have not seen him much at all." She pulled a face. "Although I suppose the Commons will keep him busy."

Madeline wondered how much free time he would have. "It sounds like it already is. The Lords keep Matt and the others occupied."

Henrietta nodded thoughtfully. "It does, but do you not think it is different with members of the Commons? After all, they receive a salary and are elected to office."

"You have a point." Peers got their positions merely by being born, and some did not even bother to attend the Lords. "Will you be at Almack's tomorrow evening?"

"Oh, yes." She laughed. "I have been told we are all expected to be present."

Madeline wanted to roll her eyes. Matt had probably insisted. "All hands on deck?"

"Exactly." They rode through the gate, and Henrietta accompanied Adeline toward Green Street.

Alice moved her horse to one side, allowing Madeline to ride between the twins.

"What do you think of Harry?" Eleanor asked.

"I think he's much nicer now that he's older," Alice said. "Madeline?" Alice raised her brows.

"Of course I did not know him before, but I like him. He

seems very steady." Her mother's words played in her head.
And handsome, but that did not need to be said.

"That is faint praise," Eleanor commented.

"I did not mean it to be. It is just that I do not know him
very well." The problem was that she might want to be
better acquainted with him. Madeline stopped her mare in
front of Worthington House and dismounted.

"That is true," Alice murmured as she joined Madeline.
"Although you will have a chance to."

She would, but she did not want her sisters to get any
ideas. "He will probably invite you to ride as well. After all,
he has just arrived in Town and does not know many ladies."

"I doubt it." Eleanor shook her head as they entered the
hall. "That would be like taking Henrietta or Dotty out."

Alice nodded.

"It does not matter why he invited me. I intend to enjoy
myself. This is the first time *I* have been asked to ride in the
Park." Eleanor had accompanied the Marquis of Montagu
and Alice had refused to ride with the Earl of St Albans. Still,
having a pleasant time was all Madeline intended to do.

Harry had breathed a sigh of relief and given a quick
thought of thanks to Fotherby for the information, and to
Dotty and Merton for offering to house him. Although Harry
had left early, it had taken some time to find the dratted committee room. As it was, he arrived as the other members
were gathering. "Good morning." He had learned not to
use the address of "gentleman" when in mixed company—
meaning members of the gentry and members with other
statuses—and inclined his head. "I'm Henry Stern for Bittleborough."

"Ah, Mr. Stern." An older man with white hair acknowl-
edged him. "Michael Taylor, Durham. We are pleased to
have you join us. New blood is always important."

A glance at some of the others showed not all agreed. "I am pleased I was able to be present."

One man's brows drew together. "Stern?" Harry nodded. "Are you any relation to Sir Henry Stern?"

"I am, sir. He is my father."

"Very good. Very good indeed. William Smith is my name, Norwich. You father and I maintain a correspondence. I will tell him I have met you."

"I think we all know Mr. Stern by now," a man in a brown jacket and waistcoat said. "Let us get down to business."

Smith immediately proposed changing the bankruptcy laws to include those other than merchants. A position with which Harry agreed, and was immediately voted down. Well, he knew reform was not going to be easy. He hadn't known how swiftly it could be temporarily defeated.

The meeting continued until shortly before the regular session began. He was joined by Mr. Taylor as he walked to the room. "Mr. Stern, I would be pleased to invite you to dinner on Tuesday next."

There was no reason to decline, and it would be useful to come to know other MPs. "I am happy to accept."

"Where should I have my wife direct the invitation?"

Harry had been trying to avoid mentioning Merton's name, but until he had his own lodgings, there was nothing for it. "I am currently staying at my sister's home, Merton House in Grosvenor Square."

The other man's lips turned up slightly. "Ah, you are from *that* Stern family. My wife will be very glad to make your acquaintance."

That sounded as if Taylor might have another reason to ask Harry to dine with him. He just wished he knew what it was. On the other hand, Dotty might know. "I look forward to meeting her."

He arrived at Merton House just in time to order one of the curricles readied and drive to Worthington House. The door opened as he reached it. He stepped in, and Madeline appeared at the top of the stairs. He'd heard of the phrase to have one's breath taken away, but he'd never thought it would happen to him. She was stunning. Her yellow carriage gown seemed to float around her, but he couldn't see how it could as the material was not muslin. It must have something to do with the way she held herself. As before, curls framed her face, this time drawing attention to her dark pink lips. Her hat was trimmed with a sparing array of flowers.

He held out his hand. "You look like spring."

Placing her fingers in his, she smiled. "Thank you. Spring is one of my favorite seasons."

Harry turned them toward the door. "The others being?"

"Oh, summer, autumn, and winter, of course." She laughed lightly. "There is something to like in all the seasons. Which is your favorite?"

"That is a very good question. I don't believe I have ever given it much thought. I suppose it would be a contest between summer and winter." He handed her into the curricle. "In summer I was out of school, and Christmas is in winter." Harry climbed up and took the ribbons. "Although, now that I think about it, spring seems to have a great deal to recommend it."

Madeline's cheeks turned a pretty shade of pink. "You might find autumn does as well."

He started the horses. "This is my first trip around the Park. I'll need your advice."

Her lapis-blue eyes widened, and he struggled to keep his eyes on the pair. "Depending on how many are in Town, it could be quite crowded. We might do well to make one trip around the carriage way."

Harry wondered how long that would take, and if he could keep her with him longer. "Have you ever been to Gunter's?"

"Yes, of course." Her lips broadened into a wide smile.

"Excellent. Is it worth a visit?"

"Definitely. What a shame you have never gone. The ices are wonderful!"

Aha. He'd found something she liked. "If you do not mind, could we go after our ride today?"

Madeline clapped her hands together. "That would be perfect!"

She was perfect. He grinned at her. "That is exactly what we'll do."

By the time they had eaten their ices, he would've been able to discover which balls and other entertainments she was attending.

CHAPTER THREE

Madeline could almost taste the ices. How sad Harry had never had them. They entered the gates and, as she feared, it was crowded. "It will take us an age to get around."

He gave her a surprised look. "Not if everyone keeps going."

She almost laughed, but that would be unkind. His sisters ought to have warned him. "But that is the problem. We will be stopped a hundred times or more by people we know."

"People *you* know." His tone reminded her of dry sand. "You forget, I am acquainted with almost no one."

He must truly think he would be an unknown. Madeline would be shocked if that was the case. "I think you will be surprised. You did attend school and university."

"I didn't know anyone in Bristol when I first arrived," he mumbled.

"London is not Bristol." It was an interesting and an almost delightful feeling to be more experienced than he was in something so commonplace. She almost added, "We shall see." But that would sound too much like the older matrons.

"That is true." He grimaced as a blond-haired gentleman on a gray gelding rode up and nodded to her. "Stern, is that you? I haven't seen you since I left Oxford."

"Salforth." Harry's clipped tone indicated he was not happy to see the gentleman. "I'm sorry to hear about your father."

The duke's smile disappeared. "As am I. He was a grand old gentleman."

"Old" was the key word. The former duke had not married until he was past his fiftieth year. Madeline waited until Harry remembered the introduction.

He glanced at her and pulled a face. "My lady, allow me to introduce the Duke of Salforth. Harry turned to the duke. "Salforth, this is Lady Madeline Vivers."

The duke's brows came together as he bowed. "Lady Madeline, a pleasure."

Why did he look as if he did not approve? "It is nice to meet you, your grace. I too am sorry about your father."

"We must be off." Harry picked up the ribbons before the duke could respond. "I'm with m'sister at Merton House for the time being."

"Will I see you at White's?" the duke asked.

"Not unless I want to be shot by my own father," Harry retorted. "We must be going."

The duke doffed his hat. "My lady."

Her mother passed in a carriage and gave a little wiggle of her fingers. Madeline was suddenly glad she had seen the duke. Although to her he seemed a little strange. Almost as if he did not approve of Harry.

He started them forward again and groaned. "So much for me not being acquainted with anyone in Town. You were right."

Two gentlemen approached the carriage on foot. One of medium height, with medium brown hair and brown eyes. The other was taller than his friend, with dark brown hair and medium blue eyes.

"I say, Stern," the shorter gentleman said. "You here?"

"As you see." Harry inclined his head. "Hereford, Bury, I haven't seen you for a while."

"Well, if you hadn't buried"—he poked the taller man's side with his elbow—"yourself in Bristol, was it? You would have."

The gentlemen glanced at her, and Harry said, "My lady, may I present the Earl of Hereford and Viscount Bury?"

Madeline inclined her head. "Gentlemen, it is nice to meet you."

"Hereford, Bury, Lady Madeline Vivers."

"I say, Lady Madeline"—Lord Hereford stepped in front of Lord Bury, who returned the favor, and the argument began.

But before she heard much of it, Harry had started the horses again. "I'm not stopping the next time. They can all go to the devil."

Madeline couldn't hold back her laughter. She did manage to make sure it was not loud enough to cause anyone to look. "You have an interesting group of friends."

"School." His voice was full of loathing.

"Look!" She pointed her chin at the gate. "We're almost there."

"Henry Stern!"

His shoulders slumped. "Dotty, I didn't know you'd be here."

"I do not know what you think you are doing, but you cannot race your—or rather my—carriage through the Park during the Grand Strut." She glanced at Madeline. "Are you crying?"

She had taken out her handkerchief because she was laughing so hard. "No. Not at all. I am laughing. He has such—such . . ." Madeline searched for a good description of his friends. "School chums."

"She met Salforth, Hereford, and Bury. I'm just glad Ashford wasn't with them."

Dotty's brows inched up to her hairline. "In that case, do not look now. Shall I waylay him while you make your escape?"

"Yes, please." He blew her a kiss. "Thank you."

She narrowed her eyes. "No racing out of the Park."

He kept to a sedate pace as Madeline worked on recovering her countenance. "Do you count them as friends or acquaintances?"

Harry slid her a look. "The more accurate description is the one you used, school chums. They were jolly good fun, and I needed some of that. I always knew I had to have a profession, and I'd disappoint my father if my grades weren't to his standards."

Knowing how high Sir Henry's standards were, she understood the burden he'd carried. "They flittered their way through school while you had to actually study."

"Indeed." He gave her a rueful smile. "There were times I desperately needed the diversions they came up with. Salforth is a real friend, or was." He shrugged. "We drifted apart after we left Oxford. Then he took offense after I won a case against him."

It was a shame to allow possibly helpful friendships to fade away. "Would it not be worth it to rekindle your acquaintance? It is possible he might come over to your way of thinking."

Harry pulled up to Gunter's and signaled to one of the many servers dashing back and forth from the carriages and to others eating outside. "I could try. I should have Dotty invite him to dine with us one evening."

"Or invite him to Brooks's for dinner?" Madeline wondered how set the duke's political ideas were. After all, others had been brought around.

"Yes." He gave her a look of approval. "That would give me an opportunity to quickly discover if he's interested in the same issues I am." He took one of her hands in his. "Thank you."

Heat rushed into her face at his compliment. "It is nothing. I like to help people."

Harry liked that Madeline was so good at helping.

The server arrived and rattled off the ices of the day, and he had to release her hand.

She addressed the server. "They all sound so interesting, but chocolate is always my favorite."

"One chocolate." He turned to Harry. "Sir?"

"You mentioned Parmesan. I'd like to have that."

"I'll be back in a moment." The man went running off.

"You live dangerously," Madeline said.

He stifled his laugh. He could see it would always be chocolate for her. "I've had ices, but never a Parmesan ice. Is eating different things part of the pleasure in coming here?"

Her eyes narrowed, as if he was trying to trick her. "Maybe."

Harry didn't know when he'd had this much fun. "Would you like a taste of my ice?"

She tilted her head, as if to study him from a different angle. "A very tiny taste."

"You may trust me. I would never attempt to talk you out of chocolate. But you may always live dangerously by tasting a minuscule bite of mine."

She looked at him from beneath her dark lashes. "Thank you, kind sir."

"Minx." Harry laughed and was pleased to see Madeline did as well. "Here are our ices."

He paid the man, then handed his small spoon to her. "Tell me if you like it."

She took a small amount, tasted it, and wrinkled her nose. "Thank you. I shall eat my chocolate."

Harry ate some of his. It was interesting, to be sure. But he might have liked the chocolate better. All too soon they had finished. "It is time I took you home."

Her eyes widened again. "I almost forgot. Almack's is tonight."

"So it is. I will see you there." He took up the ribbons again and started the carriage. "Do you know what other entertainments you will be attending in the near future?"

Madeline shook her head. "All we have been thinking about is tonight. I'm sure Grace will know."

It occurred to him that his sisters would as well. He came to a stop in front of Worthington House and managed to lift her down before a footman could reach them, then had trouble releasing her. He had to force his fingers one by one to let her go. That had never happened to him before. When they attained the door, he bowed. "Until this evening."

She executed a graceful curtsey. "I am looking forward to it."

He watched her enter the house and returned to the curricle. It was time to pick his eldest sister's brain.

When he found her, Dotty had already doffed her carriage gown and was now wearing a day dress. "I need help."

"That I did not doubt." She tugged the bell-pull and lowered herself onto the morning room's small sofa. "What is this about?"

"Madeline." He sat on the chair next to her. "I am very interested in her."

"I see." His sister sat for so long without saying anything, Harry began to wonder if something was wrong. "Do you know if she might be interested in you as well?"

"She seemed to have enjoyed my company." But how could he be sure she wanted to spend more time with *him*? Perhaps she was simply being a well-bred lady. "Are you aware of a problem?"

"Not at all. Her mother might not like the match, but she did not like Louisa's match with Rothwell or Augusta's with Phinn either."

Harry felt his mouth drop open and shut it. "She didn't like a duke?"

"Not that duke. You might not know that when Louisa met him, he was almost broke."

That made more sense. "But about Madeline? I would like to know which entertainments she is attending so I may make sure I am invited and can ask her to dance."

Parkin arrived with the tea tray and placed it on the table in front of Dotty, and she handed him a cup. "I predict you will be invited to most if not all of the events she will attend. Matt has the same rules for them as he had for Charlotte, Louisa, Augusta, and me. One event per evening, departing immediately after supper." She stirred sugar into her tea. "This evening, Grace will offer a supper at Worthington House because the only thing available at Almack's is stale bread and butter and dry cake. I can ensure you are invited." She took a sip and put the cup down. "Harry, you must make sure she wants what you have to offer. A few weeks is not long enough to truly get to know someone. Use the time wisely."

He finished his tea, took a few sandwiches, and some biscuits. "I will." After all, this was the rest of his life. "Thank you."

His sister nodded absently. "Until dinner."

How had he never noticed how knowing his sister was? It was almost as if she were the elder between them. In that way, she reminded him more of their grandmother than their mother. Yet she was correct. Madeline had told him she liked to help people, but did that mean she would like to be the wife of a politician? And would her mother cause a problem? He wished he could disregard Madeline's mother, but he could not afford to be ostracized if she disapproved. He finished the last of his sandwiches. First things first. He had to discover what Madeline wanted. But other than a husband and family, had she even thought about it?

A few hours later, he entered Almack's with Dotty and Merton.

"If you want to immediately get in her good graces, you will obtain permission to dance the waltz with her," Merton said. Dotty looked at him in shock, and he shrugged. "Even I knew that. Harry, here is exactly what you must say: 'I would like to be recommended to Lady Madeline Vivers as a suitable partner for the waltz.'" After Harry repeated it back, Merton glanced at Dotty. "Who do you suggest, my love?"

She looked around the room. "Mrs. Drummond-Burrell is not occupied at the moment. Harry"—Dotty looped her arm with his—"come with me."

"I shall be with Matt and Grace." Merton headed toward the couple.

Harry had heard about the Lady Patronesses of Almack's, but he'd never thought he'd meet one.

"Clementina," his sister said to a rather stern-looking woman. "I have brought my elder brother to be presented to you. This is Mr. Harry Stern. Harry, Mrs. Drummond-Burrell."

He immediately made his best bow. "A pleasure, ma'am."

"My lady," the woman said. "I can see the resemblance. It is a pleasure to meet you, Mr. Stern." She gave him a languid look. "Is there anything with which I may assist you?"

Harry swallowed in spite of himself and repeated what his brother-in-law had told him to say.

"Well done, sir." She placed her hand on his arm. "Lady Merton, will you lead the way?"

Harry had the feeling of being led into battle by two frigates. They arrived to where Madeline was standing just as he noticed some fribble in a light-blue suit being brought their way by another lady.

"Lady Sefton," Dotty whispered in his ear.

"Lady Madeline." Mrs. Drummond-Burrell smiled. "How lovely you look this evening. I am pleased to recommend Mr. Stern to you as a suitable partner for the waltz."

Madeline smiled up at him as if he were her hero. "Thank you, ma'am. I should be delighted."

Lords Montagu and St. Albans, whom Harry knew slightly from school, had apparently been granted waltzes with Eleanor and Alice, respectively.

Lady Sefton and the man in blue arrived. "Oh, dear," Lady Sefton said with a small pout. "I fear you are out of luck, my lord." She smiled at them. "Lord Lancelot wished to be recommended for the waltz, but unless I am vastly mistaken, the other ladies have already recommended these gentlemen to you."

Harry recognized that name from somewhere, but where? Worthington stiffened. It must have had something to do with one of the sisters.

Lord Lancelot gave a languid bow. "Ah, my dear Lady Sefton, that only means they may now waltz." The music for the first set started, and he turned his focus to Alice. "May I have this dance, my lady?"

Alice stiffened slightly as well. It was time to play knight in shining armor. "I am sorry, my lord, but Lady Alice has done me the honor of promising her first set to me."

Before the man could ask either Eleanor or Madeline, Lord Montagu had made the same claim about dancing with Eleanor, and Lord St. Albans said that Madeline was dancing with him.

"Their first three sets are taken," Worthington said, looking none too kindly at the gentleman. "We will leave after supper."

Lord Lancelot bowed and sauntered away. By then the rest of their sisters and their husbands had joined them.

"Good Lord," Phinn said. "Not him again."

Augusta frowned at Lord Lancelot, now lounging against the wall across the room. "He looks to be improved. At least he is not wearing a spotted kerchief as a neckcloth."

"But is he?" Matt raised his quizzing glass at his lord-ship's form. "I will make inquiries."

"It would be a shame not to be able to stand up with someone that gorgeous," Alice mused.

"If you like peacocks," St. Albans drawled. "He reminds me of a Gainsborough painting I once saw of a young boy in a light blue suit."

"Do you know him?" Eleanor asked.

"Not so much know him as know of him. I went to school with one of his brothers. Lord Lancelot is said to be as spoiled as his name might suggest. He fancies himself a poet."

Charlie Stanwood shook his head. "I was in school with him. He was a dead bore. Perhaps it will be easier if I have a conversation with him to see if he has changed."

"I for one will stand up with him if he asks," Madeline said. "Then we will soon know if he has improved or not."

Harry didn't like the sound of that. He waited while Worthington rubbed his forehead as if it ached. "He will not be allowed an introduction until I have determined he is the type of gentleman you should know."

Worthington had spoken and that was that. Harry would make sure the man didn't approach Madeline.

CHAPTER FOUR

After the contretemps over Lord Lancelot had ended for the present and the first set had finished, Madeline touched Harry's arm, and he immediately gave her his attention. "Are you acquainted with Lord St. Albans and Lord Montagu?"

"Yes." He smiled. "Eton and Oxford."

She tapped his arm with her fan. "And you thought you would not know anyone in Town."

"I shall once more admit you were correct." She grinned at his chagrin. "I really should have expected to see many of my old schoolmates here."

It occurred to Madeline that she could discover more information about both gentlemen that might be helpful to her sisters. "What do you think of them?"

He seemed to consider her question for a few moments. "I like both of them. I would say Montagu is solid. There is nothing to fear if Eleanor is interested in him. St. Albans has always seemed resty to me. Like a horse getting ready to kick over his traces." Harry met her gaze. "I don't know another way to describe it."

Madeline glanced at the gentleman. What Harry had said was true. There was energy, but unlike Harry's, it did not seem to be well-directed. Is that what was bothering Alice about him? "I see what you mean."

Madeline felt Harry drop his gaze to her. "Socially, it would be a good match, if that is what you're concerned about."

None of them were that concerned about not making acceptable matches. It would never be allowed. "No. It is just the effect he has on Alice. He makes her restless."

Harry frowned. "How odd."

It *was* peculiar. "I think so too." Madeline gave herself a shake. "If she wants help, we will be there for her, but this may be something she has to work out for herself."

"Sometimes being there is all one can do." His words brushed against her ear, making her neck tingle. The prelude for the waltz began. "I believe this is our dance, my lady."

Smiling up at him, she placed her hand on his arm. "I believe you are correct, sir."

He led her to the floor, where they bowed and curtseyed before he placed his hands on her waist. It was a shock to feel his warmth even through his gloves and the layers of clothing she wore. His touch was light but firm and confident, allowing her to greatly enjoy the set without worrying about any mishaps. That he was an excellent dancer did not surprise her at all. Everything he did, he would do well, or to the best of his ability.

"Dancing with you is akin to dancing with a feather. It is effortless," he murmured.

Madeline chuckled. "I was just thinking the same thing about you."

Hands overhead, he turned her into a twirl. "Would you like to go for a ride tomorrow and visit Gunther's again?"

Umm. More ices. "You can always tempt me to eat ices." She dropped her hands to his shoulders. "Did you bring your carriage from Bristol?"

"No. I don't have one that's suitable for the Grand Strut."

He'd liked the one he drove today. "I'm going to ask Dotty if I can buy the carriage from her. It will save me the time of having to wait for one to be built."

They did take time to be made. "Matt is having a high-perch phaeton built for us. It should be ready soon."

Harry looked surprised. "One vehicle for the three of you to share?"

"Yes. He did the same for Charlotte, Louisa, and Dotty."

His brows drew together slightly, as if he had been presented with a problem. "What happens to the carriage after you're all wed?"

That was the barrister talking. "The last one married gets to keep it. Augusta came out by herself, so she had one of her own."

"Interesting. I wonder why he does that." He seemed to be ruminating to himself, but Madeline had asked the same question and knew the answer.

"It is easier to keep track of us if we have to share a vehicle. I suppose because we will choose the carriage over walking in the Park."

The corner of his lips tipped up into a crooked smile. "I suppose any of us would."

"Indubitably. Think how long it would take to get around the Park and then to Gunter's on foot."

"That doesn't bear consideration." He gave a pretend shudder. "One would not even have the excuse of having to move along in order to get away from some people."

She almost burst out laughing. "Now you see what an intelligent decision he made."

Mirth lurked in Harry's eyes as he gazed down at her. He really was the most handsome gentleman she had ever met, and one of the nicest. "I hope you will invite me to ride with you one day."

"I will make sure to do so." The dance came to an end, and he escorted her back to their circle.

Madeline had been concerned no other gentleman would ask to dance with her, but when she and Harry arrived there were a few gentlemen speaking with Matt, and introductions were made, and she was able to enjoy more sets.

"It is time for supper." Matt's tone portended doom.

Harry gave Matt a droll look. "I have heard it must not be missed."

"If there was a way to do it, I would." He gathered them all with a glance. "Come along. Waiting will not make it better."

When they entered the room, Matt directed the footmen to put a long table together for them. After the ladies were seated, the gentlemen went off to fetch their bread and butter and dry cake. Harry strolled between Matt and Merton. At least Grace would have ordered a real supper to be served when they arrived home.

"What do you think of Harry?" Alice asked.

"I like him a great deal." There was no point in hiding the fact. Whether or not she wanted to wed him was another matter. And then there was Mama. Yet there was no point in worrying about that until Madeline knew her own mind and heart.

"He seems greatly improved since we were children."

"You act as if you are surprised. We all mature. Well, most of us do." Madeline grimaced, and the form of Lord Lancelot came into sight. After watching his behavior this evening, she had her doubts about him.

"True, and Harry really did not have a choice but to grow up." Alice frowned in Lord St. Albans's direction. "Unlike others."

The gentlemen returned to the table with their offerings, and Harry placed a plate in front of her. He kept his voice low. "I have been told we will not spend a long time savoring our fine fare."

She bit her lip. "Do not let anyone hear you."

"That is the reason I am whispering."

He did a noble job of pretending to enjoy the food but quickly got to his feet once Grace announced they were leaving.

He held out his hand to help her up. "I take it you, Dotty, and Merton are joining us," Madeline said.

Harry tucked her hand in the crook of his arm. "I believe that is the intention. Do you mind?"

He actually wanted her to tell him the truth, and she wanted to know him better. "Not at all. I enjoy talking with you."

Harry was more than pleased to have Madeline on his arm. She was easy to speak with, and allowed her sense of humor to show. There was nothing false about her. When they arrived in the street, Charlie Stanwood and his younger brother, Walter Carpenter, exchanged a few words with Worthington and Grace, then strolled up to Eleanor and Alice and were introduced to St. Albans and Montagu.

Walter grinned at the two men. "It is good to meet you as well. I hear you are to join us for Morning Mayhem."

Harry slid Madeline a look. "Morning Mayhem?"

She cast her eyes to the cloudy sky. "It is what they call breakfast when all the children are present."

He thought about his own nieces and nephews. "Having had the opportunity to dine with small children, I understand why he would call it that."

"Well, the babies will not be there, but the five- and four-year-olds will." She gave him a searching look. "You may join us. It is early. Right after we ride."

Harry gave her his best bow. "I am honored and accept." Grace called for Madeline, and he helped her into the coach. "I shall see you soon."

Merton waved to Harry, and he walked to their coach and took the backward-facing seat. "That was interesting. Although I'm not sure why people make a habit of going."

"Some people have nothing better to do," Dotty said in a

dry voice. "And others of us have people we need to marry off. It is not called the Marriage Mart for no reason."

"I suppose you are right." He was saying that a great deal to ladies lately. "I was surprised not to see Salforth there." But he was very glad Hereford, Bury and Salforth were not present.

"You forget that Salforth's mother is still in mourning. She would have been responsible for getting the vouchers. I doubt it will hurt his chances." His sister raised a brow, barely discernible in the carriage light. "He is a rare commodity: a young, wealthy, well-looking duke."

Mentally, Harry counted back to the old duke's death. "She should be out of it by now."

"I believe she has another week or two," Dotty said. "You will see her around after that." The coach turned, and she glanced out the window. "Here we are. Do you know Charlotte's and Louisa's husbands?"

"I made a point of introducing him," Merton said as he got out of the vehicle. "Have you met Louisa?"

Harry searched his memory but could not recall making her acquaintance. "I do not believe I have."

"Very well, then." Dotty reached out her hand to take Merton's hand. "I shall introduce you."

The others had already gathered in a drawing room, and Dotty presented him to the former Louisa Vivers, now the Duchess of Rothwell.

"We have heard so much about you." Her smile reminded him of Madeline's. "I am glad we have finally met and will see you a great deal more."

He bowed. "I am as well, your grace."

"None of that. You must call me Louisa, as the rest of the family does."

Madeline approached him and placed her hand on his arm. "Supper is laid out in the back of the room. I shall take you there."

"Thank you." He wanted to raise her fingers to kiss them but was unsure how she, or indeed the rest of the family, would react. "I am famished."

She handed him a plate and took one for herself. There was fresh asparagus, ham, lobster patties, a variety of cheeses, breads, and fruit.

Madeline sighed. "No ices. You must try some of the sauce for the asparagus. Augusta had it in Spain and brought home the recipe."

The sauce was white. "What is in it?"

"Mayonnaise, garlic, and lemon." She took a spoonful and placed it on her plate.

He did the same. "Do you ever wish to travel?"

"Not like Augusta and Phinn, but I would like to visit some foreign places." Madeline smiled. "Paris would be nice."

Unlike many young gentlemen, Harry had not been able to make a Grand Tour. But a few short jaunts would be pleasant. "It would be. Steamships are making great progress. One day soon, we will be able to sail from England to Spain or Italy in a matter of days."

She took him to a small sofa with a table in front of it. "That would be wonderful. Much better than having to travel for months at a time."

He tasted the asparagus with the sauce. It was tangy and fresh. "This is quite good."

Madeline finished chewing and swallowed. "It has become a family favorite."

It appeared everyone was involved in their own conversations. "Have you thought about the life you want?"

"A fairly simple one. I like coming for the Season. We have been doing it for a while. I also like the country. I would like to begin some sort of plan for making people's lives better." She grinned at him. "And, of course, a husband and children."

He wondered if by improving the lot of people, she would be interested in politics as one way to do it. "Are you interested in bills that are being planned or drafted?"

She popped a piece of cheese in her mouth and chewed. "Not to the extent that Charlotte and Louisa are. They help their husbands with their speeches and host large political events. Although I would like to have some say in certain bills. More the ones concerning families and the welfare of women and children."

Harry had taken the opportunity to eat much of his food while she had been thinking about and answering his questions. "There is too much power in the hands of the few and men in general. The poor must be able to find jobs and be educated."

She glanced at her brothers-in-law. "Some of the few do their best to help those in need."

He took a sip of the wine that had seemed to magically appear on the table next to him. "There are. Your family and mine are examples. Unfortunately, there are not enough."

"What happened in your committee meeting?"

That question was unexpected, but welcome nevertheless. "I was the only new member present. I met some of the gentlemen. One invited me to dine with him and his family next week, and I supported a motion to allow people other than merchants to file for bankruptcy."

She gave him a sad look. "It was defeated?"

"It was." He hated to see her distressed. "But we will try again. Eventually, the laws will change."

She huffed. "It always seems to take so long. I feel as if I could accomplish more in a shorter time."

She wasn't the only one with that belief. "Dotty is of the same opinion, but she tries to gather support for bills and, as you know, has charities to do the work the government does not."

Madeline nodded thoughtfully. Then his sister called to him. "We must be going. Tomorrow is an early day."

"Do not forget breakfast," Madeline said as he rose.

"I won't." He'd be able to ride with her, and spend time during the meal with her too.

He bid the others a good night and followed his sister and brother-in-law to their carriage. "That was fun." And productive.

"You and Madeline seemed to be having a deep conversation," Dotty said.

It was certainly a necessary conversation. "I asked her what she wanted in life."

"Ah." He knew his sister's eyes had sharpened on him. "Does she want anything you cannot provide?"

"We appear to have many of the same ideas, but I am not sure how politically involved she will want to be. Still, she has prompted me to think about my career." How far did he wish to go in politics? Was leadership a consideration?

"We are going to Lady Markham's entertainment tomorrow. I will make sure you are included in the invitation."

"Thank you." That would be another chance to be with Madeline. Hopefully, he would make more progress.

CHAPTER FIVE

The next morning, Madeline spotted Harry Stern as she and her sisters rode to the Park. She broke away from her sisters as Eleanor greeted Lord Montagu.

Harry came up beside Madeline. "Race to the tree?"

"Yes." She liked that they had early morning exercise in common. She had the feeling the other two gentlemen were only out at this time because of her sisters. "One, two, three."

Rose was never going to beat Willy and Harry, but she threw her heart into the race, and they arrived as Harry turned to see where they were.

"Excellent heart." He smiled first at her mare, then at her.

Madeline stroked Rose's neck. "I think she did not want to embarrass herself."

"She certainly succeeded." Something behind her caught his eye. "St. Albans and Alice will be here soon."

"I wonder where Eleanor and Lord Montagu are?" Madeline scanned the area for the couple. "Jemmy will not be happy that we are in different places."

"I take it you mean the groom." Harry glanced around. "He must have followed them."

Madeline did not see the servant either. "He must have."

Just then, St. Albans reined up next to Harry, and her sister came up to her.

"I wish he was not coming to breakfast," Alice said in a fierce whisper.

"What do you have against him?" Lord St. Albans seemed to be a pleasant enough gentleman.

"I do not know." Alice shook her head as she glared at him. "He unsettles me somehow."

The sound of hooves reached Madeline, and she turned to see Eleanor and Lord Montagu.

"Good morning, Stern," Lord Montagu said as they came to a halt.

"Good morn to you as well." Harry inclined his head.

Madeline caught her sisters' eyes, and without having to say a word, they agreed it was time to break their fast.

"Well, gentlemen," Lady Alice said. "Whoever is joining us for breakfast, come along. We must be going back."

"Excellent," Harry said. "I'm famished." He came up next to Madeline as they rode toward the gate. "Is it my imagination or is there an attraction between Eleanor and Montagu?"

That was perceptive of him. "Definitely an attraction. Although there are certain things she must know about him before she allows it to go any further."

Harry was quiet for a few seconds. "Such as whether he gets along with the rest of the family or, more importantly, the children?"

"Indeed." He had even more insight than she had imagined. "Could you see any of us wedding a man who could not?"

"No." He gave a short bark of laughter. "I don't think Worthington or Grace would allow it."

Now that he'd brought it up, Madeline agreed with him. "I think you are correct."

"Family is the most important thing to both of our families. I think it is one of the reasons my parents were so close to the Carpenters, and now to the Worthingtons and all of you."

That was true. Sir Henry and Lady Stern had embraced Madeline and her sisters as if they had known them all their lives. "We are fortunate in our relatives."

"That we are." They arrived at Worthington House. Harry dismounted and went around to help her. His strong hands gripped her waist. As he lifted her off her mare, all the breath rushed from her lungs. The moment her feet touched the pavement, she sucked in a large breath. His brows drew together in concern. "Are you all right?"

Not at all. "Perfectly." She smiled, as if her body was not still feeling the heat of his hands. Madeline forced herself to breathe in and out. "Shall we go?"

"Ah, yes." He grinned. "Let's see how Montagu and St. Albans react to the children. Even Dotty and Merton will be here."

Thorton met them at the door and bowed. "Gentlemen, please follow James"—her brother's butler indicated one of the footman—"He will show you where you may wash."

Madeline and her sisters went to their rooms. It would be interesting to see how the other men responded to their wider family. It only took a few minutes to freshen up and join her sister in the corridor. Eleanor appeared a bit nervous. "You will know shortly if he has passed this test."

"I will." She nodded. "Did Harry say anything?"

"Only that it was important anyone we marry get along with family." Madeline would not tell her sister what might happen if the gentleman did not.

"He is correct. Consider the efforts Grace made to bring Merton into the fold, and the concern Henrietta had about Dotty accepting Fotherby."

Madeline linked her arm with Eleanor's. "I shall keep my fingers crossed."

When the gentlemen arrived, Montagu and St. Albans

were seated on either side of Grace. Harry held a seat out for Madeline close to where his brother-in-law, sister, and niece, Vivienne, sat. The little girl grinned at him, and he tweaked her nose, making her giggle. He was obviously very good with children. His lips twitched when Charlotte and Kenilworth's son, Hugh, flipped a piece of egg on the table and Hugh's twin sister, Constance, promised to teach him his manners after the other children chastised him.

"Poor Hugh," Harry whispered to Madeline.

"He does seem to be having a difficult time." She was doing all she could to hold in her laughter.

"Montagu appears to be fascinated by everything." Harry had kept his voice low enough that only she heard him.

"But is he intrigued in a good way, or as if viewing a two-headed chicken?"

He held his napkin to his mouth as his shoulders shook. "That is an excellent question. I suppose we shall see." He brought himself under control and lowered his serviette. "I understand you are attending Lady Markham's ball this evening. May I have the supper dance?"

That was well done of him. "Yes, you may."

Talk turned to where everyone was committed for the day, and Lord Montagu excused himself for a vote at the Lords.

"I must be going as well," Harry said, rising. "I look forward to seeing you this evening."

"I look forward to it as well." Madeline knew the other two gentlemen would invite her to dance, but she had been a bit worried at having no one scheduled for the supper dance. She escorted him to the door. "Have a good day."

"You too." He took her fingers and bowed over them, and they started to tingle. She was almost disappointed he did not kiss them. "Adieu."

"Adieu." She watched as he made his way to the street.

It was a shame he was not a peer. She did not want trouble with her mother.

Madeline went back to the breakfast room to hurry her sisters along for their shopping trip. But when she entered the room, Eleanor was talking to Dotty, Grace, and Charlotte about Lord Montagu. Taking a seat, she listened. When Eleanor said Lord Montagu had asked her for the supper dance, Charlotte said she had received the order of the dances from Lady Harrington, Lady Markham's daughter-in-law, who had recently returned from Paris, and it was a waltz. It would be wonderful to waltz with Harry again.

"How does she like being back in England?" Eleanor asked.

"She has mixed feelings," Charlotte said. "She loved Paris and France, but now that her brother has started a family, and hers is increasing, she likes the idea of all the children growing up together. She and Harrington still plan to visit Paris regularly."

Madeline thought about her sister touring Europe and other places for the past three years. "I want to visit the Continent. It is a shame that ladies cannot do a Grand Tour as part of their education."

"Perhaps someday," Eleanor said. "We will have daughters one day. We could make it part of their education." Madeline glanced across the table. Dotty was staring at Eleanor, who glanced down. "Do I have a spot on my gown?"

"No. You have just given me an excellent idea. There is no reason I can think of why young ladies should not be able to travel before marrying and starting a family."

"This is the nineteenth century after all," Alice agreed.

It *was* the nineteenth century. Why did Madeline feel so constrained by what she would be allowed to do?

They all left the table, and she noticed Alice smiling

broadly as they made their way up the stairs. What was
going on with her?

Eleanor gave her twin a strange look. "You are happy this
morning."

"You obviously did not see how disgruntled Lord St. Albans
was by having to share his breakfast with the children. I do
not believe he approved at all."

"You think this will convince him to look elsewhere for
a lady?" Eleanor clearly thought that was unlikely.

"I certainly hope he does." Alice reached the landing first
and waited. "He must understand that he does not fit in with
the lives we have."

Madeline watched as her sister strolled down the corridor
to her chamber. "This might prove to be interesting."

Eleanor stopped at her door. "What do you think of Lord
St Albans?"

"I am not sure yet." Madeline wished she was. "However, I do not think he is one to give up easily. He might just
see Alice as a challenge."

"Oh dear." Eleanor pulled a face. "She will not like that
at all."

"That was exactly what I thought." Madeline gave her
sister a smile. "We shall see."

When she entered her bedchamber, her maid had her
clothing out and a bath ready. At least Alice did not have to
consider Mama. Perhaps it would not seem so when Madeline
met more gentlemen. Then again, that might make life more
problematic. She gave herself a shake. There was no point
in worrying about it, and shopping would probably help.

"You and Madeline appeared to find a lot to discuss,"
Dotty said as Harry entered her parlor to tell her he would
see her later.

As much as he appreciated his sister's help, he did not

want her overly involved. He did not want to act too quickly, but he'd had a hell of a time not kissing Madeline's fingers earlier. "We have much in common. I have asked her for the supper dance this evening."

"It is a waltz." His sister raised one brow.

"It is one dance." And supper. Merton had suggested that if Harry was interested in a lady, he should ask for the supper dance.

"Madeline would be a good choice." Dotty was obviously considering a match between them.

That was exactly what he'd been thinking, but it was early days. "It is much too soon for me to know who would be the best choice."

He started out the door when she stopped him. "I thought you might want to know that Mr. Taylor has a daughter of marriageable age."

Harry couldn't help but frown. "I wonder why she was not at Almack's."

Dotty cast her eyes to the ceiling. "The Taylors are not the type of people who are accepted at Almack's. Remember when we said blood will out?"

Harry hadn't been paying that much attention, but he did recall some of the conversation. "Then why am I acceptable—Grandmamma?"

"Indeed. Even if I had not married Merton, the fact that we are grandchildren of the Duke and Duchess of Bristol gives us a status being children of Sir Henry Stern does not." She took a letter from a stack on her desk. "As you said, there is time. Have a productive day."

Harry wished he could be certain it *would* be fruitful. "You as well."

Merton had offered to let Harry use one of their unmarked town coaches when he wished, but the day was fine, and he decided to walk. It would also give him more time to consider Mr. Taylor's invitation. Harry hoped the man hadn't made it merely to introduce him to Miss Taylor. That might be awkward. Even more so because they apparently ran in different social circles, and she might not be invited to the same balls and other events to which he was invited. On the other hand, if he was interested in her, there might be a way to receive cards for the entertainments. Yet he was fairly certain Madeline was the right lady for him. He'd just have to convince her he was the right gentleman for her.

"Stern." The shout from behind stopped him.

"That was the second time I called out," Salforth said as he caught up with Harry. "On your way to the Commons?"

"I am. Did you take your seat in the Lords?"

"Yes." He nodded. "Not long after my father died, one of his friends convinced me to do so. He said it would make it easier when I was ready to take up my duties."

"Have you decided which party you will support?" For as long as Harry had known the duke, he'd never espoused a political view on anything.

"My father was a Tory, of course. Must support the king," Salforth said. "I shall do the same." He frowned slightly. "Well, unless there is a good reason I cannot support a bill for some reason or another."

Considering all the damage the Tories had done with the Corn Laws and other legislation, Harry didn't understand how anyone could support them. Perhaps he should introduce the duke to Worthington's circle. "I say, are you attending the Markham ball this evening?"

"Mama is finally out of mourning, so yes, we shall attend." Salforth suddenly grinned. "In fact, I even wrote a note to Lady Madeline asking for a set." He looked so proud of himself, Harry almost felt badly about wanting to punch him. "I asked my mother about her ladyship, and she said your family and hers were great friends. Thank you for introducing me to her."

Harry's jaw almost dropped. Why the devil didn't the man have the sense to know that he was interested in Madeline? They had reached Westminster, and he schooled his countenance into a natural mask. "I will see you there. I hope you have a pleasant day."

"Oh." Salforth's jaw did drop. "I didn't know you'd be at the ball."

Harry gave him a pleasant smile. "Obviously, her grace did not tell you my sister is the Marchioness of Merton."

The duke shook his head. "I don't recall that she mentioned it."

Harry inclined his head. "I must go or I will be late to a meeting."

"Yes, yes. Indeed," Salforth said abstractedly.

Harry strode away, wondering if any of his other so-called friends had asked Madeline to stand up with them. It appeared that any initial advantage he had might quickly fade away. Yet he did not think she cared about whether a gentleman was titled or not. At least, he hoped that was the case. He'd formed the opinion she was like the Carpenter ladies and his sister. Merton had bemoaned the fact that Dotty thought nothing of his title except when it could be of use. Granted, Madeline's eldest sister had married a duke, although no one cared that he was one. But Augusta, her next older sister, had married a younger son. He must make a point of asking Madeline for all the supper dances and more rides in the Park, as well as meeting her in the mornings.

CHAPTER SIX

Madeline had no sooner stepped through the door when Thorton said, "My lady, her ladyship wishes to speak with you."

"Only me?" Usually when Grace wanted to see one of them, she wanted to see all three of them.

"Yes, my lady."

"I will wash my hands. then go to her straightaway." Her stomach growled. Her sisters said something about luncheon being almost ready, and she was glad she would soon be able to eat.

She and Alice ascended the stairs. Once in her room, Madeline quickly put her hat, gloves, and spencer on her bed and washed her hand. Back downstairs, she walked swiftly down the corridor, and knocked on Grace's study door.

"Come."

Madeline entered and took a seat in one of the chairs arrayed in front of her sister's desk. "Thorton said you wanted to see me."

Grace picked up what looked like several notes. "I do. You have received requests for dances from the Duke of Salforth, the Earl of Hereford, Lord Ashford, and Viscount Bury." Grace frowned. "Do you know them?"

For a second, Madeline stared at the papers in her sister's

hand; then she glanced at Grace. "I have met everyone but Lord Ashford. Harry Stern introduced them to me. They are old school chums of his."

She placed the missives on the desk before Madeline. "Very well. Aside from Lord Ashford, do you wish to accept their invitations?"

"I do not see why not." She shrugged. "They are only dances. Do they happen to mention which sets they would like?"

Grace leaned back in her chair. "Only the duke asked for a specific one. He wants the supper dance."

That he could not have. "I am already promised for that set. I shall give him another one."

Grace raised a brow. "In future, I would appreciate it if you would tell me when you meet new gentlemen. Matt likes to know of them."

Madeline should have thought of that. "I will make sure to do so, and I will tell Eleanor and Alice as well."

Her sister smiled. "Thank you. Did you have a good time shopping?"

"We did!" Madeline grinned. "We went to the Burlington Arcade and found fans, hair combs, and pins. It was such fun."

"In that case, do not let me keep you. I know you want to look at everything again."

"Thank you." She rose and leaned across the desk to give Grace a kiss on her cheek.

Her sister-in-law looked surprised. "Goodness, what was that for?"

"For being the best of all sisters-in-law."

Giving her a bemused look, she slowly shook her head. "You do not have another one."

"Not yet. But you will still be the best." Madeline wiggled her fingers. "I will see you later. Oh, I almost forgot. Luncheon will be served soon."

She went up to the parlor she shared with her sisters, but only Alice was there. "Where is Eleanor?"

"She needed to speak with Matt and Charlie about her coal mine idea. I am giving her time."

Madeline's stomach made itself known again. "I am hungry."

Alice glanced at the clock. "We should be able to go now. What did Grace want?"

Madeline showed her the invitations, then put them on the desk. "Grace and Matt also want to know about any new gentlemen we meet. I suppose it is so he can look into them."

"That sounds fair. He is, after all, responsible for making sure we are not bothered by unacceptable men." Alice slid a sly look at Madeline. "Will you make sure to see that the gentlemen are introduced to me as well?"

"Of course." She had a feeling this was her sister's way of avoiding St. Albans. "As soon as they come for their sets, I will make them known to you."

Alice linked her arm with Madeline's. "Let us go eat."

She was happy to see Charlie was still there when they entered the small dining room.

"Have we given you enough time?" Alice rushed to their brother and hugged him when he rose. "Charlie! I'm so glad you are here."

"We do not see you enough." Madeline embraced him as well. "Did you come to help Eleanor?"

"Yes. Matt thought the two of us working on this was better than one." He seemed a little taller than usual. "I am the head of the family, after all."

"You are indeed." Alice motioned with her hand. "Do sit and finish your luncheon."

"Thank you, but I am going to get a bit more food."

Next, Walter and Grace strolled into the dining room in

deep discussion about something. Her face lit up when she saw Matt. "Good afternoon."

He came around and kissed her cheek. "Good afternoon to you as well, my love. Will you serve yourself, or shall I do it for you?"

Madeline remembered before her brother and sister-in-law had met and married. He had always seemed content, but now he was happy. She wanted that too. Marriage to a gentleman who loved and cared about her. She just wished she knew who it would be. It was also exciting to be invited to dance with gentlemen neither she nor her family knew. What would they be like? She should probably send her responses as soon as possible. She finished eating and excused herself from the table.

Harry had not returned to Merton House until it was time to change for dinner and the ball. He'd been given two more committee assignments today, one on transport within the United Kingdom and another regarding the production of cotton in India.

"Sir," his valet, Burkham, said. "You received a card today. It looks like an invitation. I placed it on your desk."

That was probably the card Mr. Taylor had promised. "I'll look at it now."

It was an invitation to dinner from Mrs. Taylor for Tuesday next. He sat down and quickly wrote his acceptance. "Have this taken to Mr. Taylor's house in the morning."

"Yes, sir." Burkham held up two jackets. "The dark blue or the black for this evening?"

"The black." Harry went behind the screen to wash his face and shave again. Perhaps he should tell his valet that he wanted to outshine a duke. On the other hand, Madeline had already seen him in evening clothes, and riding clothes, and dressed for a carriage ride. He was better off dazzling her with his conversation, his dancing skills, and his ability to select foods she would like for supper.

He donned his shirt, stockings, and trousers, which were now acceptable evening wear except at Almack's. As he tied his cravat, he couldn't help but wonder which knot Salforth would use.

Stop it! If Madeline is swayed by the knot of a cravat, she is not the lady you think she is.

Finally, he was ready. Taking one last look in the mirror, he headed down to the drawing room.

"Uncle Harry." He looked up to see Vivienne, his five-year-old niece, peering down from the floor above.

He grinned at her. "What is it, poppet?"

She lifted her chin, reminding him of her mother and great-grandmother. "You should not call me that. I am a lady."

He barely kept from laughing out loud. "Very well, my lady. What is it?"

"You look almost as handsome as Papa."

"Great praise indeed." He bowed. "Thank you. But do I look more handsome than a duke?"

"Oh." She nodded so hard her curls shook. "You are much more handsome than a duke."

Poor Rothwell. He was the only duke she knew. "Thank you."

"Lady Vivienne." Nurse bustled up behind her. "You should have told Maisy where you were going."

"Yes, Nurse. I promise I will the next time."

She took the little girl by the hand. "You are right, though. Mr. Harry is very handsome. All the ladies will want to dance with him."

"Good night, Vivienne."

"Good night, Uncle Harry," she said over her shoulder.

Merton was leaning against the stair railing when he turned around. "It is gratifying to know my daughter believes I am the most handsome of men." He turned toward the stairs and accompanied Harry. "What duke are you vying against? I doubt it's Rothwell."

"Salforth approached Madeline and me when I was taking her for a carriage ride in the Park. I had no choice but to present him. This morning, he told me he'd sent a card around asking her for a set tonight."

"Ah." Merton stopped on the stair and raised a brow. "Are you afraid she'll be impressed by his rank?"

"I don't know." That was the question. "I don't think she would. At least I hope not."

"I've known her for several years now. My opinion is that Madeline will be impressed by the man."

"Not a knot and not rank," Harry mumbled to himself.

"A knot?" Merton looked at Harry as if he'd lost his mind.

"I was considering a new knot." That was embarrassing to admit.

"I'll tell you a secret." His brother-in-law waited until he had Harry's full attention. "I was terrified something would happen to take Thea away from me before I could get her married."

"But you were already betrothed."

"Yes, but no one, except my mother, was happy about it. I'd like to tell you to fight for your lady. Unfortunately, the only thing you can do is pray you are the one she wants." He started descending the stairs again. "And make sure you spend as much time with her as possible. That might mean missing a few of the later committee meetings. I'll ask Thea to arrange an alfresco luncheon at Richmond Park."

"Thank you." Harry hurried down the steps. "Why are you doing so much to help me?"

"Aside from liking you and wanting to see you happy?" Harry nodded.

"Because it will make Thea happy, and you'll finally have an excuse to get your own house." Harry was about to tell Merton he'd move out, but he held up his hand. "There is absolutely no point in renting rooms, then having to relocate in a month or so."

Harry had been ready for a long siege. "Do you think it will be that quick?"

"I do." Merton turned toward the small drawing room, which was situated next to the family dining room. "Once she makes up her mind, you'll be in a church about two weeks later."

"But how long will it take for her to decide?"

"If the rest of her sisters are any guide, not long at all."

Harry wasn't certain that was correct. "Didn't Augusta take months?"

"More like several weeks," Dotty said. She kissed Merton on his lips. "She was a special case. Other than her, Charlotte took the longest, and that was only a matter of a few weeks. I had wondered where you two were."

"I was receiving advice on courting Madeline." Harry poured a glass of sherry and handed one to Dotty. "It appears the Duchess of Salforth is participating in society again."

His sister nodded. "I understand. Her son will be at the ball this evening."

Harry took a drink of sherry. "And he's asked Madeline for a dance."

Merton poured a glass of claret. "But if Harry took my earlier advice, he already has asked her for the supper dance."

"I have." Thank the deity for his brother-in-law's counsel. "And if you have a list of balls, I will ensure I ask her for every supper dance." Until he was able to have all her sets.

"I will make a copy of the events I have accepted and give it to you." Dotty sipped her wine.

"Thank you." No man could be luckier in his family.

Dotty stared at him. "Is there anything else I can do?"

"Sell me the carriage I've been borrowing?"

"I suppose I could do that. I use my phaeton more than the curricle." She grimaced. "Actually, I use my landau more than anything these days."

"You could just give it to him, my love," Merton said. "It's in a good cause."

Dotty glanced at the ceiling and laughed. "Very well. Have your secretary draw up the document gifting the carriage to Harry."

The door opened and the butler took one step into the room. "My lady, dinner is served."

"Thank you, Parkin."

Merton placed her hand on his arm. "I have one more favor to ask of you, my love."

"Hmm, what is it?" Dotty's lips twitched.

"Could you arrange a small al fresco luncheon at Richmond Park? We will take the children, of course."

"Now that is a good idea. It will be fun to get out of London for a day." She glanced back at Harry. "Do you want me to invite all of Madeline's family?"

As much as he loved her family, that would give him no time at all alone with her. "Would it be too presumptuous to just invite Madeline?"

"I shall speak with Grace." They entered the dining room. "She will have an idea."

Only if Grace was in favor of his suit. "I'll wait to hear what she says."

Just over an hour later, he, Dotty, and Merton entered the crowded Markham ballroom, and his senses were immediately drawn to Madeline. She was dressed in a light pink gown that caught the light when she moved. Pearls and pink ribbons were threaded through her chestnut curls. Beneath a simple pearl necklace, the slope of her breasts showed above the top of her gown. If only he could taste them.

"Lead the way," Merton said quietly.

"How did you know?" It was almost as if he could read Harry's mind.

His brother-in-law just smirked. Whatever that meant. Still, Harry led them straight to Madeline's group and bowed to her. "My lady."

He would swear her cheeks were pinker than before. "Mr. Stern."

Glancing at Worthington, Harry noticed her brother was paying attention to his attentions to her. "Would you care to stroll with me before the dancing begins?"

She glanced at her brother. "Matt?"

"Yes. You have about fifteen minutes before the first set."

Now, how the devil was Harry going to discover who had her first dance? "We'll be back." He could just ask her. But would that be too forward?

She tucked her hand into the crook of his arm. "Shall we?"

Worthington raised a brow. "And please do not introduce her to any of your school chums. If an introduction is to be made, I will do it."

Thank God! Why hadn't Harry thought of that before? "Yes, my lord."

CHAPTER SEVEN

Madeline wondered if Matt had discovered anything untoward about Harry's old friends. But if Matt had, he would have had no trouble writing to them and informing them they would not be standing up with her, even Salforth.

Then she wondered if he was upset with Harry. She hoped not. She liked the feel of his hard arm under her fingers. "Do you think Matt is angry with you?"

"Not angry. Put out a bit describes it better." Harry drew her a little closer due to the crush of the ballroom. "I should have directed them to him if they wanted an introduction."

He was not being fair to himself. "How should you have known? To the best of my knowledge, you were not even present when Dotty and Henrietta came out.. Even your father might not be as wary as Matt is. Not only that, but your friends certainly expected you to present them to me."

"That is true." He glanced at her with a curious look in his bright green eyes. "It wouldn't surprise me if they decided to approach us solely because they wanted to meet you."

That was nice of him to say. But she was not going to let him berate himself. "If Lady Sefton was not aware of how badly Lord Lancelot could behave, you could not be cognizant of chums from school. And we are not even certain that any of them are unpresentable."

"Very well." He chuckled lightly. "I concede to your superior argument. I will stop chastising myself."

"Good." They reached the end of the room and crossed to the other side. "With which other ladies are you standing up?"

"No one." His eyes, which had held a glint of mirth, were now serious. "I am eligible, but not as eligible as other gentlemen. I doubt I will even be inveigled into dancing with other ladies."

She caught a glimpse of Lord Montagu being led by Lady Markham to a young lady. But he had not been standing or strolling with another lady at the time. Then she saw Elizabeth Harrington cast an appraising glance at Harry. "I would not be too sure about that."

"I was presented to some of the young ladies when my sister took me around. I don't remember their names or what they even looked like." He pulled a face. "I met a great many people that day."

"I can imagine how all the faces and names blended together. We were fortunate that Grace had us attend her at homes last year, and we knew a great many of the ladies and their daughters from having been in Town during the Season."

He stared at her for several seconds, then asked, "Who is your first dance partner?"

"The Duke of Salforth. He wanted the supper dance, but you had already asked for it." Madeline was glad Harry had asked for that set before the duke had. If she did not like the gentleman, she would not have to suffer through supper with him. "I am also standing up with Lords Bury and Hereford. Lord Ashford, the gentleman Dotty kept from approaching us in the Park, also wrote asking for a set. I believe Matt wrote to him denying his request."

"Ashford is presumptuous." Harry's tone was harder than she had heard it before.

"I must say I agree." Madeline did not think she wanted

to meet the man. "By not waiting until he was presented to me, he did not make a good impression."

The corners of Harry's lips tilted up. "However, I would dearly like to be around to hear what Worthington has to say to him."

That would be interesting. "Yes. On the other hand, I do not know what I would do if he approached Matt when I was there."

"Now that I think of it," Harry brought them to a halt, "it would not be prudent for him to approach your brother with you present, but I have a feeling that's exactly what he'd do. I just remembered that he had an outsize sense of importance because of his family's lineage."

"Oh, dear." She stifled a laugh. "Matt does not like those who are puffed up in their own consequence."

"No." Harry started them strolling again. "That was one of the first things I noticed about him when Grace brought him to meet my family."

"I have a feeling that unless Lord Ashford is contrite for asking me to stand up with him before even asking for an introduction to me, he is in for a set down." One that she would like to see. The more Madeline considered it, the angrier at his lordship she became.

Harry covered her hand with his. "Don't look now, but Ashford is approaching."

She peeped beneath her lashes. Lord Ashford was tall, with light brown hair. But what caught her attention were his lips. She could only describe them as cruel. If he did not apologize, Madeline might just give him a piece of her mind. Except that if Harry couldn't present Lord Ashford, she would not be able to speak to him at all. What would Harry tell him?

"Stern." the man stopped in front of them.

"Ashford." Harry inclined his head.

His lordship glanced at her and, for some strange reason, she wanted to slap him. "Will you present me to the lady?"

"I regret to inform you that if you wish to be introduced to her, you will have to apply to her guardian, Lord Worthington." Again, Harry drew her closer to him. "Now, you must excuse us." When Lord Ashford did not move, Harry raised one brow. "Don't be a fool. Creating a scene will not help you."

The other man stepped aside. When they strolled past Lord Ashford, Madeline gave him her haughtiest look. "He really is pompous. I have decided I do not wish him to be introduced to me. I shall inform Matt."

When Harry glanced at her, his eyes were sparkling with laughter. "I can't wait to see Ashford's reaction to that snub."

Madeline raised her chin. "In that case, he should not have been so presumptuous." The sounds of instruments being tuned made them hasten their steps. They made it back to their group shortly before the duke arrived.

Their group?

She supposed it was not odd that Harry was already part of her circle. He was Dotty's brother, after all.

"Would you like to go for a carriage ride with me tomorrow?"

"I would, thank you." He was also very good company.

Salforth came up to them and bowed. "Good evening, Lady Madeline."

She curtseyed. He was taller than he'd seemed on a horse, but slender. His shoulders were not nearly as broad as those of her brother or brothers-in-law, or Harry. And his eyes could not seem to decide if they were gray or blue. "Good evening." She glanced at Grace. "Grace, please allow me to present the Duke of Salforth. Your grace, my sister-in-law, the Countess of Worthington."

Once again, he bowed. After that, everyone else had to be introduced. By the time Madeline was finished, dancers were taking their places for the quadrille, but Salforth was not paying attention to them. "Your grace, if you wish to stand up with me, now is the time to go to the dance floor."

He flushed slightly and excused himself from Matt. "Dreadfully sorry, my lady."

That the duke was flustered made her think better of him. "I do understand how one can get caught up in conversation."

"Thank you." They took their places and waited as the first two couples began the set, which gave them time to talk. "You have a very large family."

"I do." Now was the time to find out what he thought about that. "There are more of them. You only met the adults. We are very close as well."

He looked surprised. "Ah, that would explain why you are part of such a large group this evening."

Madeline was not going to tell him it was because each one of them was tasked as a chaperone. "Yes. We also spend every other Christmas together, and every summer we have a get-together."

"Very interesting." She could tell nothing by his bland tone.

It was their turn to dance, and the conversation ended. When they had the opportunity to speak again, he told her about his holdings. "I'm very busy directing my stewards."

"Have you tried any of the new farming methods?" Grace had made sure Madeline and her sisters had a working knowledge of agriculture and estate management.

His brows drew together slightly. "I am sure my stewards would not be interested in anything new."

This was not promising. "Hmm. Do you have schools on your estates?"

He appeared surprised. "For what purpose?"

Fortunately for him, it was their turn to dance again. Was he ignorant, or did he not care? Ignorance she could do something about. However, if he did not care about the welfare of his dependents, she did not know if she could fix that.

When the set ended, he escorted her back to her family. Instead of staying, the duke left, and Harry came up to her and whispered, "Ashford's approaching."

She stepped over to her brother. "Matt, I do not wish to meet Lord Ashford. He attempted to press for an introduction while Harry and I were strolling. My opinion of him is not high."

Her brother nodded. "Very well. You go on. I'll take care of Ashford."

"Thank you." She and Harry joined her sisters and Lord Montagu.

Alice, keeping her voice low, asked, "Who is that gentleman?"

"Lord Ashford. I'll tell you everything later. Suffice it to say, I do not care to meet him."

From the corner of her eye, she followed the man as he approached Matt.

"Is he not eligible?" Alice asked.

"I am certain *he* believes he is the most eligible gentleman here." Madeline hoped her sister would not be interested in the man. Ashford's visage darkened. "Oh. I wish I could hear what Matt is saying."

Just then, Lord Bury came up to them and bowed. "Lady Madeline."

"My lord." She curtseyed. Alice slid her a look. "Alice, may I introduce Lord Bury? My lord, my sister, Lady Alice Carpenter."

"It is nice to meet you, my lord." She dipped a shallow curtsey.

He took her hand as he bowed. "A pleasure, my lady. Do you have a dance free this evening?"

"I do. The one after the next set."

Madeline tried to remember which of their relatives was supposed to have led Alice out but could not.

"What luck." He smiled. "I am free for that set as well."

"Fribble." Harry's voice was so low, she almost did not hear him.

The sounds of the next set began. "Lady Madeline." Lord Bury held out his arm. "Shall we?"

This set was a country dance, so there was very little chance for a discussion. Therefore, as he escorted her back to her circle, she mentioned her large family.

"Do you mean to tell me everyone you were standing with is related to you?"

"Everyone but Mr. Stern, and he is the brother of my cousin by marriage."

"Good Lord." His lordship's eyes widened. "And you all get along?"

Madeline forced herself not to laugh. "We do."

"Remarkable." After excusing himself from her, he went straight to Alice.

"What did you say to put that shocked look on his face?" Harry asked.

"I told him everyone in our group was related, and that we all got on well." She covered her mouth to keep from laughing too loudly. Harry did not help. He pressed his lips tightly together but couldn't stop them from twitching. "Stop it. We're going to create a scene." Finally, she got herself under control. "I must assume his family is not as close as ours."

The smile disappeared from Harry's lips. "Apparently, there is outright war at his home."

"How sad." She could not imagine living in a family like that.

He nodded. "From what I understand, it is extremely uncomfortable."

"My lady." Madeline glanced up to see Lord Hereford. "My dance, I believe."

She smiled politely. "It is, my lord."

The set was a waltz. Lord Hereford was a good dancer, but he did not dance nearly as well as Harry. Although the set gave her a chance to discover more about his lordship. As she had with the duke and Lord Bury, she told him that all the people with her were related.

"I see." He sounded indifferent to the information. "That must be interesting."

What did he mean by that? "It is, rather."

"My family is large as well, but we rarely see one another. We are scattered over the country, and everyone is involved in their own lives."

"As you see, my family is frequently together."

"I say." He acted as if they had not been having a conversation. "Would you like to tool around with me in my carriage tomorrow for the Grand Strut?"

Madeline was glad Harry had already asked her. "I regret I cannot. I have a previous engagement."

He looked taken aback but smiled. "The next day, then?"

Persistence had to be a mark in his favor. "I must ask my sister-in-law, but if she agrees, I would be pleased to ride with you."

When the dance ended, he escorted Madeline back to her family but did not remain. She had not even had the opportunity to make him known to Alice.

The next set was the supper dance. She was about to put her hand on Harry's arm when Lady Markham approached them. "Lady Madeline"—her ladyship looked around and smiled—"and Lady Alice, may I present Lord Normanby?

My lord, Lady Madeline Vivers and her sister, Lady Alice Carpenter."

"My ladies, it is truly a pleasure to meet you." He bowed. "Dare I ask if one of you has the supper dance available?"

Matt heaved a sigh, and Grace stepped over to them. "I am sorry, my lord, but they both have partners. Perhaps you could make arrangements for another time."

Lord St. Albans joined them. "Normanby."

"St. Albans." It was clear the gentlemen did not like each other. "Lady Alice." He bowed and held out his hand. "My dance, I believe."

From the expression that briefly passed over her face, Alice would have switched partners if she could have done so. Instead, she placed her hand in his. "It is, my lord."

This Season seemed to have a great many pitfalls when it came to gentlemen.

"Lady Madeline?"

Harry's voice brought her out of her reverie. "Yes?"

"The dance," he drawled.

"Oh. Oh, yes." She placed her hand on his arm, and he led her to the floor.

As they took their places, the palm of his hand seemed to burn into her. "You are concerned about Alice."

"I do not know if 'concerned' is the right word. I simply do not understand what is going on between her and Lord St. Albans."

"He does not appear to be a danger to her," Harry said thoughtfully.

"Only to her nerves."

He glanced at Madeline and chuckled lightly. "I have noticed she behaves much like an aggravated cat when he's around."

That was the best description she had heard yet. "She

does. Well, there is nothing I can think to do about it. She will not even discuss what she is feeling."

The music began, and they started twirling around. "I suppose we will have to trust them to work it out."

Madeline supposed that was the only thing she could do. With that in mind, she relaxed into the dance, happy to follow Harry's lead. After all, she had a husband to find as well. It was a shame none of the other gentlemen danced as well as he did.

After the set ended, they rejoined their circle and made their way down to the supper room. Harry selected seats for them, then went off with the other gentlemen to secure their meals.

Alice sat next to her. "I have not had a chance to talk with you all evening."

That was strange. What was stranger was that Madeline had not even noticed. "It has been quite busy."

Her sister grinned. "Harry staying next to you might have something to do with it."

Alice was right. He had remained with Madeline the entire evening, except when she was dancing with other gentlemen. He had been correct when he said Lady Markham would not present him to other ladies. "You know he would not have minded if you joined us."

"I know." The way Alice responded reminded Madeline that they had been practically raised together. "What I really want to ask about is the other gentlemen. What did you think of them?"

"I decided to start seeing if they met our requirements and drew attention to the size of our family." Madeline had to stop herself from pulling a face. "None of them gave me truly satisfactory answers. Although Salforth came the closest."

A faint line formed between her sister's brows. "That is disappointing."

It was. Next time she was simply going to have to be more direct in her questions.

CHAPTER EIGHT

Merton strolled next to Harry as they approached the buffet. "I'm glad to see you're taking my advice and remaining next to Madeline."

"For all the good it's doing me." He'd wanted to growl at each of the men who'd claimed a set with her.

"Didn't like seeing her dance with other gentlemen?" His brother-in-law chose asparagus and peas, then lobster patties. Harry did the same.

"No. All I wanted to do was throw her over my shoulder and carry her out." He hoped they had ices. Madeline always liked them.

"I think we've all had the same urge." Harry raised a questioning brow. "Ask any one of us. They'll confirm it."

"I'm taking her for a carriage ride tomorrow, and thanks to Worthington, I don't have to present anyone to her."

Merton nodded absently as he perused the next offerings. "He's being extremely cautious this Season. More so than before."

"It's because he knew all of us," Kenilworth said. "We're of an age. None of us knows these new gentlemen. We're all too old, and Charlie's too young."

Harry grimaced to himself. "Unfortunately, I only knew them in school, then lost track. I have no idea what they've been doing since then." Not that he wanted any of them around Madeline. "For all I know, they've lost their fortunes and are into moneylenders."

"Probably not Salforth," Rothwell said. "I hear the duchess has kept a tight rein on him."

"Poor sod," Kenilworth muttered.

Harry had to agree, but Salforth's mother having so much power over him would not endear him to Madeline. She wasn't the type of lady to suffer interference in her household once she wed.

"Not all of us got to run free when we came into our titles." Merton's tone was dryer than usual.

Kenilworth gave him a broad smile. "Quite true, but I do not regret a moment of my previously debauched life. It's made me a much better husband and father."

His brothers-in-law scoffed.

"I'll remind you of that when your son and heir starts to run wild," Worthington commented.

Kenilworth gave Worthington a considering look. "I wonder if having cousins so close in age will temper him. I had no one to keep a check on me."

Worthington shrugged. "I suppose we'll find out."

"When do you think you'll hear about Hereford and Bury?" Merton asked.

Harry was glad his brother-in-law had posed the question, as he wasn't in a position to ask. Learning more about the competition would be helpful.

"Tomorrow or the next day at the latest," Worthington replied. They had been making their way along the line and had finally reached the desserts. Thank God there were chocolate ices! "I must add Normanby and Ashford to the list. Madeline might not want him to be introduced to them, but Alice may."

Harry was very pleased that Ashford had set Madeline's

back up. He selected a chocolate ice for Madeline and a lavender ice for himself.

Worthington signaled to a footman and asked that wine, champagne, and lemonade be brought to their table. Harry noticed each of the gentlemen slipped vails into the hands of the servants carrying the trays, and he did the same.

As they strode back to the ladies, Salforth approached Worthington. "My lord, to whom do I apply to take Lady Madeline out for a carriage ride?"

"You may send a card inviting her around to Worthington House."

"Thank you." The duke stepped out of the way. "I shall do as you suggest."

"Slow top," Phinn muttered.

The man had been so quiet, Harry had forgotten he was there. "How so?"

"It's much more difficult to refuse a man to his face." Phinn glanced at the table. "I speak from experience."

Harry knew he wouldn't be able to ask Madeline to accompany him every day, but he could set up a series of rides with her. Perhaps every other day. "Good point."

St. Albans and Montagu had followed them but had taken no part in the conversation. Had they been gathering the hints the other gentlemen had been dropping as Harry had? Not that it mattered. They were interested in her sisters, not Madeline.

Harry motioned to the footman to place the dishes in front of Madeline. "They had chocolate ices."

"Oooh. I see." She beamed up at him. "Thank you."

"I also have asparagus and lobster patties." He took his seat next to her.

"You did very well indeed, sir."

"Thank you, my lady." He placed the foods she indicated on her plate, then filled his own. "Would you care to ride with me in three days' time?" He had no doubt Salforth would ask her to accompany him the day after tomorrow.

"Yes. I would be delighted." She smiled, and Harry's body tightened.

She would be his.

They devoted the next few minutes to eating as the others conversed around them. It wasn't until St. Albans mentioned one of their old school chums that Harry thought to ask him what he knew of Bury, Ashford, and Hereford. St. Albans had been on the town for a few years now. Yet not at the moment. Tomorrow morning would be soon enough. If the man could arise in time to join them.

The next day, Harry awoke to rain spattering on his window.

Hell and perdition!

There'd be no riding this morning. He prayed it stopped by this afternoon. He should do something to remind Madeline of him.

Flowers. Something bright to make the day less dreary. Reaching over, he tugged the bell-pull.

A moment later, Burkham entered his room. "Sir."

"I'd like to send a lady flowers. Something cheerful. Can you arrange that?"

"Of course, sir. Give me a few minutes. When I saw it was raining, I brought up your wash water."

"Thank you." Harry threw back the covers and strode behind the screen. By the time he'd washed and shaved, his valet had returned.

"I asked one of the footmen to accompany a maid. I am certain she will be able to select a suitable arrangement."

"Good idea. I'll write a note after I'm dressed." Never

one to dawdle over his toilet, he was ready a half hour later. Fortunately, Dotty had ordered stationery for him. He pulled out a piece of pressed paper and took out an already sharpened pen. Now, what to say?

My dear Madeline,
    I'm sorry the weather has caused us to miss our ride this morning. I hope the—

"Burkham, do you have any idea what kind of flowers?"
"I believe the maid mentioned she had seen daffodils."
"Thank you." Harry went back to the note.

the daffodils will make your day brighter.

> *Yr. Servant,*
> *H.*

Short but appropriate. He should add something about their ride.

PS I hope it will stop raining by this afternoon. If not, I would still like to visit with you.

That ought to do it. He sanded the letter, folded it, and affixed his seal.

"Burkham, make sure the flowers are daffodils before this goes out. If not, I'll have to write another note."
"Yes, sir."
As Harry rose to go down to breakfast, it occurred to him that his day was going to feel much longer without having seen Madeline first.

* * *

Madeline had just returned from her sister's bedchamber when her maid handed her a card. "This came for you, along with the last of the season's daffodils."

The flowers had been put in a vase, and the note had already been opened. As she perused it, she was surprised that her heart started to behave as if there were butterflies in her chest. "It is from Mr. Stern. He hopes the flowers brighten my day."

"That was nice of him."

"It was." And very sweet. She hoped the rain would stop this afternoon as well. Today was the day Charlie took his seat in the Lords. Would Harry be there? Had he been invited to the celebration taking place afterward? She would have to ask Grace. "I must dress quickly."

Even though she rushed through her toilet, she arrived on Alice's heels. Eleanor, already at the table, burst into tears. Oh dear. What had happened? Madeline rushed to her sister and hugged her, and pressed a handkerchief into Eleanor's hands. "It will all be fine."

Alice gave up hers as well.

"What on earth brought that on?" Matt's fork was suspended halfway between his plate and his mouth.

"I think she has finally understood the magnitude of what this Season means," Charlie said.

Madeline glanced at him. What did that mean?

"I knew it was a good idea Constance, Vivienne, Alexandria, and I decided not to have a come out," Elizabeth's tone conveyed her disgust at the idea of a come out. Well, that would most likely change.

"Did you?" Grace was clearly trying not to laugh as Eleanor wiped her tears.

Matt leaned back in his chair and crossed his arms over his chest. "I knew you were clever girls. You have made me and the other fathers very happy."

"That is what Aunt Eleanor said." Elizabeth looked pleased with herself.

Theo swallowed a piece of toast. "Enjoy it while you can."

"It will not last." Mary had one brow raised.

"I don't understand," Gideon had been staring at Eleanor but now glanced at the table as a whole. "Why is she sad?"

"You are too young to remember," Mary said calmly. "But when one has a Season, a lady marries, and then she has to move away and live in a different house. Just like Charlotte, Louisa, Henrietta, and Dotty did."

Gideon's face puckered. "But I don't want them to move away. Papa, you must take us all home right now."

Matt dragged a hand down his face. "Can we please eat our breakfast and have this conversation later?"

Theo whispered something to a footman and rose. "Come along, Gideon. I will explain it to you. It is not as bad as you think it is."

She took him by the hand and left the room. A footman followed them with their breakfast plates.

"I am sorry." Eleanor placed the damp handkerchiefs on the table.

"It is fine." Grace gave their sister a soft smile. "This was bound to happen sooner or later. You have been here his whole life."

"Better he gets it out now than at the wedding," Mary took a sip of tea. "The hardest was seeing Charlotte get married and go away. Then I realized I just would not see her as much, but she was still my sister. And we all really like Con."

That was true. "And we like Rothwell, Merton, and Phinn too."

Phinn's lips twitched. "Thank you. I'm very happy to be part of the family. In fact, I'm very much looking forward to the next get-together."

That was it. What made her family so strong. Madeline

regarded her brothers and sisters. "Indeed we never lose
people, we just add them to our family."

Grace looked at Matt over her cup. "That we do."

Madeline patted Eleanor's shoulder. "And that is the
reason we have that one requirement on our list."

"So it is." She gave a just slightly watery smile.

It was something Madeline had to put in the forefront of
her mind when choosing a husband. He had to be willing to
marry all of them. So to speak.

They took the large family coach to the Palace of
Westminster, where Charlie, very regally dressed in a robe,
took his seat in the House of Lords. Afterward, they had a
small family celebration before Harry departed for his
house across the square for the more formal one attended by
his peers.

Fortunately, the rain had stopped, and Madeline would
be able to enjoy her carriage ride with Harry.

While they'd been gone, several bouquets of flowers had
been sent. Two were red roses, obviously hothouse flowers;
the others pretty arrangements of carnations, delphiniums,
and fragrant freesias. None of them were prettier than the
daffodils Madeline had received from Harry that morning.

Grace opened the cards that had been placed in front of
the bouquets and read them.

"Madeline, the roses are from Salforth. The mixed bouquets are from Lords Bury and Hereford. There is one for
you and one for Alice. Alice, the other roses are from St.
Albans." Grace handed the cards to them. "Salforth asks that
you accompany him on a carriage ride tomorrow. Lords
Bury and Hereford simply ask to be allowed to drive you
out. Alice, they asked the same of you." Grace smiled. "I
suppose they left it to you to decide on the dates."

Alice kept scowling at the roses St. Albans sent.

"They are very pretty." Madeline hoped her sister would not throw them away.

Finally, Alice sighed. "They are. What are we doing this evening?"

"We are staying home." It would be nice not to have to go anywhere. "Tomorrow Lady Brownly is hosting a musical evening."

"We are very busy today. There is just enough time for a light luncheon before we must make morning calls," Grace said as she turned toward the small dining room.

Their first stop was at Exeter House. Dorie greeted them, then Grace exclaimed, "Anna, I did not know you were in Town."

Anna rose and hugged Grace. "We just arrived the other day. My sister-in-law, Althea, had her first child, and we felt as if we should be there for her." She smiled. "They have a little boy."

They sat together on one of the sofas. "She had been traveling with her husband, if I remember correctly."

"Indeed. They returned last autumn to await the birth." Anna accepted a cup of tea from Dorie.

"That is excellent news." Grace took a cup from Phillida Endicott, Dorie's sister-in-law.

Once everyone had been served tea, Madeline, Alice, Eloisa Rutherford, Anna's other sister-in-law, and Phillida gathered around one of the tables. Phillida and Eloisa were both in their second Seasons.

"How are you enjoying your Season so far?" Phillida asked.

"It has been interesting," Alice said. "We are starting to meet more gentlemen, but our brother insists on having them investigated before he will allow introductions."

"At least he is not threatening them with bodily harm," Eloisa mumbled.

Madeline was sure she had heard incorrectly. "What exactly did he do?"

"It was last Season. The gentleman was very handsome and quite charming."

"And a cad," Phillida said.

Eloisa gave her a look of agreement. "He was a fortune hunter. To make a long story short, Rutherford told him that he had two choices: leave me alone or he would make him disappear."

"I assume he left you alone," Eleanor said.

"No, the idiot decided he should elope with Eloisa." Phillida's lips formed a thin line.

Madeline had heard about Lord Rutherford working for the Home Office during the war. "And?"

Eloisa shrugged. "I have not seen him since."

Madeline could not but think the gentleman must have been very stupid indeed to have not listened to Lord Rutherford. It did make her wonder if Matt would do something of the sort, and decided he probably would. "I am glad our brother has decided to investigate ahead of them being presented to us. It will save a great deal of trouble."

Just then several ladies were announced, and Grace signaled it was time to leave.

Madeline prayed neither she nor her sisters would have to contend with fortune hunters.

CHAPTER NINE

Harry arrived at Worthington House promptly at five o'clock for his appointment with Madeline. This week was going to be busy, and he needed to make as much time for her as possible. Fortunately, as he had the dinner at Mr. Taylor's house to attend, there were no other entertainments planned for this evening. But he must ask her to sit with him at the musical evening tomorrow.

Parkin opened the door and bowed. The next second, he was almost knocked off his feet by two exuberant, young Great Danes. "Sit." Remarkably, they did. "You must be Zeus and Posy. Good dogs. Now, if only I had a treat for you." To the side of him, someone coughed. When he looked, a footman handed him two biscuits. "Thank you." The Danes' tails began to thump. "Stay." He handed the first to the female. "Ladies first." Then to the male. "I know you're not normally left wandering around to greet visitors."

Sounds of feet running down the stairs caused him to look up. Elizabeth, Gideon, Mary, and Theo looked at him in horror and stopped.

"We're sorry," Gideon said. "They got away from us."

"Completely understandable." The dogs, no longer sitting, went to the children.

"Oh dear." Madeline's voice came from above.

"It's no matter." He gave her a reassuring smile. "They merely wanted to see who was here." He started to brush off his trousers.

"Allow me," a footman said. Wielding a brush, he made quick work of the dog hair.

Harry was finally able to pay full attention to Madeline. She was a vision in a pale pink carriage gown trimmed with ribbons in a deeper pink. He held out his arm. "Shall we? I am hoping to miss at least some of the crowd."

"I wish you good luck with that." She tucked her hand in the crook of his arm. "Are you still borrowing your sister's curricle?"

"No." He glanced down at her, but the brim of her very fetching bonnet hid her face. "It is now mine."

"Excellent!" Madeline turned her head enough that he could see her smile. "That will make your life easier."

"It will. I was told the names of your dogs, but not their ages."

"Zeus is three and Posy is two. We got them from two different breeders." She raised one shoulder in a shrug. "They are mostly Gideon and Elizabeth's. Except when they are hiding. Then they sneak into one of our rooms."

That baffled him. "Hiding from what?"

"This morning it was from their walk." Her lips twitched. "They do not like to walk in the rain."

"Ah. I can't say I blame them." He didn't like to get soaked either.

"Do you have dogs at home?"

"My father always has an older dog in the house, but they usually stay close to him in his study." He sensed there was a reason behind her question. "I would love to have a dog of my own."

Madeline slid him a look. "In the house, like ours are?"

"Of course. I remember the Great Danes the previous Lord

Stanwood had. They always greeted us when we visited. That was how I knew to tell yours to sit."

"Oh." She'd turned her head, and, once again, he couldn't see her face, but she sounded happy.

They drove through the gates to the Park, and he was pleased to see it was not yet overly populated. "This is much better."

"I must not forget to thank you for the flowers. They were beautiful." She moved slightly so that he could see her and smiled. "They really did brighten up the morning."

"Thank you." He returned her smile. "I hoped they might. I find I missed riding. It seems to steady one's day."

"Yes." She nodded. "I find it helps me work off any excess energy." He could find other ways to help rid her of her excess energy. "How was your day?"

He took a breath and let it out. "Frustrating. Several of us are working on a bill to allow all women, not just those who can afford lawyers, to keep their possessions and earnings, and the like."

"That would be helpful." Madeline sounded thoughtful. "It is not fair that one must have a contract in order for a female to keep what is hers."

It didn't surprise him that she was aware of the law. Knowing the ladies around her, he would have been shocked if she had not. "I also wonder how many women know they can make an agreement to protect their possessions."

"That is something I had not considered. Yet you are correct. In fact, I imagine most females, even ladies, do not know." She was silent for several seconds as he drove at a respectable pace around the carriage way. "There must be something we can do about it."

He liked the "we." "What do you suggest?"

"I must give it some thought. A pamphlet comes to mind, but would ladies read it, and what about the women who cannot read?"

"A person can draw up their own contracts. They need not be done by a solicitor." From the corner of his eye, a horse and rider approached. *Salforth*.

"Matt writes the contracts for any of our dependents who wed. Did I not hear that your father does the same?" Obviously, Madeline hadn't seen his so-called friend.

Perhaps Harry could pretend Salforth wasn't there. "He does. He also agrees there must be a law protecting women who wed."

Her fine brows drew together. "What about a whispering campaign to get the word out?"

"Good afternoon." The duke's voice was cheerful.

Madeline glanced up at him, frowning. "Yes, I suppose it is."

Harry almost laughed out loud at the look of dismay on the other man's face.

"I take it you were discussing something serious." Salforth lifted his hat. "I shall leave you to it." And rode off.

Madeline's frowning gaze followed him, and Harry wanted to get her back to the subject at hand. "The other problem is that a man must agree with the proposal."

Her brow cleared. "I suppose that is a fence that must be crossed. If he was marrying her for her possessions, he would be unlikely to agree."

"Indeed. Hence, we are back to a law." To Harry's shock, they were already driving out of the Park.

He glanced over to find Madeline staring at him. "I would like to assist in drafting a law for women."

This was exactly what he wanted in a wife. Someone who could give him ideas and help with the formation. "We could certainly use a female perspective."

Her expression changed from concerned to satisfied. As if just being able to do something to help would be sufficient for the time being. There was no reason to tell her how difficult it would be. A bill like the one they were planning might take years to pass. Still, it was a beginning. "Ices?"

Her face was suddenly alight. "Yes, please."

He wondered what flavor he'd try today. They pulled up at Gunter's, and there was a distinct lack of carriages. A servant ran out. "I'm surprised it's not busy."

"The weather, sir." The man glanced up, and for the first time, Harry noticed an almost black cloud overhead. "I suppose everyone expects it to rain."

"You are right," she said. The long line of her throat was visible as she stared up at the sky. "That does not look good."

They had better eat quickly. "The lady will have a chocolate ice. What do you have as specials?"

"Pineapple, bergamot, and custard."

"I will try pineapple, please." He liked pineapples, ergo he should like the ice.

"I'll be right back with them."

As they waited, Harry decided to raise the convertible hood. It wouldn't keep them completely dry, but it would help. Fortunately, the man was back soon, and Harry paid him.

Harry held out his ice to Madeline. "A tiny taste?"

She grinned, took a little on her spoon, and ate it. "This is much better than the last one."

"But chocolate is still your favorite."

"Yes." She dipped her spoon into the confection and opened her mouth. He were completely attuned to the way her lips closed around the spoon. "Are you not going to eat yours?"

Damn. He dragged his gaze away from her and tasted his ice. The pineapple was tart and sweet at the same time and much better than the Parmesan. A fat drop hit the convertible top. "We'd better go." He gave the server their cups. "Fortunately, your house is not far."

They dashed around the corner and down the street to

Worthington House. When he lifted her down, their eyes locked, and their lips were closer together than they had been before. If he didn't leave now, he'd kiss her right in the street. "Come, I need to get you in before this starts in earnest."

"Yes, I suppose you must go home before you are soaked."

He took her hand and kissed it. "That doesn't mean I can't walk you to the door."

Thorton stood in the entrance. and Madeline waved to Harry. The musical! "Will you sit with me tomorrow evening at the musical?"

"Yes." She nodded. "I shall see you then."

He hoped it wasn't raining in the morning.

Madeline turned to watch Harry depart, but the door was already closed. She hoped he did not get soaked on his way home. When she reached her bedchamber, her maid already had her clothing laid out for dinner, and she glanced at the clock. She would have just enough time to write accept-ances to the other gentlemen. But first, she'd change into a clean gown.

A few minutes later, she pulled out a piece of pressed paper. Salforth first. But before she could dip her pen into the ink, Alice strode into the room. "I thought we should coordinate the carriage rides. It will not do us any good if we accept rides for the same days."

"I should have thought of that. Bring that chair over here." Pushing the pressed paper aside, Madeline took out a piece of cut foolscap. "I thought of telling Salforth he could take me out tomorrow."

"That is an excellent idea." Her sister's tone was a bit too pleased.

"Why are you so happy about that decision?" She dipped the pen in the ink and wrote his name.

"Your mama stopped by while you were out with Harry. She wanted to speak with Grace about who was courting you."

After the uproar over Augusta, Madeline did not think Grace would provide Mama much information. "What did Grace say?"

Alice waved her hand in an airy gesture. "You know Grace. She merely said it was early days, and several gentlemen had asked you out for rides and for dance sets." Then Alice huffed. "Then your mama asked specifically about Salforth."

Madeline sighed. Of course her mother would want her to wed a duke. Then again, she had only just met him.

"Grace repeated herself and asked how your mother was, because you know she is pregnant again."

"I do know." One would think her younger children would keep her too busy to interfere with Madeline. "Salforth it is, then. Who are you thinking of first?"

Alice tapped a finger against her chin. "Lord Hereford. He was a good-natured dance partner. Then Salforth, and Lord Bury. I do hope Lord Normanby soon passes muster with Matt."

"Hmm. I will ride with Lord Bury, then Lord Hereford. But with a day in between the rides." Harry would ask her to ride with him again, and Madeline wanted to spend more time with him. Of all the gentlemen she had met, he had by far the best conversation.

Alice grinned. "What a good idea. If we meet other gentlemen, we will have time to ride with them as well." The corners of her lips dipped down. "Although if St. Albans asks, I do not know what I will say."

"I am sure you will think of something." Madeline would really love to be able to read her sister's mind when it came to his lordship. "I must get these missives sent before dinner."

"I too." Alice jumped up and strode to the door. "I will see you in the drawing room."

"Yes, I will see you then." Madeline finished making notes on the foolscap and pulled the pressed paper in front of her. Her acceptances would be short.

> *Your grace,*
>   *Thank you for the lovely roses.*
>   *I would be pleased to ride with you tomorrow afternoon at five in the afternoon.*
>
> > *Cordially yours,*
> > *M. Vivers*

She read it over once, signed it, and wrote the next two. Once they were sanded and sealed, she took them down to the round table in the hall and left them on the silver salver to be delivered. Then it occurred to her that if they must go out today, she would have to immediately send a footman. She picked them back up again and turned to the footman at the door. "Can you please call for Roberts? I have an errand for him."

"Of course, my lady." The footman stepped inside the green baize door, and Roberts entered the hall.

"My lady?"

"These letters must go out this afternoon, but I am afraid I do not know where the gentlemen reside."

"Leave it to me." Roberts took the missives.

"Thank you." It was a mystery to her how the servants seemed to either know or could easily discover the direction of everyone.

Grace descended the stairs. "A moment of your time."

This had to be about Mama. They strolled to the family drawing room, where Matt was waiting. "I heard my mother came by this afternoon."

"She did." Grace accepted a glass of sherry from Matt.

"Madeline?" He held up the decanter.

"Yes, please." Once she had her glass, they sat in the chairs in front of the fireplace. "I heard some of what she said."

"Alice?" Grace asked.

"Yes. She told me when we discussed the carriage rides. Mama is interested in Salforth."

"Of course she is." Matt barked a laugh. "The higher the better for her daughters."

"Madeline, this is your life," Grace said firmly. "You must choose the gentleman with whom you can be happy. We did not allow her to interfere with either Augusta or Louisa. We will stand by you as well. If it is Salforth, so be it. But if it is another gentleman, that is fine as well."

"If need be," Matt said, "I will speak with Wolverton."

"Thank you." Madeline appreciated their support, but that would not stop Mama from making demands, or being upset if Madeline picked a gentleman with whom she did not agree. And she *wanted* to please Mama. Madeline would have to spend more time with the duke.

Alice and Eleanor entered the drawing room, followed by Theo, Mary, and Walter. He poured lemonade for their younger sisters, and Matt gave the older ones sherry. The talk turned first to Charlie's induction to the Lords. Then Matt said, "I have received reports on Salforth, Hereford, Bury, and Ashford. They are all financially solvent, and other than the normal things young men get up to on the Town, I can find nothing objectionable."

It was comforting that her brother was so careful with Madeline and her sisters. Perhaps during the carriage rides she would make a point of knowing the Duke of Salforth better.

CHAPTER TEN

It was still raining when Harry set out for Mr. Taylor's house in one of the Merton unmarked town coaches. He had been looking forward to the evening until Dotty had mentioned the man's marriageable daughter. As it was, Harry was concerned the daughter was the primary reason for the invitation. If that was true, he'd have to be polite and noncommittal. The coach turned into Russell Square and rolled to a stop.

The footman he brought with him opened the carriage door. "There's a stable not far from here, Mr. Stern. Your coachman can go there and wait for you to summon him."

He did not know the area well at all. In fact, he'd never been here before. "Thank you."

"I'll stay in the kitchen until you're ready to leave," the footman said.

Harry almost felt as if he were being protected from the unknown. "I appreciate that."

"Our pleasure, sir." The servant stepped back. "I hope you have a good evening."

"So do I." He'd soon see. He strolled to the door and was almost surprised that it didn't open at his approach. Then he remembered mannerisms would be different here.

"Shall I knock for you, sir?" the footman asked.

"No, I'll do it." He plied the brightly shined knocker in the shape of a lion, and a second later it opened.

"Good evening." The butler bowed, then glanced at the footman. "Your servant can wait in the kitchen. I shall take your coat and hat."

"Thank you."

The man betrayed a brief look of surprise. Harry supposed he was not used to being thanked, but that was how he was raised. His mother always said being kind to servants was the least one can do for their steadfast service. As he was being divested of his coat, hat, and cane, Harry noticed the decoration lent itself to the Egyptian style popular a few years earlier.

"If you will follow me," the butler said.

The man led Harry to a drawing room just off the hall and opened the door. "Mr. Stern."

He stepped into the room. Mr. Taylor and an older matron, who had to be his wife, bustled up to greet him. A younger woman followed behind them.

"Stern, I'm glad you could join us," Taylor said. "My dear, may I introduce the new MP from Bittleborough, Mr. Stern." Harry bowed. "Stern, my wife and helpmeet, Mrs. Taylor." She curtseyed.

Mrs. Taylor looked to be a few years younger than her husband, with blond hair and brown eyes. "A pleasure, ma'am."

The woman signaled for a younger version of herself to come forward. "Emily, I'd like you to meet Mr. Stern."

Emily Taylor appeared to be in her early twenties. Harry bowed as she curtseyed. "Miss Taylor, I am pleased to meet you."

The younger woman blushed. "We have heard so much about you, Mr. Stern. Papa is quite impressed with the way you have so quickly taken up your duties."

"I am fortunate that I am able to reside with my sister and her husband for the nonce."

Mrs. Taylor smiled broadly. "Your sister is the Marchioness of Merton, is she not? She is very active in Whig politics."

He inclined his head. "Yes, she is. She and her husband both. They have been extremely helpful."

Taylor led him to a sideboard, also in the Egyptian motif. "A glass of wine before dinner?"

"Yes, please."

He handed Harry a glass of claret.

"It must be useful to be able to have firsthand knowledge of what is going on in the Lords. There are times when I feel as if they are purposely acting against us."

Harry got the feeling he was being encouraged to discuss politics, which was not what he expected when a young woman was present. Other than in his broader family, of course, it was not considered polite. "I believe my brother-in-law and his friends would support a new bankruptcy law. Quite frankly, I don't know why it would not have considerable support in the Lords. After all, it's their family members who are frequently imprisoned and must be helped."

"A good point. I had not thought of that," Taylor said.

"Oh, Mr. Taylor, may we not speak of politics all evening?" his wife said rather archly. "I would be very interested in hearing more about Mr. Stern."

Taylor might have invited Harry over to learn more about his political leanings, but Mrs. Taylor clearly had other plans.

He opened his hands in a gesture of surrender. "I am happy to discuss whatever subject you would like, ma'am."

"Excellent." The woman tittered. It was then that Harry, who tried not to notice the way people spoke, noticed her speech was not of the gentry.

"Mama," Miss Taylor said. "We must not interrogate Mr. Stern."

Mrs. Taylor patted her daughter's hand. "You are correct, as always." She turned to Harry. "Emily attended a very select seminary in Bath."

Miss Taylor blushed. "It was the only school that would agree to allow me to read all the newssheets Papa insisted upon."

Mrs. Taylor fidgeted with her wine. "You can be sure she also learned everything a lady should."

Harry's cravat was tighter than it had been, and he resisted the urge to tug on it.

"Did your sister attend school?" Mrs. Taylor asked.

"No. My father taught them alongside my brother and me until we went to school. He was a vicar until his brother died and he inherited the baronetcy."

The woman made a pout but didn't answer.

The butler opened the doors and bowed. "Dinner is served."

Mrs. Taylor placed her arm on her husband's, leaving Harry to escort her daughter. He held out his arm to her.

Miss Taylor grimaced slightly at her mother's not expecting him to escort the older woman. He was pleased to note that she did not make the error of either correcting her mother or apologizing for the slip in manners.

He wanted to make it less painful for her, and it wasn't as if other mothers hadn't done the same type of thing, albeit with more finesse. "She means well."

"Yes." Miss Taylor smiled. She really was a pretty young woman. "She loves me a great deal."

The table had been shortened to seat four, and he was placed across from her. There was no center table arrangement to make discussion difficult. Harry could not complain of the food. A white soup was served, followed by two types of fish and removes of buttered artichokes. Next came the meat: rare roast of beef, rabbit, and chicken. This was removed with haricots verts with shaved almonds, a salad of greens and spinach, as well as braised fennel. For dessert, he was offered a selection of small tarts, strawberry, currents, and preserved pears.

While they ate, the conversation ranged from politics to the Season. He knew the Season Miss Taylor was attending would be quite different from his own in the quality of entertainments.

"Do you plan to situate yourself to move into a leadership position in the party?" Miss Taylor asked.

That was something to which he'd not given a great deal of thought. "I have not decided yet." He gave her a wry smile. "I am still finding my feet."

"Ah, I understand." The answer didn't seem to impress her. Did she aspire to be a political hostess?

Taylor pulled Harry back into conversation about the bankruptcy law, and he ventured to mention the idea of protecting the property of married women. "It does not seem right to me that women who cannot afford a lawyer, or someone able to write the agreements, or whose prospective husbands will not agree, have their property put at risk."

Before Taylor could give his opinion, his wife said, "But do you not believe women should be able to trust their husbands?"

"That is, of course, what we all would like to believe, ma'am. Yet how many men gamble either at the table or with investments, leaving their families with naught."

"Although I will be no great heiress"—Miss Taylor turned to her mother— "I would like to know that my husband could not bankrupt me. How would you like to have me living in debtors' prison?"

"Oh." Mrs. Taylor's eyes rounded. "I see your point. I

have had a wonderful marriage, and your papa has been very prudent, but I suppose one cannot know what the years will bring."

"Well said, my dear." Mr. Taylor's smile was warm as he regarded her. "I think it is a good idea, but don't expect it to sail through."

"I don't." It could take years. "In fact, I only hope that we will be able to pass it on to benefit our daughters or granddaughters."

Mr. Taylor nodded. "First we must rid ourselves of the Corn Laws that have plagued the country for much too long."

They went in for tea as the clock struck ten. He should be leaving soon.

"How do you like your tea?" Miss Taylor asked.

"Just a bit of sugar, thank you."

As he took the cup, her mother said, "We are planning a dance in the near future. May we send you a card?"

Harry took a sip of tea and tried to decide how to answer her query. He'd be noncommittal. "Yes, of course."

"Perhaps I should invite the marchioness as well," Mrs. Taylor mused.

Harry let that pass. Dotty was well up to snuff and would know how she wished to handle any card she received from Mrs. Taylor.

He finished his tea and set it on the low table in front of the sofa. "Thank you for a very pleasant evening." Rising, he bowed to the women. "However, I must be going. I do not keep late hours."

Taylor got to his feet. "I'll walk you out."

As Harry was donning his coat and hat, a knock came on the door. The butler opened it, and his footman bowed. "Your coach is ready, Mr. Stern."

"Thank you."

"We're glad you could join us," Taylor said. "I'll see you tomorrow."

Harry shook the other man's hand. "I had a lovely time. Until tomorrow."

He climbed into the coach and sank into the soft cushions. There was no doubt Dotty would want to hear about this evening. He wondered what she'd say about the forthcoming invitation to a dance. She would probably be fine with it. Merton, on the other hand, would be a fish out of water. Remembering the assembly his brother-in-law attended in the town near Harry's parents' estate, he chuckled.

When he arrived home, Parkin informed Harry that both her ladyship and his lordship had retired for the evening. He decided to do the same. The sun was coming up earlier every day. Meaning he'd have to be up even earlier to ride with Madeline. "Thank you. I'll see you in the morning."

The next morning rain hitting the windows woke him. "Well, hell."

"Did you say something, sir?" Burkham asked.

"I'll need more flowers." Harry got out of bed. "One bouquet for Lady Madeline to make up for the gray start to the day. I should also get one for Mrs. Taylor, thanking her for inviting me last evening."

"I'll see to it." His valet left the room.

He wouldn't get to see Madeline until this evening.

Madeline opened her eyes and groaned. "It's raining again."

"Yes, my lady," Harper said from the dressing room. "But William Coachman said it would stop around noon."

"Did he happen to say how long these wet mornings would continue?"

"For the next day or two." She came out carrying a green morning gown.

When she disappeared back into the dressing room, Madeline got out of bed and padded next door to Eleanor's bedchamber.

Alice was lying in bed next to Posy, yawning. "I am tired, but I am not, if that makes any sense at all."

It did to Madeline. "I think rain makes one tired." It was hard to be energetic when the skies were gray and rain pattered the windows. "At least it always seems that way." She tried to stifle her yawn but gave up. "When I think of a rainy day, I think of reading a good book." She'd rather be riding. What was Harry doing? Was he wishing he could ride this morning?

Alice glanced at Madeline. "If we did that every time it rained, we would never get anything done."

"That's true." This reminded her of when they were younger, and Daisy would cuddle with them in bed.

"This is where you all are," Eleanor's maid said. "My ladies, your maids are looking for you. Miss Posy, there is a footman who needs to take you out."

Madeline sat up and pushed herself off the bed. "I'll see you at breakfast."

She went into her room, where her maid was waiting with a cup of chocolate. "I thought this might help."

"Thank you." She picked up the cup and drank it. "I do not know why it is so hard to become motivated on rainy days."

"Did they find Posy?" Harper asked.

"Yes. We were all in Eleanor's chamber." It occurred to Madeline that all three of them in bed with a dog might not happen again. Soon they would all have their own homes and families.

"It is interesting the way Posy and Zeus try to hide when it's raining." Harper gave a small smile. "He tried to crawl under Lady Elizabeth's bed this morning."

The bed was very low to the floor. Madeline wished she

had seen his attempt. Great Danes truly did not know how large they were. "That must have been funny."

Harper gave a small smile. "The nursemaid telling the story barely got it out, she was laughing so hard."

Madeline dressed quickly.

A knock came on the door, and Harper opened it. "These are very pretty!" She turned around with a bouquet of yellow and pink tulips in a vase. "For you, my lady."

They were beautiful. Madeline did not even have to read the card to know who had sent them. No one else would have a reason to send flowers so early. Suddenly she felt happier. "They are from Mr. Stern. He has excellent taste in flowers."

She glanced at the missive to see what he had written.

My dearest Madeline,
 I hope the flowers bring some sunshine into your morning.
 I look forward to seeing you this evening.

   Yr. servant,
   H.

She looked forward to seeing him as well. Even more than she expected she would, and she was not ready for what those feelings might portend. Madeline folded the card and put it in her desk drawer. Today was another full day of visits, and she had her ride with the Duke of Salforth. Madeline gave herself a shake. If her mother was set on him, she would do her best to ensure he met her qualifications.

CHAPTER ELEVEN

At breakfast, Madeline was listening to her brother's conversation with Eleanor about a meeting he was having today that included Lord Montagu. They had agreed to continue the conversation at luncheon. Alice asked about Lady Brownly's musical evening, and something prompted Elizabeth to remember a monkey with a fellow playing a pipe and deciding she would like to have one as well. That caused Grace to firmly quash the idea of a monkey in the house. Seeing that the little girl was not ready to concede the argument, Madeline quickly excused herself from the table. Alice and Eleanor followed, and they had to stride swiftly into the hall before they could let out their whoops.

"A monkey!" Eleanor held on to her sides.

Madeline could not conceive how a musical evening could equate to a monkey. "It never would have occurred to me that she would think of the fellow playing the pipe."

"The things they come up with." Alice fanned her face with her hand. "Who would have thought?"

"Montagu will be here this morning for Matt's meeting," Eleanor said, sobering. "I must find a way to listen to them. He cannot be as dim as he acts around me."

"We will help you." It was the least Madeline and Alice could do. That and pray that Lord Montagu did not disappoint Eleanor.

Madeline made her way to her chamber and tried to imagine what the Duke of Salforth, or the other gentlemen, would say to a monkey in the house. Indeed, what would they say to large dogs in the house? The only one who might understand would be Harry Stern, and that was no help at all. Her mother would not approve. Would he be at the meeting today?

She went to the music room and practiced piano pieces. At some point, she supposed she would have to play them. She had been there for over an hour when a footman entered the room. "My lady, Lady Eleanor asks you to join her in the Young Ladies' Parlor."

Had this to do with Lord Montagu? Madeline put her music away. "I'll be straight there."

When she entered the parlor, Alice was already there.

"Madeline," Eleanor said, "Charlie said he would help us. He is leaving the antechamber door slightly open and placing a chair in front of it so that it cannot swing open."

Well, that would keep them from falling into the room while they were listening. "When do we go down?"

Eleanor bit her lip. "He will send a note."

Ah. They were waiting. "With any luck, it will not be long."

Fortunately, within a few minutes, a footman knocked on the open door. "Lord Stanwood said this is for Lady Eleanor."

The servant handed her a folded scrap of paper. "Thank you."

Eleanor's hand shook as Alice urged her to open it. Madeline went to her sister's shoulder and read the note.

In five minutes.

S

She had been hoping it was the summons. "Why do you think he wants us to wait?"

Eleanor frowned. "They will spend time greeting each other before settling down to business."

"There is that." The clock seemed to tick more slowly; finally, they slipped quietly down to the antechamber. As Charlie had promised, the door had been secured, and they could easily see and hear the meeting. Lord Montagu was not the only younger gentleman there. Harry was seated next to Merton. Madeline was impressed to hear Harry taking an active part in the discussions.

They listened to the men discuss mine reforms for several minutes, and Madeline could see the moment Eleanor knew that Lord Montagu had proven himself. They quickly made their way back to their parlor.

"I assume it answered your questions?"

"It did." Eleanor smiled. "I will see you at luncheon."

"What will you do about Montagu?" Alice asked.

"I shall continue discovering more about him." Eleanor left the room.

They all seemed to be doing the same thing regarding gentlemen. Madeline just wished the process could be easier. "I would like to draw up a list of questions we could pose to our possible suitors."

"It might be better if we could require them to write the answers," Alice said.

That was an interesting idea. "And we could quiz them afterward to make sure we understood their answers." Madeline glanced out the window. The rain was finally growing lighter. "There must be an easier way to find the right husbands for us."

"I wish there was." Alice threw herself into a chair. "Just look at the lengths to which Eleanor has gone, and she is not finished."

"Very true." Madeline would have to be more subtle than she had been during her dances. It was all just so frustrating. "I have decided to simply attempt to get to know the gentlemen, and not apply our criteria yet."

Alice tilted her head as if she was considering the idea. "That is a good plan. It will not move things along as quickly, but it might have the benefit of letting us know if we like the gentlemen."

"That is what I thought." Madeline started fidgeting with a letter opener. "I need something to do."

"I agree, but what?"

"Shopping." She nodded to herself. "We have enough time before luncheon to go to a few stores."

"Excellent. We will have to change." Alice jumped up from the chair. "We had better take a carriage. I'll call for that, and you tell Grace."

Madeline found Grace in the library. "Grace, Alice and I wish to go shopping. We will be back before luncheon. Do you mind?"

Her sister-in-law looked up from a journal. "Not at all. In fact, if you go to Hatchards, you can pick up some books I ordered."

"Thank you. We will do that first." How wonderful to be out of the house.

Madeline's maid was waiting for her when she returned to her chamber, and a yellow walking gown was already out. "I must hurry."

Soon she was in the town coach with Alice, their footmen standing on the back in waterproof coats. Madeline leaned back against the squabs. "It makes no sense, but I feel as if I have made an escape."

"I understand," Alice said. "Perhaps it is because everyone has something important to do but us."

Madeline glanced at her sister. "I had not thought of that, but you are right. Grace has the family and estates. Matt has the Lords. Eleanor has her mines. We seem to be at loose ends."

"We will find our causes." Alice patted Madeline's hand. "Everyone else has."

They spent a pleasant hour in Hatchards. Madeline was in the process of handing the books she had purchased to her footman when the sound of a scuffle caught her attention.

A boy had his hand on a flower girl. "Lemme go. I don't wanna join ye."

The lad, slightly larger and stronger, was pulling the girl in his direction despite her feet being dug into the road. Madeline was not going to stand by and do nothing.

She strode up to the boy. "Unhand her. Now."

"An' who do ye think ye are?" the lad sneered.

"Someone who is going to ensure this girl does what she wants to do and not what you want her to do."

"Won't do ye no good." He scoffed. "Sooner or later, she's gonna be with us."

Madeline brought down her umbrella on his wrist, breaking his hold.

He snatched back his hand. "Ow! That hurt!"

"It serves you right." She fixed the lad with her best stare. "Leave."

The boy shot the young girl a look. "I'll be back. Next time don't fight me."

She spat at him before bending to pick up her spent blooms.

There had to be more Madeline could do. "I will pay you for them."

When the girl looked up, tears blurred her eyes. "He's right. I can't stop them."

"What is your name?"

"Suky." She finished picking up the flowers.

"I take it he is part of a kid gang and he's trying to get you to join?"

She nodded. "I ain't no thief." She straightened her thin shoulders. "An' I won't be no whore."

What a horrible situation to be in. "Do you have any family?"

Suky shook her head. "I had an older sister, but she disappeared. I ain't seen her in three or four days."

Madeline wished she could do something about the sister, but right now, she had to help Suky. "If you could do what you wanted to do, what would it be?"

"I dunno." She shrugged. "Be safe. Have food in my belly."

The girl's basic needs could be easily resolved. "Would you like to remain in London, or do you think you would like the country more?"

Suky shrugged. "Don't know nothin' but Lunnen."

Madeline had to think of a different approach. "How did you come to be selling flowers?"

A ghost of a smile entered the girl's face. "They's pretty."

Now they were getting somewhere. "What if you could work with flowers and other plants, and be safe, and well-fed, and be paid to do it?"

For the first time, Suky looked as if she did not quite trust Madeline. "That's all I hafta do?"

"My promise." Madeline wrinkled her nose. "You will have to take a bath and accept new clothing."

Suky looked around Madeline toward the coach, and the child's expression changed. Something there must have made up her mind. "I'll do it."

Madeline glanced at her brooch watch. "We had better be going, then. Come, you can ride in our coach."

Suky's eyes rounded. "A coach?"

"Yes indeed. But first I must pay you for the flowers." Madeline took several coins from her reticule. "Is that sufficient?"

The girl nodded. "Thank ye."

She almost held the child's hand but decided it was better if Suky came of her own accord. "If you will follow me, please?"

Roberts opened the door and assisted Madeline into the coach before picking up the girl and setting her on the backward-facing bench.

Suky sat next to Alice, who was already there, reading a book. She glanced up and smiled. "How do you do?"

"Good. I think." Suky looked around the small town coach.

The door closed, and the carriage started. The child looked fearful, so Madeline gave her a reassuring smile. "We will be home soon. Then Mrs. Thorton, the housekeeper, will show you around and introduce you to the others in the house."

Suky nodded and sat quietly until they stopped in front of Worthington House. Roberts went to the door, while Alice's footman helped them from the coach.

By the time they entered the house, one of the maids was there. "I'm Molly. I'll take you to Mrs. Thorton. She'll make sure you're right at home."

After Thorton took Madeline's coat, she decided to go see Grace. "Is her ladyship still in the library?"

"Yes, my lady."

Alice grinned. "You found your cause."

"I did." At least helping Suky was satisfying. "I believe I am meant to help people. But is that enough?"

"I do not know why it would not be," Grace said later after Madeline told her what she had done. "One does not have to have an established charity to make a difference in people's lives. Stepping in and helping are very useful. In this case, you saved a child from prison or being violated. That is just as important as what others are doing. Once Suky is settled, you will have to work out with Mrs. Thorton what the child's role will be."

"Thank you." Madeline had been looking for something big, such as what Dotty did, or a mine like Eleanor's, but Grace was right. Helping people was important as well. Madeline would just have to keep her eye out for those she could assist.

She had reached the turn into the hall when she heard Matt say, "Your ideas about bankruptcy reform are thought-provoking. I don't know how many peers would be interested. Naturally, peers cannot be jailed, but any unentailed property can be seized. I've seen the threat of debtors' prison used to keep a dependent under control or convince them to seek employment, or even to move overseas."

"I hadn't thought of that aspect of it," Harry said. "Power." He sounded disgusted.

"Indeed. I'm not saying it can't be done. You will need to find a way to convince those for whom coercion is a useful tool."

She changed her position sufficiently to see Harry rubbed his chin. "I believe I would be better served by drafting a bill before I discuss it with anyone else. It's too easy for someone to shoot down a spoken idea. If there's a written proposal, it might make the idea easier to grasp."

"That's an excellent idea. We should do the same thing with mine reform," Matt said.

A feeling of pride in Harry filled Madeline. Did the Duke of Salforth or the other gentlemen even care about politics? She would have to find out.

"Oh, there you are, my lady." One of the younger footmen

came up behind her. "Mrs. Thorton wished to speak with you about Suky."

"Certainly."

"Suky?" Matt asked as he and Harry strolled to her.

"Er, yes." There was no reason not to tell him. Grace already knew. "Alice and I went to Hatchards earlier, and as we were leaving, I saw a boy trying to pull a smaller girl away with him. She clearly did not wish to go, and I intervened."

"And brought her home?" Matt sounded resigned.

Harry's lips started to twitch.

"Naturally." Her brother knew better than to ask. What else would she do? "She needed help."

"You did what you ought to have," Matt agreed. "Do you have any plans for her?"

"Not yet." Madeline did not even know how old the girl was. Although she looked to be about ten. "At the moment, all I know is that she was selling flowers because she likes them, and her only relative, an older sister, disappeared a few days ago." She really should try to find the sister. "May I send a few of the grooms out to see if they can discover what happened to the sister?"

"Of course. Don't get your hopes up, though."

"I will try not to." Madeline did not even want to contemplate what could have befallen the sister. None of it was good. "I will not tell Suky unless she gets the idea to search herself."

"Good idea." Matt nodded.

Harry seemed to focus on Madeline. "You said she likes flowers. Do you think she might like to be trained as a botanist?"

She could not help but grin at him. "Only if her interest in flowers goes beyond their being pretty when her life has been anything but."

"There is that." He shrugged. "I suppose you will give her opportunities to discover her true calling. After she is no longer starving and learns how to read and has her other basic needs met."

"Yes." After she feels safe. She wished she could linger and talk with him, but she had work to do. "I must go to Mrs. Thorton. I shall see you this evening."

"Until then." He smiled as he bowed, and a warm feeling crept into her body.

She went to the green baize door, and as she opened it, Matt said to Harry, "Let me see your proposal when you have it drafted."

"I will. Thank you." The front door opened and shut, and Madeline descended the stairs to the housekeeper's domain. She was looking forward to discussing the bills and Suky with him that evening.

CHAPTER TWELVE

Harry caught up with Merton and fell in beside him. "Worthington wants to see a draft of the bankruptcy bill I'm going to write."

"You will find him helpful. He's good at legislation." They were silent for a few seconds; then Merton asked, "How was your dinner last night? Was Thea correct that Mrs. Taylor would attempt to matchmake?"

"Dinner was excellent, and she was right. Fortunately, Mrs. Taylor seemed to be the only one interested in matchmaking. Mr. Taylor wanted to discuss legislation. Miss Taylor seemed disappointed that I was unsure of what I wanted from a political career. Particularly a leadership position."

"From what I noticed, positions in the government are all-consuming." Merton swung his cane as he walked. "I will do all I can to enact bills to help others, but I also want time for my family and my estates."

Harry considered his brother-in-law's many holdings. "In your case, managing your estates well equates to helping the population at large."

Merton flashed Harry a smile. "I see we think alike. I must also raise my heir with the same sense of duty I have."

"Poor Edwin. I see no chance of him being allowed to run wild on the Town."

"Not for his brother either," Merton said grimly. "They both will be raised to make themselves useful to others."

It would be easy to think that was Dotty's influence, but Merton had a strong sense of duty before they met. Granted, it was misguided, but it was there. Madeline had that same sense of responsibility for others. That she found a child in need and brought her home hadn't surprised him at all. It was what anyone in his family would do, and what her elder sisters would do. Harry looked forward to hearing about her protégée this evening.

Harry remembered the ball Mrs. Taylor had mentioned. "I should warn you, Mrs. Taylor is planning a ball and intends to invite you."

Merton's brows shot up. "Do you have any idea when it will be?"

"None at all." Harry couldn't understand why that would matter. "I suppose we'll find out in due course."

"I shall speak with Thea about it." Merton sounded as if he was considering attending. "It might give me an opportunity to meet some like-minded members of the House."

Ah. That made sense. Harry had thought about it as merely a social event. He must start considering all the possibilities. For a second, he wondered how Madeline would fit in that sort of event, but almost immediately knew she would be fine. Like him, she would have been raised with village children and have attended the entertainments in the area. He wished he could monopolize her time, but even if he would be allowed to do so, his time was not his own. Not only that, he also had competition for her hand. He definitely needed a better scheme if he was to succeed in having her as his wife. It was time to call in reinforcements. He prayed Henrietta and Nate would join them for luncheon.

They frequently did. She and Dotty wanted the children to have close relations with their cousins.

He strode into the family dining room and saw his wish had been granted. Both his sisters and their husbands were seated at the table. "Excellent."

"What is excellent?" Henrietta asked as he took an empty chair.

One of the footmen served him what smelled like chicken soup. "It occurred to me that I need an actual strategy to convince Madeline to marry me."

Henrietta stared at him for several seconds. "If she is attracted to you and you to her, what is the difficulty?"

"There are three other gentlemen vying for her hand. One is the Duke of Salforth. The other two are Lords Hereford and Bury."

"I do not know Madeline as well as I know her sister, Augusta, but I cannot believe she would pick a husband based on his rank."

"She would not," Dotty said. "The only reason Louisa married Rothwell was that she fell in love with him, and he with her. It was the same with Charlotte and Kenilworth."

Merton coughed. "It was a bit more than that with Kenilworth. After they were seen together when she'd been abducted."

Dotty raised one shoulder in a shrug. "If you think any of us would have stood by and seen her forced into marriage, you are sadly mistaken."

"No, no, you would not," Merton conceded. "But you must admit it was harder for him. He had to prove himself."

"More overtly prove himself, you mean," Dotty countered. "Much as you did."

Merton inclined his head. "Indeed."

Dotty shook her head. "No, it will not be rank. It will be Lady Wolverton."

Henrietta picked up a forkful of salad and frowned. "Her mother?"

"Yes," Dotty said. "She is very high in the instep and wants her daughters to marry well. Her standard is to a wealthy peer."

Not a mere mister.

"You are right." Henrietta broke off a bit of her bread roll. "She was quite upset when Augusta turned down so many offers, and apoplectic when she inadvertently announced she wanted to study at a university. But so may any number of other ladies be upset."

"I agree," Dotty said. "But she is determined her daughters make advantageous marriages whether they wish it or not."

Henrietta appeared to think about Dotty's statement for a moment. "You think she might convince Madeline to act against her inclinations merely to make her mother happy."

"Precisely." Dotty applied herself to her soup.

This was all very interesting. Harry hadn't known about Madeline's mother. "The question is, what can I do about it?"

"You cannot compete on the basis of rank or wealth," Henrietta mused.

It was irritating that those two things were always mentioned as what he was lacking. "I am aware of that."

She glanced at him with a startled look. "Forgive me. I was thinking out loud. You must offer her something she wants that the others cannot provide."

He knew that. "Such as?"

Merton and Nate shared a look. "You do what Merton and I did. Help her with her causes."

Dotty's brow creased. "She might not have discovered hers yet."

"I think she did." Harry thought back to other conversations he'd had with Madeline. "She told me she likes to help others, but I don't think she realized what she meant to do until today. This morning, she brought home a young girl who was being accosted by an older boy." He told them about the conversation she'd had with Worthington.

Dotty's brow cleared. "It is just the type of thing most gentlemen would discourage."

Merton cast his gaze to the ceiling. "Thea started out doing the same thing. That's how I ended up with Cyril."

The cat who insisted on riding in the carriage with him. "She'd been doing that sort of thing her whole life. I have a feeling for Madeline it's new."

"You must also continue to remain by her side," Merton added. "You did an excellent job of it at the ball the other night."

"I'm sitting with her at the musical evening tonight." Harry was looking forward to the event.

Merton took a drink of ale. "Separate her out from the rest of us. Otherwise, you will never be able to converse with her alone."

That was good advice. "I shall. Is there anything else?"

"Her come out ball is next week," Dotty said. "Ask her for the opening dance. If her ball is anything like ours, she will not have a great deal of time to spend at supper."

Harry never would have thought of that. "Thank you for the advice."

He finished the sandwich he'd made during the discussion and bit into it. Some of his scheme would rely on blind luck, such as being with her when she came across someone to assist. But he'd follow his family's advice, and pray the other gentlemen somehow made a mull of it.

By the time Madeline was dressing for her carriage ride with the duke, she had spoken with Mrs. Thorton, Suky, and the head gardener. For the time being, she would remain with them in Town. All three had decided it was best to allow Suky to discover what she wanted to do. Naturally, she would also spend part of the day in classes for reading and arithmetic. From there, their governess would be able to work out her strengths and weaknesses before adding other subjects. Unfortunately, finding her sister was not going to be an easy task. Still, they had to try. At least they were now armed with her name (Nan); her age (fifteen); a description; and from where she might have disappeared. Madeline could only pray it all went well. She looked forward to telling Harry about Suky that evening. He might have some ideas she had not considered.

"The pink carriage gown, my lady, or the blue?" Harper held up the two gowns.

"The pink, and my pearl earrings." After all, what else did one wear with pink?

"The bonnet with the pink and white flowers and ribbons, then," Harper said. "And you must take your parasol. The sun is getting stronger."

Madeline washed her hands, then turned for her maid to unhook the gown she had worn that morning. By the time the clock struck five, she was ready. Now all she had to do was wait to be informed the Duke of Salforth had arrived. She almost wished she had arranged for Posy to meet him, but she had agreed with herself she would not pose any more tests for a bit.

A knock came on the door and Harper opened it. "My lady, the duke has arrived."

Madeline glanced at the clock. It was ten past the hour. "He is late." She trusted that he did not think that because of his rank he did not have to be timely. Then she bit her lip. She should not be so hard on the duke. He might have a very good reason for being late.

Rising, she went to the stairs. Thorton had left him waiting in the hall. The duke was handsome enough, in a Prussian blue jacket and buff trousers. His cravat was neatly but not extravagantly tied, and she was pleased to see he did not wear more than three fobs.

Madeline reached the last tread before addressing him. "Good afternoon."

"My lady." He bowed. He held out his arm. "I do apologize for arriving late. Shall we depart?"

She placed her hand on his arm. It was neither too soft nor was it hard, as if he did any exercise or physical work. "Certainly."

A black curricle with gold piping, black cushions, and matching black horses stood in the street. "My mother required my assistance in deciding which bonnet to wear."

"It was kind of you to be so helpful." Madeline could not imagine any of her sisters asking a gentleman for advice. Although there were gentlemen who accompanied ladies shopping and, apparently, gave excellent advice. "Did she take your advice?"

He donned a wry look. "No. Just the opposite. She did take my father's advice."

"You will most likely have to gain her trust. Will she be at the Park?" One could always learn more about a gentleman from his mother. She supposed it worked for ladies and their mothers as well.

He waited while the footman assisted her into the carriage. Hmm, what was she to think about that? "Yes, she mentioned going riding with a few other ladies."

Madeline smoothed her skirts. "Perhaps we will see her there."

The duke climbed in and picked up the ribbons. "I imagine we will see a great many people we know."

"You are probably correct." She held on to the carriage arm as he started his pair. They would also be slowed down by the amount of traffic.

"I understand your mother is Lady Wolverton?"

"Yes. She remarried several years ago to a gentleman

she knew in her youth. She was still quite young. And had been widowed for several years." Madeline remembered the uncertainty her mother had felt at taking a new husband. But she and her sisters, as well as Matt and Grace, had convinced her that she should live her own life. Matt was their guardian, so there was no need for Lord Wolverton to take on that role. All in all, it had worked out well. Mama now had two sons and another child on the way.

"She must be a great source of comfort to you as you navigate your Season."

Not precisely. "Of course."

He smiled. "I'm very glad my mother is here to advise me."

They were approaching the gate, and already the Park was overly crowded. Madeline grinned to herself as she thought of what Harry's reaction would be. "I am not sure we will find anyone in this congestion."

The duke smiled at her again. "We will let them find us."

Fortunately or not, they were easily discovered. The first carriage they approached was Lady Bellamny's, which was drawn up along the verge. "We must stop and greet her ladyship."

The duke appeared unconvinced. "Who is she?"

"Lady Bellamny, a longtime friend of my family." Not to mention one of the leaders of the *ton*.

He suddenly appeared to remember her ladyship. "I understand her lines go back to William the First."

Madeline was aware of her ladyship's bloodlines, but it was not the first thing she had learned about her. "They do. Lady Jersey is with her."

"Was her grandfather not a banker?" There was disapproval in his tone. He had better not let Lady Jersey hear that.

Madeline decided to save him from himself. "She is also one of the Patronesses of Almack's."

"Oh, I see." The duke was definitely not happy about that.

He pulled up next to the landau and waited.

"Good day, my ladies. I would like to make the Duke of Salforth known to you. Your grace, Lady Bellamny and Lady Jersey."

He inclined his head somewhat haughtily.

"Lady Madeline, how good to see you." Lady Bellamny raised her lorgnette and peered at the duke. "I had heard you were in Town. Now that your mother is out of mourning, I will expect to see you at the entertainments."

"She has applied for vouchers to Almack's," Lady Jersey said. "I shall discuss the matter with my other Patronesses."

That did not sound promising.

"Thank you, my lady. I trust we will receive them soon." His tone this time was slightly more conciliatory, but his words were not.

Madeline had the feeling his mother would hear about this conversation. As well she should. "We must be moving on before we hold up the other carriages for too long."

He glanced behind him. "Yes, of course." He lifted his hat. "Ladies, it was a pleasure to meet you."

Lady Jersey gave him a skeptical look as they drove forward. Madeline wondered if she should give him some advice but decided to leave it to his mother. On the other hand, that might be where he got his attitude from. She gave herself an inner shrug. In any event, he probably would not appreciate her counsel.

They nodded to several people walking and riding horses. The next landau they came across on the verge held Mama. "My mother is in the next coach."

He glanced over. "That's my mother's landau. I did not know they were acquainted."

Neither had Madeline. He pulled up next to the coach.

"Mama, may I present the Duke of Salforth? Your grace, my mother, Lady Wolverton."

She inclined her head. "A pleasure." She turned to the duke's mother. "Your grace, I'd like to make my daughter, Lady Madeline Vivers, known to you. Madeline, her grace the Duchess of Salforth."

"Lady Madeline, I have been hearing a great deal about you." The duchess smiled graciously. "All to the good, I must say."

"Thank you." Madeline returned the smile. "It is delightful to meet you."

"I trust we will see each other again." She glanced behind them. "Salforth, you must move on. Even dukes are not allowed to keep others waiting."

His mother seemed nice enough. Madeline wondered if the duke was a bit shy. That often caused people to behave in an affected manner. She would have to get to know him better to decide if that was it.

When they arrived at Worthington House, a high-perch phaeton was standing in the street. It looked like the one Matt was having built for them. The door opened, and Alice strolled out. "You are just in time."

The duke came around and waited for the footman to assist Madeline down. She looked at her sister. "Now?"

"Why not?" Alice grinned. "It arrived while you were gone, and there is still time before dinner."

Madeline curtseyed to the duke. "I had a lovely drive, your grace."

"I see you're about to have a more adventurous one." His lips tilted up. "Don't let me keep you. Your sister obviously wishes to test the carriage."

Their footmen helped them in. Alice took the ribbons, the groom stood back, and off they went. Madeline wondered if any of the gentlemen other than Harry would drive with her.

Chapter Thirteen

That evening, after Harry passed through Lady Brownly's receiving line, he entered a drawing room where the doors had been opened to another room. Chairs were lined up facing a stage. He immediately sought out Madeline and had no problem finding her at all. It was as if he could sense her in the room.

He started working his way through the other guests, stopping only occasionally to greet them, and when he neared her, she turned. He hoped that meant she felt the same thing he did.

He bowed. "Good evening."

"Good evening to you." She dipped a shallow curtsey. "Have you heard about the singer?"

"No." He took two glasses of champagne from a footman. "I assume you have."

Madeline took the glass he handed her and sipped. "I have. We saw Dorie Exeter and she told us who it is. Her name is Senora Giuditta Pasta. She is said to be excellent. Do you enjoy opera?"

"I do. Not that I have had the opportunity to attend here in Town. I'm looking forward to going." He thought Merton had a box. Harry would have to ask.

"You should get up a party if either Dotty or Henrietta

will act as your hostess." Madeline's smile made him want
to do just that.

"That is the difficult part about being a single gentleman.
One must have a hostess." The only problem was, he did not
want any gentleman who was interested in her to be there.
Perhaps he could make it just family.

"I suppose it is to ensure that everyone behaves." Madeline tucked her hand in the crook of his arm. "It will be a
while until the performance begins. Shall we stroll?"

"What a good idea." With any luck, he could keep them
from being stopped. Except by their particular friends. "How
was your day?"

"Busy." She told him about her plans for Suky.

"I'm glad you came along when you did. I don't like to
think of any child made to be a criminal." There were too
many children running around London without anyone
to take care of them.

"Once she was settled, I went for a ride with the Duke of
Salforth. When we returned, our new phaeton had arrived,
and Alice wanted to take it out. We arrived home just in time
for dinner. Fortunately, when we are dining early with the
children, we are not required to change. What did you do?"

"Your day sounds much more interesting than mine. I attended meetings, a vote, and started drafting the bankruptcy
bill and our bill for married women's property. I would like
you to review that if you are still interested. Speaking of
carriage rides, would you like to join me tomorrow?"

"I would like to look at your draft bill and go riding with
you." Her mien brightened. "Perhaps I will be allowed to
take you out in the phaeton. I will have to ask Matt and
coordinate with Alice and Eleanor."

"Excellent. I'd be privileged to drive in it with you."

They greeted Eleanor and Montagu, coming from the
opposite direction. After they parted, he glanced at Madeline. "Do I sense there is something in the wind there?"

"Very possibly." She nodded. "There are still some things she needs to discover about him. But I think it is headed in that direction."

Harry wished he was making as much progress with Madeline. He wondered if he should bring up Salforth, but decided the duke was better out of sight and out of mind. If she brought him up, Harry would be honest, but careful not to criticize the man more than strictly necessary.

"I understand your come out ball is next week. Would I be presumptuous in asking for your first set?"

"Not at all." Her lips tilted into a beautiful smile, and it was all he could do not to drag her into his arms. "I know it is customary for a family member to lead a lady out, but neither Matt nor Charlie has mentioned it. Therefore, I accept."

The chairs were filling up. "We should probably decide where we are going to sit."

Madeline glanced around. "Toward the back, I would think. She is used to projecting her voice." Suddenly, she frowned. "What is she doing?"

Harry followed her gaze. "Who?"

"Alice. She walked away from St. Albans and went to sit with Penelope and Eloisa. I hope nothing is wrong."

"We'll join them and find out." Harry was beginning to feel sorry for St. Albans. He was clearly infatuated with Alice but seemed to be doing everything wrong. He steered them toward the ladies and claimed the seats next to them.

"Now what happened?" Madeline asked her sister.

Alice scowled. "He assumed I would sit with him without even asking me ahead of time or at all."

The man was an idiot. "Not the brightest thing to do."

The other two ladies nodded in agreement.

"You see, even Harry agrees," Alice said pointedly.

Lady Brownly stepped onto the stage, clapped her hands, and called the guests to order.

"If you will take your seats," she said, "I will introduce our special guest for the evening."

Harry was amused to hear people actually sigh with pleasure even before Senora Pasta began to sing. Phinn and Augusta slipped into the seats next to him.

Augusta leaned over. "We heard her in Milan. She is fantastic. I do not think there was a dry eye in the opera house when she finished."

As Pasta began to sing, he immediately understood the reaction of the guests. Her voice was clear and so full of emotion, even those who could not understand the words had to understand the passions. Soon ladies' lace-trimmed handkerchiefs were dabbing teary eyes. Even the gentlemen looked affected. After she finished, footmen circulated with canapés and champagne. Phinn and Augusta went to join Eleanor and Montagu, but Alice remained determinedly in her seat. "I'll summon a footman."

Thank you, Madeline mouthed.

Harry brought back a footman with plates of cheese and chicken canapés for the ladies.

"Thank you," Alice said. "I am afraid if I get up, *he* will come over to me."

He was tempted to ask what it was she didn't like about St. Albans, but having sisters, he knew better than to start that conversation here. Harry scanned the room, and sure enough, St. Albans was lounging against the wall, staring at Alice. Waiting for a chance to approach her. One would think he'd learn from his mistakes with her, but apparently not.

Madeline must have seen the same thing. "It is all very strange."

Harry agreed. "If he wants a chance with her, he needs to change tactics."

She raised a brow and shrugged. "How did you like Senora Pasta?"

"She is every bit as wonderful as Augusta said. I'm looking forward to the next aria."

"As am I. Will you ride tomorrow morning?"

"Unfortunately, I've arranged a very early meeting with some gentlemen I hope will be interested in the bankruptcy bill. We're breaking our fast at Brooks's." He did hope she'd be able to take her carriage out. "If you can take the phaeton, send a note around and I'll walk over. There's no point in you bringing a groom with you only for him to go back to Berkeley Square."

"That is a good idea." The look of approval she gave him had his chest puffing out. "Thank you."

There was something else going on tomorrow as well. "I almost forgot. Henrietta's ball is tomorrow. May I have the supper dance?"

"You may." Madeline had hoped he would ask for that set. It was a waltz, and none of the other gentlemen she had waltzed with were half as good as Harry. Not to mention he was a wonderful conversationalist during supper, and he brought her ices. "I am surprised she is not here this evening."

"The baby's been cranky."

"Ah." That would do it. When one of Madeline's nephews or nieces was not feeling well, neither Grace nor Matt got much rest. "I hope he feels better soon."

Harry grinned. "So do we all."

Lady Brownly went to the stage and clapped again, causing everyone who had got up to take their seats. "The performance will continue."

Perfect silence awaited Senora Pasta. She really could not have had a more appreciative audience. During the performance, Madeline could not help sighing and wiping away a tear.

Harry leaned closer to her. "It is beautiful."

"Yes, it is. I cannot wait to see her full performance. Grace is going to take us. Would you like to come as well?"

Harry grinned. "I'd love to."

How nice that he loved the opera as much as she did. "I shall let you know when it will be."

The next morning, it was clear spring was finally here. The air was warm, lilacs bloomed, and the trees were in leaf. It was amazing what a few days of rain could do. Unfortunately, Alice was casting a pall over the beautiful day.

Madeline wished she knew how to help her sister. "What do you have planned today?"

"Montagu is coming over to discuss positions he needs filled," Eleanor said.

"Other than a wife." Alice really was grumpy.

"On his estate." Eleanor shook her head.

They discussed her plans for helping him and her decision to introduce him to one of the Danes. Madeline wished she was that far along with any of the gentlemen. Fortunately, Alice perked up and actually made some helpful suggestions.

"Would you mind if I took the phaeton today? I am going riding with Harry and wanted to drive."

"I had thought we could go out after tea," Eleanor said.

That would not work. There were three of them. "Yes, but only two of us fit in it. You can take it out after Harry and I return."

Eleanor glanced at Alice. "Do you mind?"

"No." She shook her head. "No. I want some time to myself."

"It is settled, then." Madeline was relieved. "I shall take Harry out, then return for you."

"Where is Harry?" Alice asked.

"He had an early meeting this morning." Madeline hoped he was successful. "Where did Alice go?"

Eleanor looked around and closed her eyes for a second. "She is leaving. We had better go."

They urged their horses to a gallop and caught up to her halfway to the gate. Madeline rode on one side of Alice, while Eleanor rode on the other side.

Eleanor pressed her lips together. "You should have said you were ready to leave."

"I do not wish to remain long enough for anyone else to arrive," Alice said.

"Anyone such as St. Albans?" Madeline could not understand what was going on between the two of them.

When they reached Worthington House, Madeline remembered some conversations she had had with some of Charlie's dependents at Stanwood. "You said Lord Montagu required people. Charlie might be able to help you. When I went to Stanwood with Grace in March, more than one mother was concerned about her older children."

"That is an excellent idea," Eleanor said.

"Would you like our help with the list?" Alice asked.

Eleanor smiled at her. "I would love your help, and Madeline's."

"Good." Alice nodded sharply. "We shall meet after breakfast."

They would have to be quick. "Do not forget we have fittings for our ball gowns. Our come out ball is next week."

Eleanor blinked. "So it is."

"I asked Grace not to invite St. Albans," Alice said.

They were back to that again. But she would not tell him she did not want to see him. Madeline was going to give up thinking about them. She quickly washed and dressed for breakfast, then went to find Grace, who was with Elizabeth.

"I would like to take Harry Stern out in the phaeton this afternoon. Eleanor and Alice agreed."

"I do not see a problem. You are an excellent whip."

Elizabeth tugged on Grace's skirt. "Mama, when will we get to ride in the new carriage?"

"During a quiet part of the day. You should ask Madeline to take you out some time."

The little girl turned her big lapis-blue eyes on her. "Will you, Aunt Madeline?"

"Naturally, I will. Let us think of a time to go. I believe after the morning deliveries have been made and before luncheon. How does tomorrow sound?"

"That sounds very good. Can Gideon come too?"

They were both small enough to fit together on the seat. "Yes, if he likes."

"Oh, he will." Elizabeth grinned. "Wait until I tell him."

"I shall see you at breakfast." Madeline went to the hall and sent a messenger to Merton House to inform Harry that she would be driving today.

After breakfast, Madeline and Alice helped Eleanor finalize her list of people. Then they took the town coach to Madame Lisette's for their fittings. Madeline's gown was a beautiful blue silk with a sheer fabric embroidered with flowers and figured lace that draped near the hem. The sleeves were made of embroidered sheer fabric over the silk and puffed and very short. It was perfect.

Eleanor's gown was a deep cream, and Alice's was a pale yellow.

"My ladies," Madame Lisette said, "you must purchase gloves that come just above your elbows. That is the newest fashion. I have sent the silk to the shoemaker. They will be delivered with the gowns."

They spent the rest of the morning shopping, returning home in time for luncheon. Then there was the round of morning visits.

Before Madeline knew it, the family, including Charlie, Phinn, Augusta, Elizabeth, Gideon, and both Danes were gathered in the morning room for tea. Thorton announced Lord Montagu. If he was surprised to see children and dogs, he did not show it. She had almost laughed aloud when Elizabeth and Gideon told Lord Montagu about the mandatory family meetings. Yet, Lord Montagu even seemed to take to that in stride.

Thus far, he seemed to be meeting all the requirements. Other than Harry, Madeline wondered whether the gentlemen she was looking at would agree. Then again, any man she married would have to approve, or he would not be the right gentleman for her.

Her footman entered the morning room and whispered, "Miss Harper sent me."

"I'll be right there." Madeline caught Grace's eye and left the parlor.

She met Alice in the corridor holding their list of requirements. Eleanor joined them, and Alice said, "I think he has met all the qualifications."

"All except one."

The final and most important one. "Love."

"Yes. Although I am hopeful that will come." Eleanor sounded determined that it would. "I am going back down to the morning room. Are you coming?"

"I have a book I want to finish," Alice said.

"Harry is meeting me for our carriage ride." And she could not dally. Harry was never late. "I shall be down soon."

"I will wait for you," Eleanor said.

"Very well. Give me a moment."

Eleanor's concerned gaze followed Alice back to her room "Do you think Alice is upset with us?"

"No." Madeline knew it was not them. "She refused St. Albans's offer of a carriage ride."

"When did that happen?" Eleanor looked confused.

"When you were with Lord Montagu." Madeline looked at her brooch watch. She had to hurry.

"Today?" Her sister frowned.

Madeline touched Eleanor's arm and started toward the stairs. "No, yesterday." When they reached the bottom stair, she linked her arm with Eleanor's. "She will be fine."

"I suppose so." She turned and went toward the morning room.

The front door opened, and Harry stood in it, sunlight shining around him. He looked almost like a dark angel, or an avenging warrior. Madeline gave herself a shake. That was a fanciful thought. Still, she could not help but to notice how much more powerful he appeared than before.

"My lady." He held out his hand, and she was drawn to him as if there was an invisible string connecting them. "I am looking forward to our ride."

She touched his fingers and placed hers on his arm. "As am I. You must promise not to be nervous."

"Not me." He turned and led them out. "I have two sisters who are excellent whips. I expect nothing less from you."

Warmth flowed through her. This was a man who would support everything she wanted to do.

CHAPTER FOURTEEN

Harry escorted Madeline to her high-perch phaeton and waved the footman aside. It was too high for him to lift her into it, but he could and would assist her. He placed his hand beneath her elbow as she held her skirts with the other hand.

Once she gained the bench, she smiled. "Thank you."

"It is my pleasure." If she knew his main goal in life was to find ways to touch her, she'd be shocked. He climbed into the other side of the carriage, and she signaled for the groom to let the matched grays go. The pair were the perfect color for the phaeton, which had been painted the color of a dunnock's egg, with gold piping and light brown seats. The convertible cover was in the same color blue. The seat on the back was also upholstered in light brown and had handrails. "Did you select the colors?"

She was dutifully watching the traffic, but the corner of her lip tipped up. "Eleanor, Alice, and I selected the colors and made some changes to the standard design. Because there are times we might have a groom with us, we wanted to make it comfortable for him and changed the back-seat design. Although you probably could not see it, we also added a box, in the event there was something we needed to carry."

That was clever. "Such as a package?"

"Yes." When she looked at him, her eyes twinkled. "Or a kitten or a puppy. One never knows what one might find."

They were turning into the gate to the Park, and her response made him laugh out loud. Several people turned to stare at them. "I've done it now."

"I think it is silly that we are not supposed to laugh loudly," she said staunchly.

He not only appreciated her defense of him, he felt as if they were growing closer. "Thank you. Nevertheless."

"I know." She used the same tone of long-suffering his sisters did. Come to think of it, the ladies in her family probably did the same. "Ah, well. There is nothing we can do about it."

"We need one of the leading matrons to start to change the rules." Dotty and Madeline's sister Louisa might be the ones to do it, but not for several more years, and who knew what the future would bring.

"Perhaps one of our sisters." Madeline flashed him a quick look. "But not for a long time."

He liked that they thought along the same lines. A minute or so later, they were hailed by a young gentleman Harry didn't know.

"Lady Madeline," the man said. "May I have a dance at Lady Fotherby's ball?"

Harry leaned back against the squabs, congratulating himself for having already secured the supper set.

"You may have the second set, my lord."

"Thank you." He tipped his hat and went off.

"Who was that?" Harry hoped the competition was not growing.

"Lord Brinkley," Madeline said as she started the horses again. "He is quite young, but a good dancer."

That made him feel safer. "Quite young" was not a term used by a lady for someone she considered a suitor.

Unfortunately, Hereford and Bury were approaching. Harry scanned the crowd. There was no way to avoid them.

"Lady Madeline, Stern, good afternoon." Hereford bowed.

"Good afternoon," Bury parroted.

"Good day, gentlemen." She inclined her head.

"Hereford, Bury." Harry was not going to encourage them to stay any longer than necessary.

"Bang up rig," Bury said admiringly.

"Thank you." Madeline gave him a genuine smile, and Harry could only hope it was because he'd complimented her phaeton.

They both requested sets for his sister's ball, and she accepted. That made four sets for which she was promised.

"Gentlemen, I must move on." They stepped back, and she and Harry resumed their slow circuit.

Lady Bellamny hailed them from a carriage on the side of the verge. She cast an eye over the carriage. "Lady Madeline, that is a lovely phaeton."

Madeline colored with pleasure. "Thank you, my lady. My sisters and I helped to design it and selected the colors."

"I remember when your older sisters did the same. You have excellent taste." She turned to Harry, and he was very glad that she appeared to approve of him. "How are you enjoying your ride?"

He surmised what she was really asking was how he liked being driven by a lady. "Exceedingly well, my lady. But I expected nothing less."

"You two enjoy the rest of your ride." She waved her folded fan at them.

"Enjoy your day, my lady," Madeline said.

"I am sure we will." Lady Bellamny had an enigmatic look on her face. What the devil was she thinking?

"After we finish, do you want to stop at Gunter's?"

Madeline flashed him a smile. "You know I do."

He did know, and he was fairly certain Salforth hadn't

taken her there. Thinking of the devil, he was on a horse next to a landau ahead of them. Unfortunately, Madeline would have to stop.

She pulled up next to the landau. "Good afternoon, your grace."

It was then that Harry realized she was speaking to one of the ladies in the carriage. He glanced at the duke. "Salforth."

"Stern." The man didn't seem at all happy to see Madeline with Harry.

"Mama," Salforth said, "may I present Mr. Stern? He is an MP."

"Mr. Stern, how nice to meet you." The duchess's countenance was a cool mask.

Harry inclined his head. "A pleasure, your grace."

Madeline lifted one imperious brow. "Mr. Stern is the grandson of the Dowager Duchess of Bristol, and his uncle is the duke. His sister is the Marchioness of Merton."

Her grace's mien seemed to thaw. "I see." She cast a look at Salforth, and Harry knew from being on the receiving end of one of them, it boded ill for the man. "I hope you have a lovely ride."

"You as well, your grace." Madeline looked at Salforth. "Your grace."

Harry couldn't work out what Salforth was doing, but Harry didn't like it. On the other hand, he did like Madeline standing up for him.

They made it to the gate without any more interesting experiences, and she headed straight to Gunter's, and came to a stop on the side of the road.

A server ran up to them. "Would you like to hear about our ices today?"

Harry nodded. "I would. The lady will have chocolate."

Madeline beamed at him as the man recited the short list. "Hmm, the prune ice sounds interesting."

No more than a minute or two later, the server came back

with their ices. Harry held his cup of ice cream so she could take a taste.

"That is much better than the others, but I—"

"I know." He laughed. "You will stay with chocolate."

Smiling, she dipped her spoon into the bowl.

Once he'd finished, it occurred to him that this might be a good time for her to read the draft bill of the married woman's act.

"If you wouldn't mind coming to Merton House, you can read the draft bill. If not, I can bring it to you." Harry swore his heart stopped as he waited for Madeline to decide.

"I do not see why I should not go to Merton House. I assume you would not have asked me if Dotty was not present."

"Indeed." He sent up a prayer of thanks to whatever deity had listened. "She is spending time with the children today."

Madeline handed him her empty ice dish. "In that case, let us not waste time. I must be home in time for dinner."

"Or you could join us." He held his breath. Did she have any idea how important she was to him? "We dine early as well, because of Vivienne."

"Excellent." Madeline smiled. "That will give us more time to study the draft. If Grace agrees, that is. I do not see why she should not."

Harry didn't think she would have a problem with Madeline dining with them. Unless, of course, some event was going on that Madeline didn't know about. "We'll soon find out."

"We shall." When she glanced at him, her eyes were sparkling.

By the time they arrived at Merton House, they had close to an hour to go over the bill. First, he must inform his sister Madeline would be dining with them. "Parkin, where is her ladyship?"

"In the nursery. One of the twins is being fussy. No doubt

the other one will soon be crying as well." That didn't sound promising.

"Please send a message to Burkham to bring me the draft of the married women's bill, and bring tea to the morning room." There was a large table there he and Madeline could use to review the bill.

"I will also send a maid to sit with you," the butler said rather archly.

"Of course." How could he have forgotten they could not be in a room alone together?

He took her hand and started down the corridor. "I don't know what will happen to dinner."

"It is no matter. Perhaps you can dine with us." She tilted her head and frowned. "Another option would be to make time tomorrow."

"I'm sure we'll think of something." The document arrived, and he placed it on the table. "And here is our tea. Would you like to pour?"

"Yes." She fixed his cup, then her own. "Now, let us see what we have here."

She spent several minutes carefully reading the draft before setting it down. "I think you have remembered everything but the wages a woman might earn and the potential of owning a business." She tapped her pencil on the table. "I also think there should be something about children. It does not seem to me that women should have to rely on their husbands to appoint a guardian. I think it should be in the law that a husband can appoint a second guardian, but the mother must have rights under the law as well."

He could only stare at her for a second. "Why didn't I think of any of that?"

Madeline shrugged lightly. "Perhaps because you are not closely acquainted with working women, or have not given much thought to men who would deny mothers their children." She patted his hand. "You have done an excellent job.

I would not have expected you to remember everything. After all, you are not a female."

That was a fact. If he was, he probably wouldn't be doing his best not to think about kissing her deep, rosy lips. He pulled a piece of paper to him. "Let me write down your additions."

She selected a lemon biscuit and took a bite. "This is wonderful."

For some reason, the biscuit reminded him of the al fresco luncheon he'd asked Dotty to plan. "What would you think about a luncheon in Richmond Park? I would ask my sister to arrange it, and we could take the children."

"That sounds delightful."

He heard a soft patter on the carpet but assumed it was the maid, until a childish voice said, "I like eating outside." Vivienne. "I will invite Elizabeth and Gideon, and Constance and Hugh, and—"

Harry closed his eyes and groaned.

Madeline burst out laughing. "Perhaps it would be better to have the luncheon in the garden. If we went to Richmond Park, it would involve several carriages, nursemaids, footmen, and who knows who else."

Vivienne stared at them as if they had violated some rule or another. "I was not yet finished."

"Oh yes." Madeline's voice shook with mirth. "How rude of us to interrupt."

His niece regally inclined her head. "As I was saying, we must invite . . ." She recited the names again and added, "and Alexandria and Damien. I think that is everyone."

So much for Harry's romantic idea of taking Madeline for a walk in the wood while his niece played quietly or took a nap. "You should ask your mama about it."

The little girl turned toward the door, stopped, and screwed up her face. "I cannot do it now. Edwin and Andrew are both crying, and Mama always says 'no' when the babies are upset."

"Perfectly understandable," Madeline said. "Grace is the same way. Perhaps you would like a biscuit or a tartlet."

Vivienne nodded and climbed into a chair. "Thank you. I am hungry." She glanced at Harry. "Uncle Harry, I am supposed to tell you dinner will not be served in the dining room. You will have a tray."

"Why do you not dine with us?" Madeline asked.

"Oh." His niece looked horribly unhappy. "I had hoped we would be able to eat dinner together. Otherwise, I will have to dine in the nursery, where the babies are crying."

"Hmm." He glanced at Madeline. What was she thinking? "I have an idea. You can both join us for dinner. I will take the carriage back, and you can come over when you have washed."

Suddenly, Vivienne's wobbly lip transformed into a smile. "May we, Uncle Harry?"

"I'll ask your father." Better yet, he'd send a message to Merton that he was taking Vivienne to Worthington House. "I am certain he will not object."

She jumped down from her chair and gave both of them a hug. "Thank you so much! That is much better than being around crying babies."

She ran out of the room, and Harry quickly cut a piece of paper, and summoned a footman. He'd keep it short.

> *Merton,*
>   *I'm taking Vivienne to Worthington House to dine.*
> *Tell me quickly if you have any objections.*
>
>   *H.*

Harry folded the note and gave it to the now waiting footman. "I need an immediate answer, and a groom to escort Lady Madeline to Berkeley Square."

"Yes, sir."

Only a few minutes had passed when the footman returned. "His lordship said to tell you you have his undying gratitude."

"Wonderful." Madeline rose. "I had better go home and tell Grace."

"We will be there as soon as possible." Harry wondered how long it would be before his niece was ready. He took her hand and walked with her through the front door to the waiting carriage. A groom ran from the side of the house, and Harry helped Madeline into her phaeton. "We will see you soon."

She chuckled. "I will not expect you too soon. I have some experience of getting little girls ready to go out."

"Hopefully, we won't miss dinner."

"Remind her of that." Madeline took up the ribbons and started the carriage. "Good luck."

He felt for his sister and the babies, but this would give him an opportunity to spend even more time with Madeline. Which was exactly what he wanted to do, and what everyone was telling him to do.

CHAPTER FIFTEEN

Madeline drove home and gave the reins to the groom Harry sent with her. "Thank you for accompanying me."

"Weren't no problem at all, my lady."

She strode to the open door. "Thorton, Mr. Stern and Lady Vivienne will be joining us for dinner."

The butler bowed. "Very good, my lady. I shall send a message to Cook."

"You had better tell her ladyship as well." Madeline knew neither Grace nor Matt would mind two more at the dinner table, but forewarning was always appreciated.

"Yes, my lady."

From the corner of her eye, Madeline saw Lord Montagu follow a footman up the stairs.

Eleanor smiled as her gaze followed him; then her sister saw her. "I have never seen the Park so busy."

"Neither have I. The Season is really underway now." It appeared as if they would have three guests at dinner this evening. "I take it Montagu is staying for dinner?"

"Yes." Her sister smiled broadly. "I'll tell you the rest after we have changed."

They mounted the stairs together, and she went to her chamber. Thankfully, they did not wear evening gowns when dining at home with the children. "Harper, I'd like to change. My blue day gown."

A knock came on the door as Harper was arranging Madeline's hair. "Come."

Alice strolled into the room. "Did you have a good ride?"

"I did. Harry is coming with Vivienne to dine with us. The twins are not feeling well, and I thought they would have a better time with us."

"Lord Montagu will join us as well." Alice took the beehive chair next to the toilet table. "I think dinner with the children will be the last test. Although he did well at breakfast."

"He did." Funny. That was one of many requirements Harry met. If only he was a peer. Or if only his status would not matter to her mother. If that was the case, she would— no. Madeline could not change the facts of Harry's status, and her mother did care. "How was your ride with Lord Bury?"

Alice shrugged. "He talked a great deal about his estate. At least he does not leave a steward to take care of it, but neither does he truly take care of his dependents."

"Ah." That did not sound promising. Madeline glanced at the clock. "We should go. Eleanor has something to tell us."

Madeline and Alice entered their parlor to find Eleanor already there and pacing with excitement. "We do not have much time, but I wanted to tell you Montagu has asked for my opening set at our come out ball *and* the supper dance."

"Oh my!" Alice's eyes rounded. "Eleanor, he must be getting ready to ask for your hand."

Madeline agreed. "I am so happy for you." She hugged Eleanor. "After this afternoon, I was more certain than ever he was the right gentleman for you."

Eleanor bit her lip. "Let us not get ahead of ourselves. He must still tell me he loves me."

"It will happen." Alice sounded certain of the outcome.

Madeline prayed her sister was right. "Would it not be wonderful if he proposed at our ball?"

"I do not want to even think about that." Eleanor nibbled on her lip again. "We must go to the drawing room."

When they entered, Montagu was already there with Matt, Grace, Gideon, Theo, Mary, and Elizabeth. Matt immediately rose. "There you are. Your sister set dinner back a bit."

He handed them glasses of sherry.

Alice glanced at Madeline. "When do you think Harry will arrive?"

"He has to wait until Vivienne has been dressed." Elizabeth always seemed to take an inordinate amount of time when she thought someone other than family was dining with them. "It might be a while."

Thorton had just announced dinner when a knock came on the door. The under butler opened it.

Harry and Vivienne walked in. "Are we too late?"

"Not at all." Madeline went to them. He took her hand and bowed.

"One of us had trouble deciding which dress she should wear."

"Vivienne!" Elizabeth rushed to her friend and cousin. "I did not know you would be here. That is a very pretty gown." She glared at Madeline, probably for not telling her Vivienne would be there. "Come with me. We can sit together."

Grace signaled to Theo and Mary, who nodded and followed the little girls into the dining room.

"Stern, glad to see you," Lord Montagu said.

"Harry." Grace strolled to him. "How are the twins doing? I hope it is not serious."

"Nurse believes it is teething. The problem is that when

one of them is fussy, the other one gets fussy as well. I hope it's over soon."

Grace gave him a sympathetic smile. "I'm afraid you are only about halfway through the process. We have all been fortunate that Edward and Gaia have not been bothered overmuch."

"But Gideon and Elizabeth were miserable," Matt added.

They strolled to the family dining room. Harry held a chair for Madeline and sat next to her. "Merton's secretary agreed to rewrite the bill for our further study."

Harry was fortunate he could rely on his brother-in-law's servants and employees. "What will you do when you have a home of your own?"

"Hire staff." He placed the serviette in his lap. "That is all I can do."

What sort of residence was he considering? "You will require either a large set of rooms or a house."

"I have been thinking of a house." A footman brought around the soup, and Harry served them. "I do plan to wed soon. Ergo, there is no reason to lease rooms when I will need a house for my wife."

For some strange reason, Madeline's heart fell to her stomach. She had known he was searching for a wife. Why had she not remembered it? Did he have a lady in mind? She did not want to know. All she could do was enjoy his company for as long as she could.

Madeline was silent while they finished their soup. Was she merely hungry, or was it something else? The footman came around with pieces of roasted capon, followed by asparagus. "Madeline, would you like the capon and asparagus?"

"Yes, please." Her smile seemed overly bright.

Something was definitely wrong. Harry reviewed what they'd discussed just before she became quiet. Ah. He was talking about taking a wife. Did she think he had referred to someone other than her, or was she afraid it was her? And how would he find out which one it was? Quite honestly, he'd never thought to have this sort of problem. But he couldn't very well ask her or anyone else. "The chicken is excellent."

"Jacques is a wonderful cook." She busied herself with eating.

Harry had to think of something to draw her out. "Would you like to review the document tomorrow? Perhaps after we take a ride and go for ices?"

An expression he could only describe as distraught entered her eyes. "I am already committed to riding tomorrow. Perhaps the next day?"

"Of course, whenever you like." Who the devil was taking her out for a ride? Or was she driving? "Are you going in your phaeton?"

"No." She shook her head but didn't expound.

Well, then. He'd just have to take a ride through the Park to see with whom she was meeting. While he was at it, he'd do his best to ensure whoever it was knew she was his.

"Sir, would you like to try the lamb?"

"Yes, please. Madeline?"

"Thank you." It was time to get her to talk to him again. "How is Suky settling in?"

A subtle shift in her posture took place, and she glanced at him. "She is doing well. Our gardener is very pleased with how quickly she understands what he wants her to do and said she asks good questions. Mrs. Winter said it was as if she just remembered how to read. Although Suky says she never learned. Mrs. Winter said that sometimes people are simply ready to be taught. Suky is very intelligent."

That was heartening to hear. "Have you had any luck finding her sister?"

"Unfortunately, no." Madeline's eyes became a bit watery,

and she blinked back the tears. "We are beginning to think she might have been murdered."

He wanted to take her in his arms to comfort her. "It is a sad fact of life that one cannot save everyone. I wish we could."

She cut a piece of the capon. "That is what Grace says."

"She is wise." It seemed as if everyone relied on Grace for advice. Maybe he should ask her for some. "I've heard how she helped Dotty and Henrietta."

The smile he'd been trying to prompt appeared on her lips. "Alice, Eleanor, and I helped as well, when Henrietta was concerned about Dotty's reaction to her marrying Fotherby."

Harry took a sip of wine. "What did you do?"

"We were in the antechamber next to Grace's study. . . ." He laughed when Madeline told him how, when attempting to hear what Henrietta was saying to Grace, they fell through the door but were able to give his sister some advice. "When Dotty came to talk to Grace, we decided just to use the door to the study, and we were able to help her as well."

"I'm very glad you were able to aid them. Henrietta is extremely happy with Fotherby, and he and Dotty have become friends." It occurred to him that Madeline and her sisters might still be using the antechamber. He remembered Stanwood putting a chair in front of the door leading to Grace's study but leaving the door open slightly. He wondered what they wanted to know and if they achieved their goal.

"Helping people is important," Madeline said firmly.

"It is. Both on a personal level and more broadly in government. That was the reason I decided to become an MP. Too many times, the laws that are enacted cause misery to those who do not have wealth."

She finished chewing and swallowed. "Matt complains

about how long it takes to make changes. For years, he has been trying to have the Corn Laws rescinded."

"It's a matter of great frustration to many of us. Change will come eventually, and I want to be part of it." If only he knew what had caused the change in her earlier.

Her fine, dark brows formed a line between her eyes. "I cannot fathom why the Tories do not understand that having a starving populace is not good for our country."

"Because they care about nothing but themselves." And funding the regent, who was now their new king.

Madeline heaved a sigh. "Sometimes I feel as if those of us who want progress are banging our heads against a brick wall."

It did seem that way at times. "And that is when helping individuals or even groups of people is the most necessary." He wanted to put his hand over hers. "What you are doing is important."

She gazed at him and seemed to be searching for something, then glanced across the table. "I think you have a tired niece."

Harry looked at Vivienne. Both little girls were trying to hide their yawns. "She and Elizabeth both. Although they will deny it."

"They will." Madeline chuckled. "I think we have all gone through that."

"I'm sure we did." Finally, she was happy again. "The question is, how do I take her home without her arguing with me?"

Madeline glanced at Grace, who was also looking at the girls. She rose. "I think it is time for some people to seek their beds."

"Mama." Elizabeth pouted. "I am not tired at all."

"Which is the reason you look as if you are about to fall asleep at the table," Worthington commented drily.

"I don't know why you bother arguing," Gideon piped up. "It never works."

Elizabeth shrugged one shoulder in a perfect imitation of her aunts. "I know." The footman helped her and Vivienne from their chairs. "I am very glad you were able to come to dinner."

"I am too." She hugged Elizabeth. "Uncle Harry, we need to go home."

"And that is how it is done," Madeline whispered to him.

"I must take notes." He wanted to hold her hand as he walked to the door and kiss her. Better yet, take her home with him.

"Uncle Harry." The whiny tone in his niece's voice made him realize he really did need to take her home.

"We're going, sweetie."

"I'll walk you out," Madeline said.

At least he'd get part of his wish. "Thank you."

When they reached the front door, he took her hands in his. "I thoroughly enjoyed myself this evening."

"I did too." She smiled softly and, again, searched his face. Could she see how much he cared for her? "Will you ride in the morning?"

"Yes. I shall see you then." He raised first one hand to his lips, then the other.

She seemed a bit sad. "Good sleep to you."

"And to you." He'd rest better if she was with him.

"Cousin Madeline." Vivienne tugged on Madeline's skirt.

"A good sleep to you." She bent down and hugged the little girl. "I am very glad you could join us."

Vivienne nodded. "Me too." She held her hand out to him. "Uncle Harry, home."

"Yes, my lady."

Madeline's lips twitched. "Good night."

She was still in the doorway when he climbed into the carriage, and they waved good bye.

Vivienne yawned again. He'd be lucky if she didn't fall asleep on the way home.

"Uncle Harry." She slumped against him.

"Yes, sweetie."

"Do you want to marry Madeline?"

Out of the mouths of babes. "Where did you get that idea?"

"Elizabeth." His niece yawned. "She is very knowing."

He was in trouble now. "Is she?"

"Yes. She said that you and Madeline look right together, and she thinks you should get married."

That *was* interesting. "What do you think?"

"I think it's a good idea too. She is very nice."

"Yes, she is." He just needed to work out a way to end this conversation without giving away that he did indeed wish to wed Madeline. If his niece got any hint at all, he'd have Vivienne and Elizabeth trying to play matchmaker.

"I'll consider your idea, but you are not to tell anyone. Do you understand?"

Her head moved up and down his side. "I won't tell anyone."

"Thank you. And I promise, you will be the first to know when I decide."

She reached up and kissed his cheek. "I'm tired."

"I know." They pulled up in front of Merton House. What would it be like to have his own children with dark brown curls and perhaps his green eyes? An image of Madeline heavy with his child appeared in his mind. Yes, he was going to marry her. He just needed to find a way to get her to agree. But what would it take?

CHAPTER SIXTEEN

Madeline and her sisters rode to the Park early the next morning as the sky was lightening. Birds sang, and spring flowers had popped up everywhere. Even the trees were now filled with leaves.

As they made their way, Henrietta Fotherby and her friends joined them. "It is a glorious morning."

Madeline thought so as well. "It is."

Harry rode up beside her. "Good morning."

Butterflies took up residence in her chest, making it hard to breathe. She could not feel this way. Her mother would be livid. If only there was someone in whom she could confide, but everyone she knew would tell her to follow her heart. And that was no help at all. She did not even know if he was interested in her other than as a family friend. Well, he had kissed her hands yesterday. But did that mean anything? "Good morn to you. Did Vivienne fall asleep on the way to Merton House last night?"

He laughed. "Just about. If we had been in the coach any longer, she would have."

Madeline was glad that her older nieces and nephews had formed a close bond with Harry's niece. "Sometimes I wonder what they will be like when they are older."

He cast his eyes to the sky. "The girls will all be ladies to be reckoned with. I have no doubt they will set their own rules."

"No doubt at all. Elizabeth has already asked Augusta what making a Grand Tour would be like." Madeline was certain that when they were her age, the girls would all insist on going to Europe.

Harry went into whoops. "I can see the look on Merton's face."

"Oh, dear." She started to laugh. "He will send an army with them."

"And tell them to be discreet." Harry's voice trembled with mirth. "It wouldn't surprise me at all if by the time they returned to England, they will have gathered puppies, kittens, and people in need of help."

"You are right." Rose swung her head around, as if to tell Madeline to pay attention to her riding. She tried to get herself under control, but another thought came to her. "Even Augusta brought back a Great Dane and a cat."

"And she is not a reformer," Harry pointed out.

"I wonder if we are correct in thinking the girls will follow their mothers." None of Madeline's Vivers sisters had followed their mother's example.

He gazed off, as if he was thinking, then glanced at her. "I suppose it *could* happen. Although, Dotty, Louisa, and Charlotte have all taken their girls to the home in Richmond where some of the women and children they rescued reside."

"Involving them at a young age will have an influence." It was probably much more interesting than being constantly told one could not do things. "I think you are correct. They will be forward-thinking."

"How did Grace and your mother influence you?"

When Madeline looked at him, he was studying her with an intent gaze. "I have to say, Grace was more of an influence. She allowed us to be children and guided us into being young ladies. My mother only seems to be concerned with propriety and marrying to advantage." That reminded her of at least one thing her mother would not like. "Do you want to race to the oak tree?"

He grinned. "On the count of three."

The second he said three, Madeline touched her knee to Rose's side, and the mare sprang forward. Madeline knew Harry would pace her, but she wanted to give him a run, at least once. They reined in at the tree.

He patted his horse's neck. "Willy almost didn't catch her."

Willy looked at Rose and snorted. She raised her head, shaking it. As if to say, *I do not care what you think.*

Madeline and Harry glanced at each other and laughed.

Dorie rode up with the others. "It looks as if your horses are having an argument."

It does." Madeline stroked Rose's neck. "You did very well."

She nodded her sleek head, as if she knew it.

Harry laughed again. "She is definitely proud of herself. Whereas Willy looks a bit put out."

"Typical male," Alice said. "Trying to control a lady."

Madeline met Harry's gaze. They both knew to whom Alice referred. Was that the problem with her and St. Albans?

As if Harry could read Madeline's mind, he imperceptibly inclined his head. How interesting that they knew what the other was thinking.

"I cannot believe how quickly the past week has gone by. We had better go home," Alice said. "Today will be extremely busy."

"You have your come out ball this evening," Adeline Littleton said. "What else do you have planned for today?"

"I am riding with Lord Hereford," Alice said. "Madeline

is riding with Lord Bury and Eleanor will ride with Lord Montagu."

Harry did not like hearing that Bury was taking Madeline out for the Grand Strut. At least he now knew who it was. He grinned to himself. Interfering would be a pleasure.

When they reached the gate, Henrietta glanced at him. "Harry, would you escort us, please?"

Madeline gave him a quick smile. "I will see you this evening."

"Until then." He joined his sister and her friends. It was strange that Henrietta had asked him to accompany them to their houses. "What is it?"

"It occurred to me that you might need a little help with Madeline."

He wanted to raise a brow, but she was right. He required all the assistance he could get. "What do you suggest?"

Adeline Littleton rode up on his other side. "When Littleton was courting me, although I did not realize it at the time, he would appear in the Park when I was riding with another gentleman and remain with us until we left."

Harry was glad to hear he wasn't the only gentleman to think of the same plan. "It seems as if his strategy worked."

"It certainly irritated the other gentlemen, which had the effect of making them show a side they did not normally display to a lady."

"I do not know much about Lady Wolverton," Dorie said. "But she has been seen in the Duchess of Salforth's company a great deal recently."

Could Madeline's mother be pressuring her to wed Salforth? And was Madeline listening to Lady Wolverton?

"Harry," Henrietta said, "I know enough of Madeline to know that if you win her heart, she will eventually choose you."

He wasn't sure about that. "Even over her mother's influence?"

Dorie Exeter nodded. "If you could have witnessed the scene that was created when Augusta decided to attend university, and the way Lady Worthington in particular stood up for her, you would understand that Madeline will have a great deal of support for her decision."

"Although I would not be at all surprised if her mother will have found a way to pressure Madeline into marrying as she wishes her to," his sister added.

Lady Wolverton sounded like his Grandfather Bristol when he attempted to convince Mama to marry someone other than Papa. Perhaps Harry needed to show her that he was not just a family friend but a suitor for her hand. "Thank you. I think I will take Willy and go to the Park this afternoon."

At ten past five, Harry entered the Park gate and joined the Grand Strut. Despite the crowd, he found her almost immediately. Getting around carriages and walkers was most definitely easier on a horse than in a vehicle. When he reached Bury's curricle, it was stopped next to a landau holding Lady Jersey and Mrs. Drummond-Burrell. The latter said something to Bury that made the man flush.

"Mr. Stern." Lady Jersey gave him a polite smile. "How nice to see you could take some time away from your duties."

He executed what he knew was a neat bow. "My lady, ma'am. It is a pleasure seeing you again. I trust you are enjoying the lovely weather we're having."

"We are indeed," Mrs. Drummond-Burrell said. "I must say, I wish other gentlemen had your address. It makes life much more pleasant."

Bury scowled, prompting Harry to make a point of looking at Madeline. He leaned over and took her hand. "Lady Madeline, a pleasure to see you here."

She gave him a polite smile. "Mr. Stern, I too am glad you could make some time for recreation."

"Lord Bury." Lady Jersey waved her hand in a shooing motion. "You had better move on."

Harry kept pace with Bury's carriage and engaged Madeline. "I spoke with Worthington earlier, and he told me he plans to breed Zeus and Posy this autumn. I've asked for one of the puppies. What do you think, a male or a female?"

"I like them both, but I am partial to the females." Something caught her eye. "Lord Bury, you must stop next to the green landau."

The carriage was Lady Bellamny's.

"I say, Stern, thank you for mentioning dogs. I almost forgot to tell Lady Madeline about my hunting dogs." Bury glanced at her. "Best ones in East Anglia."

"Lord Bury." There was a definite bite in Madeline's tone. "The green landau."

"What did you say?" He quickly glanced at the verge. "Oh, yes, green carriage. I've never had to stop so much before. Don't understand why we must." Something seemed to draw his attention. "Should I tell her that purple turban don't go with that green?"

Harry stifled a laugh when Madeline turned her head toward him and closed her eyes, as if she were in pain. He could imagine her response to Bury's inane chatter. "You are stopping because Lady Madeline is quite well-connected."

"Yes, yes, of course. Must do the pretty," the man muttered.

This time she almost rolled her eyes, and Harry had a harder time maintaining his countenance. Fortunately for Bury, he did as she told him to.

"Lady Bellamny." Madeline smiled at the older woman. "How are you this afternoon?"

She raised her brow at Bury. "I am doing better than you

are, I suspect." Lady Bellamny glanced at him and nodded. "Mr. Stern, at least you speak with sense."

He bowed to her. "Thank you, my lady. I do try."

"From what I hear, you are succeeding." She waved her fan at Bury. "Lord Bury, it is time for you to drive on. Do try to be attentive to those behind you."

Once again, he flushed a deep red. "Yes, my lady." He started the horses, and before they were out of earshot, said, "She scares me to death. Always has. Never know what to say around her."

Madeline placed the tips of her fingers on her forehead.

Harry suspected she'd had enough of Bury. "My lady, do you have the headache?"

She threw him a look of gratitude. "I feel one coming on."

Bury, however, seemed oblivious. "Bury, perhaps you had better take Lady Madeline home. She has the beginning of the headache."

He glanced at her, as if surprised she was still there. "I say, my lady. It's probably from talking to all those old ladies. I'll take you straightaway."

Madeline rubbed her temples, and Harry hoped she wasn't really getting a headache. "Thank you, my lord."

He accompanied them to Worthington House. Once the curricle had stopped, he dismounted and helped Madeline from the carriage, whispering, "If you don't really have a headache, perhaps we could go for an ice in about fifteen minutes or so."

Her eyes began to sparkle. "That is an excellent idea. I shall see you soon."

"I'll hurry Bury along."

Harry waited unit she was inside and went back to his horse. Bury was still sitting in his carriage.

"Do you think she will be all right? Tonight is her come out ball. Hate for her to miss it."

Even if she wasn't feeling particularly well, Harry couldn't imagine her missing her own ball. "Most likely lying down will see her right again."

"Yes, of course." He nodded. "That's what m'mother always does. A shame I couldn't tell Lady Madeline about my dogs. I did tell her about the hunting. Not as good as Melton, but we have some fine grouse."

No wonder Madeline had had enough of Bury. "I'd better be getting back home."

"I should go too. No sense in staying here."

"I'll ride with you part of the way. Where do you live?"

"Got rooms on Jermyn Street," Bury said in an injured tone. "M'father wouldn't open up the house because they weren't coming this Season."

"I'm lucky to be able to stay with my sister." Harry accompanied Bury to the corner of Hay and Berkeley Streets. "I'm off to Grosvenor Square." Once Bury had turned onto Hay Street, Harry traced his way back to Worthington House. A footman came out to take Willy. "Lady Madeline is waiting for you."

"Thank you. Can you find someone to take my horse to Merton House?"

"Happy to, sir."

Harry slipped the man a coin. "Thank you." The door opened as he approached, and Madeline was waiting in the hall. He held out his arm. "Shall we?"

Smiling, she tucked her hand into the crook of his arm. "I cannot wait."

They reached the pavement and turned toward Gunter's, at the other end of the square. "I wonder what they'll have on the menu today."

"We will soon find out. Thank you for rescuing me from Lord Bury."

That was one gentleman Harry didn't have to worry about. "He's a good person, but not much in the brainbox."

"Making conversation with him was rather difficult. I will say that he knows his estate. That must be in his favor."

"It is almost all he talks about." Perhaps Harry should have warned her. "Even at school, he was obsessed with the subject."

Madeline tilted her head. "His parents must have taken pains to instill a sense of duty in him. He will need a lady who is happy to let his holdings be her primary concern as well."

"I never actually gave any thought to the type of lady he should wed." She had a good point. Perhaps he should work out who Hereford and Salforth should wed and nudge them in the direction of other ladies. They arrived at Gunter's, and a server came up to them.

"Would you like to hear our ices of the day?"

"Please."

"Lavender, Gruyère, and violet."

Harry hadn't been impressed by the Parmesan. He didn't think the Gruyère would be better. "I will take the lavender and the lady will have chocolate."

"Yes, sir." The man ran to the shop.

"Not the Gruyère?" Her laughter reminded him of chimes.

He made a face reminiscent of their nieces'. "I will forgo the cheese ices."

The server returned with their ices, and as was becoming his habit, he held his out to her.

She took a small taste and nodded. "That is good. Perhaps one day I will try it."

Harry chuckled. "After you have had enough chocolate?"

Madeline assumed a serious expression. "I'm not sure I could ever have enough chocolate."

"Will the children be allowed to stay up to see you and your sisters in all your finery?"

"They will." She took a spoonful of the ice and looked

as if she was in heaven. "They will also be able to taste everything we will have at supper."

"That was my favorite part." Dotty had been more interested in what their mother and Lady Stanwood were wearing.

"Where did your parents hold their balls?"

"My parents did not hold balls, but Lord and Lady Stanwood did. When we were young, Dotty and I were allowed to go to Stanwood."

"That was extremely kind of them. I wish they had lived." Madeline quietly finished her ice.

His family had been distraught when they died. "As do I. You would have liked them. Grace is the very image of Lady Stanwood."

He gave himself a shake. "Nevertheless, it all turned out well for your family and the Carpenters."

Madeline gazed at him as if in thought. "It has. I could not imagine my life without Alice and Eleanor and the others."

Harry wanted to tell her that if she married him, they would always live close to her family. "We should go. You must have a great deal to do before this evening."

"I do. There are all the arrangements to be inspected." She gave her bowl to the server and tucked her hand into Harry's arm. "Lead on."

They strolled back to Worthington House. "Do you know what the first set will be?"

She slid him a playful smile. "A waltz."

Thank God for that. He'd be able to hold her in his arms.

CHAPTER SEVENTEEN

Madeline climbed the stairs slowly, thinking about the warm grin Harry had given her when she had told him the first set was a waltz. It made her want to kiss him, which he would most likely see as a sisterly one. And that was probably for the best. She was trying very hard to do what her mother wanted her to do, but it was more difficult than she thought it would be. She sighed as she walked to the Young Ladies' Parlor. Hopefully, Alice would be there. Madeline had a few words for her.

She opened the door and found her sister reading a book. "Why did you not tell me what a bore Bury is?"

Alice glanced up and stared at Madeline. "Because I thought he was quite entertaining."

"Indeed. I had no idea you enjoyed hearing about the properties he will inherit someday."

Her sister's eyes widened. "I would not have. We discussed fashion. He has a great many good ideas about colors. He even told me that when I can wear colors, I should make Pomona green my signature."

"Fashion?" He had mentioned Lady Bellamny's turban and how it clashed with her carriage.

Alice narrowed her eyes. "Did you happen to ask him about his future properties?"

"Yes, but not to talk about every crop and animal. I wanted to discover how he treated his dependents." Madeline would have enjoyed hearing his ideas about fashion more than his lands, but it still would have him crossed off her list of suitors.

"Sometimes one must be careful of what one asks," Alice said archly. "I liked that he listened to my ideas and considered them."

"I barely got a word in edgewise." Madeline would decline any other requests for carriage rides from him. Thank God Harry had rescued her. And took her for an ice. "Maybe he listened to you because you were discussing something ladies usually talk about."

Her sister's forehead wrinkled in thought. "You might be right. In any event, I would go out with him again, but he is not someone I would wed."

"That is something upon which we can agree." She went to the sofa and sank into the cushions. "Who is standing up with you for the opening set?"

"Rothwell." Alice smiled and shook her head. "He insisted. Have you decided with whom you will dance?

"Harry Stern asked me, and I accepted." Madeline looked forward to dancing with him. No other gentleman could compare with his skill in the waltz. "Salforth asked for the supper dance."

"Lord Bury asked me. I shall be careful not to ask him about his home, and encourage him to critique everyone's choice of headdress and gown."

"In that case, you had better sit far away from Grace. You know how she feels about gossip."

"You are right. I will sit at the other end of the table." Alice glanced at the clock. "We had better go down to dinner."

Even on evenings they had entertainments they dined

THE HUSBAND LIST   155

with the children, then ate something light before going out. "They will be allowed to remain up late this evening."

Alice looked confused. "Why—oh, yes. To see us in our ball gowns."

"And to sample the foods from the supper table." That was something Madeline and her Vivers sisters never got to do before Matt married Grace.

Alice's eyes grew misty. "I remember my mother dressed for a ball. She was beautiful."

Madeline got up from the sofa and linked her arm with her sister's. "Come. Everyone will be waiting for us."

Theo and Mary crept into the anteroom next to Grace's study. Theo's mother had asked to speak with Grace, and they were now seated on the chairs in front of the fireplace.

"Are you sure this is necessary?" Mary whispered.

"Shhh." Theo put a finger to her lips. "We need to hear what they are saying."

Thorton came in with a tea tray and placed it on the table between the chairs. After Grace poured, Mama said, "I should tell you that I have been spending a good deal of time with the Duchess of Salforth. She and I believe Madeline would make an excellent wife for the duke."

Grace sipped her tea, which was what she did when she was thinking. She put the cup in the saucer. "You know Matt and I are in agreement that all the girls must find the husbands who are right for them. Have you spoken to her about your wishes?"

"Not yet," Mama said. "If she decides Salforth is the one, you will not object?"

"*If* Madeline chooses Salforth, then no. But neither will we push her in that direction. It is not at all clear to me that she has formed a preference for a gentleman." Grace took another sip of tea. "I should tell you that Harry Stern is standing up with her for the opening set."

Mama's lips formed a thin line. "I suppose he is in the way of being part of the family."

Mary raised her brows, and Theo went back to peeking out the door.

"Our families are extremely close," Grace said noncommittally.

"As long as that is all it is." Mama rose. "I do not consider him suitable."

Grace rose as well. "You are entitled to your opinion."

Mama's eyes narrowed. "She is my daughter."

"Indeed, she is." Grace inclined her head. "I shall see you out. It is time for me to start preparing for the evening."

Once Grace and Mama left the study, Theo turned to Mary. "What do we know about the Duke of Salforth?"

She pulled a face. "He waited for the footmen to help Madeline in and out of his carriage. None of our brothers-in-law did that, and neither did Harry."

She was right. "Nor Lord Montagu."

"Do you remember when Lady Bellamny visited the other day?" Mary asked.

Theo nodded. "I was practicing the piano."

"Yes, well, she said that the duke looked down his nose at Lady Jersey, and she almost did not give vouchers to Almack's to his mother for them."

That was not good. In fact, it was actually rather stupid. "He does not sound like he would make a good husband for Madeline. She did not like Lord Bury either."

"How do you know?" Mary asked.

"I was looking out the schoolroom window when he drove her home." It was amazing what one could see from there. "Harry was with them, and Madeline looked as if her head ached. Once Lord Bury left, Harry took her to Gunter's."

"Ha. Madeline never gets headaches."

Theo gave Mary a look. "If she really had one, she would not have gone to Gunter's with Harry."

"That is true. Who else is a possibility?" Mary mused.

"The only other one who has sent flowers is Lord Hereford. We shall be able to look at him when Madeline takes a carriage ride with him."

Mary nodded. "The day after tomorrow."

"Who is she riding with tomorrow?" Theo did not think her sister was staying home.

"Harry," Mary said. "I heard her tell Grace."

"Hmm." There was one way to get the measure of a gentleman. "Perhaps we should let Posy meet Lord Hereford."

A smile grew on Mary's face. "That is an excellent idea."

Harry arrived at Worthington House with his sister, brother-in-law, and Vivienne well before the ball began so his niece could join the other children to see Madeline and her sisters in their ball gowns. He wished he'd been allowed to go with them, but he was no longer a child.

Worthington handed Harry a glass of sherry. "I have been told you are to stand up with Madeline for the opening dance."

"I am." Waiting to see if her brother would say anything else, he took a sip of wine.

Worthington opened his mouth, closed it again, then said, "Enjoy your evening." And strolled away.

What was that about?

The door to the drawing room opened, and Madeline, along with her sisters, seemed to float into the room. His breath caught, and for a moment he couldn't breathe. God, she was beautiful. The blue gown enhanced her eyes, and the lower neckline gave him an enticing view of the upper swells of her breasts. What he wouldn't do to be able to touch them. Unfortunately, every other gentleman—at least the ones she wasn't related to—would have the same idea. When she moved again, he noticed it was the sheer fabric over the silk that gave the impression of floating. That and her innate grace. Her gloves came to just above her elbows, leaving a long glimpse of creamy skin between them and the tiny puffed sheeves.

The next thing he knew, she was standing in front of him. "My lady." He bowed and took her hand. "You are enchanting."

Beneath his fingers, her pulse quickened. Could she be as affected as he was?

"Thank you." She gazed at him as he placed a brief kiss on her hand. "You are quite handsome."

He straightened. Her hair was an intricate arrangement of braids through which a blue ribbon dotted with pearls was threaded. Chestnut curls framed her face. If only he could reach out and twine one of them around his finger. "Thank you."

She blushed slightly, bringing a lovely pink to her cheeks. "It seems as if I have been waiting for this particular ball since I was a little girl."

"That doesn't surprise me. It's a special night." He glanced down at their hands and realized he was still holding hers. How long would she allow it? "I suppose our morning ride will be canceled. I doubt your brother will make everyone leave after supper."

"No." She chuckled lightly. "We will be up until the early morning hours. Would you like to see the ballroom? My sisters and I designed the decorations for this evening."

"Of course." He wanted to see anything she created. "I imagine it is interesting."

"We think so. It is different from other themes we have seen this Season." She let go of his hand to tuck hers into the crook of his arm. "We are going to the ballroom."

"We will be along soon," Grace said.

Madeline led him toward the back of the house. "I only saw it completed before we went to the drawing room. It is a garden theme, using flowers that are presently in bloom."

"I can't wait to see it." He couldn't wait to have her in his arms, if only for one dance.

"We also added papier-mâché birds and other woodland animals." Excitement radiated through her.

They entered the ballroom and his jaw dropped. It was the most original idea he'd ever seen. Green and yellow swaths of silk wound with netting scattered with purple spangles that caught the light hung from the ceiling above the windows and doors. The chandeliers were decorated with flowers and ribbons in the same colors. Against the walls were branches of forsythias and lilacs in vases on pedestals.

Madeline smiled and pointed to one of the windows. "The birds and squirrels turned out well."

He glanced in the direction she pointed and laughed. Papier-mâché birds and animals were placed on a few of the swags, where they were sure to catch an attentive guest's eye. Finches perched on some of the curtain rods, and squirrels peeped shyly from behind some of the vases. "Excellent job. The *ton* will be talking about these decorations for weeks."

Madeline colored with pleasure. "We wanted something different that reflected us as well."

Just then, he knew part of what she contributed. "You thought of the animals?"

"I did." She glanced at them.

"This is a beautiful and creative ballroom. I'd say you succeeded magnificently."

"Thank you." Her smile broadened. "I am glad you like it."

The others joined them, exclaiming over the room.

"Dotty, Louisa, and I knew you would think of something unusual," Charlotte said. "And you exceeded our expectations. Congratulations."

Madeline hugged her older sisters and Dotty. "Thank you. That means a lot to us."

Looking pleased and proud, Alice and Eleanor hugged the other ladies as well.

"The children would love this," Louisa said.

"Speaking of the children," Grace said. "Alice, Madeline, and Eleanor, you must go up to your parlor and let them see you."

"Then it will be time to take your places in the receiving line," Worthington added.

Madeline untucked her hand from his arm. The loss was almost painful. "I will see you later."

"I'll be here." He searched her face, looking for any sign of how she felt about him, but couldn't see anything or didn't know what he was looking for. "I don't envy you the receiving line."

She grimaced slightly. "I have heard it can be tedious. Charlotte told us to make sure our slippers were slightly larger than normal."

Harry grinned. "I wonder if that advice holds for gentlemen as well."

Madeline laughed. "I have no idea. You will have to try it and tell me."

"Madeline," Grace said.

"I must go." She hurried out of the ballroom.

"How long do receiving lines last?" he mused to himself.

"Until most of the guests have arrived," Dotty said. "They

will not have sent out too many invitations. Matt does not like the rooms to be overly filled."

Wonderful. Harry had who knew how long to wait until he saw Madeline again. "I'm going to stroll around and look at the decorations."

"I'll go with you, if you don't mind," Rothwell said. "I feel as if I'm in a forest."

"Not at all." Rothwell fell in with Harry as they wandered around the ballroom. "It's like something in a fairy tale."

"They have always been a bit fanciful." Rothwell stopped at a vase with one of the squirrels. "Remarkable. Look how they have made the eyes larger, and with lashes on this one." They went on to look at one of the birds. "Are you serious about Madeline?"

Harry supposed he should have expected to be questioned about his intentions. "I want to marry her. What I don't know is if she feels the same."

Rothwell nodded and moved on to the nearest swag. "I understand her mother has been seen in the Duchess of Salforth's company quite a bit. I have come to know Salforth from the Lords. Dukes must sit together, you know."

Harry did know the Lords sat by rank. Was he going to learn Rothwell's impression? "Yes."

Rothwell stared up at a bird. "He's quite rigid in his beliefs, and a Tory."

"He could change parties. Others have." Merton had been the most changed, from what Harry had heard. Exeter as well.

"From what he's said to me, I highly doubt it." Meaning that Rothwell had tried.

Salforth did not sound like someone with whom Madeline would be happy. Yet that begged a question. "Why talk to me about Salforth when there are other gentlemen who seem to be attempting to court her?"

Rothwell raised a brow. "Lady Wolverton has been busy."

Harry didn't like the sound of that. "Do you know if she has said anything to Lady Madeline?"

"Not thus far." He glanced at Harry. "To the best of our knowledge, she has not spoken with anyone."

If she wanted her daughter to wed whom she wished, one would think she'd mention it to someone. "Do you know how much influence she has over Lady Madeline?"

"I couldn't tell you." Rothwell shrugged slightly. "Although we really haven't seen it yet, we all believe Madeline can be as determined as Louisa and Augusta."

Harry had sensed the same inner strength as well. "Thank you." At least now Harry knew who he was up against, and it probably was not Salforth, and it might not even be Lady Wolverton.

"A pleasure." Rothwell gave him a rueful look. "We all needed help."

That was what Merton had said. "I'll take all the assistance and advice I can get."

"An intelligent decision." Rothwell's tone was as dry as dust. "I wish I'd done that." He strolled off toward another vase.

Well, then. How did Harry capture Madeline's love? Dotty had said something about it being important that Merton had seen who she was and what she wanted. It seemed to Harry that Madeline would want the same. If only there was a list.

CHAPTER EIGHTEEN

Madeline had never been so glad for advice in her life. Although her slippers rarely hurt her feet—they were handmade for her, after all—she knew that standing for so long had made her feet swell. She would thank Charlotte as soon as she saw her.

"The Duke and Duchess of Salforth," Thorton announced.

Grace and Matt greeted the duchess first, casually making sure she knew Eleanor, Madeline, and Alice's names.

The duchess had a polite smile on her face when she greeted Eleanor. Then she came to Madeline.

"Lady Madeline, how lovely you look." Her grace smiled warmly as Madeline made a low curtsey.

"Thank you, your grace." Salforth appeared to hover over his mother. Was she still fragile from her husband's death?

"I trust your mother is already here?" the duchess asked. "I am very much enjoying her company."

"She is, your grace." Mama was one of the first to arrive. Madeline knew her mother and the duchess were spending a great deal of time together. What she could not explain was why the back of her neck was pricking her as if something was wrong. She was probably just tired from standing there.

The duchess moved on to Alice, and Salforth bowed to

Madeline and took her hand. "I am delighted to be here, my lady."

His voice was deep and smooth, but she felt nothing more than she had with the other gentlemen who had passed through the receiving line. Then again, she hadn't felt anything when she had danced with him. Nothing like what Eleanor was experiencing with Montagu.

"I am happy you could come." Madeline smiled politely.

He greeted Alice, then followed his mother into the ballroom.

Lord Montagu arrived with his mother, sister, and brother-in-law. It must be almost time to go to the ballroom.

Then Thorton announced, "The Duke and Duchess of Cleveland."

Next to Madeline, Alice stiffened. "*He* had better not be here."

Goodness, she was prickly. Yet, for Alice's peace of mind, Madeline hoped St. Albans would not appear. He had not been invited.

Eleanor and Madeline curtseyed and greeted the duchess.

Before Alice could utter a word, the duchess took her hands and smiled. "My son is not with us. I, however, am pleased to see the lady who has him tied in knots." Madeline wondered what Alice thought about that rather remarkable statement. "I have no doubt he has done something stupid."

The duke bowed and strolled off after his wife.

"Well." Alice looked after the duke and duchess as they ambled away. "What do you think of that?"

"I think she is having a grand time watching her son hang in the wind." Charlie grinned wickedly. "The three of you will have all the gentlemen tripping over themselves."

Kenilworth walked up to them. "One of these days, Charlie Stanwood, you are going to have to court a lady, and when you find you've made a muddle of it, I'm going to take a great deal of pleasure laughing at you."

Madeline glanced at her sisters. They were all struggling not to go into whoops.

"Let's repair to the ballroom and join our guests," Matt said. "It is almost time for the first set."

A thrill of anticipation shot though Madeline as Harry made his way through the crowd toward her. He kept his gaze on her, as if she were the only other person in the room. She could not explain why she was so drawn to him, but it must be *those feelings*. Still, she had her mother's wishes to consider, and did she truly want to be the wife of a politician? Could she have feelings for another gentleman? Could they be made to develop?

He was in front of her, bowing and taking her hand. "How was the receiving line?"

"At first it was exciting to be greeting our guests, then it became tedious, then the Duke and Duchess of Cleveland arrived, and she said the drollest thing to Alice."

After Madeline repeated what the duchess had said, Harry chuckled. "That sounds like something my grandmother Bristol would say."

Madeline raised her brow. "Alice asked that Lord St. Albans not be invited."

"Even more interesting." He glanced at Alice. "This is starting to remind me of one of Miss Austen's books."

For a moment Madeline was speechless. She had never met a gentleman who had read the author. "I had no idea you read Miss Austen."

The corners of his firm lips tipped up. "Oh, yes. She has a wicked wit and crafts remarkable situations for her characters to overcome. I quite enjoy her." He looked thoughtful for a moment. "Why doesn't she tell St. Albans to go away?"

Madeline sighed. "Eleanor asked her that very question. She said she was not going to allow him to defeat her. Before you ask, we have not a clue what she meant, and she never explained it."

"Curious." Harry's forehead creased. "What do you think will happen?"

"I wish I knew." She glanced at her sister. "I suppose we will find out in the end."

"I suppose we will." He smiled. "In the meantime, St. Albans is amusing his mother."

Madeline struggled to hold in her laughter. "Apparently."

The strains of the violins announcing the first set floated through the air. She was about to take his arm, but her hand was already on it. When had that happened? And how had she not noticed it? She must have been too engrossed in their conversation.

"Shall we take our places?" Harry asked. "The set can't begin without you."

"Oh, I had not thought of that." She and her sisters would be the first ones to dance. "How did you know?"

"How do you think? I was thoroughly instructed in first-set protocol for a come out ball by Dotty."

A burst of laughter escaped Madeline. "Of course, you were. Dotty does not do anything by half measures."

Madeline exchanged glances with her sisters as they took their places. Once they had bowed and curtseyed, she put her hand on Harry's shoulder, and he placed his palm on her waist. Suddenly, all her breath rushed out of her, and she had trouble breathing. He took her other hand in his, and warm tingles traveled from her fingers to the rest of her body. Madeline thought she was becoming used to the reaction she had to him. But apparently not. Finally, she was able to suck in a breath.

He bent his head, and his breath caressed her ear as he asked. "Are you all right?"

"Yes. I am just a bit nervous."

"Perfectly understandable." His voice was warm, and kind, and deep, and started the tingles all over again. "It is almost like being on a stage. I felt the same way the first time I argued a case."

His hand on her waist caressed her slightly. He probably only wanted to soothe her, but it made her want to lean against him. Fortunately, the music began, and he began guiding her around the dance floor. Soon others joined in.

He glanced down at her and captured her gaze with his. Concern lurked in his deep green eyes. "Better?"

"Yes. Much better. It *was* almost like being on a stage. I felt as if everyone was staring at us."

Harry chuckled lightly. "They were."

"I suppose you are right." Had anyone seen her reaction to him?

Eleanor and Montagu twirled next to them. Harry's gaze followed them briefly before focusing on Madeline. "Do you think he will offer for her?"

"He asked for two sets. The first and the supper dance. We all think he will propose to her soon. Alice thought he might do it tonight, but Eleanor was not sure about that."

"If he did, it would take attention away from you and Alice. He'd do better to pick another time."

Harry had an excellent point. She tried to sound offended. "You are being right a great deal this evening."

He grinned. "Only because you are distracted by your ball."

Madeline smiled back. "There you go again."

His lips twitched.

"Why is it I can see you throwing your head back and laughing?"

"Because that is exactly what I'd like to do."

His bright green eyes stared down at her; then his gaze dropped to her lips, and they tingled. Madeline wished she could dance the supper set with him as well. If only her mother was not set on a peer. If only she was braver, and pleasing Mama did not mean so much to her. But surely one could have these feelings with a gentleman who was acceptable to her mother. There had to be another gentleman who met all the requirements on the list. For some reason Madeline once again seemed drawn to Harry's firm, well-shaped lips. Perhaps she could try a little harder with Salforth.

Without seeing her eyes, Harry knew she was looking at his mouth and responding to him. He wished he could kiss her. Here. In front of everyone. But wouldn't that cause a scandal? Instead, he guided her into the next twirl. Thinking about kissing and making love to her was not at all helpful. What he needed to do was exactly what Merton and Rothwell had said: engage her affections. Lady Exeter's ball was tomorrow, and Harry hadn't asked Madeline for a dance. "Will you stand up with me for the supper set at the Exeter ball?"

Her lapis eyes met his. "I will."

It was time to twirl again. "If Montagu can restrain himself from proposing tonight, he will surely do it tomorrow evening."

Madeline's eyes began to sparkle. "That would be perfect."

They passed a squirrel that seemed to be rolling its eyes at him. His imagination was working overtime. His musings about Madeline were completely understandable, but the squirrel? "It would certainly make Dorie Exeter's night."

Madeline smiled. "She would be in alt. The *ton* would be talking about the ball for at least a week."

He almost laughed out loud. "One would hope no one else did anything to shorten the period."

She started to giggle and then stopped. "I so wish one could show more of one's feelings in public."

Harry had the same thought. "We do seem to be made to constrain ourselves when in Town."

Her head tilted, and she stared at him. "Yes indeed. One is freer in the country to behave more naturally."

The last notes of the set were played, and he brought them to a stop. All he could do for the rest of the evening was remain as close to her as possible. He escorted her back to their circle. Eleanor and Montagu joined them. They both looked as if they would burst with happiness. If Harry wanted that with Madeline—and he did—he'd just have to work harder, and find a way around her mother. Or perhaps not do anything that would make Lady Wolverton notice him, or think of him as Madeline's suitor. He drew her a little closer, and she glanced at him. What was she thinking?

"Have you been to the local assemblies in Stansbury? It's been a few years since I attended one, but I remember them being rather lively."

Madeline smiled up at him. "They are. We spent a fair amount of time at Stanwood when Charlie was making his Grand Tour."

"I remember that Worthington was watching over the estates for him. He brought you all along?"

"Oh yes." She nodded. "Only Theo and I had not been raised there, and they enjoyed seeing their neighbors again. I liked it too. We don't really have close neighbors at Worthington." She frowned a bit. "Well, we did not until Grace came. She has a talent for bringing neighbors together."

"Lady Madeline." A gentleman bowed. "If I remember correctly, this is my set."

She inclined her head. "Mr. Cornish, it is."

He really didn't like watching her dance with some other gentleman. Someday soon, he hoped he'd have all her dances. He forced himself to look away and glanced at Lady Wolverton. Fortunately, she was alternating between speaking with the Duchess of Salforth and glancing at Madeline. If it wasn't so important to remain by Madeline's side, he'd leave. But he would not give another man the opportunity to claim her attention. He wandered over to Rothwell, who was standing next to Merton.

Hidden among her family and his, he watched her as she went through the steps of a country dance. At least her partner could only touch her hand. "Is there a reason we cannot simply throw ladies over our shoulders and ride off with them?"

"Thea has always thought it would have been very uncomfortable for the lady," Merton mused.

"I believe Louisa expressed the same opinion," Rothwell said. "If I'm not mistaken, we have all had the same desire."

At least Harry was in good company. Speaking of good company, where had Montagu gone? Harry scanned the room and found the man speaking with another couple. "Who is the gentleman and lady with Montagu?"

"His twin sister and Lytton, her husband," Merton said. "He was interested in Augusta when she came out. Why?"

"No reason in particular." The set ended, and Madeline was with Harry again. When she placed her hand on his arm, tension he'd not been aware of melted away.

She looked around. "Where is Eleanor?"

He glanced to where Montagu had been. "She is with Montagu."

"And they are gazing into each other's eyes," Alice said. "They had better not do it for too long. People will talk."

Harry noticed the couple was drawing attention. "I think they already are."

Madeline looked at the other guests. "They do not need to become an *on-dit*."

That was true. This ball should be remembered for the stunning and original décor and what was no doubt going to be excellent food, not Eleanor and Montagu drawing everyone's attention. "Do you want me to go to them?"

"No." Madeline shook her head. "Alice and I had better do it."

"It will appear more natural," Alice agreed.

They strolled across the room, greeting guests as they went. Soon they were speaking with their sister and Montagu.

Harry's attention was drawn away from the sisters to Kenilworth and Rothwell, who were also watching Eleanor and Montagu.

"That's a proposal waiting to happen," Kenilworth said.

"The Season will be over by the time he gets around to it," Rothwell retorted.

"No." Kenilworth shook his head. "It will be much sooner than that."

Madeline and Alice were accompanying Eleanor back to the family circle.

Rothwell huffed. "Take it from me. Nothing is going to happen in that direction anytime in the near future. He hasn't even spoken with Worthington yet."

Kenilworth raised a knowing brow. "I'll wager you a pony he'll ask her within the next few days."

Rothwell smirked. "I shall be happy to take your money."

"We shall see." Kenilworth smiled smugly.

Harry glanced at his brother-in-law, who also raised a brow. "Montagu is the best of her suitors."

They all knew. Every blasted gentleman in this family had been keeping a closer eye on the ladies than he'd imagined. Nothing escaped their notice, and they, apparently, had their favorites. That was the reason Rothwell had spoken with him this evening. Harry was glad for the help, but he didn't like the idea of being so closely watched. Yet if it would help him marry Madeline, he'd put up with it.

CHAPTER NINETEEN

The next evening, Madeline and her sisters entered the Exeter ballroom accompanied by their relatives.

Eleanor's excitement was infectious. "If his behavior last night is any indication, I think he will propose tonight."

Madeline was about to look for Harry; then he was suddenly by her side.

He took her hand, kissed it, then gazed into her eyes. "You are beautiful."

Pleasurable sensations raced through her. "Thank you, sir, and you are very handsome."

He placed her hand on his arm, and it occurred to her that she liked it there. It felt right. Unfortunately, it would not last long. The quartet had taken their places, and the prelude of the set was being played.

Dorie Exeter strode up to them. "Mr. Stern." She took his other arm. "I have a young lady who requires a dance partner."

That had never happened before. Madeline was amazed at how disappointed she was to have him taken from her.

"My lady." Lord Folliot bowed. "This is my set."

She forced herself to assume a polite smile. "It is, my lord."

He led her to the dance floor, and they took their positions in the quadrille. Harry was across from and one person up from her. Again, their eyes met, and it was as if he was saying he'd rather be dancing with her. All Madeline could think was that at least it was not a waltz. But Dorie had more than two planned for the evening. Perhaps she would leave Harry alone after this set. Unfortunately, not long after the dance was over, she took him to meet another lady, and Madeline's partner came to claim her.

When Lord Bolingbroke returned her after the third set, Harry joined her again. "Dorie is ensuring there are no ladies sitting on the side this evening."

"I noticed that." Well, she had noticed Harry was being pressed into service for every set so far.

Alice came up to them. "There is no unclaimed gentleman who is safe."

Madeline glanced around. "Where is Eleanor?"

"She is outside with Montagu," Alice said. "Con is going out after them."

Their brother-in-law was headed for the doors to the terrace but keeping well back. "Do you think Montagu is going to ask her to marry him?"

Alice lifted one shoulder and dropped it. "We shall find out soon."

Madeline prayed Con did not interfere with her sister and Montagu.

A few minutes later Con strolled up to Matt. "You will receive a request for her hand before the night is out," Kenilworth said, looking pleased. "They are well matched. And Rothwell owes me a monkey."

Matt stared at Con. "How the deuce did that come about?"

He shrugged. "You know how he can be. He went on and on about Montagu being a slow top. I got tired of it and finely wagered five hundred quid."

"That will teach him," Matt said.

"Until the next time." Kenilworth grinned.

Eleanor was betrothed! Madeline could not keep the smile from her face.

Alice took her hands. "This is wonderful! And he met all the requirements."

Harry placed a hand over Madeline's. "Here they come, and looking extremely happy."

"I could not be more thrilled for them."

"Worthington." Montagu bowed. "I wish to have a word with you."

Matt inclined his head. "My study, no later than ten o'clock tomorrow morning."

Montagu smiled at Eleanor, and she smiled back. "I'll be there."

She stepped over to Madeline, and Harry moved back. She and Alice hugged Eleanor. "I am so happy!"

"We are happy for you." Madeline laughed as Alice said the same thing at the exact same time.

"He told me he loves me."

"The most important requirement," Alice said.

The prelude to a dance began, and Eleanor appeared surprised. "We did not miss the supper dance?"

Alice gave her a look. "If you had been gone that long, Matt would have had our brothers hunting for you."

"He would have, wouldn't he?" Eleanor said. "But now I can waltz with my betrothed."

Madeline was beginning to think the supper set would never arrive. Where was Harry?

He placed her hand on his arm again. "Shall we?"

"Of course." And she did not have to worry about her mother watching. Neither Mama nor the Salforths had been invited.

She reveled in the familiar pressure of Harry's palm as he placed it on her waist. She held her hand up and he closed his much larger one around it. They moved with the music so easily, there was no need to even think about steps or feet. The progress of the dance had placed him behind her.

"I think they will be happy," Harry said, his breath caressing her ear and neck.

"Yes." Madeline's breath quickened. "We will be very busy until the wedding."

He twirled her back around. "Too busy for morning rides?"

"Oh, no. We will need them more than ever." She searched his face for some sign of his feelings. Not that she should. Her mother seemed set on Salforth.

"I imagine you will help her plan it."

"No. Grace will do it. Alice and I will make sure it is done as Eleanor would want it. Not that Grace would do anything she did not like, but I have a feeling Montagu's mother will want to be involved."

Comprehension appeared on his lean face. "Ah, I understand. It is easier for you two to disagree with his mother than for either Eleanor or Grace."

"Precisely." He was quick to recognize the subtleties of her family. Why could he have not been a duke?

When the set ended, they found Lady Montagu and Lady Lytton were already in conversation with Grace.

"How long will it be to the wedding?" Harry whispered in Madeline's ear, causing the wonderful feelings again.

"I do not think it will be more than two weeks. That seems to be the length of time, once there is an agreement to wed."

Lady Montagu took a seat down the table from Grace, and Alice sat next to her.

"Let us sit near Alice."

"As you wish." He seemed as if he would like to ask for a reason but decided not to.

While the gentlemen were fetching the food, Lady Montagu began to tell Alice and Eleanor about her ideas for the decorations. "I think dark green and maroon would be lovely."

She and her sister exchanged a look. Alice took a breath and simply said, "No. Eleanor would not like that."

Her ladyship's eyes flew open in shock.

Madeline decided to explain. "Our sister—indeed all of us—prefer to be surrounded by brighter colors that will make a room look lighter." Her ladyship did not appear to understand. "Such as the colors we had at our come out ball."

Alice glanced at her, and Madeline nodded. "Perhaps you should come to our house, and you can see what we mean. Even the rooms that face north do not look dark."

"If you really believe Eleanor would not like the colors I suggested, I will ask Lady Worthington to show me around when I arrive for tea."

Madeline breathed a sigh of relief. Still, they would have to keep a close watch on the wedding plans. What was keeping Harry and the others? She glanced toward the long table on the side of the supper room. He, and Athersuch, Alice's partner, were watching them. Madeline smiled, and they signaled to the footman following them.

He took the seat next to her. "I was afraid to interrupt what looked to be an important discussion."

"You were wise to wait. Did Montagu say anything?" She would not want him upset. Her sister had been quite firm with his mother.

"Nothing of importance." She dipped her spoon into the chocolate ice Harry had brought for her. "He merely wondered what was being discussed."

He looked pointedly at her ice. "Did you not want to taste the bergamot and orange ice?"

"Oh, no." Madeline glanced at her ice cream. "I totally forgot." She pushed it aside and drank a rather large sip of champagne to clear the chocolate taste. "Yes, I would love to try yours."

He handed her his spoon, and she took a small sample and tasted it. "That is actually very good."

Harry grinned. "But not as good as chocolate."

She smiled at him. "No, but it is closer than the others."

How well he knew her. Still, she must try to concentrate on Salforth as a husband. Lord Hereford as well, she supposed. Rain had put off her ride with him, but he had asked for a set at Lady Bellamny's ball. Although, as much time as Mama was spending with the Duchess of Salforth, Mama would be happier for Madeline to wed the duke.

Wedding plans swirled around Harry as Madeline, Alice, and Lady Montagu discussed them. Several times he had to stifle a chuckle at her ladyship's expressions. As hard as the woman tried, she could not keep an expression of bemused horror from her mien.

"I do think the dogs should be dressed up a bit," Alice said. "Not as much as we dressed Duke and Daisy, but something."

"We can leave that to Mary and Theo," Madeline said.

"Dogs at a wedding?" Lady Montagu's voice was so faint he barely heard it.

"Not at the service, of course," Madeline assured her ladyship. "At the breakfast."

"They are very well-trained," Alice added. "Most of the time."

"All the children must have new clothing." Madeline took a pocketbook with an attached pencil from her reticule and made a note.

"For the wedding breakfast." Lady Montagu's tone was stronger this time. As if she finally knew how things would work.

Madeline gave her ladyship a wide-eyed look. "At the

service and at the wedding breakfast. The children always attend."

"Not the babies." Alice waved her fork before taking a bite of cake.

Harry glanced at Athersuch, who had apparently been forgotten. He could not be much older than twenty and appeared to be listening with rapt attention.

"I say," the man said. "Have you thought of peonies? M'sister had them at her wedding."

Alice graced him with a look of approval. "That is an excellent idea."

Worthington stood, putting an end to the discussion. "It is time for us to depart."

Exeter strode over. "I must say congratulations to Montagu and Lady Eleanor. I trust you all had a good evening."

"We did." Grace smiled. "It was an excellent evening."

As a whole, they made their way to the hall. Used to the schedule, their carriages were already waiting.

Harry drew Madeline aside and took her hands. "Barring rain, I will see you in the morning."

"I will see you then." She gazed up at him, excitement making her glow. "I am not sure how many events we will attend before the wedding. There will be a great deal to do."

"I can imagine. Two weeks is not long at all to plan a wedding. I remember Dotty needing a whole new wardrobe."

Madeline's mouth dropped open for a second, and she closed her eyes. "I had not even thought of that. And they will take a wedding trip. I sincerely hope Montagu will take care of those arrangements, but she will need luggage, as well as new gowns and other things."

Harry pressed his lips together to stop himself from laughing. "I heard Paris mentioned."

"In that case, we must remember to ask Madame Lissette for recommendations."

Fortunately, he knew Madame Lissette was the dressmaker

to whom they all gave their custom. She, it seemed, was extremely accommodating when it came to rushed weddings. "I'm certain she will be helpful."

"Yes." Madeline nodded, her thoughts clearly on the wedding preparations. "Oh, dear, forgive me. I cannot seem to think of anything aside from the wedding."

"That is entirely understandable." He squeezed her fingers. "I remember the week before Dotty's marriage. It was a madhouse."

"Madeline," Worthington said.

Harry placed her hand on his arm. "Come. I will escort you out."

"Thank you." She flashed him a smile. "For your escort and for understanding."

"I need no thanks. I enjoy seeing you happy." Once he handed her into the large coach, he recalled Alice's remark about Montagu meeting all the requirements. Harry thought he might know what she meant, but he was sure Dotty would know. He would have preferred to walk. Merton House was not that far, but Dotty's slippers would have been ruined. He went to the Merton town coach and climbed in, taking the backward-facing seat. "I have some questions."

"What would they be?" Merton asked.

"When Kenilworth told Worthington Montagu had proposed, Alice said that he, meaning Montagu, met all the requirements. Do you have any idea what she meant?"

Dotty chuckled lightly. "I have no doubt they made a list of requirements a gentleman must meet to be a husband."

Harry wished he could find a way to read the list. "Such as?"

"Love will be the most important. She must love him, and he must love her in return."

"Did you have a list?" Merton asked.

"Charlotte, Louisa, and I discussed what was important. I do not think we actually wrote them down."

Harry was impatient to know the rest. "Other than love, what would be on it?"

"The usual things for our families. Love of children, dogs, cats, the rest of the family." There was a little light from the gas streetlamps, and he could see her smile.

"Worthington would require that the gentleman was capable of supporting her," Merton added.

"They have seen all of our marriages," Dotty said. "I am quite sure they will want the same thing."

That would include respect and a partnership. Harry had seen that with her sister and brother-in-law and the others. It seemed as if the list Madeline had included the same things he wanted.

"Harry." Dotty leaned over and put her hand on his knee. "You were raised by the same parents as I was. I am quite sure you already meet any requirements they have."

"As long as you love her." He knew without seeing Merton the man had raised a brow.

"Yes," Dotty agreed. "That is the most important requirement."

The coach rolled to a stop, and Harry jumped out. Merton followed him. "I wish there was more we could do to assist you."

A footman put down the carriage stairs, and he turned to help Dotty.

"I know you do." Harry did not know why he'd not thought of love. Of course that would be necessary. Yet he didn't have to agonize over it. He was in love with Madeline and wanted to spend the rest of his life with her.

Chapter Twenty

Two mornings later, Harry met up with Madeline and her sisters before they entered the Park. Once again, she had to admire his seat. "Good morning."

Willy nickered at Rose, and she returned the greeting.

"Good morning." Madeline smiled at him. "It is glorious weather."

"It is. Especially after the annoying drizzle yesterday." He came up beside her. "How is the bride-to-be this morning?"

"Good morning, Harry," Eleanor said. "I cannot stop thinking about everything that must be accomplished. Nothing got done yesterday."

"Feel free to task me with anything with which I can assist you." He didn't expect her to accept his offer, but if she did, he'd be happy to help.

Eleanor gave him a grateful look. "If I can think of anything, I will tell you."

"As a matter of fact, a great deal was accomplished yesterday." Madeline's voice was low, so that only he could hear her. "Matt spoke with Montagu and Eleanor about the settlement agreement." She glanced at her sister. "Still, it will be a short ride this morning."

Harry's father had told him about Worthington's idea of

a settlement agreement. He was determined any lady under his protection would be well cared for.

"Will you be shocked that I am not at all surprised?" Disappointed, but not surprised.

"Let us race." She pulled a face. "Although it cannot truly be called a race when you insist on pacing with me."

"Not me." He assumed an expression of mock indignation. "My horse. I'm starting to believe Willy is smitten with Rose."

Madeline let out a peal of laughter as she and Rose raced ahead.

"Come, Willy, we must catch up to them." The horse snorted and started to gallop after his ladylove. "We'll be in a bad way if she doesn't marry me."

As it was, Madeline and her mare had covered about two thirds of the distance to the tree when they reached them, and Willy slowed slightly to keep pace with Rose.

They reached the tree and dropped to a walk. "I wondered how long it would take for you to catch us."

Willy sidled up to Rose. For a moment it appeared as if he'd put his neck on her withers but thought better of it.

Alice and Eleanor rode up to them.

"I hope Madame will be able to see me today," Eleanor said to no one in particular.

"If not today, tomorrow," Madeline said.

"Yes." Eleanor heaved a sigh. "I just want everything done. Two weeks is both too long and not long enough."

He wondered if he'd think the same way. Then again, he'd have been searching for a house to keep him busy. "Do I understand correctly that you are traveling to Paris after the wedding?"

"Yes." She nodded. "Dorie is going to take me to the luggage maker she used and advise me as to what I will require."

As if by mutual agreement, they turned and walked the

horses back to the gate. He glanced at Madeline. "It is going to be like this until they are married."

"I think you are correct." She glanced at Eleanor. All of them looked distracted. "We are making lists of what needs to be accomplished. A great deal of time will be spent shopping."

He recalled the relatively short journeys he had made. "Do not forget books. I realize they will be newlyweds, but travel can be tedious."

"That is an excellent idea." Her countenance cleared, and her lips curled into a lovely smile. "None of us have thought of needing books."

Harry wanted to see Montagu's face when his bride revealed a trunk of books. But even newlyweds couldn't make love all the time. "I'm glad I could help with something."

Madeline's gaze lingered on him. He'd give a fortune to know what was going through her mind. "I know you were unable to make a Grand Tour, but did you ever wish to travel?"

"Yes, and I'd still like to visit certain places." He attempted to read her look again and could not. "I was seriously considering the Foreign Office, but my father pointed out that studying the law was better preparation for managing the estate when the time came."

They reached the gate, and she stopped staring at him. "Did you never contemplate the Church?"

"Not at all." He barked a laugh. "I don't have the temperament for it. My younger brother might be a good candidate."

When they reached Worthington House, he dismounted and got to her before one of the servants did. Although she was probably perfectly capable of alighting from her mare without help. She had already released her leg from the upper pommel and was sitting sideways. He took hold of her small waist and lifted her down and, resisting the urge to allow his hands to slide up under her lush breasts, he set her feet carefully on the pavement.

She picked up the train of her skirts before glancing up at him. "Thank you."

He gave her a courtly bow, and she smiled. Yet he sensed something else was bothering her. Unfortunately, this was not the time to ask about it. "It was entirely my pleasure."

"Madeline," one of her sisters called. "We must go in."

She glanced over her shoulder. "I will be right there." She turned her attention back to him. "I must go."

"Have fun making your lists and shopping."

Madeline got the same strange look in her eyes. "I am sure we will."

Had she forgotten she was to ride with him today? "Will you still have time to ride with me this afternoon?"

Her eyes widened slightly. She had forgotten. "Yes. I will see you then."

Harry had to find a way to spend more time with her, and the wedding was going to take more and more of her attention. "I have an idea. Would you mind if I accompany you while you are shopping? I have some things I must purchase. I could use your advice."

He held his breath until she smiled. "By all means. We would be happy to have your company."

He sent a prayer of thanks to the deity. "When should I return?"

"In about two and a half hours. Matt is meeting with Eleanor and Montagu to finalize the settlement agreements. We must take the town coach when we go shopping. It looks as if someone is attempting to harm Eleanor, and Matt insists we take extra footmen and the coach wherever we go on an excursion."

That must have been what had been bothering her. He'd bring his sword stick. "I'll help keep an eye out as well."

"Madeline." Alice's tone was urgent.

She glanced behind her. "I really must go in."

"I'll see you in two hours." He wanted to shout "Hooray," but settled for escorting her to the door.

When he reached his horse and mounted, he glanced back at the house. Madeline was standing there looking at him. She gave a small wave before going inside. He hoped that meant he was making progress.

At the appointed time, Harry strolled up to Worthington House. A town coach stood on the street in front of the door.

It opened, and the butler bowed. "Mr. Stern, please come in. The ladies will be down shortly."

No sooner than the butler had finished his sentence, the swishing of skirts and the sound of footsteps floated down from above.

Eleanor and Alice greeted him and proceeded out the door. He held out his arm, and Madeline placed her hand on it. "I am glad you are joining us. Although now Alice has decided we should ask Lord Bury to accompany us some time."

It was as if his brain had stopped working for a second. "Bury? Why would she want him to go shopping with you?"

Madeline glanced at the sky. "When she went for a carriage ride with him, they discussed fashion. He gave her several suggestions."

Bury? Harry gave himself a shake. "He's interested in ladies' fashion?"

"I never would have known." Madeline lifted one shoulder in a shrug. "In any event, she finds him witty."

"I definitely must accompany you when he does." If only to see what he recommended.

She chuckled quietly. "I will tell you when she arranges it."

The first stop was at the elegant shop of Madame Lissette.

Surprisingly, it did not take long at all. Madeline came out first, and he raised a brow in question.

"She already had sketches and fabrics," Madeline whispered. "We are on to order shoes and hats."

Her sisters joined them, and they left the shop and turned to the right.

"Stop that boy!" the vegetable vendor down the street shouted as a lad was passing them. Harry grabbed the child by his grubby shirt, his legs still running hard.

"Let me go!"

Madeline and her sisters, who had stopped to look in a shop window, hurried up to him. She glanced at him and the boy. "What is going on?"

The vendor, a short, thin man with thinning hair, scowled. "That thief was stealing apples. I'm sending for a constable."

Frowning, she studied the man, then the boy. That was when Harry noticed that although the child's clothing was dirty, it was not poorly made. Had this been a dare?

The lad was still struggling. "Calm down and tell me and Mr."—he cut a glance at the vendor.

"Robbins. Mr. Fred Robbins."

"Tell me and Mr. Robbins why you took the apple."

"He st—" Harry held up his hand, stopping the man from speaking. If one wanted information, it was better not to use words such as "theft" or "stealing."

Madeline approached more closely. "It will be all right. Tell us why you took the apple."

The boy sniffed loudly. "I'm hungry."

Harry was about to question the child further but stopped as Madeline crouched down to the lad's level.

"Where are your mother and father?"

"My mama died when I was little. It was just Papa and me, then he died when some men tried to rob him."

She glanced at Mr. Robbins, then back to the child. "Can you tell me your name?"

"Bobby Fields." The boy sniffed again.

"I am pleased to meet you. I am Lady Madeline Vivers, and the gentleman holding you is Mr. Stern, a friend of mine. Do you not have any family who could care for you?"

Bobby shook his head. "Not that I know of."

"Look here, my lady," Mr. Robbins said. "I got to make a living. I can't have people taking my produce and not paying for it. It's hard enough being by myself to look after everything."

The instant he said he was by himself, a light came into Madeline's lapis-blue eyes. "Bobby, how old are you, and have you attended school?"

"I'm nine, my lady." He shuffled his feet on the pavement. "I went to a school in Brentford, where we lived."

That caught Mr. Robbins's attention, and his frown deepened. "Why are you in London?"

Bobby shrugged. "We lived over the office, and when my papa died, the landlord said I couldn't live there anymore and sent me here."

Harry had heard versions of this story before. There were always too many people willing to take advantage of orphans.

Mr. Robbins went to attend to a customer, and Madeline asked, "What did your father do?"

Bobby screwed up his face, thinking. "He organized things. He was going to teach me to do it too, but I had to go to school."

Harry made a note to himself to find out exactly what Mr. Fields organized, and if the landlord or anyone else had stolen from Bobby. He'd wager his new carriage they had.

"Do you know how to read, write, and figure your numbers?" Madeline asked.

The lad nodded vigorously.

Madeline rose gracefully as Mr. Robbins returned. "Sir, it appears to me that you would do much better to have an assistant. Bobby can already read, write, and knows basic arithmetic. He could be helpful to you."

The man's jaw dropped and his eyes widened. "I–I can't afford to take anyone on."

Harry expected Madeline would have to come up with another solution when she said, "It would not cost so very much to feed the child. I would be willing to pay a sum to cover his board until you know if he would be of assistance to you."

At the mention of money, Mr. Robbins's demeanor changed. It was clear he hoped to earn a good deal extra for taking the boy in. "And how much would that be, my lady?"

Harry watched her closely. She might be young and wellborn, but she was also very intelligent and knowing. "One shilling per week."

The merchant's face fell for a moment, but one shilling was more than fair. It would pay for Bobby's food and then some.

The lad had stilled as he watched Madeline and Mr. Robbins. Harry leaned down and whispered into the boy's ear. "Are you willing to work for Mr. Robbins?"

Not taking his gaze off Madeline and the merchant, he nodded.

"I must also inform you," Madeline said, "that either I or someone I trust will come by now and then to make sure Bobby is being well-treated."

The man was silent for several seconds before glancing at the boy. "If you're willing to work for me, I'll teach you the business and treat you well."

"Yes, sir." Bobby nodded. "I'll work hard."

Madeline stuck out her hand. "Then we all have a deal."

Mr. Robbins seemed flummoxed but took her hand and shook it. "We do, my lady."

"I will have him cleaned up and brought to you this evening." She took the boy's hand. "Come along."

It had surprised Harry that Eleanor and Alice had stood off to the side and not added their voices to the process until Alice gave him a sly smile before following Madeline to their town coach.

"He'll be very happy until he realizes he must bathe," Eleanor mumbled.

He almost laughed, but instead hurried to the coach to hand Madeline in. "The store is on my way to Westminster if you would like me to look in on him in a day or two."

"I would appreciate that." She placed her foot on the first step. "Thank you for not interfering."

"It was my pleasure." He handed her sisters into the coach as well before stepping back. "I shall make my own way home. Shall we postpone our carriage ride until tomorrow?"

A line creased her forehead, and he wanted to smooth it away. "That would probably be for the best. I do not know how long it will take to settle everything."

Instead, he bowed. "I will see you at the ball this evening."

She gave him a grateful look, and the coach started forward.

On the walk back to Merton House, Harry had an opportunity to consider the boy's situation. Now that Bobby was settled, it was time to find out exactly what happened to his father and any possessions he might be entitled to. An investigation must be conducted as soon as possible. Harry wanted to do it, but he might not be able to get the answers someone else could.

He walked through the door as it opened. "Parkin, is his lordship in?"

The butler took Harry's hat and gloves. "Yes, sir. He's in his study."

"Thank you." He made his way down the corridor to the left and knocked on the study door.

"Come."

He was not surprised to find his sister there as well. "Good morning."

"Good day to you," Dotty said. "To which of us do you wish to speak?"

Harry took the other chair in front of the large walnut desk. "Both or either of you. We found a boy today who had taken an apple. Madeline arranged for him to work for the merchant. But there is a question about why the boy is in Town. He said his father died after being robbed." He told them the rest of the story. "In my opinion, something is not right about the whole situation. Who, for example, would put a young child on a coach to London?"

Dotty raised a brow. "Someone who wanted him dead, I should think."

"Would you like me to send someone out to ask questions?" Merton asked.

Harry appreciated the offer but wanted to be there himself. "I would like you to let me borrow someone to go with me and help me ask questions."

Merton nodded. "Very well. When are you free?"

"I have nothing pressing tomorrow morning. It will take about an hour to get there. I'd like to leave immediately after breaking my fast."

"I'll have someone ready." Merton wrote something down. "Take the unmarked town coach."

Harry rose. "Thank you."

As he strolled to his rooms, he thought back to the twins allowing Madeline to take the lead. Were they trying to support her efforts to be more independent, or was she the best one to handle the situation? The way she convinced Mr. Robbins to take the child had impressed Harry. What impressed him even more was how she came up with the idea. He had been willing to simply pay the shopkeeper for the apple. She had thought of a more permanent solution. Ideas like hers could benefit some of the people in his constituency, and in England as a whole.

CHAPTER TWENTY-ONE

Madeline sat next to Bobby on the way home. He needed a bath, something she was not going to mention. He'd find out soon enough. A change of clothing, a meal, and probably a pallet, a pillow, and a set of linens. Mr. Robbins was unlikely to have a second bed, and she did not want the boy sleeping on the floor. When they arrived at Worthington House, she explained what she needed to Mrs. Thorton, who took Bobby with her.

Madeline repaired to join her sisters in their parlor, and a tea tray had already been brought up.

"That was really well done," Alice said. "How did you have the idea that the shopkeeper might take him in?"

"He said he was alone." And he appeared sad when he said it. "It cannot be easy for him to look out for thieves, serve customers, and do all the other things necessary to run a busy store. By the way Bobby spoke, it was clear he is a bright boy and had some schooling." Madeline had been a bit surprised with the alacrity he displayed when accepting the job. "What I do not know is how permanent a situation this will be. He might not know of any relatives who could raise him, but someone in the town he comes from might know."

Eleanor took a ginger biscuit. "Will you ask Matt to look into the boy's father?"

"No." Madeline sipped her tea. "I am going to ask Harry. He is already involved, and he said the circumstances needed to be investigated."

"Clever." Alice nodded approvingly.

"He admitted he would not have thought of arranging for Mr. Robbins to offer Bobby a position, but he fell in readily when I suggested it." She took a sip of tea. "It is time to start separating the wheat from the chaff, as it were." She finished her cup and poured another. "I will present the story to the other gentlemen at the ball this evening and ask what they would have done."

The afternoon was spent on morning calls, and Madeline was glad to see Eleanor was the center of attention. Everyone who had not wished her happy on her betrothal did so then. It never failed to amaze Madeline how quickly word spread.

Shortly after arriving home, Mrs. Thorton came to Madeline's chamber. "Master Robert has been scrubbed, fed, and his clothing has been cleaned. I also found some of Master Phillip's old garments that are in good condition." The housekeeper smiled fondly. "He met our Suky at luncheon. When she asked if he was going to live here as well, he straightened his shoulders and informed her that he was going into business."

Madeline had to laugh. "I suppose he is. His father was a merchant of some sort. It wouldn't surprise me if he does not become one as well."

Mrs. Thorton pressed her lips together in thought. "He'll need more schooling. Perhaps, after a bit, you can arrange a time for him to come here for an hour or so during the day."

"That is a wonderful idea. Thank you." After all, his father had him in school. "I want him to settle into his new life first. Then I will approach the idea with Mr. Robbins."

Not long afterward, Madeline was presented with a clean,

clothed, and fed Bobby. He gave her a look that clearly meant he'd been betrayed. "You didn't tell me I had to have a bath."

"No?" She schooled her countenance into a look of confusion. "I must have forgotten. Cook never allows anyone to eat in his kitchen unless they are clean." She held out her hand. "Did you enjoy your meal?"

He nodded enthusiastically. "It was the best meal I've ever had, and I had cake."

"He is a very good cook. Come along. It is time to go to Mr. Robbins's store."

The town coach was waiting for her, along with the driver and her footman. Roberts handed her up, then lifted Bobby into the carriage. It was not long before they pulled up in front of the store.

Bobby seemed fascinated as he watched Mr. Robbins briskly take care of his many customers. "I can help him. I know how to count out money and weigh things."

It was interesting that Bobby already knew some of what a business required. "We shall wait until he has time to greet you and show you where you will sleep."

Still staring out of the coach, Bobby nodded; then he glanced back at Madeline. "I think I will like working here."

Tears stung her eyes. He was so young, and his recent life had not been easy, but he seemed determined to press on. She would make a point of asking if her family and friends could give some of their custom to Mr. Robbins.

The last customer left, and Mr. Robbins stood back and glanced around. A slight smile appeared on his face as Bobby waved to the man. In no time at all, her footman had delivered Bobby and his few possessions to Mr. Robbins, along with the first payment.

"Did you see where he will sleep?" Madeline asked Roberts.

"Yes, my lady. He has a small room. Mr. Robbins said

something about a bed. The place is clean and kept neat. It looks like he might have had a wife or a sister living with him. There's a woman's touch."

"That is good to know. Thank you." Even though she knew she could have dealt with the situation herself, she was glad Harry had been there earlier. If not for him, poor Bobby would have run off to who knew where, and he might have eventually been arrested and put in prison.

Later that evening, Madeline and her sisters entered Henrietta Fotherby's ballroom.

Lord Hereford came to claim the opening dance. He bowed. "My lady."

She placed her hand in his and curtseyed. "My lord. Good evening."

As he led her to the dance floor, she had the feeling he thought claiming her for the first dance was significant to him. Fortunately, it was a minuet, which gave her enough time to tell the story but no time to argue about it.

She performed the first steps of the dance. "My lord, an interesting question came up today."

He circled around her. "What was that?"

They were separated by the steps, then came back together again. "If one catches a young child stealing an apple, what would you do about it?"

She waited until they met again. "Call the constable, of course. Thieves should be punished. Pity the poor shop-keeper."

As he circled around her, she tried again. "Do you not think it would behoove both parties to have a different solution proposed? A position, for example."

He took her hand as they performed the next steps. "Most

of these street urchins are lazy and uneducated. What good would they be?"

Did he not know that many people, from farmers to mill workers, could not read or write? "But what if the child was not completely uneducated?"

"I do not understand why anyone would take the time to find out." By his tone, he was extremely unconcerned about the plight of the child and did not care to speak about it.

Madeline was glad when the steps of the dance called for him to drop her hand. "I believe more should be done to help the unfortunate."

"Yes, yes, of course. All you ladies are interested in charitable endeavors. It is your soft hearts." He took her hand as they danced toward the couple across from them. When they were in the next position, he continued, "It is a good thing we harder-hearted men rule."

What tripe. If she could have walked off the dance floor, she would have done it. Despite the fact that her mother approved of Lord Hereford solely because he was a peer, Madeline struck him off her list. At the end of the set, he escorted her back to her circle and bowed. "I enjoyed our dance very much, my lady."

"Thank you." She wished she could return the compliment. And was very happy she had not gone for a carriage ride with him. She looked for Harry. He had been pressed by his sister into dancing with a young lady. He was now speaking with Dotty.

"Stand aside, Hereford. You had your set. It is now my turn." The Duke of Salforth stepped in front of Lord Hereford. Madeline's next partner bowed. "My lady, shall we?"

"There are several more minutes before the next set," Hereford huffed.

"I am well aware of that fact. I hoped to convince Lady Madeline to converse with me before the dance."

She gave him a sweet smile. "I would be pleased to speak with you until the next set, your grace."

Lord Hereford took himself off, muttering as he went. With any luck, he would not bother her again.

"What did he say to make you look so murderous?" the duke asked.

Good Lord! It had not occurred to Madeline that she had let her feelings show. That was not well done. On the other hand, she could now ask the duke what he would do. She repeated the story. "What would you do, your grace?"

He appeared to consider his answer. "I would have paid for the apple and have him taken to a workhouse where someone could care for him. Despite what the law states, I do not think it is right to arrest and imprison young children."

"Could you not have thought of something to help the child?" Madeline hoped he would pass her test.

His brows drew together. "I would, naturally, like to help all the poor children. I suppose I could ask him if he would like to be trained in a profession and arrange it for him."

"I think that is a good idea." He might not know how to go about it, but his heart and mind were in the right place.

The music for a country dance began, and he led her out. "What did Hereford say?"

"He'd put the poor child in prison."

"Ah." They took their places. "That is what most people would do. I suppose you can't blame them. It is the law."

Her opinion of him lowered. "You are in the Lords. You could sponsor a bill to help unfortunate children."

"I suppose I could think about it."

The steps of the dance separated them, and Madeline was glad of it. Salforth could sponsor a bill to help, but he would not. Then again, if he had someone to guide him, he might do it. He had enough potential that she would still consider him. If only for her mother's sake.

When the set ended, the duke took her back to her family and bowed. "Forgive me, my lady, I must find my next partner."

A second or two after he left, Harry was by her side, and her hand was on his arm. "How is your protégé?"

"Mine? I really think of him as *our* protégé. If you had not caught him, I do not care to think what would eventually have happened to him."

Harry gave one of his ready smiles. By looking at his lean, aristocratic face, one would not think he smiled so easily. "Very well, then. *Our* protégé."

"He is doing well." She told him about his objection to bathing and what he told Suky.

"I have made arrangements to go to Brentford in the morning. I'll see what I can discover."

That was fast. "Thank you. I hope we find he has some family who will be willing to care for him."

Harry's eyes narrowed slightly. "Perhaps. Although, he might like it better with Mr. Robbins. He seemed keen to start working."

That was true. "But his father wanted him in school. I will be interested to find out what his business was or is."

Harry gave her a sharp look. "That makes me wonder if it was someone who wanted to take over the business who tried to get rid of Bobby."

What a good point, and it made horrible sense. "Do you think you will know soon?"

He inclined his head. "That is my plan." He raised one dark brow. "Hereford didn't appear happy when he left."

"He was not." Madeline was surprised he had noticed, and told him about her conversations with him and Salforth, and what the duke had said to his lordship. "Have you thought about what could be done to help small children who are left alone?"

"Or with parents too poor to care for them?" Harry said. "I have been giving it a good deal of consideration. London isn't the only city with orphaned and abandoned children, either by lack of care or not having parents. We have them in Bittleborough as well. Although not to the extent larger cities have. The problem is, I have not been able to find one answer for every case."

Madeline considered what he said. "Perhaps there is no one answer, but instead there must be several."

Harry's intent gaze was instantly upon her. "Such as?"

"Some children would like to work in some sort of trade. While there are others who clearly have the intelligence to attend university and enter a profession. Yet, for all of them, the most pressing problem is finding a place or places that will take good care of them and make sure they are fed and clothed and bathed."

Harry barked a laugh that drew the attention of the others around them. Fortunately, it was, for the most part, their families. "I agree, bathing is important. Do you know your nose wrinkled just before you said that?"

Madeline touched her proboscis. "It was remembering Bobby's odor. He cannot have been on the streets for long, but . . ."

Harry's shoulders shook in suppressed mirth. "He *was* rather pungent." The prelude for a waltz started, and he glanced around. "Do you not have a partner for this set?"

"No." Madeline was tired of dancing every set. "I wanted to take a pause." She was about to suggest they stroll, but because she was dancing with him later, that could be considered two sets with him. Which would no doubt draw the attention of her mother. And for some reason she was not prepared to consider, Madeline did not want Mama's focus on Harry. "It will give us time to discuss ways to help homeless or orphaned children."

"Our list of projects and potential bills is expanding," Harry said.

"I suppose they are." It was gratifying that he was so willing to include Madeline in the legislation they discussed. It also gave her a better idea of what an MP did.

CHAPTER TWENTY-TWO

The wedding of Eleanor and Montagu had, unfortunately, consumed most of Madeline's time and energy for the past two weeks. Two days before the wedding, Harry met Madeline and her sisters for their morning ride. Their cheerfulness seemed forced. He wished Madeline would confide in him, but she was determined to focus on riding.

Once again, they raced to the tree, and once again, Willy refused to run ahead of Rose. Harry patted the stallion's neck. Despite their horses becoming friendlier, he could not say the same for himself. It was as if he were in purgatory, waiting to either ascend into Heaven or descend into Hell. "You are definitely not a racehorse."

Madeline chuckled as the horses nicked at each other. "I think you were right when you said there is something going on between the two of them." They began to walk the horses. "If you return in time, will you come to tea?"

"Yes." He'd had to put off his information-collecting excursion to Brentford. Naturally, she would want to know the results of his trip as soon as possible. "I hope I'll have something useful to relate."

"I am sure you will. There is something tricksy about all of this." The horses ambled along companionably. "I wish I could go with you."

"If only you could." He tried to keep the wistful tone from his voice. She would be a great deal of help. Madeline had a way of talking to people that made them want to trust her.

Alice and Eleanor rode up to them, and Madeline glanced at Eleanor. "Is there anything of importance we are doing today?"

"Nothing that I can remember. Why do you ask?"

"Harry is driving to Brentford, near Kew Gardens. I have decided I would like to go with him."

They all turned back toward the gate.

"What is in Brentford?" Alice asked. Her eyes narrowed. "Oh, wait. That is where Bobby is from."

"Yes." Madeline nodded. "He is going to try to discover more about him."

As much as Harry wanted her to accompany him, there was the problem of the closed coach. "I had planned to travel in a town carriage with one of Merton's men."

She gave an airy wave of her hand. "He may ride in the coach, and we can take your curricle. It is only around an hour's journey. I will ask Grace as soon as I am home."

The question now was, would she give her permission?

Madeline slid him a look. "I will send a running footman with the answer. Although I am certain she will allow me to go. After all, you will be there, as well as one of Merton's guards."

The scope of his investigation quickly broadened. She could easily speak with the women and ladies in the town. They generally knew everything that happened. "Thank you."

"No, no. I want to be involved in discovering how he came to be alone in London."

Harry wanted to lean over and kiss her. "If you'll excuse me, I'll advise the stables about the change in plan."

She inclined her head and left with her sisters. He had to give this new plan more thought. If they did not arrive at the same time as Merton's man, Higgins, he could act as if he was conducting his own inquiry. That, in and of itself, would cause a great deal of talk in a small town. And Harry would have most of the day alone with Madeline. If only he was going to the ball this evening, but Mrs. Taylor's invitation to her entertainment had arrived and been accepted.

It occurred to him there was no reason to send a message to the stables when he could ride there.

"Mr. Stern." The stable master hurried toward him. "What brings you here?"

"I have a request." Harry swung down from his horse. "I will require my curricle in addition to the town coach."

"Of course, sir. Is there a change in time?"

"No. I'll be ready in an hour." But would Madeline be prepared to leave by then? "I'll let you know immediately if anything changes."

"We'll have 'em around front."

"Thank you." In the meantime, he'd be on pins and needles until he heard from Madeline.

He strode to his chambers and quickly washed and dressed. When he entered the breakfast room, he was surprised to find himself the first one there. As anxious as he was to eat and go, he had to wait for Madeline's note. He would just have to use the time to formulate more of a strategy. Harry filled his plate from the sideboard, then poured a cup of tea.

A scheme started to take form. They could be a couple who had planned to visit Kew Gardens but decided to go by way of Brentford. They had heard it was a charming little town. He hoped the place actually was charming. If not, they'd have to think of something else. They would walk along the streets. At some point—he'd leave that up to Madeline—they or she would ask about Mr. Fields and his son. Someone was bound to tell them the story. Once they did, she could ask what had become of the boy. Harry trusted there were at least a few busybodies who would have made it a point to discover everything about Bobby and his father and provide them the direction of Mr. Fields's solicitor. Or someone who would know. Harry might even be able to speak to the man today. In the meantime, Higgins would go to the inn or inns and gather as much information as he could while pretending to be conducting a more official inquiry. It occurred to Harry that he didn't know how either Madeline or he would have known Mr. Fields.

"Good morning," Merton said as he strolled to the sideboard.

"Good morning." An idea popped into Harry's mind. "You don't happen to have any properties around Brentford, do you?"

"Not in the immediate area. Why?"

Harry explained the circumstances around Bobby. "I had thought that if you had a property nearby, I could mention you not hearing from Mr. Fields."

Merton poured a cup of tea and stirred a lump of sugar into it. "I do know we use an intermediary to sell our crops. However, I do not know who he is."

Ergo, it could be or have been Mr. Fields. "Would you mind if I use your name? I may not have to. I could simply say it was my brother-in-law."

"I don't have an issue if you need to use my name and title." Merton grimaced. "It seems to be the only use your family has for it."

Laughter came from the direction of the door, and Dotty strolled into the room. "Why does Harry need to use your title?"

Parkin strode into the breakfast room. "Mr. Stern, a message from Lady Madeline. She said she has permission to go with you. You may fetch her in half an hour."

Elation replaced the trepidation that had been plaguing him. "Excellent."

Merton looked at Harry over his cup. "Madeline is going with you?"

He blotted his mouth with his serviette. "Yes. It was her idea. I think she will be able to discover information neither Higgins nor I could."

"You are correct, she will." Dotty took a plate and inspected the egg offerings. "I predict she will be a great help in discovering what happened."

Harry rose. "I'll see you later."

"I want to hear all about it," Dotty called after him.

Exactly thirty minutes after he received Madeline's message, he arrived in front of Worthington House.

Madeline met him at the door. "Good morning."

"Good morning." Her face was pinched, as if she was suffering a great deal of tension. Madeline's groom came up the outside stairs. "Bringing Finnigan was a condition of my accompanying you."

"In the carriage?" Harry hoped not.

"No, he can ride in the coach."

Thank God for that. He lifted her into the curricle, went around to the other side of the carriage, climbed in, and started the pair. Should he ask what was wrong or leave it to her to tell him? Perhaps discussing their course of action would make her feel better. "I have some ideas about how we can approach acquiring the information we need."

Madeline nodded. "I have thought of some things as well. You tell me your ideas first."

Due to the morning traffic, it was not until they reached Kensington Park that he was able to explain everything. From Kensington, they took the toll road. Madeline was a very good listener and had not interrupted him once. "What do you think?"

"I think it is a splendid scheme." Madeline was determined

not to think about her sister's problems until they returned home. Earlier, when she had suggested she go with him, she had not really considered the ways in which she could be an asset. She had just wanted to know how he was going about discovering the information, and she had not wanted to wait to hear what he had found. Yet he had made her understand how useful she could be. She could not imagine any other gentleman doing that. "The only thing I would add is visiting one of the shops, such as a fabric shop, and speaking with the vicar. Since we have Finnigan with us, he can go to the stables and ask questions, or to one of the other places."

"Excellent. I would not have thought of going into shops. Have there been any more problems concerning Eleanor?"

"Unfortunately, yes. Thankfully, Walter had a sword parasol made for her, and she was able to use it on her attacker." Madeline took a breath. "Then Montagu made the situation even worse. He came up after the attack and expressed the opinion that she should not do what she wanted to with her mine. In fact, he told her that he would forbid her from doing so." She glanced at Harry to gauge his reaction.

He frowned. "That was a stupid and useless thing to say. Are they still getting married?"

That was a question to which she had no answer. "I do not know. She has been with Grace. I suppose Matt will have a conversation with Montagu."

Harry gave her a quick glance. "I would not want to be Montagu."

"You would not be stupid enough to say what he did to Eleanor." Harry was intelligent enough to put the blame where it belonged: on the person attempting to harm Eleanor, not on Eleanor.

For a brief moment, the corners of his lips rose. Then his jaw tightened. "You're right. I wouldn't. If I was concerned for my betrothed, I would find some way to keep her safe so that she could accomplish what she set out to do."

"It is out of our hands. At least for the moment." Madeline prayed Montagu could be made to see his error and beg her sister's forgiveness, so that Eleanor would accept his apology.

They rode for a while in a comfortable silence, allowing her to look at the scenery around them. Wildflowers and trees dotted the landscape.

Then Harry said, "I seem to remember Merton and Dotty's wedding was at risk. I'm not sure what happened, but I know Worthington spoke with him." Harry glanced at her. "He appears to have a way of getting things worked out."

He was right. Matt did seem to be able to fix problems between couples. "I think—I hope you are right. He did it with Charlotte and Kenilworth, and with Louisa and Rothwell as well."

"Shall we leave it with him, then?" Harry smiled.

They would. Madeline was glad he had said what he had. "I suppose we must. We have Bobby to help."

"I believe we are coming into Brentford."

She glanced ahead. They were quickly approaching a small town. "Shall we use our real names?"

"I will use mine," Harry said. "You will be Lady Madeline. There is no reason to tell anyone your surname."

"That is probably for the best." There was most likely no chance at all this could be dangerous for her, but there was also no reason to tempt fate. She looked behind her and could not see the coach. "Where did they go?"

"We decided they would arrive long enough after we did so no one could think we were in any way connected. I do not expect to see them for a while."

Madeline turned back around as they entered the town. The first houses were medium-sized cottages with low stone walls. Behind the walls were gardens. It looked to be a fairly prosperous area. "It is charming."

"It is said that one of the American presidents lived here for a few years before he was made president."

She was impressed. "You did your research."

"I like to know what I'm walking into, and it was not difficult to discover information about the town."

He might have had to put off this trip, but he had not been idle. "You sent someone to look at it."

Harry smiled. "I did. Apparently, the local citizens are proud of their town and ready to talk about it. The inn has a large parlor set up for women to dine or drink tea."

That was good news. "Let us hope they will also talk about one of their citizens and his son."

He pulled into the larger of the two inns on the main street, and a boy ran out to take the horses. "Good day to you. I do not know how long we will be here."

"Ain't no problem," the boy said. "I'll take proper care of 'em."

He flipped the lad a coin. "Thank you."

Madeline tucked her hand in the crook of his arm. "Mr. Stern, I would like to stroll around this lovely town."

He inclined his head. "As you wish, my lady."

She had been about to suggest they make arrangements for luncheon but remembered they were not supposed to be familiar with the town. She wrinkled her brow. "If only there was a place we could drink tea. I do not suppose it is proper for a lady to be in the common room."

"We have a parlor fer women here," the boy said. "Mrs. Walker, the landlord's wife, insisted."

Madeline smiled at the lad. "How clever of her." She dropped his arm and started toward the main door of the inn, then glanced at Harry. "Shall we ask for a table?"

He grinned at the stable boy. "By all means." Swiftly passing her, he opened the door. "My lady."

A woman Madeline supposed to be Mrs. Walker was next to the front desk, speaking with a man who was probably her husband. The landlady had medium-brown hair styled into a neat knot at the back of her head. She wore a white mobcap decorated with lace. Dressed fashionably, but in plainer fabrics than one would find among ladies in the *ton*, she was younger than Madeline expected, but, then again, so was her husband, who was taller than his wife, but not as tall as Harry, with blond hair.

"Excuse me." She smiled as the landlady turned to her. "I am Lady Madeline, and this is Mr. Stern. We would like a table for luncheon, if that is possible."

Mrs. Walker threw her husband a look that clearly said, *I told you so* and dipped a curtsey. "Naturally, my lady." Mrs. Walker had a lovely, slight French accent. She pulled one of the two ledgers on the desk toward her. "Would twelve thirty be acceptable?"

Madeline resisted glancing at Harry. "Indeed. That would be perfect."

"Very well. We will see you then." She bobbed a curtsey.

Harry inclined his head, and they strolled out through the door. His green eyes were twinkling, but he maintained a merely contented countenance. "Well done, my lady."

"She is French, or her family is." Madeline took his arm again. Augusta had told them that in France, ladies dined at restaurants and cafés. "I had the feeling the dining room for women was her idea, and her husband was not fond of it."

Harry shrugged. "He probably had to give up a room he used for something else."

They had gone no more than a few feet when Madeline noticed a shop selling fabric. A glance in the window told her they were doing a brisk business. Now, how to go about asking the initial question?

Harry opened the door and she entered. She looked at the

fabrics laid out in the shop and listened to the conversations. Finally, she heard what she wanted to hear.

"Bobby knows how to write," a woman in her middling years said. "I do not know why we have not heard from him. He promised Mr. Phelps he'd send word as soon as he reached Newcastle."

CHAPTER TWENTY-THREE

Harry resisted giving Madeline a sharp look. This was what they had hoped for. She was subtlety making her way toward the three women speaking while pretending to look at trimmings.

"Perhaps his cousin, Mr. Fields, is keeping him busy," a lady in a hat with purple ribbons said in a kind tone. The way she spoke told him she was of the gentry as was the first lady.

"I could accept that, but Mr. Phelps has not heard from the headmaster of the school he had arranged for Bobby to attend." The lady heaved a sigh. "I just know something has happened to that poor boy. If only his father had let one of us care for him."

Madeline glanced at Harry and indicated he should speak. "Excuse me, are you speaking of Bobby Fields? The son of Mr. Fields who has a business here?"

The lady with the purple hat narrowed her eyes at him. "We are. What is it to you, sir?"

That didn't go well. Before he could think of a response, Madeline interceded. "That is what you get for not introducing yourself properly." She used the same tone his sister used with his niece when she did something she ought not to. Madeline turned toward the lady. "Ladies, I am Lady

Madeline, and this is Mr. Stern. Please allow him to make his excuses."

Well done, Madeline.

He bowed, which appeared to mollify the women somewhat. "Please forgive me. I am concerned that we have not heard from Mr. Fields in some time. You see, my brother-in-law's steward wrote to him about two weeks ago and has not received an answer."

The lady in the purple hat raised a brow. "And your brother-in-law is?"

"Lord Merton." Harry looked for any signs of recognition. The lady wearing a bonnet with yellow flowers, who hadn't spoken, widened her eyes. "He has an estate several miles from here."

The yellow-hatted lady said, "I am sorry to inform you Mr. Fields was attacked and died from his injuries. His will appointed a distant cousin as Robert's guardian." She glanced at her friends, then back to Harry. "As you probably heard, none of us thought that a good decision."

"Oh, I agree with you." Madeline voice was full of sympathy. "When my father died, it would have been horrible to have had to leave my home. Fortunately, my brother was of an age to be my guardian. Even if he had not been, I am certain Papa would have made someone who lived near us our guardian."

"I know it is a great imposition," the lady Harry assumed was Mrs. Phelps said. "However, is there any way you can discover where Bobby is and if he is well?"

Madeline had tucked her hand into the crook of Harry's arm again. "Of course we will help." She glanced at him. "Will we not, Mr. Stern?"

"Naturally. If you could direct me to the solicitor Mr. Fields used, I will be able to gather the information I need to begin."

The lady in the yellow hat inclined her head. She must be one of the higher-ranking ladies in the town. "Mr. Bankborough is the solicitor Mr. Fields patronized. My husband recommended him when the other solicitor died several years ago."

"Thank you, ma'am." Madeline had let go of Harry's arm so he could bow properly. "Can I find him along the main street?"

"Yes," Mrs. Phelps said. "Along to the right on the opposite side of the street. He is in the same building as the jeweler."

"Thank you." He turned to Madeline. "Would you like to remain here and look around?"

"No, thank you. I found what I was looking for." She stepped over to the lace she had been regarding. "I would like to purchase a length of this lace, and then I will accompany you."

The lady in the purple-flowered bonnet put her hand over her mouth, but the rest of her face betrayed her mirth. This was obviously a town of strong women.

"Very well. I will wait outside for you to complete your business." He bowed again. "Ladies, thank you."

"Thank you, Mr. Stern," the yellow-flowered bonnet lady smiled politely.

He strolled out of the shop. Madeline had been absolutely correct when she said a shop ladies patronized would be the place to gather information. He now had more information than he'd hoped. Behind him, the door opened and closed, and she was with him again. "That was perfectly done."

She took his arm again and gave him a slight smile. "Thank you. However, I am afraid the details of our trip here will soon be talked about."

That was not good news. "How so?"

"The lady in the green gown with the bonnet with yellow flowers is Lady Masters. The shopkeeper said her name as I was leaving. If I am not mistaken, her husband is a baron, and she is the sister of Lady Greenly, who lives on Mount Street."

All roads led to London. "I take it Lady Greenly is a gossip?"

"One of the worst." Madeline's lips formed a thin line.

Even if the female was a gossip, what was there to tell? "We have your sister's permission, and we arrived in an open carriage. What could she possibly find amiss?"

"I hope you are correct, but do not be surprised if the story is changed beyond all recognition."

In that case they would wed, but Harry did not want Madeline forced to marry him. "I'll warn Dotty."

"Yes." Madeline nodded. "I will tell Grace as well."

They came to the building with the jeweler. The sign indicated Mr. Bankborough's office was on the first floor. With any luck, they would soon have all the details.

Harry knocked on the door, and a clerk answered it. "Do you have an appointment?"

It was going to be like that, was it? He heaved a sigh. "I am here on the Marquis of Merton's business. We would like to speak with Mr. Bankborough immediately."

The clerk gave Madeline a curious look but led them into a large room. "I'll see if he's in."

Fortunately, a short, rather rotund man with a balding pate came out from a door as the clerk knocked. "What is it?"

"Sir, this gentleman and the lady would like to speak with you. Something to do with the Marquis of Merton."

"Lord Merton, eh?" He studied Harry and Madeline. "Well, come in, then." The solicitor took a seat behind a solid desk, but not so massive it would dwarf him. He picked up a pencil and drew paper to him. "In what capacity do you represent the Marquis of Merton?"

"I am Mr. Stern, his brother-in-law." He motioned

toward Madeline. "This is Lady Madeline Vivers, the Earl of Worthington's sister."

Mr. Bankborough folded his hands on the desk and regarded them. "What can I do for you?"

For the time being Harry would stick to the story they'd related to the others. He told the man about not being able to contact Mr. Fields, adding what the ladies had said about Bobby being missing. "Were you aware that the boy did not, in fact, arrive in Newcastle?"

The man's face drained of color. "Not in Newcastle?" He rang the bell on his desk so loudly it could be heard outside.

The clerk ran in. "Sir?"

"Get me the Fields file. Immediately."

The clerk ran out, and Bankborough said, "I have a letter from the cousin informing me that Bobby arrived and is in good health." The clerk rushed back into the office and placed a file on the desk. The solicitor opened it and produced a piece of paper. "Ah, here it is."

He handed it to Harry. Madeline leaned over to read it as well.

Dear Mr. Bankborough,

As I agreed, I am writing to inform you that Bobby has arrived safely and is going about settling in. He will begin school next week. You may make the first deposit in my account for his support.

Yr. Servant,
C. Fields

Madeline's jaw firmed. "The information in that letter is false. Bobby is in London, living with and working for a grocer."

"And how would you know that?" Bankborough asked in disbelief.

Harry fixed the man with a look meant to intimidate and raised one brow. "Because her ladyship saved him from being taken to jail."

Bankborough seemed to shrink in his chair. "Tell me."

"I was shopping and heard a man shout that he'd been robbed and to stop the thief. Mr. Stern was with me, and he grabbed the boy by his collar. I ascertained that he had some education, and he told me his name, that his father had been murdered, and that the landlord put him on a coach to London. He had been living on his own for about a week before we found him."

"Alone? On the streets in London?" It took a minute for the solicitor to fully appreciate the implications of Madeline's account. Color rushed back into his face. "By God, I'll have the authorities on him for attempted murder and theft."

Harry expected the other man's reaction. "You have to prove it first."

"It's clear from the facts." Bankborough was so sure of himself. As were most people who did not have much to do with criminal law.

"Not to a court." Harry placed the letter on the desk. "Fact one, Bobby is very young. He didn't even give us the full story. We came here expecting to find a landlord who had thrown him out." He held up his hand when the solicitor started to speak. "Fact two, the ladies said someone was to have met Bobby in London. It is, unfortunately, very easy to say the person couldn't find the child. Fact three, when you lose the case, as you will, because you have no proof the man failed to have someone meet Bobby, the cousin is still Bobby's guardian. The only thing you have proof of is his greed. Yet even that can be explained away." Harry let that sink in before continuing, "Mr. Fields will only find another method to do away with him."

Madeline leaned forward slightly. "We are convinced that

at some point in the future, you will be informed that Bobby has died."

"Long after he has illegally received the funds for the boy's maintenance," Bankborough said faintly. He straightened and narrowed his eyes at Harry. "You don't happen to be Mr. Stern the barrister from Bristol, do you?"

Harry inclined his head, but Madeline was not going to leave it at that. "He is also the MP for Bittleborough."

"I have heard of your success in court. Congratulations on becoming an MP." Mr. Bankborough looked at her. "What is it the two of you suggest?"

She glanced at Harry, who gave her a signal to carry on. "Bobby is currently attending classes at my brother's house with the younger servants. Mr. Robbins, the grocer, is extremely happy to have Bobby. He said he has been a great help and his customers like him a great deal. And Bobby is happy working there." She smiled to herself. "He, very importantly, told one of the girls we took in that he was in business."

For the first time since they arrived, Mr. Bankborough smiled. "That sounds just like him. He was very proud that he was going to be taking over his father's business someday."

She exchanged another glance with Harry, then turned back to the solicitor. "That brings us to the question of how to proceed in a way that would benefit him and achieve what his father wanted for him. Were you in his confidence and can you tell us if the business is continuing? The best way to thwart the cousin is by taking care of Bobby."

"Indeed I can." Mr. Bankborough picked up the pencil. "He went to the school Mr. Phelps, our vicar, has for the local boys. He is—was—studying the basics, but also Latin and French. His father also wanted him to attend a school in Bristol and apprentice with himself. He was already taking Bobby around with him when he spoke with farmers and craftsmen who wanted to sell their goods in London and other larger cities."

"He will continue to learn those subjects with our governess and tutor. Do you know when his father planned to send him to Bristol?"

"When he was twelve. It is rather late, but that was what Mr. Fields wanted."

"Twelve is perfect." She remembered Matt asking them if he could be their guardian when she was that age. "At twelve, he can choose his guardian. Do you think Mr. Phelps would agree to become his guardian?"

"I know he would. Mrs. Phelps was not happy when Mr. Fields chose his cousin. But the man represented himself as a well-to-do merchant who could train Bobby."

That was one fence cleared. "I suppose he can live with them when he is here learning his business. He will have to learn from someone." It occurred to her she did not know if the concern continued. "If there is still a business."

"Yes, my lady," Mr. Bankborough said. "Mr. Fields had an assistant who is quite knowledgeable. He will be able to instruct Bobby on how to go on."

That was good news. "Excellent. In that case, the only thing left to do is to coordinate with everyone involved." Including Mr. Robbins and Bobby.

"I would be happy to speak with Mr. Phelps and Mr. Egerton, who was Mr. Fields's assistant and is managing the business. I'll also ask if the cousin has written to Egerton about the business."

"Yes, I imagine the man might be interested in ensuring the concern was continuing to make money." She glanced at Harry. "Can you think of anything else?"

He shook his head. "Not at the moment. We must proceed carefully until he is of an age to select a new guardian. By the time that new guardian has been appointed, we will have enough evidence of theft, breech of his fiduciary duty, and general malfeasance to get a conviction. In the meantime, I'll have Merton investigate this Mr. Fields. However, I don't expect to find any good of him."

There was one thing they had not discussed. "May I ask, how wealthy is Bobby?"

"Mr. Fields was quite warm, my lady. He will come into a goodly sum."

Another reason for the cousin to wish Bobby harm. "An inheritance the cousin will receive if anything should befall Bobby."

The solicitor appeared a bit surprised at first, then nodded. "Just so, my lady."

They would have to keep a close eye on him when he was in London. "I do not think that Bobby should know about that yet. We should wait until he is older."

"And wiser," Harry agreed.

Mr. Bankborough just nodded.

Harry opened his pocket watch. "We shall leave it to you." Harry handed him his card. "I would appreciate hearing about your discussions with Mr. Egerton and Mr. Phelps."

"Of course. I will keep you informed." The solicitor came out from behind his desk. "Thank you for saving Bobby. I shudder to think what could have happened to him. I am one of his trustees. Mr. Phelps is the other. Once I speak with him, I will make funds available to you for his upkeep. I assume he has none of the possessions he took with him."

"No." Madeline hoped he had not had anything of senti-mental value. "We will talk with Mr. Robbins when we return to Town."

Harry held out his hand and Mr. Bankborough shook it. "I have one more question. Where did Mr. Fields and Bobby live?"

"They made their home above the office. He has a modest

house on the edge of town, but they spent most of their time in the rooms."

"That is where the landlord comes in." Madeline wanted to know what part the man had actually played. "Was he the person who took Bobby to the stagecoach?"

"Indeed, my lady. The poor boy didn't want to leave, but the cousin was going to take him, and he couldn't remain there by himself."

Another question answered. This had been a very productive day. She peeped at Harry. Particularly when it came to him. It must be almost time for luncheon. She smiled and held out her hand. "It was a pleasure speaking with you, Mr. Bankborough."

He blinked before shaking it. "It was a pleasure meeting you, my lady. I would like it if you could send me notes from time to time about Bobby."

"Of course we will."

He walked them to the door and bowed. "Until we meet again."

As they left the building, Madeline tucked her hand in Harry's arm. She was to take a carriage ride with Salforth this afternoon. Yet she did not believe he could come close to Harry in the way he thought or acted. Still, she must give him a chance to prove himself. Perhaps it was time he met Posy.

CHAPTER TWENTY-FOUR

Harry and Madeline ate a delicious luncheon of roasted chicken, peas, new potatoes, salad, and, for dessert, a strawberry tartlet. The meal was accompanied by a crisp, dry white wine. The Ladies' Dining Room, as it was called, had been almost fully occupied. Even the ladies from the fabric shop were present.

He took the last bite of the tartlet and swallowed. "Do you think it's always this busy?"

"Probably not *as* full." She sipped her tea. "I appreciate her not putting us in the center of the room."

"Lord, yes." That would have been embarrassing. But, quite frankly, it was something a typical landlord would do if an important customer arrived. "She appears to be savvy enough to know we would not like being so exposed."

Madeline lips tilted up slightly. "She is French, and she wants this restaurant to prosper."

Since the war ended, the English had been very taken with many things French, but in France, not in England. That was an interesting observation. "Will you tell your friends about it?"

"I will. After all, this is a short drive from Kew Gardens." She was clearly planning on helping the landlady. "It is about time ladies had a place to frequent for luncheon, and even dinner, without it being a scandal."

"Very true." He took out his pocket watch and glanced at it. "What do you have planned for this afternoon? If it was morning visits, you will be hopelessly late."

"No. I am to go on a carriage ride in the Park with your friend Salforth."

He wasn't much of a friend. Still, Harry thought Madeline looked more resigned than happy about it. "I heard Grace canceled all your engagements until after the wedding."

Madeline nodded. "I suppose I should go back to find out if anything has changed."

Clever of her not to even allude to the problems her sister and Montagu were having.

The landlady approached them. "My lady, was everything to your liking?"

"Yes. The meal was wonderful," Madeline said. "I will certainly tell my friends about your restaurant. Some of them have been to France and will be glad of someplace here to which they can give their custom."

The woman curtseyed. "Thank you, my lady. I greatly appreciate your recommendation."

Harry wondered how the bill was paid here. "As much as we are enjoying your restaurant, we must get back to Town."

She raised her hand, and a waiter appeared. "Please see to our guests' bill."

"Yes, ma'am."

"I bid you a good trip back." After bobbing another curtesy, she went back to the door.

The waiter had a small slip of paper with the amount of the meal on it, and Harry settled the bill. Standing, he held out his arm for Madeline. "Shall we?"

"I suppose we must." They were outside, waiting for his curricle, when she spoke again, "We must meet with Mr.

Robbins. After dinner would be a good time. He will not have many customers."

"You're right." The sooner the better. "Fortunately, both our families dine early."

"Would seven suit you?"

"Yes. I'll come for you." If he had his way, he wouldn't take her back at all.

Finnigan and Higgins met up with them after they left Brentford. Higgins leaned out of the coach window. "When do you want to hear what we found out?"

Harry glanced at Madeline. She'd want to know as well. "Shall we go to your house or mine?"

She chewed on her bottom lip for a second or two. "Mine. My only reservation is that I do not know if Dotty will be at your house."

That was a concern, but Alexandria's governess would be there. "The governess."

The cloud in Madeline's face cleared. "Of course. You need one for Vivienne."

The drive back to Mayfair was taken up with attempting to decide on a schedule for Bobby that would allow him to work with Mr. Robbins, attend lessons, and meet with his father's customers, as he was accustomed to do. It would become even more complicated when he attended school in Bristol, but that wasn't for another three years.

"Perhaps we should ask Matt's man of business," Madeline said. "He is in a position to know how a merchant's son is trained."

"Now that is an excellent idea." Harry hadn't realized he'd spoken out loud, until he saw her beaming.

"Thank you. I will ask Matt to send him a note." When she turned her head to face the road, she was still smiling.

He drove around to the back of Merton House. There was no reason to draw attention to her being there, particularly when he didn't know if his sister was home. When he lifted her down, he forced himself not to hold her close to him. Although just the feel of her hands on his shoulders made his resolve almost impossible to accomplish. A groom unlocked the back gate and they strolled to the house.

Madeline peered around. "The gardens are even lovelier than they were at Easter."

"I believe Dotty has a few more projects to complete before they are done." He recalled his niece wanted an alfresco luncheon for all the cousins. "I wonder when Vivienne's luncheon will be held."

Madeline's tinkling of laughter warmed his heart. "After the wedding. That is all I know."

"It is amazing how everyone in the family seems to be waiting for Eleanor and Montagu to wed. I hope they work it out."

"I do too."

They reached the morning room and found Dotty playing with the twins. She glanced up. "What did you discover?"

Before he could answer, four pairs of arms were wrapped around his legs. "You got me."

"Uncle Harry." Edwin started climbing up his leg. He picked him up and took Andrew's hand. "Shall we sit?"

Dotty tugged on the bell-pull.

He moved the twins to his lap. "May we wait to tell you until Higgins and Finnigan arrive?"

"Yes. There is no point in repeating yourself." A footman came into the room. "Tea for the ladies, and three ales."

"Madeline, good afternoon," Dotty said.

"Good afternoon," Madeline said, then grinned at Harry. "You have your hands full."

"Favorite uncle."

The tea tray arrived, and the twins jumped off his lap.

Finnigan and Higgins knocked on the French windows before entering and bowing. Harry pointed to the ale, and the men each took a mug.

Madeline sat on the sofa next to Harry. "Let us tell you what we discovered, then you can tell us what you found. . . ." She related their conversations with the ladies and, more importantly, with the solicitor. She looked at Finnigan.

"I didn't find out much." He shrugged. "Mr. Fields kept a coach and four at the inn. It's still there. He was a good man. Always ready with vails for them."

Harry glanced at Higgins. "Hopefully, you discovered something more."

"Yes, sir." He set down his mug. "Mr. Fields had or has an assistant. The man stops in after work for an hour or so, regularlike. He came the other day looking like he had a problem, and the landlord asked what was wrong. Crampton's his name. He got a letter from the cousin who is supposed to have Bobby, wanting to know how the business was going and asking for regular reports. He said he wasn't goin' to do it. It wasn't the cousin's business. If he wanted to know anything, the man should ask Mr. Bankborough. What he was more upset about was the cousin didn't even tell him how the lad was doing. Right fond of the boy, he is."

Madeline let out a soft breath. "That's excellent. Good job."

Harry agreed. "Yes. Well done. It will also make what we are arranging much easier." He glanced at her. "When do you want to meet with the man of business?"

"Tomorrow, if possible."

"Whose man of business?" Dotty asked.

Madeline answered. "Matt's."

"Dom uses the same one. Shall I write a missive to him for you?" Dotty rubbed her forehead. "All the gentlemen are at your house, dealing with an emergency."

The problem must be serious for a council of war to have been called. It was then he noticed his nephews weren't in the room any longer. How had that been done so quietly?

Madeline was frowning, and he placed his hand over hers. "I should take you home."

"Yes, please. I wish I knew what I will find when I get there." The frown deepened. "And I have to freshen up for my ride with Salforth."

Harry wanted to cheer. She definitely didn't want to go with the man. If only there was some way to get Salforth out of Town. But the only thing that might do it was a problem at one of his estates, and he'd probably leave it to one of his stewards to solve. Not only that, Harry would have to cause the problem, which would be committing a crime. It appeared his only path forward was to capture Madeline's heart. Unfortunately, it hadn't happened yet, and he'd tried everything he could think of.

Madeline arrived home to a relieved and happy house. There was going to be a wedding after all, and they were all going to attend the opera the following evening to show the *ton* that the families were united. Even Alice, who had been suffering from a cold, was feeling more herself. Madeline had just enough time to refresh herself and change her carriage gown, which was now sadly creased. A few minutes before five o'clock, she stepped into the corridor and heard footsteps and a dog's whine.

"Quiet, Posy, you will be allowed to greet the visitor as soon as he arrives," Theo whispered.

Madeline moved to a position where she could see what her sister was doing.

"Ow!" Mary jumped back and went to the other side of the Dane. "Her tail got me."

A knock came on the door, and Thorton answered it. "Your grace, I shall tell Lady Madeline you have arrived."

"Now!" Theo whispered.

Posy flew down the stairs.

"Miss Posy, you must not snuggle against the duke," Thorton said.

Madeline walked to the head of the stairs and started down them. Posy was trying to wind herself around Salforth. He was alternately grimacing and trying to fend her off. Sounds of quiet laughter came from the floor above. It was time to save the duke, and the girls obviously were not going to do it.

"Posy, come." Madeline pointed her finger to the stair beside her, and the dog bounded happily to her side.

A footman arrived with a lead. "I'll take her."

Thorton was busy brushing dog hair off the duke.

"Thank you." She summoned a polite smile, finished descending the stairs, and curtseyed. "Good afternoon, your grace."

"My lady." He bowed, then held out his arm. "Shall we?"

"Of course." She had thought he would say something about the Dane, but perhaps later. If he did not mention it, she would.

As had happened the other times she had ridden with him, he allowed the footman to assist her into the carriage. It occurred to her that Harry would never, had never, done that. In fact, the first time she rode in his curricle, he had signaled the servant away. Was this what marriage with Salforth would be like? Only touching when necessary?

The carriage had started without Madeline knowing it, and they were moving out of the square. "Posy does not usually greet visitors."

"She is quite large," Salforth said in a polite tone. "I am not used to having dogs in the house."

He had not said he did not want them in the house, keeping him on the list. "We have always had at least one Great Dane. When my brother married, his wife's family also had a Dane. Since then, we have had two. They live in the house."

"How interesting." How frustrating. His comment told her nothing at all.

They drove through the gate into the Park. It was a nice day, and it seemed everyone in the *ton* had decided to be seen out and about. As she usually did, she greeted friends and acquaintances. They eventually came upon Salforth's mother and hers.

He pulled up beside them. "Mother, Lady Wolverton, good afternoon."

Madeline waited until they had greeted them before bidding their mothers a good afternoon.

"I understand your sister had a public disagreement with Lord Montagu," her grace said in a disapproving tone.

Madeline resisted the urge to give the woman a narrow-eyed look and a piece of her mind about gossiping. Instead, she widened her eyes innocently. "I was not present, so I could hardly know. Lord Montagu was at our house earlier, and no one mentioned any difficulties. If there was a difference of opinion, I assume it is because of the wedding preparations. They can be stressful."

"Indeed." The duchess appeared taken aback. "The wedding is quite soon, I take it."

Madeline inclined her head. "It is the day after tomorrow."

"Oh, my, yes. This is a difficult time," her grace said.

"Mother, my lady, we must be on our way." The duke picked up the ribbons. "Enjoy the rest of your ride."

"You as well, Salforth," his mother said.

"Madeline, I am happy to see you," her mother said.

It was strange that she did not see her mother very much at all. Yes, they visited in summer for a few weeks. Yet in Town they seemed to occupy separate worlds. In fact, the only time Mama had come to Worthington House was to attempt to convince Grace that Madeline should marry the person whom Mama wanted her to. And she did not speak to Madeline about it at all. It was very odd. Perhaps it was because she was increasing. Although no one else she knew seemed to be affected by their pregnancies.

"Will you be at Lady Thompson's ball this evening?"

Salforth's question brought Madeline out of her thoughts. "No. Our only event will be attending the opera tomorrow."

"I understand. The wedding." He did not sound as if he truly did understand.

"Yes. Not to mention the children and my other sisters."

He looked perplexed. "What have children to do with it?"

"All my married sisters have children with whom they must spend time." Why was that a difficult concept?

"Oh. I really had not considered the idea that one must placate children."

She was not going to continue this conversation. He would only express ignorance, minimizing his potential. Did she want to work that hard on a husband? Then again, did she want to be the wife of an MP? And then there was her mother. There was a great deal to consider, but no time for it until after the wedding.

CHAPTER TWENTY-FIVE

Harry drove to Worthington House immediately after eating his dinner, and knocked. A footman opened the door, and he strode into the hall. "Has Lady Madeline finished dining?"

The young man bowed. "I'm not sure. I'll ask."

"Thank you." He wondered if the servant was new and just being trained.

The under butler arrived and bowed. "Mr. Stern, Lady Madeline asks that you give her a few minutes."

"Certainly. I'll wait here." Where he could watch her descend. She always appeared to float.

"Harry." She smiled at him from the landing.

Not able to wait, he ascended the stairs. "Madeline." He searched her face, and she searched his; then they both looked away. He held out his arm, and she took it. "Hopefully, there will not be too much traffic. Are you ready to tell them what we discovered?"

"Yes. I have thought about how much to tell Bobby. We agreed not to mention our suspicions about his cousin."

"Yes. He'll need to be told at some point, but not now." Harry couldn't imagine being told at the age of nine that someone was trying to murder him.

They reached his curricle, and he lifted Madeline up into

it. While she arranged her skirts, he took his place on the other side and picked up the ribbons. Fortunately, the traffic was light, and they were able to park the carriage a few yards from the store.

He lifted her down, and they turned to find Mr. Robbins and Bobby closing the shop.

"Good evening." Madeline strode to them. "Mr. Stern and I have discovered some things you will be interested to hear. May we go upstairs?"

Mr. Robbins appeared nervous. Was he afraid Bobby would be taken from him? In actuality, this was the best place to hide the boy.

"As you wish, my lady." The man made a belated bow.

Bobby copied him. "Will I like it?"

"I think you will like most of it." Madeline took his hand in hers.

When they reached the small parlor, she took a seat at the square table in the center of the room. Harry sat on one side and Bobby on the other. Mr. Robbins took the seat across from her and waited.

"We went to Brentford this morning." She glanced at Bobby. "I spoke with Mrs. Phelps and your father's solicitor, Mr. Bankborough. The landlord put you on the coach to London because someone was supposed to have met you and taken you to York to a distant cousin."

"York? I don't want to go there. I want to stay here." Bobby crossed his arms over his thin chest.

"We agree." She nodded. "You are much better off here. For the time being. You must still attend classes and learn everything you can about the grocery business."

He nodded his head so hard it could cause damage. "I will." Bobby turned to Mr. Robbins. "I've been a great assistant, haven't I?"

"Yes, you have. I don't know what I did before you started

working for me." He snuck a look at Madeline. "There is more, my lady?"

Harry reached into his pocket and pulled out some coins. "Go buy some meat pies for your dinner."

"Mrs. White always has a full meal waiting for us."

"Then fetch that." Harry grinned at the boy. "Get going."

As Bobby ran out of the room, Madeline looked at Mr. Robbins and bit her lip. "Yes. Several things. Bobby is quite wealthy. His father was a middleman who represented the goods from farmers and other businesses who wanted their products to be sold in London. Your fruit and vegetables, for example. There is an assistant who can carry on the business . . ." She quickly and concisely related their conversation with the solicitor, what they had been told about the assistant, and their suspicions about the cousin. "You will be given funds to keep Bobby and train him."

"I'd do it for nothing, my lady. I've earned more since he's been here than I ever have. He's looked over my books. Imagine a young'un doin' that. He's a clever one."

Madeline beamed with pride. "He is clever. You must also send word if anyone asks about him."

"We'll send employees of ours around occasionally to make sure you and Bobby are all right."

"At some point—and we do not know exactly when yet—Mr. Crampton, the assistant, will want him to go with him to speak with the customers, and possibly the buyers. We will send someone to you to help when Bobby's away."

The man nodded. "Had a feelin' he was more than he said." He looked up at them. "I'm a bit worried about the lad, my lady. He don't seem to mourn his da."

That was unusual, but everyone took death differently. "I shall see if he will talk to me about him."

Madeline leaned across the table and patted Mr. Robbins's folded hands. "You will have him for at least three years.

After that, his father wanted him to attend a boarding school in Bristol. But that is a long way off."

"Yes, my lady," he said, but he didn't sound as if he believed it. The clattering of feet sounded on the uncarpeted stairs. "He's coming back."

She rose. "We should leave. We do not think Bobby should know about his wealth."

"No, my lady. That's a fact." Mr. Robbins broke into a smile. "He chatters as much as a squirrel."

An apt description of most happy children. "When we know more, you can tell him he's to go around with Mr. Crampton." Harry turned as Bobby entered the parlor carefully carrying their dinner. "We shall see you later."

Madeline stayed Harry. "Bobby, would you like to talk about your father sometime? You really have not had time to mourn him."

The child shook his head. "My papa said I wasn't to think of him as dead, because he'd always be with me here." He pointed to his heart. "And he'd watch over me from Heaven." His lips had started to tremble; then he smiled at all of them. "And he is. He found you for me."

Harry felt tears prick his eyelids, and a look at Mr. Robbins and Madeline showed they were suffering from the same emotion. "We will always be here for you."

She touched Harry's hand. "We should go and let you eat."

When they were back on the pavement, she whispered, "I think he is starting to think of Bobby as his."

"I agree. That could work to both their benefits." Bobby needed a father figure, and Mr. Robbins needed someone to care for. Harry had a feeling he and Madeline were also thinking of the lad as part of their family.

She tucked her hand in his arm as they strolled to his carriage. "This has been a successful day."

"I agree." It was also an indurant project. One that would be much easier for her to manage if they were married.

"Dotty heard from Merton's man of business. He can come to Merton House the day after the wedding, if that suits you."

"It does." She sighed. "I do not imagine much else will be accomplished until then."

"I agree. Even Dotty has canceled her evening entertainments in the event she is needed."

Madeline laughed. "She is probably remembering Louisa's betrothal ball. If it was not for her, there would not have been one."

"I'll have to ask her about that." No matter what it was, it seemed as if his family and the Worthingtons were closely intertwined.

They reached the carriage and were soon on their way. "Will you ride tomorrow?"

Madeline glanced at him. "Yes. Will you?"

"I wouldn't miss it."

The next three days passed quickly.

The morning after the wedding, Harry woke up in a cold sweat. He'd dreamed the madman who had tried to murder Eleanor had attacked Madeline instead. Dragging his hand down his face, he threw back the bedcovers. The sky was just beginning to lighten. Intellectually, he knew she was safe, but he had to see her to satisfy his fears. Throwing his legs over the side of the bed, he went to his washstand. He came out to find his riding garments already out, and dressed.

"Sir," his valet said, "I've brought you a cup of tea and a piece of toast."

"Thank you, Burkham."

None of the family had eaten much yesterday. Even though the attack at the end of the wedding had ended successfully, the horror of it lingered. Thankfully, Eleanor and Montagu were on their way to France for their honeymoon and the madman had been arrested.

Harry finished the tea and toast, then quickly dressed. He was not going to miss Madeline this morning. Willy was waiting in front of the house, and Harry mounted the horse. "Let's find our ladyloves."

He caught up with her just before the Park gate. Harry was damned glad the other gentlemen interested in Madeline either couldn't get up early in the morning or hadn't discovered the morning rides. Although with his sister Henrietta and her friends, he didn't get as much time with Madeline as before, it was still better than seeing her only at balls and other events.

This morning, their group was smaller than usual. Aside from Madeline, only Henrietta and Georgie Turley were present. They settled into their usual pattern of riding to the oak tree, but neither seemed to want to engage in their usual banter. Madeline and Harry bid the others goodbye, and he continued down Mount Street with her in the direction of Berkeley Square.

When they reached the corner of South Audley Street, Madeline stopped. "That young woman is crying."

Indeed the female was weeping into a plain handkerchief and was also carrying one black suitcase.

Madeline slid off her mare and handed her groom the reins. "Good morning. May I be of assistance?"

The woman, little more than a girl, gave Harry a frightened glance. "I–I–I don't know what to do," she wailed. "We were all told to leave this morning. He didn't even pay us."

Madeline patted her back. "That is dreadful. Where will you go?"

And criminal. Harry worked to keep the scowl from his countenance. The girl was frightened enough. As soon as they got the whole story from her, he'd look into what could be done for her to at least get her paid.

"I don't know." The girl started crying again. "I want ta go home, but I don't know how ta get there. I was hired in the country."

Frowning, Madeline looked over her shoulder at Harry.

His horse shifted underneath him. "Your house or mine?"

After a moment, she gave a decisive nod. "Mine." She looked at her groom. "Finnigan, please carry her bag and escort her to Worthington House. I shall ride ahead with Mr. Stern and tell Mrs. Thorton to expect Miss . . . ?"

Tears still leaked from the woman's eyes, but shock was the expression on her face. "Parker, miss. But I don't know you."

Madeline smiled. "Nor do I know you. But you are in need of help. If you can promise me you are not a thief or some other sort of criminal . . . ?"

"Oh no, miss. We were all turned off without any notice this morning."

"In that case, I am able to assist you to go home or to find another position. My groom will walk with you to my home, and Mrs. Thorton, our housekeeper, will take care of you until it is decided what we should do. Will you come with us?"

The seconds ticked by slowly until Miss Parker finally nodded. "I will."

"Excellent. That is much better than wandering around London by yourself." Madeline glanced at the bag, and her groom took the suitcase from Miss Parker.

"I'm Finnigan. Don't you worry none, miss. The family's all good people. Us servants too. We'll all help you."

Miss Parker seemed to notice Finnigan for the first time and gave a tremulous smile. "Thank you, Mr. Finnigan."

Harry got down and helped Madeline mount her horse, then regained his own, and they set off down the street to

Berkeley Square. "I have a feeling there is something other than being let go. She kept looking at me as if I might harm her."

Madeline's forehead wrinkled, and he wanted to run his thumb over it to soothe her. "I noticed that as well. Yet she was fine with Finnigan."

"Perhaps it was my status." He made himself remain calm, but anger at whoever had harmed the girl was growing.

"That blackguard." Madeline's voice was harder than he'd ever heard it. "Mrs. Thorton will get the whole story. She is very good at that sort of thing."

Harry urged Willy to a faster trot, and Madeline matched his pace. "The sooner we get her settled, the sooner we'll know with what we are dealing. There might even be something I can do about getting the wages she's owed."

"That will be helpful." She glanced at him. "Thank you."

"There's no need to thank me. As you know, that's the way I was raised."

"Yes." Her smile filled him with an urge to take her into his arms. "You should stay for breakfast."

"Thank you. I will." And be able to spend more time with her, but, again, not alone.

They arrived at Worthington House, and he rushed around to help her down from Rose, making sure to lower her slowly, brushing her body slightly against his. Her breath caught, and he knew she felt the heat between them. He also knew she had been told what happened between a man and a woman, but did she know what passion felt like? Probably not. It would be up to him to teach her what that meant for them. She couldn't possibly feel the same about the other gentlemen. Still, that had not stopped other young ladies from marrying for a higher rank. Not that he would or could believe Madeline cared about rank, but it was still something about which to be concerned.

By the time he'd placed her feet on the pavement, a

footman had the horses. "Did something happen to your groom, my lady?"

"Ah, no." Her cheeks were pinker than usual, and her breathing faster. "We met an unfortunate young woman. He is escorting her here."

The man nodded.

The door was open before they reached it. Thorton bowed. "My lady, Mr. Stern."

Madeline smiled when they both greeted him at the same time. "Thorton. Finnigan will arrive soon with a young servant who has lost her position. She was standing on a corner with a bag in her hand. It appears all the servants were dismissed without notice this morning. I will need Mrs. Thorton to take care of her and discover the whole story. Mr. Stern thinks something horrible might have occurred."

"Certainly, my lady. I will notify her." He glanced at Harry. "Will Mr. Stern be joining you for breakfast?"

"He will."

"Very well. I will have a footman escort him to freshen up."

Madeline looked at him. "I will see you soon."

He wished he could touch her again. Once she reached the stairs, he turned to the butler.

"Thank you. How much time do I have?"

"Enough time for a short bath, if you wish. I can have a message sent to Merton House for a fresh set of clothing."

That was odd. "I'm surprised the children are not up and around."

"Master Edward had a bad night, and Master Gideon and Lady Elizabeth were up with him as well. Thankfully, Lady Gaia was taken to another room where she could sleep. Everyone is moving a bit more slowly this morning."

"That makes sense. The same thing happens at my sister's house."

"Just so, sir." Thorton signaled for a footman.

It struck Harry that the normally starchy butler had treated him like a member of the family. He supposed it was because his brother-in-law was Worthington's cousin. But could it be something else? Did the man think Harry might become one of the family? He was afraid to hope.

CHAPTER TWENTY-SIX

Harry was bathed, dressed, and making his way toward the landing to the stairs in less than forty minutes. His first idea was to wait in the hall for Madeline, but Mary and Theo joined him before she did.

He bowed as they bid him a good morning.

Both girls curtseyed as gracefully as any young lady just out did.

"Good morn to you. Were you awakened last night as well?"

"We were up with him for a bit," Mary said.

"What are you doing here so early?" Theo asked. "Not that you are not welcome, but I did not know we were having visitors."

He told them the story of the young servant, and they nodded.

"Mrs. Thorton will allow her to break her fast, then give her a nice cup of tea in her parlor," Mary said.

"Then she will find out everything there is to know about the poor maid," Theo added.

As he accompanied them down the stairs and into the breakfast room, he wondered how often this sort of thing occurred.

"You must sit here." Theo pointed to a seat midway down the long table. "That way you will be next to Madeline."

Harry only just kept his jaw from dropping.

"And ask her for the supper dance at the ball this evening. The Duke of Salforth sent a note, but she has not seen it yet. Grace will not give it to her until after breakfast."

"Are you matchmaking?" he teased them.

Both girls lifted one shoulder and dropped it.

"Maybe a little," Theo said without a hint of contrition.

Mary gave her sister a wry look. "Maybe more than a little." She put the serviette on her lap. "You see, we have had the opportunity to meet the other gentlemen when they came to call on Madeline."

Theo wrinkled her nose. "And we are not impressed."

"No. They are not for her." Mary shook her head. "The duke is the best of them, but he is not for her either. There is nothing there."

Nothing there? If they were older, he would know what she meant by that. As it was, he was at a loss. "What do you mean?"

Theo looked at him as if he were a slow top. "You must know how all of our older sisters and Dotty are around their husbands. It was the same before they wed."

Mary sighed, as if she was having to explain something he should know. "It's the way their eyes follow them, and the way their husbands always seem to know where they are."

"All of them appear to have softer looks on their faces," Theo added.

"Except when they are aggravated with them," Mary amended. "But even then, there is something there."

"Do you understand now?" Theo's look told him they were done explaining. "We do not know of another way to put it."

"I do, and thank you." They were not the first people who'd told him Salforth wouldn't be a good match for Madeline. Rothwell had hinted at the same thing. What

Harry hadn't noticed was that Madeline looked at him in a particular way.

Voices floated from the corridor, and Mary whispered, "Yes." As if she'd been reading his mind.

"Mama is the problem," Theo said softly.

Just as Dotty had said. "A title."

Theo nodded.

Well, at least he had confirmation of what he was up against.

He rose as Grace, Madeline, and Alice entered the breakfast room, followed by Worthington and Phillip. It was odd not seeing Eleanor. "Ladies, gentlemen, good morning."

As everyone greeted him, he paid particular attention to Madeline's expression and thought he saw a light enter her eyes when she saw him. What would he have to do to counter Lady Wolverton's objections to his lack of a title? And why did she care? He was of excellent birth, and even if he wasn't the wealthiest gentleman, he had more than enough to support a family. Harry didn't like the idea of having to recruit more help, but he might need to. He'd have to find out where his grandmother Bristol was.

He held out her chair for Madeline. "I've been told it was a rough night for much of the family."

She lowered herself onto the seat. "Yes. Edward has an earache. We were just up to see him. He appears to be doing better. Thankfully, it's not contagious, so little Gaia cannot catch it."

Harry took the seat next to Madeline. Just what everyone needed after the wedding, a sick child. Or perhaps it was just the thing to take everyone's minds off a lunatic attempting to kill Eleanor. "Did he have a cold recently?"

Madeline gave him a surprised look. "They both did. How did you know?"

"Henrietta used to have earaches after she'd been particularly stuffy with a cold." The footmen came around with the breakfast dishes. "Eggs?"

"A soft-boiled one."

"I will have the same," he told the footman. After they were served toast, tea, and rare roast beef, he remembered what Theo had said. "Do you have the supper set available tonight, and if you do, may I please have it?"

The corner of her lip lifted as she picked up her teacup. "I do and you may."

He hid his grin. Salforth could go hang. "Thank you."

"You are most welcome." She glanced at him and smiled. "Is your day very busy?"

"Not as much as some. I'd like to ask for you for a carriage ride, but I have meetings this afternoon and I'm not sure when they'll finish." If that happened too often, it was going to be a problem. He hated to do it, but for the time being, courting Madeline had to take priority. And he knew his so-called friends had already ridden with her when he had been otherwise occupied. "Is tomorrow possible?"

"Yes. Alice and I planned to take our carriage out today. I would not cry off from that."

"And leave her alone?" He raised his brows, feigning an insulted expression. "I should say not."

She chuckled lightly. "Just so. One must take care of one's family members."

"None of us are very close in age, but Dotty and Henrietta have shown me how important relationships between sisters can be."

"And friendships too." Madeline finished chewing and swallowed. "Look how close Dotty and Charlotte have always been and still are."

He glanced around the table. "Where is Walter?"

"With Augusta. She is teaching him Spanish."

"I remember hearing that. I hope the family I have will be as close as yours."

Madeline tilted her head as she gazed at him. "I do not know how it could be different. You have excellent examples."

They finished eating, and as he rose, Worthington caught Harry's eye. "Stern, will you walk with me to Westminster?"

"Of course." He bent down to Madeline, who was still drinking tea. "Until this evening."

She gave him what he could only describe as a soft smile, and his heart began to thump harder. "I am looking forward to it."

"My lady, I wish you a good day."

"I wish you one as well. I hope you are able to slay some dragons." Madeline could not look away as he strolled from the room with her brother. What on earth made her mention slaying dragons? It must be the fear Miss Parker displayed, or the scare they had at the wedding ceremony. Madeline gave herself a shake and bit into a piece of toast.

"I wish Harry was not like a brother to me," Alice said.

What was she talking about? "Why is that?"

Alice shrugged. "What I really mean is that I wish I would meet someone like him. Have you noticed he meets all the requirements on our list?"

Unfortunately, Madeline had been forcefully struck by that very fact. "But do you not think it would be a great deal of work being the wife of a member of Parliament?"

Her sister took a drink of tea and looked at her over the rim. "I suppose it would be if he was interested in being in leadership. Yet I do not have the impression that is what Harry wants. After all, he will also inherit his father's estate and the work along with it."

But that was the type of work they were raised to do. Harry had never mentioned being a minister in the government, but this was still his first year. "I wonder if you are correct."

"Do you not think it would be the same if a peer wanted

to be in leadership in the Lords?" Alice raised one brow as she made her point.

"I had not considered that. I suppose you are right. It would be much the same thing." If only Madeline knew more about what being the wife of an MP was expected to do. Closing her eyes, she stopped her thoughts. Why even bother when Mama would not approve? Madeline had begun this Season vowing not to upset her mother and do her best to wed the person whom she wanted her to. That was obviously Salforth. Although another titled gentleman would do. Or should do, but Madeline was having doubts about that.

She finished eating and rose. "I brought a young servant home today. I must speak with Mrs. Thorton about her." Madeline had to find something to keep herself from thinking about Harry. She strode out the door and to the hall, where one footman was manning the door—she was learning a great deal of military talk these days—and another was standing by to provide assistance. She glanced at him. "Can you find out if Mrs. Thorton is free to speak with me?"

"Yes, my lady." He bowed, then strode swiftly to the green baize door and through it, and returned a short while later. "She said she would meet you in your parlor."

"Thank you." Madeline went to her chamber to brush her teeth, then to the Young Ladies' Parlor to wait. Even though she would have gone to their housekeeper, Mrs. Thorton insisted they behave as they must when she became the mistress of a house. Well, if nothing else, it was good training. Madeline picked up a book but kept staring at the same page.

Fortunately, Mrs. Thorton knocked on the open door and entered. "My lady." She bobbed a curtsey. "Do you wish to speak about Miss Parker?"

"Yes, indeed." Madeline would have offered Mrs. Thorton

a seat, but she would not have accepted it. "Can you tell me exactly what occurred?"

She folded her hands in front of her waist. "She worked for Lord and Lady Witherspoon. Lady Witherspoon's brother was staying with them as well." Her face darkened. "He made unwanted advances. Once, he caught her alone. It was pure luck the housekeeper happened upon them and ran him off. It scared Miss Parker a great deal. She was never alone after that. Fortunately, the gentleman"—she practically spat out the word—"left a few days later." Mrs. Thorton's lips formed a thin line of disapproval. "Yesterday, Lord and Lady Witherspoon left in their coach for what was supposed to be a house party, taking most of their clothing and all of the valuables. This morning, their man of business—at least that's who she was told he was—came and turned everyone off."

That answered that. "One would think that even if one was experiencing a reversal in fortune, one could at least pay one's servants."

Mrs. Thorton looked resigned. "As you know, my lady, not everyone cares about their duties as your family does."

Madeline tapped the open book. "She mentioned going home."

"She said the same to me." The housekeeper nodded. "Howbeit, one of our maids quit to go to Montagu House, so I have an open position. I asked her if she'd like to take it, with the understanding that she must work well. If not, we can send her home."

Trust Mrs. Thorton to find the perfect solution. "That takes care of that, then."

"Is there anything else, my lady?"

"No, thank you." Madeline smiled at the housekeeper. "And thank you for solving this problem. If only we could help the rest of the servants who were turned off."

"I wouldn't waste my time. They left her there on her

own. I have a feeling most of them knew what would happen. I'd like to see her get her wages, but I suppose there's no hope for that."

This was something with which she could assist. "There might be a way. Now that I have the employer's name, Mr. Stern might be able to assist in that regard."

Mrs. Thorton nodded again. "Mr. Thorton said he was impressed by Mr. Stern. I hope he can get Ann what she's due." She bobbed a curtsey and left the parlor.

Madeline stared at the door. "There is a lot about Mr. Stern about which to be impressed." She slammed the book shut. There had to be something to pass the time until luncheon. After they'd dined, she could count on morning visits and her ride in the Park to keep her busy until the ball.

Alice strode into the parlor. "Did Mrs. Thorton settle everything?"

Madeline placed the book on the small cherry table next to the chair. "Most of it. I'll ask Harry to see about acquiring the girl's wages."

Her sister sat on the sofa. "We need to go out."

"We are attending the ball this evening." Had Alice forgotten?

She frowned. "No, I mean we need to go shopping." Madeline stared at her. "*I* need to go shopping. If I do not, I might never go again. It is like falling off a horse. One must get back on again. I was not there when Eleanor was attacked, but I felt her fear."

It must be because they were twins. As close as Madeline was to them, there was a bond that enabled them to share some thoughts and feelings. "I understand what you are saying." She would probably never experience the feelings. She had been horrified by the attack on Eleanor but had not felt it. "Call for the town coach and change into a carriage gown."

Alice let out a breath. "Thank you."

A knock came on the still open door and a footman said, "Flowers for you, Lady Alice, from Lord St. Albans."

She turned around and sneezed.

"I'll take them to the servants' parlor," the footman said.

"Please do." She assumed a look of long-suffering. "Hyacinths. When I was ill, it was lilies."

"Does he not know you have a bad reaction to them?" That was one of the differences between the twins. Alice sneezed when around some flowers and not others. They did not affect Eleanor at all.

"He has never even asked if I liked the flowers he sends." Alice had a disgusted tone. "He obviously thinks I should be happy to receive them."

For weeks, Eleanor and Madeline had tried to work out what it was about Lord St. Albans their sister did not like. This was the first real clue. "Does he do that a lot? Believe you should be pleased he pays you attention?"

Alice raised her chin, and a mulish look entered her eyes. "I do not wish to discuss him. I must call for the coach."

She turned around and stomped out of the room.

"What is she upset about?" Mary said from the corridor. What was she doing here? "Do you not have lessons?"

"I am on my way to the music room," she said.

Madeline wondered what this was about. "This is not on the way from the schoolroom to the music room."

"If you go shopping today, could you pick up ribbons for Theo and me?" Mary had an innocent look on her face, but she and Theo were becoming quite devious.

"Yes, of course." Was that all?

Mary smiled. "Oh good. We were afraid Alice might not want to go."

Ah, that was it. They were worried about their sister. "Alice came to ask me if we could go shopping. I am sure she will conquer her fear."

"Very well, then, I shall see you later."

Madeline's throat closed with emotion as she rose from the chair. No matter what happened, the family she had with her husband, whoever he was, would be like this one. She would make sure of it.

CHAPTER TWENTY-SEVEN

Harry stared into the mirror and scowled as he tied his cravat. He'd sent a note around to his grandmother's house and was told she was traveling and had not told them when to expect her return.

Bloody hellhounds!

He needed someone with greater social standing than Lady Wolverton and who was not related to her to convince her that Harry would be a much better choice of husband for Madeline than a dratted duke. But who?

Burkham was standing by with more neckcloths on his arm. Harry rarely ruined his cravat, but tonight was an exception. After his second attempt, the valet ducked into the dressing room and came out with more.

He carefully lowered his chin until the folds were just right and breathed a sigh of relief. "Done."

His valet let out a breath as well. "It was touch and go there for a while, sir. I'll take the rest of these back."

Harry stifled a laugh as the man went to put the neckcloths away. A valet's reputation depended on how well his employer was turned out. He carefully added an emerald tiepin and waited for Burkham to attach his watch and quizzing glass. Harry rarely used the quizzer, but it was a useful thing to carry.

Once that was accomplished, he opened the door to the corridor. "I won't be much past midnight."

"Yes, sir," Burkham said.

Maybe Dotty would have an idea about whom Harry could approach for help. She and Merton were already in the drawing room when he strolled in and poured a glass of claret. "Dotty, I have a question."

Merton groaned. "Why do you all insist on that name? Thea is much nicer."

She pressed her lips together, but her eyes were sparkling with hilarity. "My love, I greatly enjoy that you have your own name for me. It would lose that value if everyone called me Thea."

"I suppose you're correct." Merton shuddered. "Harry, you may continue."

Dotty turned to Harry. "What is your question?"

"I received confirmation this morning that Lady Wolverton is indeed pressuring Madeline to marry for rank. Specifically, I believe, Salforth. Who could convince her that I am a better match for Madeline?"

"Lady Bellamny," Dotty said instantly. "However, you must ensure yourself that Madeline will accept you."

"In other words, I must first propose. And if she accepts me, we can approach her ladyship."

"Exactly." She took a sip of wine. "Have you decided when you will ask her?"

"No." Harry almost moaned. "I think it must be soon. Before Salforth does it."

"You'd better speak with Worthington first," Merton said.

"I already did. This morning. He said he'd accompany me to Westminster, and I took the opportunity to ask him. He said he thought it would be a very good match, but it was ultimately up to Madeline. I think he knows her mother's wishes."

"He would have to." Dotty's tone was as dry as dust.

"She has been to Worthington House more than once to express her desire concerning Madeline's potential spouse."

Harry drank half his glass of wine. "I had no idea she was being so forceful about it."

Dotty tilted her head. "Interestingly, she has not spoken with Madeline herself."

That was strange. "Do you have any idea why?"

"Not really." His sister shook her head slightly. "I think, at first, she was attempting to convince Matt and Grace to support her, but that was never going to happen. As to not speaking to Madeline, perhaps she is afraid Madeline will openly defy her."

Harry could not see her doing that. Not unless her feelings were already attached. Were they? If only he knew how to ask her what she felt for him. Why were relations between males and females always so difficult? "I am at a complete loss as to how to proceed."

"Continue as you have been doing," Dotty said. "I am not the only one who believes she prefers you."

"Don't take that for granted," Merton added. He glanced at the clock. "We must be going."

"I won't." Harry strolled after his sister and brother-in-law into the hall. This would be another evening of standing with her, watching her dance with other gentlemen, and trying to discover if she wanted him more than Salforth. When what Harry wanted to do was take her in his arms and carry her to the bedchamber in his nonexistent house.

When they entered the rooms Lady Turley had opened for the ball, Harry walked directly to Madeline, bowed, took her hand, and kissed it. "Good evening."

She stared at him, perplexed for a moment. "Good evening to you. You are later than usual."

He was stunned that she had noticed. "A bit. How did your day go?"

"Miss Parker—Ann—settled in. Our housekeeper told me she had a position for a maid and hired her."

"Excellent." That was the best solution. "What else did you do?"

"Alice and I went shopping." Madeline glanced at her sister, who was standing with Eloisa Rutherford and another lady. "It had not occurred to me how affected she had been by the attack on Eleanor before the wedding until she told me she would not be afraid of going shopping."

"The twin bond."

"Twin bond?" Madeline's brows came slightly together. "Is that a new term?"

"It is something I've noticed with my nephews. When something happens to one, the other one seems to feel it. It's my name for the phenomenon."

"It is an apt way to put it." She pressed her lips together in what he now knew was thought. "I have always seen it in Alice and Eleanor, and with the babies as well. I had not realized how deep it went. It appears Alice felt Eleanor's fear."

"I would not have guessed it could be as strong. I suppose there are many things we do not understand about that type of bond."

Something caught her attention and did not appear to please her. "Lord Bolingbroke is approaching for his set."

Harry decided to remain until his lordship took her to the dance floor. That, however, did not work in his favor. The second he saw her off, Georgie Turley approached. "I am sorry, Harry, but there is a young lady who requires a partner."

He bowed. "At your service."

She gave a quick smile and shook her head. "You must learn to hide better."

He couldn't very well do that if he wanted the other gentlemen to see he was with Madeline. "I usually do."

Georgie gave a trill of laughter as they approached a lady who seemed rather shy. She made the introductions, and Harry led Miss Appleby out to dance. He must have missed the first set, because it was a country dance, and no ball would open with that. No wonder Madeline had noticed he was late. He made a point to draw the lady out and soon had her smiling. She danced well when she wasn't thinking about her steps. When he returned her to her mother, he was not surprised to see another gentleman approach her. This one was leading Georgie to Miss Appleby.

She blushed prettily and curtseyed. "Thank you, sir. I enjoyed the dance."

Harry bowed. "It was a pleasure."

He hurried back to his circle and to Madeline. This time he'd move them closer to the others.

"I see Georgie is busy with her hostess duties." Harry thought Madeline's tone was a bit tight.

"She could do no less. Did you enjoy your dance with Lord Bolingbrook?"

"He dances well." Something was upsetting her. If only Harry knew what it was. "Not as well as you."

"Thank you." She had placed her hand on his arm, and he covered it with his own. "It was the same with Miss Appleby. She'd do better if she could strive to be less shy."

Madeline gave him a that-is-not-as-easy-as-you-think look. "I am thankful none of us suffer from shyness. It cannot be enjoyable."

"No, exactly the opposite." For ladies especially. Gentlemen could hide in the cardroom or simply not attend events. "Particularly when one is expected to put oneself out during the Season."

"Yes." She smiled at him, and he wanted to crow. "You understand so many concepts other gentlemen do not."

He didn't believe that of the men in her family. But there might be one gentleman to whom she referred. "I have been surrounded by people who care about others and their suffering."

Madeline worried her bottom lip. Something she did not normally do. "What is troubling you?"

She shook her head. "I cannot explain it." The sounds of the next dance intruded. "Even if I could, there is no time now."

Salforth was making his way through the crowded room to Madeline, yet Harry remained by her side. The next set was a waltz, and it occurred to her that she would rather be standing up with him. There was nothing wrong with the way the duke waltzed, but it was more enjoyable with Harry.

Salforth gave Harry a hard look and bowed. "Lady Madeline, Stern."

"Salforth." Harry never called him "your grace" or "duke." It was always by his name.

He lifted his hand that had covered hers, and Madeline had the fanciful feeling she had been set adrift. She curtseyed to the duke. "Your grace." And placed her fingers on his sleeve. Something felt wrong, but what? She had done this dozens of times before. Why should it be different tonight? They went through the motions of the dance, but she knew that unless she brought up a serious topic of conversation, he would limit himself to polite talk.

After the set, Salforth returned her to her family and the Rutherfords. Eloisa drew Madeline aside when the duke appeared across the room and leaned against one of the columns. He reminded her of a character in one of the Minerva Press novels, dark and brooding, except for his blond hair. He had potential to meet all the requirements on the list and the two others she had added for herself, but he was not quite there. Would he ever be?

"He is magnificent." Eloisa sighed. "Every time I see him, I get tingles in my neck and shoulders, and when we stand up together I never want to stop dancing with him."

Tingles? With Salforth? Madeline caught herself frowning and resumed her polite mask. Naturally, she knew how important a physical reaction was for attraction. The question was, how important were those feelings? The tingles and butterflies in the breast, the warmth that heated one's blood when the right gentlemen touched one. Were they absolutely necessary for happiness? All her sisters seemed to believe they were. Yet Madeline did not feel anything at all when she danced with his grace. And if her friend was having tingles with the duke . . . well, that might complicate things, or it might make her decision easier.

First, she needed to know more about Eloisa's emotions. "How long did it take for you to have that reaction?"

She glanced at Madeline. "No time at all. The first time he touched my hand I had them." Her friend's blond brows drew together. "Have you not felt them, or a certain warmth, more than just a normal feeling, with any of the gentlemen?"

Madeline had. With Harry Stern, and only with him. And that was the dilemma. He was perfect in every way. He met all the requirements on the list. The problem was, her mother would assuredly be extremely unhappy. On the other hand, Mama had not said a word when Madeline danced or went riding with Harry, and she had to know that she did. If not for her mother's calls upon Grace—which was the only time she voiced her desires—Madeline would have thought her mother had given up the idea of her marrying Salforth or another titled gentleman. The only other complication was that life with him would not be what she thought she wanted. The life of a Member of Parliament was not the same as the life with a member of the Lords. She did not think she even knew anyone who was wed to someone in the Commons or had any knowledge of that life.

"Is there something particularly interesting on the opposite side of the room?" Lady Rutherford, Eloisa's sister-in-law, said.

Eloisa shook her head slowly. "No. We were discussing 'tingling.'"

"Ah." The corners of her ladyship's lips rose. "An important topic." She seemed to scan the ballroom, and her gaze stopped on someone. "My brother says Mr. Stern is starting to make a name for himself in the Commons."

Madeline looked at her ladyship. "Your brother?"

"My brother has the seat my father had when he was an MP."

And to think Madeline had never known that. "What was it like for him? Being in the Commons?"

Anna lifted one shoulder in a Gallic shrug. "He was, naturally, involved in our local community, as was my mother. When one represents people, one must know what their needs are. We were here in spring and autumn and on our estate during winter and summer. Why?"

Madeline was not going to answer that question. "I had just been thinking I did not know anyone who had much to do with the Commons."

Lady Rutherford grinned. "I suppose it can seem like a different world, and, depending on the constituency, it can be quite different. If one represented a city or an area of the city, one would spend more time there."

Yet Bittleborough was more of a large market town than a city. "I would think one would miss the country."

Her ladyship chuckled. "Most, if not all, MPs have estates. After all, one must have a certain amount of wealth to be eligible to be one."

"I had not thought of that." Madeline caught sight of Harry Stern, and a pleasurable shiver slid across her shoulders. "Is spending time with one's constituency the same as visiting dependents on an estate?"

"Hmm." Her ladyship seemed to gaze off. "It is not as intimate. But I suppose it could be if the effort was made."

Her face softened and a look appeared in her eyes as

she lifted her hand. "Rutherford, have you finished your conversation?"

"For now." He raised her fingers to his lips. "Is there someone to play chaperone so that I may waltz with you?"

She turned her head slightly. "I believe Eloisa and Madeline will be dancing as well."

Madeline glanced in the direction Lady Rutherford had looked. Harry and the duke were cutting through the crowd, making a direct line for them. She had already stood up for one set with the duke. He must be dancing with Eloisa.

Harry arrived first and bowed. "My lady, I believe this is my set."

"It is." Madeline smiled as the duke did and said almost the exact same thing to Eloisa. Perhaps it was time to learn more about what an MP's wife was expected to do from the Member of Parliament himself, and a waltz was the perfect time to do it. She would also have supper to ask questions.

They took their positions and started the first steps before she realized she did not know quite how to pose her questions. She could not say, *What would your wife do as an MP's spouse?* This was frustrating. As she twirled, an idea came to her. "Are many of the MPs with whom you associate married?"

"Most of them." He took her back in his arms. "Why?"

She kept her tone light, as if she was merely interested, not interviewing him. "I was curious if the wives did the same sorts of things the wife of a member of the Lords did. It occurred to me that I am fairly ignorant about the Commons."

"That's not surprising." They twirled slowly around the room. "Just like the Lords, it depends on how ambitious an MP is for his career. Those who are interested in being prime minister or a cabinet member put most of their effort into their positions at Westminster. Those of us who want to concentrate on helping the people of this country and our constituents try to discover their needs and how bills that have already been passed help or harm them."

It occurred to her that she already had been assisting him to do some of that. "I understand that members of the Commons must have an estate or something of the sort."

"Yes." They increased the pace of their steps. He sounded as if he did not approve. "Land is still everything; therefore, one must have property of some sort no matter how wealthy one is. Then again, anyone with a certain amount of wealth will have at least a house."

"You never mentioned having an estate." Madeline wondered why he had not.

Harry quickly pulled a face. "I am embarrassed that I have only visited it once before coming up to Town. I must spend more time there. It was a gift from my grandmother to ensure I met the requirements to run for the position. Unfortunately, I didn't have the opportunity before the Parliamentary session began."

That was something with which she could help. "How frustrated you must be about that."

"I am. Extremely frustrated." The musicians played their last chords and the set ended. "Come. We can continue this discussion during supper."

That was exactly what she wanted to do. "Yes. I find this very interesting."

CHAPTER TWENTY-EIGHT

A surge of hope rushed through Harry at the interest Madeline was showing in being the wife of an MP. Did it mean she was seriously considering him as a husband? He chastised himself for not realizing she would know very little about what he did. After all, she'd been raised as the daughter and sister of an earl, not an MP. But this was an opportunity to discuss it with her. A chance to show her that the skills she'd been taught fitted well with her position as his wife and helpmate.

He and the other gentlemen were approaching the table where the dishes had been laid. Harry hoped there were ices for Madeline.

"Damn Netherby," St. Albans muttered.

It occurred to Harry that the man was not at their table this evening. "Who?"

"Netherby. He had the supper dance with Lady Alice." St. Albans's tone resembled a low growl.

"Ah." Harry had some sympathy for the man. He wouldn't like any man who stood up with Madeline, particularly for the supper dance. "Do you not like him because he had the supper dance, or do you know something that makes him ineligible?"

"I don't trust him." St. Albans frowned. "He's making her laugh."

This was ridiculous. "Bury makes her laugh. If you can't do it, perhaps you should change your approach."

They reached the table, and Harry took two plates.

St. Albans followed him. "What do you mean? She's a lady. She wants what the rest of them want. Wealth and status."

No wonder St. Albans hadn't made any progress with Alice. "You mean to say you have spent weeks chasing after her and you haven't learned a single thing about her? She could not care less about status or great wealth. None of them do."

St. Albans's jaw dropped. It was still hanging open while Harry selected the ices. Finally, the man's mouth snapped shut. "Then why is she with Netherby?"

Harry almost rolled his eyes. "Why do you think? He asked her to dance." He signaled to a footman to help with the plates and glasses of champagne. "If you really want her, I suggest you find out what interests her."

When he attained the table and Madeline, he placed a chocolate ice in front of her. "I brought some others as well."

"Brilliant!" She smiled. "I shall have a taste of the others first."

Once she had finished her ice, he brought the conversation back to the duties of a Member of Parliament and his wife. "What else do you want to know about members of the Commons?"

Madeline took a sip of champagne. "I imagine there are political entertainments."

"Yes. Just like in the Lords. If one wishes, one can hold soirées to discuss politics." He remembered Mrs. Taylor's ball. "There are other entertainments as well. After all, the Members have families and girls who make their come outs."

Madeline appeared to consider what he'd said. "Of course. Why had I not thought of that before?" She took another sip of wine. "The Commons is made up of gentry and people of other statuses."

"Indeed there are younger sons of peers, as well as at least one heir to a peer who decided to remain in the Commons." He wanted her to understand how much more diverse the Commons was than the Lords.

Worthington stood, signaling it was time for his family to depart. Harry rose and held out his hand to Madeline. "Is there anything else you wish to know? If I don't have the answer, I will be happy to find it for you."

"Not at the moment." She placed her fingers in his. I will tell you if I think of anything."

"As you wish." She'd given him no indication how she felt about the information he'd told her. And despite his earlier elation over her questions, he had no idea of how she felt toward him. Would the fact that he was an MP be a problem? Did she want the life of a normal lady who was married to a peer? He'd not thought of that before. Drat St. Albans for putting the idea in Harry's head. Naturally, Madeline would want to know what life would be like if she married him. Any thinking woman would.

He escorted her to her coach and assisted her in. "Tomorrow morning?"

She smiled at him again, and his heart hurt with longing. "Until then."

Two days later, Madeline sat in her favorite chair in the Young Ladies' Parlor and frowned at the book she had been trying to read. Her choices of a husband were Salforth and Harry, and, despite her mother's ire if she did not choose Salforth, he had also asked Matt for permission to address her. Although Harry had done the same and still had not proposed. The problem was that she could not bring herself to consider a gentleman who had potential when there was a perfectly good gentleman, one with whom she was almost certain she was in love, who met all the requirements on the list. As long as he loved her too, that was, and that was what she intended to discover today. She leaned her head back against the velvet wing chair. She was tired and bored with indecision. Salforth had given her no indication at all that he loved her. Yet if Harry loved her, her decision was made. If he did not . . . Well, she would jump that hurdle if she must. She had tried her best to do what her mother wanted her to do.

Sorry, Mama, but I have found my husband, and he is not a duke.

She was going to be difficult, but it was Madeline who would have to live with whomever she chose to marry. And Harry was the one. She had spent the past month trying to persuade herself that she could have the same feelings for another man that she had for Harry, not to mention how bereft she had been when she thought he might be courting another lady. Even though it was soon obvious that he spent all his time at balls and other events with her. If Madeline had confided in any of her sisters, they would have told her she was mistaken to consider anyone she did not think she could love. But she had not because she also knew they would also tell her to ignore Mama. And Madeline could not. Yet, in the end, that was exactly what she was going to do. She put down the book on the small round table next to the chair and rose. The al fresco luncheon for the children was today, and Harry would be there. There was nothing to do but ask him if he loved her. If he did not . . . well, that was something she would deal with later.

A knock sounded on the door before it opened. "Madeline," Alice called. "Everyone is downstairs waiting."

"I will be just a moment." Madeline rose and stepped across the corridor to her bedchamber. It was right that she be surrounded by her family when what she hoped was that a betrothal would take place.

Harper entered the room from the dressing room with a wide-brimmed bonnet. It was not the most fashionable hat Madeline had, but it was the most practical for the day. "Here you are, my lady."

Madeline donned her gloves while her maid fixed her bonnet on her head. She picked up her reticule and straightened her shoulders. She would soon know whether or not she and Harry would make their lives together.

She was halfway down the stairs when Elizabeth ran up to her. "You will make us late."

"We will be fine." Madeline took her niece's hand.

Elizabeth closed her eyes and shook her head. "That is what you always say. Everyone always says it."

Madeline fought the urge to smile. Her niece would not take that well. "Have we ever been wrong?"

"No, but there is always a first time for everything," her niece said darkly.

"I cannot argue with that." Elizabeth was an old soul in a young body. "But maybe not today."

"My lord, the coach is waiting," Thorton announced as she reached the last step.

She glanced at the child holding her hand. "You see, we are not late after all."

Elizabeth fairly bounced with excitement. All her closest friends would be there. And from the food to the games, the afternoon had been planned around the children. Even the babies—toddlers, really—had been invited. Madeline just had to find the time and place to speak with Harry alone.

"Children, hold hands," Matt said, reminding her of when they were all younger and Grace had told them the same thing.

Elizabeth clasped Gideon's hand. Mary took Edward's and Theo had Gaia's. The twins looked very cute and clean in their white dresses. By the time they arrived home, the gowns would be stained with grass and grime. Gaia was no better than her brother.

The nursemaids would travel in a smaller vehicle behind the family coach.

Matt and Grace led them to the carriage, and the footmen assisted everyone into the vehicle.

A few minutes later, they arrived at Merton House.

Dotty was at the door, grinning when their butler opened it. "Welcome. Charlotte and Louisa are already here. Henrietta should arrive soon with her little boy." She turned and led them down the corridor to the garden. "We have an area set up for the toddlers and their nurses. Vivienne has put herself in charge of the games." Dotty glanced at Grace. "That should be interesting. Hugh is already challenging her role." Dotty grinned. "The only thing for us to do is play referee and relax."

"A happy change of pace," Grace said. "With the wedding over, we are back to our rounds of balls and other events."

"As are we all," Dotty said drily.

"And we thank you for it," Grace said.

Madeline looked around for Harry. With any luck, after today they would only have Alice to worry about.

Dotty continued as they strolled through the house to the garden. "Dom refused to allow Vivienne to paint a hopscotch design on the grass, so she convinced me to give her a sheet upon which to paint the pattern."

They entered the morning room, and Gideon and Elizabeth dashed to the garden as the rest of them ambled through the French windows. Harry was inspecting a croquet court. At the same time Madeline stepped into the garden, he glanced at her and started striding her way. It had only been a few hours since they had last seen each other. Still, her breathing increased, and her chest was so tight she could barely breathe.

"Good afternoon." The corners of his eyes crinkled when he smiled at her.

"Good afternoon." She glanced at the croquet court. "Were you pressed into service?"

He tucked her hand into the crook of his arm. "Yes. But only due to my superior knowledge." He looked at Vivienne and Hugh. Both children had their hands on their hips. "He's going to catch cold if he thinks he can tell her what to do."

"I hope he learns his lesson before he's ready to look for a wife." Although, recalling what Con went through to convince Charlotte to marry him, she did not have much trust in that occurring. Hugh was very like his father.

"Now Gideon's going to become involved," Harry said.

Naturally, Elizabeth followed him. "And Elizabeth."

Harry grinned. "There goes Constance and Alexandria as well. Hugh doesn't stand a chance against those four."

"You sound as if you speak from experience. Was it like that with Dotty and Charlotte when you were all growing up together?" What would it have been like to have such close friends when one was young?

"Very much the same." He nodded as he watched their nieces and nephews. "Although I was a few years older and at school. That sometimes gave me the advantage."

Madeline wanted the same thing for her children. Hugh had a pained expression on his little face, but he bowed to the girls, and he and Gideon walked off toward the croquet court. "That is a friendship that will last their lifetimes."

"The girls as well." Harry was still watching the boys. "Did you not have close friends as a boy?"

"Not like those two. The Stanwoods were the only other gentry in our neighborhood at the time with younger children. The boys I played with took different paths than I. Hugh and Edward will go to school and university together."

Which was where Harry formed friendships that were not that close.

Although insightful, this conversation was not getting her what she wanted. The children were settled, and no one was paying attention to her and Harry. "Shall we take a stroll? I want to see the result of the changes Dotty made."

"Of course.. She made sure it was all completed before today." He glanced to the side, where there was an enclosed area for the toddlers and they were being entertained; then he looked a little more toward the back of the garden. "There is a new path you might want to explore."

Dotty had told them of the changes she was making, but Easter had been cold and wet, and none of them had wanted to venture out to see what she had done. The last time she was here, they walked straight from the gate to the house with no time for her to explore. He led her to a flagstone path bordered with thyme and other fragrant plants. The path led to a small, raised, marble fountain of a girl pouring water from a jug. "That is very pretty."

"And safe." Harry glanced at Madeline. "The babies cannot accidentally fall into it."

"Perhaps that is the reason we do not have one in our garden." She scanned the area in case any of the children had followed them. But no one was there. "Harry." She turned so she was facing him, gazed up into his eyes, and took his hands in hers. "I have something to ask you." This was much harder than she thought it would be. Should she kiss him first? Yet, if he did not love her, what would he think? "I love you. Do you—"

"Desperately." Suddenly, she was in his arms, and he was kissing her. Madeline quickly overcame her surprise, threw her arms around his neck, and kissed him back. His tongue touched her lips and she opened them, allowing him to explore her mouth. This was as good as she had been told it would be. She copied what he was doing and melted against him. And to think there was more to come. He pulled back from their kiss and stroked her back. "I love you too. Thank God you—"

Harry started to go down on one knee, but she pulled up on his hands. "No. Let us be equals from the beginning."

"As you wish." He kissed her fingers. "Madeline, I love you. Will you marry me and be my wife, my helpmate, my lover, and the mother of our children?"

A thrill tripped down her spine. "I will. Harry, I love you. Will you be my husband, my partner, my lover, and the father of our children?"

"I will." He drew her to him, and his lips touched hers.

Madeline sighed and opened to him. She placed her fingers on his cheeks, cradling them. His hands stroked her back and sides and touched under part of her breasts. Frissons of pleasure raced through her and curled her toes. She wanted more. If only they could wed today.

CHAPTER TWENTY-NINE

"Are they supposed to be doing that?" a high voice sounded from the bushes.

The children.

Harry groaned quietly and they stopped kissing. Bending his head, he placed his forehead against hers. Madeline wrapped her arms more tightly around his neck. So much for being alone. They remained still, listening for what would come next.

"It does not matter." That was Constance. "They are going to be married."

"How do you know that?" By the suspicious tone, it had to be Hugh.

"Because that is what Mama and Papa do." Superiority colored her tone.

"She is right. Our mama and papa do it too," Elizabeth said.

How many of the children were watching them?

"Uncle Harry was supposed to have told me first." Vivienne sounded aggrieved.

There was a rustling in the shrubs, and the next thing Madeline knew, Hugh and Elizabeth were shouting, "Harry and Madeline are getting married!"

"It is a good thing I've already spoken to Worthington," Harry muttered.

Madeline laughed silently for several moments. "I suppose we should go back and make our own announcement."

"That would probably be for the best." He took her hand in his, and they strolled toward the terrace. "We need to find our own home. Soon."

She agreed. As much as she loved her cousins, she did not want to live with them. "Do you have someone looking for you?"

"An agent recommended by Merton and my grandmother. I shall send a note around to him, informing him we are ready to view the properties he's found."

At least she would not be refurbishing a house her mother-in-law had decorated. "Eleanor!"

"You must write to her." Harry grimaced. "Do you want to wait until she returns?"

Madeline wanted her sister there, but Eleanor had said they would depart Paris immediately upon hearing of a betrothal and return home. "No. Matt will have a message sent through the embassy. It will arrive in a few days."

That relieved Harry's mind, but there was a cloud on the horizon. "Your mother?"

"I do not know how to tell her. She will not be happy." A worry line creased Madeline's forehead and shadowed her eyes. If only he could make this easier for her. "I did try to do what she wanted, but I could not." Madeline glanced at him. "I love you, and I would never have been happy with another gentleman. No matter his rank."

"I am extremely glad about that." Harry squeezed her hand. "I don't know what I would have done if you'd agreed to wed someone else."

"No. Thank you for showing me who you are." It had taken her too long to realize he always showed his true self.

He wanted to do something to help her. "Perhaps we should go to see her together."

"I do not know. Let me think about it."

For the moment, that would have to do. They entered the open part of the garden and, as he suspected, their families were all waiting. He and Madeline glanced at each other. They were both smiling broadly. "We have decided to spend our lives together."

Everyone came forward, meeting them halfway to the terrace.

"I knew you would be perfect together." Alice hugged them.

Merton and Rothwell exchanged glances and grinned. What was that about?

Grace, Charlotte, Louisa, and Dotty took turns hugging Harry and Madeline. Parkin, the Merton butler, arrived with champagne for the adults and lemonade for the children. "Congratulations, Mr. Stern. You could not have picked a better gentleman, my lady."

Merton assumed a pained expression at his butler's informality.

Dotty laughed. "Indeed she could not have. Although I must admit to being partial to my brother."

"Stern," Worthington said. "My study no later than ten tomorrow morning."

"I'll be there." Harry was glad Merton had told him what would happen and what would be in the settlement agreement.

Once the glasses were handed around, Merton raised his. "To Madeline and Harry and another wedding."

Then it was Worthington's turn. "Harry, welcome to the family." He nodded at the children. "If you have any questions, I'm sure they will be happy to answer them."

Madeline had told Harry that her nieces and nephews had

informed Montagu about the family get-togethers. "I will be sure to do so."

The children went to the croquet court, and Worthington nodded sharply. "Merton, if I may have paper and pen, I'll write a note to Eleanor and Montagu, informing them they must return straightaway if they do not wish to miss the wedding."

"Follow me," Merton said. "I'll have it sent immediately to the foreign office."

Worthington strode after him. "I must also send someone after them. If they stopped along the way, they may not yet be in Paris."

Harry was ecstatic that everything was happening quickly. Then again, he suspected it would. Madeline had been taken away by her sisters and his. He was about to join Kenilworth and Rothwell when Theo and Mary came up and hugged him.

"Well done," Theo said.

Mary smiled. "We are happy you are joining our family."

"I appreciate the help you gave me." In fact, he'd been thankful for all the help he'd been given. "This has been a busy Season for you."

"We expected that," Theo informed him.

"And we still have Alice to settle," Mary added.

Harry was fascinated by their machinations. "Do you have a gentleman in mind?"

Theo's brows drew together, and for a moment, she appeared much older than her years. "We do, but he requires a great deal of assistance."

"Indeed." Mary nodded. "He can be quite a sapskull."

"Buffle-headed," Theo agreed. "When it comes to our sister, that is.

"I am certain you will be able to set him straight." Harry thought he knew to whom they were referring. When he saw the gentleman, he'd give him another hint. He glanced at

Madeline. She was in deep discussion with her sisters. Now would be a good time to send a short letter round to the housemonger. He'd ask if they could view some houses tomorrow. He went to the desk in the morning room, dashed off a missive, and gave it to a footman to have delivered, then returned to his betrothed.

He joined Madeline and placed his hand on the back of her waist. She flashed him a smile and resumed listening to what Grace was saying.

"Two weeks." Grace raised a brow to him. "You are responsible for obtaining the special license and reserving the church. Ten o'clock is the time we usually choose. The wedding breakfast will follow."

"Yes, ma'am." Harry wouldn't have any trouble at all in remembering those two tasks. "I should tell you I will be purchasing a town house and have written to the person who has been recommended, asking him to show Madeline and me the properties he's found on the morrow. Will that be convenient?"

The muscles in Madeline's back stiffened as they awaited the answer.

"Yes, after her appointment at Madame Lissette's. I will write to her today."

"You may use the desk in the family room if you wish," Dotty said.

"Thank you. I accept your offer." Grace took herself off toward the house.

Madeline relaxed, and he rubbed the small of her back. "Is this what I can expect from the next two weeks?"

"Yes." She nodded. "Just like with Eleanor, the days will mostly be devoted to fittings and other things to do with the wedding and finding a house."

He thought of something else they must do. "Once we decide where we will live, I imagine you will want to decorate it to your standards."

She grinned as the others chuckled. "Grace knows an excellent decorator and a builder, if we decide to make structural changes."

Answers to the letters that had been sent arrived in short order. Madame could see Madeline as early as she could arrive. Mr. Bennett, the housemonger, had time to show them the houses after luncheon. He had one in particular he thought they would like and a few more as well, and the Foreign Office stated they would put Worthington's letter in that day's diplomatic pouch. Everything was proceeding smoothly thus far. The only thing that would upset Madeline was her mother's disapproval. Somehow, Harry would need to see what he could do to help her. Until then, he must do his part to prepare for the wedding.

"First the town house, then the special license, after that the church."

"First the church," Rothwell said. "You will be surprised at how difficult that can be with everyone marrying."

"The license is only good for fourteen days," Kenilworth said wryly. "I made the mistake of procuring one immediately and had to buy another."

"Right, then. Church, town house, license." That would be easy to remember. "My parents and Grandmamma! I knew I was forgetting something."

Merton barked a laugh. "My darling wife is writing to them. Your grandmother blames herself for not being in Town for Henrietta's first Season. She has been hovering not far from here since you arrived."

That didn't make any sense. "Why would she not stay in Town?"

"Unlike your sisters, you did not require her to chaperone." He indicated ladies around Madeline. "We had it well in hand."

Merton was right. The "family" had guided him since he came to the metropolis. It had felt like years since he'd arrived, but it had only been a matter of weeks. He'd expected to take his time choosing a wife. A wife who would help him acquire more power in the Commons. A position he now knew he didn't want. He'd never even considered love. Although, with the examples of his parents and sisters, love must have been somewhere in his mind. He absolutely had not thought he'd find the lady he wished to wed almost immediately. Nor had he considered that any lady he chose might not be so quick to realize how well-suited they were. He gazed at Madeline surrounded by her sisters and his. She was beautiful on the outside, but it was her inner beauty, strength, and caring about others that attracted him the most. "I am the luckiest man in the world."

"No, no." Rothwell shook his head. "*I am* the luckiest. You may only be lucky."

"You only think so," Kenilworth said. "I am actually the luckiest man."

Merton shared a glance with Worthington. "You are both wrong. I am the luckiest."

Harry hadn't noticed the ladies had joined them until Madeline was by his side, and Grace said, "What on earth are you talking about?"

Worthington put his arm around her waist and smiled at her. "These fools each think they are the luckiest man on earth when I know I am."

As the debate continued around them, Madeline clasped Harry's hand. "Who started this?"

"I'm afraid I did. I was mulling over what had happened since I arrived in Town and said I was the luckiest man in the world, and that started it. Are they always so competitive?"

She cast her gaze to the sky. "You have no idea. It is especially bad between Con and Rothwell."

Harry had noticed the ladies referred to the gentlemen by their first names, all but Rothwell. "Do you call him by his title because he is a duke?"

"Oh no." She laughed. "It is because his first name is Gideon. He was quite puffed up when he thought Grace had named my nephew after him. However, it was her father's name. Fortunately, it is all in good fun."

He raised her hand and kissed it. "I'm going to enjoy being in your family."

Henrietta and Fotherby came up on his other side.

"What did we miss and why are they arguing?" she asked.

Madeline leaned around Harry. "Debating over who is the luckiest."

His sister gave her head a quick shake. "I do not understand."

He quickly explained it to her, and Nate laughed. "We are all the luckiest men for finding the perfect wives for us."

Merton glanced at Fotherby. "Fotherby, glad you could make it. What did you say?" He repeated himself. Merton glanced at the others. "Well, I agree, and I think that ends this discussion."

Dotty looked toward the house. "Aside from that, luncheon will be served shortly."

While they had all been talking, the servants had been setting up tables and bringing out food.

Henrietta's eyes widened. "You are betrothed!"

Madeline grinned at her. "We are."

"You may now wish us happy." Harry hadn't had a chance to tease his sisters in a long time, and it felt good.

"I do." Henrietta immediately hugged Madeline. "I knew you were perfect for each other."

Fotherby shook Harry's hand and slapped his back. "Congratulations. I agree with my wife: you are perfect for each other."

"Everyone keeps saying that," Madeline mused.

"Because it's true," Louisa said. "I know what took you such a long time to realize it. Defying one's mother is not as easy as some seem to think. Perhaps you might want to talk to Augusta about it." Madeline appeared almost afraid, and Louisa frowned. "You have not told her yet?"

Madeline shook her head. "Not yet. I must do it soon."

Her sister's frown deepened. "Do you want me to go with you?"

"No. This is something I must do myself." She gave herself a shake and glanced around. "Where is Augusta?"

"Probably buried under some translation or another." Louisa chuckled. "You won't see her at a children's party until she has a child of her own."

"I never thought about it, but I suppose you're correct." Madeline would have to go to Stanwood House and inform Charlie and Augusta about the betrothal. At least they would be happy for her and Harry.

Somehow, Madeline had got separated from Harry and he didn't like it. He slipped his arm around her waist. "I do not know her well, but I'm getting to know her husband. They will most likely treat having their baby with the same diligence they go about their research."

She gazed up at him. "I do not know whether to be worried or happy for the poor thing."

"The child will be reading by three and translating foreign texts by six," Rothwell said.

"I concur," Louisa said. "But he or she will have cousins, and the rest of us will teach him or her how to play."

Harry studied Madeline. What would their children be like? Chestnut hair and green eyes? Black hair and blue eyes? Or some other mix? The eldest male would be the heir, but what would be his interests in life? What would the girls want? He couldn't see into the future, but surely it would be different. With any luck at all, females would have more choice. There were so many things he'd not considered before today.

"You look as if you're having revelations," Worthington said.

That was exactly what Harry was having. Terrifying ones. "You could say that. I was thinking about children."

"We all wonder what they'll look like, and what their future will be." His soon-to-be-brother-in-law's tone was thoughtful. "Until the birth." Worthington's jaw tightened. "Then all you want is for your wife to live."

Harry had a faint recollection of his father pacing the room, and him being hustled to the nursery. Still, his mother's shouts could be heard. That must have been when Henrietta was born. He'd been at school for the others. "What did you do?" Other than wait. "I mean, how did you get through it?"

"I demanded to be allowed into the room with her." Worthington glanced at Grace. "Fortunately, all three labors have gone well." He clasped Harry's shoulder. "We'll be there for practical and moral support."

"Thank you." He looked at Madeline, surrounded by her family. And it suddenly occurred to him that no matter what the difficulty, they would always be close at hand, not only for one another but for the children as well.

CHAPTER THIRTY

Madeline woke up the next morning, tossed back the covers, and jumped out of bed. Outside, the sky was beginning to lighten, birds chirped, and a squirrel jumped from branch to branch in a nearby tree. There had never been such a wonderful morning.

I'm marrying Harry!

Her maid entered the room with a cup of chocolate and a piece of toast. "Good morning, my lady."

"Good morning." Madeline quickly washed and tried not to fidget as her maid dressed her.

"Her ladyship said to invite Mr. Stern to break his fast here."

That made sense. He had to speak with Matt this morning about the settlement agreement. She and her sisters had read a copy of the agreement he used, and she could not believe Harry would disagree with it. In fact, none of her sisters' husbands had refused to sign it.

She drew on her gloves. "I shall see you soon."

"Yes, my lady."

Alice walked out of her bedchamber as Madeline entered the corridor.

"Good morning." She could not stop smiling.

Her sister peered at her. "Good morn to you. I suppose you are going to look like that all day."

"More than likely." She laughed. "I feel like champagne bubbles are flowing through my veins."

"You are certainly sparkling." Alice quickly turned her head away. "We should go."

If only Madeline could do something to help her sister find true love. "Yes, we should. Today will be busy."

To her surprise, Harry was waiting for her when she walked outside. He was smiling as well. "Good morning."

"Good morning to you." Last night, she'd dreamed he kissed her again. Perhaps her dream would come true.

"Alice, good morning." Harry grinned.

She glanced around, took a breath, and returned the smile. "It is."

At least she was trying to put on a good show. Harry helped Madeline mount Rose, then swung fluidly onto Willy. "What made you decide to come here instead of meeting me along the way?"

He rode between her and her sister. "I wanted to spend as much time with you as possible."

A happy warmth joined the bubbles. "I am glad you did." Her horse snorted, prompting her to mind the street. "Before I forget, you are invited to break your fast with us today."

"It would be my pleasure." He looked to the side, where a dray was delivering milk. "I suppose I'll meet with Worthington directly afterward."

"*We* will meet with him." She held her breath until he nodded.

"Have you already read the contract?"

Madeline did not think it would be a problem for him, but now would be a good time to find out if it was. "Matt reviewed the agreements with us before the Season began."

Harry flashed a grin. "Merton told me he did the same

with Dotty. He also told me what was in them. I don't expect to have any objections."

She let out the breath she had been holding. "They are the same as the others. All my brothers-in-law accepted them."

He barked a laugh. "I have no doubt." He reached his hand out, and she took it for a moment. "I will as well."

She was trying to find a way to include Alice in their conversation when Henrietta, Dorie, and Georgie joined them. They all greeted one another, and the ladies took Alice with them, leaving Madeline alone with Harry. "I do not know what to do about my sister. She seems unhappy."

He was distracted for a second, then said, "Now she'll have the opportunity to be aggravated."

Lord St. Albans spurred his horse and rode up to Alice. Her back immediately stiffened. "You are right about that."

Harry's brows drew together. "If he is serious about her, he'll have to change his way of thinking."

They passed through the gate. "What do you mean?"

He told her about the short conversation he had with his lordship, and Madeline fought hard not to roll her eyes. "No wonder she is not impressed with him."

"I gave him a hint." He glanced at Alice and Lord St. Albans. "Perhaps he'll take it."

Madeline looked at them as well. "I suppose only time will tell."

Harry turned his attention to her. "I want to help her as well. But do you think we can get married first?"

A peal of laughter escaped Madeline. She had never been so happy. "I agree. We should wed first."

"I'm glad we are in accord." He led them farther away from the others. "I heard from the housemonger. We have five houses to tour today."

"Five!" That would take most of the day. "I had no idea there would be so many houses available during the Season."

Instead of racing to the tree, they let their horses amble along toward it. "None of them are rentals."

Did that mean they would be in better condition or not? "I suppose offering a house for sale during the Season makes sense."

Harry shrugged. "We'll soon know."

"We will." Although first, they would have their meeting with Matt. "What time is the first viewing?"

"Ten thirty."

They reached the oak, and Madeline continued around to the back side of the wide old tree. He followed her. Could one kiss on horseback?

"Are we hiding?" He was as close as one could get under the circumstances.

Mentally, she measured the distance. It seemed possible. "Will you kiss me again?"

His lips rose slowly, and his eyes lingered on her. "Or you could kiss me."

She could. Why had she not thought of that? Madeline leaned toward him, and he leaned toward her, closing the distance. Somewhere, not quite in the middle, their lips touched, sparks flew, and she wished she was in his arms. Unfortunately, the best she could do was to place her hand on his broad shoulder to keep from falling. He teased her mouth, and she opened it, tangling her tongue with his.

Rose shook her head, whinnied, and stepped away. Madeline quickly straightened. "It is doable, but not very practical."

Harry stroked Willy's neck, and she imagined his large hand on her. "Maybe with practice." The look Harry gave her was so hot, she almost went up in flames. "However, I think we can find better places to kiss and make love."

The image of a bed popped into her head. She sent a prayer of thanks to her sisters and Dotty for being honest with her about what happened between a husband and wife.

"Much better." And sooner rather than later. "We had better go back."

Harry agreed. It was time to sign the contracts. If there was an opportunity before seeing the first house, he'd take Madeline and go by St. George's to arrange a date for the service. He followed her out from behind the tree. "Where is everyone?"

She gave a light shrug. "They look to be gone." She opened her brooch watch. "We are late."

It was amazing how quickly time passed when he was with her. "Race to the gate?"

"Yes." She urged her mare into a trot. "Do you think Thorton will be sufficiently prescient to have sent a message to your valet?"

Damn! He'd forgotten about having to change. "He is efficient."

Encouraged by them, their horses were in a full gallop. They reached the gate and slowed to a trot, not speaking again until they reached Worthington House.

He reached her as she unhooked her leg from the horn, and clasped his hands around her waist, letting her slide down his body as he lowered her to the pavement.

Her eyes widened, but her lips curved into a smile. "I wish I could kiss you here."

"I wish the same."

"My lady," Thorton said from the door. "Mr. Stern's valet is waiting for him, and your maid is pacing the floor."

Harry held out his arm. "We'd better hurry."

"Yes."

He'd never bathed and dressed so quickly. He'd wager Madeline hadn't either. He met her on the landing to the stairs. Fortunately, there were footsteps behind them. They wouldn't be the last ones down, but as they strode through the breakfast room door, he saw they were the last of the older members of the family.

There were two empty seats next to Alice, who looked as if she was in deep thought about something. He gave himself an inner shake. Madeline first. Then they could attempt to help Alice.

He held the chair for Madeline, and she smiled her thanks. "Good morning."

Worthington pulled out his pocket watch, then opened it and closed it without saying a word. Right, then. Harry should have been paying more attention to the time. He and Madeline ate quickly.

As soon as they set their serviettes on the table, Worthington rose. "Madeline, Stern, my office in fifteen minutes."

Harry inclined his head. Wonderful. More than enough time to brush his teeth and let his nerves take over. He didn't even know why he was so on edge. He knew what was in the settlement agreement. His father had approved of them for Dotty. Harry wanted Madeline to be equally protected. He was never nervous. It must be because this was another concrete step on the way to marriage. But he wanted to be married to Madeline. None of this made any sense at all.

Madeline squeezed his hand. "I am tense as well."

He looked down at their intertwined fingers. He hadn't even noticed they were holding hands. "How did you know?"

She gave him a small smile. "You *look* nervous."

Harry shook his head "I don't understand why I am."

Madeline lifted one shoulder and let it fall. "I do not either. It is not because I do not want to wed you. I do. I think it must be the change it portends."

"Hmm. That sounds logical." They reached the landing to their chambers. There was no more time to talk. "I'll see you in a few minutes."

"Yes. I will see you soon." Madeline smiled at Harry. The poor man. Eleanor had told her how on edge Montagu had been before meeting with Matt. Her betrothed would soon discover he had nothing about which to worry. The agreements were all clearly written. She kept all her property in a trust her brother controlled. She also kept everything that she acquired either by purchasing it herself, as a gift, or inheritance in the future. There was a list of what she currently owned. It was all very straightforward. In the future, every quarter, she was required to send a list of any new items to Matt, and he'd keep an updated account.

She brushed her teeth and started to leave the room.

"My lady." Harper's hands were folded in front of her waist. "When you're looking at houses, could you ensure the servants' quarters are in good condition?"

"I will do so." Madeline was glad for the prompting. "If they are not, we will not relocate until they are."

The dresser breathed a sigh of relief. "Thank you, my lady. I was not sure you'd thought of them."

To be honest, they had not been foremost in her mind. "I am glad you reminded me." Her maid gave a sharp nod. "Once we have chosen the town house, you and I will tour the servants' quarters."

"Thank you, my lady."

Madeline glanced at the clock. It did not seem possible, but fifteen minutes had almost passed. "I must go." Harry was already waiting when she arrived, and she clasped his hand. "Ready?"

"Never more so." He grinned.

She could not tell if he was over his bout of nerves, or whether he was very good at hiding his fears.

They reached her brother's office, and Harry knocked on the door.

"Come."

Madeline exchanged a glance with Harry, and they entered the study.

Matt glanced up. "Have a seat." Three sets of documents

were lined up on the desk facing the chairs she and Harry took. Matt fixed his attention on Harry. "As you know, Madeline has read them and is in agreement with all the provisions. I don't need to tell you to read them carefully."

He picked up the first stack, glanced through them, and put the copies back on the desk. She could not help but study him as he read. At one point, he nodded. Both brows rose on a few pages, and he continued to peruse the documents. When he was finished with the first, he went to the second set. His mouth flattened, but he gave no other indication of what he might be thinking. Was there something with which he disagreed? Matt would not change anything in a way that disadvantaged her. As Harry had before, he set down the documents and picked up the last set. Madeline reminded herself to breathe.

Finally, he placed the last set on the desk and looked at Matt. "I pity the gentleman who thinks to profit from a marriage with your sisters. In general, I agree with what has been written. However, I would like to add a provision stating that any property that either I acquire or is acquired during our marriage or before, whether by me or her or jointly, aside from the estate I will inherit from my father, is to be her sole property upon my death."

All her breath rushed out of her. She had never heard of such a generous gift.

Her brother raised one brow. "You do not wish it entailed after you ascend to the baronetcy?"

"No. I see no reason to enrich any heirs." Harry glanced at her, then back at her brother. "Madeline may leave the property as she wishes. One never knows what one's heirs will do." He reached over and squeezed her hand.

Matt nodded. "Very well. I shall have that provision added. It will be ready by tomorrow morning for our signatures."

Harry inclined his head and stood. "I shall see you then. We have houses to tour."

"Good luck," Matt said. "I'm immensely thankful I did not have to purchase a house."

She flashed a smile at her brother. "I think I shall have fun looking at them."

He groaned and waved them out of the room. "Tell me that when you return."

"I will." She took Harry's arm, and they strolled to the hall. Once they were in his curricle, she decided to discover the reason for his change. "Why do you want me to have any property you own?"

"For your protection. My father has set aside a house for Mama if he predeceases her. However, it is only a life estate. I do not want you to ever think that you are a tenant in your own property."

Madeline knew that houses belonged to men, but she had never thought of a lady as being a tenant. Yet he was right. Once one's husband was dead and an heir took over, they could do what they wished within the bounds of the settlement agreement. "Thank you."

The corners of his lips rose. "Matt isn't the only one who wants you to be cared for well."

And this was one of the reasons she had chosen Harry Stern.

CHAPTER THIRTY-ONE

Harry feathered the corner onto Mount Row and almost kept going. It was only the presence of the man showing them the properties that made him stop. The houses on the small street were of the same stature of the previous street and built in red brick.

He glanced at Madeline and saw a moue of distaste on her beautiful lips. He drew up to the side of the street. Mr. Bennett was in his midthirties and in a fair way to taking the business over from his father. "Mr. Bennett, this street will not do."

"Yes, sir." He took out a piece of paper. "The next house is on Mount Street."

Harry hoped Mount Street would be an improvement. "If you care to ride with us, you may climb up on the back."

"Thank you, sir." The carriage dipped a bit as the man climbed into the groom's seat.

He drove to Mount Street and stopped at the house Bennett indicated. One glance at Madeline told him she was skeptical but would withhold judgment. What did she know that he did not?

"The front is nice." She peered through the window on the side of the door.

Bennett drew out a key and opened the door. "As you see, the hall is in good repair."

Madeline circled it. "The size is adequate." She glanced at him. "I am not at all certain about the black marble."

"It does make the entrance dark." Even with the sun shining in through the windows around the door, the hall was dim. "Let's see the rest of it."

They looked in the main rooms before entering the servants' hall. After inspecting the kitchen, the housekeeper's chambers, and the butler's rooms, Madeline shook her head. "This will never do. It must be completely renovated." She glanced at Bennett. "What does the garden look like?"

"I will show you, my lady. It is a bit shabby. It's been several months since anyone has lived here."

Once again, she inspected the area with a critical eye, and pointed to the gate. "That leads to the cemetery."

Bennett appeared as if he wanted to loosen his cravat. "I believe so, my lady."

"Mr. Stern." Her lips pressed together. "I do not wish to live adjacent to the cemetery."

He couldn't blame her. He particularly didn't want any of their children getting into the cemetery. "I agree." He glanced at the agent. "What else do you have?"

"Hay's Mews," the man croaked.

"If I am not mistaken," Madeline said, in a tone that dared anyone to disagree with her, "there is a coaching inn on the street."

Bennett swallowed. "Yes, my lady. I do have a house on Carlos Place."

Her eyes narrowed. "Near the hotel?"

"A few doors down."

Harry had had enough. "What do you have that is suitable?"

This time the man appeared hopeful. "You might like the house on Hill Street."

"We will see it." Madeline tucked her hand in the crook of Harry's arm and lowered her voice. "It had better be more to our liking than the last three."

They drove to the house that Mr. Bennett indicated and stopped. The residence was midway between the Park and Berkley Square. The location appeared to be perfect. The street was quiet and lined with good-sized houses. They entered the house through a portico with four columns. The front door was painted Prussian blue, and the knocker had been polished to a high shine. Pink marble covered the floor. The walls and alcoves in the hall were painted light yellow.

He leaned down so that only she could hear him. "What do you think?"

Madeline's eyes sparkled with delight. "It is beautiful."

In fact, the hall seemed to have been decorated with her in mind.

"We will have to find statues or something to put in the alcoves."

"I have some ideas. Come." She dropped her hand from his arm. He took her hand, twining their fingers. "Let us see the rest of it."

"My lady, sir, I will wait here for you," the housemonger said.

That suited Harry perfectly. Although he didn't think she would hold back, he wanted Madeline's honest opinion of the house.

They passed through three drawing rooms with pocket doors. The wood paneling on the bottoms of the walls had been painted to complement the silk paper covering the upper part of the walls. Every room on the ground floor was either painted or papered in the sort of light colors Madeline liked. The furniture was tasteful and in good condition but sparse, giving them the opportunity to put their own mark on the house. They moved into the corridor. The wood floor was covered by a long Turkey rug. Unlike the drawing rooms, the wood on the lower part of the walls had been waxed instead of painted. Polished wall sconces had been affixed at intervals along the entire length. Madeline had taken a pocketbook from her reticule and made notes as they inspected the rooms.

"I am glad there is not so much furniture," she murmured, then pointed to the curtains. "These are a lovely shade of light green."

"They are. What do you think of the wallpaper?"

"I like it a great deal. It reminds me of the paper in the music room at Worthington Place. It is the same type of open flower design."

The more she approved of what she saw, the more excited he became. He was almost positive they had found their home. He opened a door and stepped back as she strolled in, looking around her. It was obviously a morning room. Butter-colored curtains embroidered with butterflies and small colorful birds framed wide windows that gave a view to a garden of rosebushes on one side and the back garden on the other. French windows opened to the garden. The upper walls were painted cream and the lower walls were paneled in undyed, waxed oak.

He pointed them out to her. "They will stand up to whatever young children might do."

Her cheeks bloomed a beautiful pink. "I agree." Turning her head, she gazed out at the garden. "It is lovely." A line marred her forehead, and he wanted to kiss it away. "Before I fall in love with this house, we must tour the servants' quarters and bedrooms."

"Of course." Naturally, she would think of their servants. It was one of the things he loved about her. "Up or down first?"

"Up. That way we can view the rest of the house as we descend."

They found the servants' stairs, and he preceded her up

to the floor that held the attic and the servants' rooms. The rooms were a comfortable size and large enough for two servants to sleep in one room without being cramped. "Well?"

She scrunched up her mouth, and once again, all he could think of was kissing her. "They need painting."

They were rather dull. "They do."

She gave him a brilliant smile. "The nursery should be below."

Dear God, give me strength. His thought went immediately to having her in bed.

He led the way into the schoolroom and was stunned by all the light. "Is this usual?"

Madeline glanced around, turning as she did. She stopped with a perplexed look on her face. "I do not know. Both the Stanwood House and Worthington House schoolrooms and nurseries have a great deal of light. Grace renovated them."

"Indeed?" Being a barrister had made him a suspicious sort of man. He was beginning to think that the horrible properties they had been shown first and this jewel of a house were not by accident. Then again, the schoolroom at Stern Hall was bright. Perhaps he was imagining interference where there was none. On the other hand, it also had a well-lived-in look. This did not.

"There is not much to do here." She blushed again. "At least not for a while."

"The bedchambers should be on the next floor." They held hands as they descended. He opened the first door they came to and opened it. The wallpaper had brown stripes and pink flowers, and it was yellowed and stained in places, fortunately not near the ceiling. "Good Lord! Who would have chosen those colors for a bedchamber?"

Madeline's brows rose. "It will have to be changed."

"I should say so."

"Grace will know who to call upon." Madeline backed

out of the room. "I hope the others are not as horrible. I do want to make some changes, but I do not know if I am capable of a whole house."

Harry drew her into his arms. "You, my love, are capable of anything you want to do."

"Thank you for your confidence." She raised her face to his, and he kissed her.

If only they could remain here. "We must see the rest of the house."

She laid her head against his shoulder. "Yes. Mr. Bennett will think we have got lost."

The rest of the bedchambers were a mix of well-decorated and not. He opened the door to what was either the master's or the mistress's bedchamber. A massive dark oak bed anchored the room. He hoped she intended to share a bed with him. "What do you think?"

"It reminds me of Matt's bedchamber." She walked to a door and opened it. "Oh, this is a lovely parlor."

Harry stuck his head into the room. It was beautiful, and not a bed in sight. "If you want to make it into your bedchamber . . ."

"No." She blushed a deeper rose than he had seen before. "I mean, only if you want me to have a separate chamber."

That was the last thing he wanted. "Not at all. Unless you find another parlor you like better, this can be yours."

She strolled into the room and paused. "I can see this being a place we share with the children and spend time in ourselves. Our private oasis, as it were."

That was an excellent idea. "We will make a rule: No one other than the children can bother us here."

"Agreed."

Madeline strolled to the corridor, and he followed. "Where are we going next?"

She glanced over her shoulder. "The kitchen. We must know if it needs any substantial changes."

Taking her hand in his, they made their way down the servants' stairs to the kitchen and the housekeeper's rooms. Knowing nothing about kitchens, Harry stood back while Madeline inspected the stove and other furnishings. When she nodded her head a few times, he knew this was their house.

"Well?"

"Everything is perfect." Her smile made him want to swoop her into his arms and carry her up to their bedchamber.

"Let's tell Mr. Bennett and make the arrangements for the keys. I imagine you will want to start on what must be accomplished before our wedding."

She wrapped her arms around Harry's neck and kissed him. "You make such good suggestions."

The more he was around her, the more he needed to touch her, taste her, make her his in every way. Drawing her closer, he swept in for another kiss. This time, he teased her lips with his tongue, and she opened for him. He placed his hands on her waist. Thank the deity she wore short stays. He moved his palms down over the flair of her hips, then slowly up to her breasts, and brushed his thumbs up over her full breasts to her nipples. Even through the layers of linen, he could feel them furl into tight nubs.

Madeline moaned. "That feels so good."

"It will feel even better when they aren't hidden beneath your stays and gown." He moved his lips over her jaw to her ear. "When I can kiss and caress them as I'm doing to your neck."

She shivered and pressed closer to him. "You know that I have been told what happens."

He touched the tip of his tongue to the shell of her ear. "I had a good idea you might have been."

Harry swept one hand from Madeline's neck over her derrière while his other cupped a breast. Can one actually swoon from pleasure? Her breathing quickened, and an achy feeling began between her legs, begging for attention.

"My lady, Mr. Stern," Mr. Bennett called from the hall. "Have you made a decision?"

She dropped her forehead to Harry's chest. "We had better tell him. It is a shame we cannot stay here."

Harry placed his thumb under her chin and raised it up. "We can come back tomorrow to take measurements."

"Taking measurements sounds very interesting." If only they did not have to wait until then. But there was nowhere else they could be alone.

"Let's put him out of his misery."

Hand in hand, they climbed the stairs to the hall. When they arrived, Mr. Bennett was pacing nervously. He gave them a concerned look.

"We will take it," Harry said. "There are a few rooms that require immediate attention. Therefore, her ladyship would like the keys."

"Yes, of course." The man fished them out of his bag. "When would you like to sign the purchase contract?"

Madeline hoped Harry had a better idea of what that involved than she did. She glanced at him. "Today?"

He, in turn, focused on the housemonger. "We will sign them as soon as they are ready. Please ensure her ladyship is also included on the contract as an owner."

The man's jaw slackened. "Yes, sir. Yes, my lady." He handed her the keys. "I can have them ready by nine in the morning, if that is not too early."

That would give her most of the day with Harry.

Harry squeezed her hand. "Bring them to Worthington House."

"As you wish." He ushered them out of the house, shut the door, then looked at her.

"Oh, yes." Fortunately, the keys were all marked, and the lock slid easily. She dropped them into her reticule and tucked her hand into the crook of Harry's arm. "We should tell our families that we have a house."

He lifted her into his curricle, and frissons of pleasure shot through her. Tomorrow. Tomorrow she would discover for herself what it was like to be with the man she loved.

Harry climbed into the other side. "Mr. Bennett, can we drop you somewhere?"

"Thank you, sir, but no. I will either take a hack or walk."

Her stomach growled as Harry started the horses, prompting her to look at her brooch watch. "We missed luncheon, but we will be in time for tea."

"Good. I'm famished." He drove straight to Berkeley Square and turned the corner.

Never having been on Hill Street before, she was surprised how short a drive it was. "It is not at all far from Worthington House."

"It isn't. You will be able to walk if you wish." He pulled up to the house, jumped out as soon as a footman had the horses' heads, and came around to lift her out.

This time she understood what he was doing when he lowered her slowly down, brushing her body lightly against his. Madeline had always experienced sensations before, but now they were ten times stronger. All she wanted to do was throw her arms around him and kiss him. Well, other things too.

His lips were soft against her ear. "We should go in before we create a scandal on the street."

She dragged in a breath. "Why am I never the voice of reason?"

Harry placed her hand on his arm and grunted. "Because you've never wanted to kiss a gentleman before."

That made sense. Thorton bowed as they strolled through the door. "Everyone is in the morning room, my lady."

"Thank you, Thorton. I should tell you we have found a house and I will need your help hiring servants."

He bowed again. "I would be honored."

CHAPTER THIRTY-TWO

Madeline and Harry strode down the corridor to the back of the house, entered the morning room, and she stopped. Not only was her family present. His was there as well. Everyone turned and looked expectantly at them.

Merton lounged against the fireplace. "Did you find a house to your liking?"

Alice and Henrietta exchanged an excited glance. What was that about?

Harry put his hand over Madeline's fingers on his arm. "We did. It was, in fact, the only one suitable."

Madeline pulled Harry as she walked forward into the parlor. "Indeed it was. It is about halfway down Hill Street."

"Excellent." Alice smiled smugly.

"We are signing the contract tomorrow." Harry glanced at Matt. "You will need to be there, as Madeline is a minor."

Matt inclined his head. "We can sign the settlement agreement and the contract for the house at the same time."

"Harry," Henrietta said, "you and Madeline should sit with Alice and me. We would love to hear about the house."

Nate stared at his wife and shook his head.

Merton raised one brow. "I think all of us would like to hear about their new home."

Madeline did not know Henrietta nearly as well as she

did Alice, but something was going on and Madeline intended to get to the bottom of it. She and Harry took cups of tea from Grace. "One of my favorite parts of the house is the morning room. It reminds me of the music room at Worthington Place." Madeline sank onto one of the two chairs next to the sofa upon which her sister and Henrietta sat. "It made me quite comfortable."

Alice's eyes widened and she appeared a bit too innocent. "Did it?" She tilted her head. "Come to think of it, I suppose it would."

Harry lowered himself into the seat next to Madeline. "I was interested to see there was only one bedroom for the master and mistress. The other was a parlor."

"Yes." Madeline took a sip of tea. "It was an unusual configuration for a house being sold. The other ones all had two bedrooms. Of course, they were all horrible."

"Especially the one on Mount Row. I don't even know why the agent thought it would be at all suitable."

Elizabeth put a plate of tartlets and biscuits at the end of the sofa table near where Madeline and Harry sat. He took a biscuit and bit into it.

Henrietta's eyes shifted to Alice and back to Harry. "Yes. Er, Mount Row could hardly be appropriate."

"I agree. That made no sense at all." Madeline selected a lemon tartlet. "It was almost as if we were being guided to the house we decided upon."

Nate drifted over to stand behind his wife and placed his hands on her shoulders. "You two are horrible liars. You might just as well confess. They will work it out soon if they haven't already."

Harry munched his biscuit and picked up another. "Yes. Why don't you tell us what you've been doing?"

The two of them kept their lips firmly shut. They might need just a little help. Madeline tried to think of a tastefully decorated room she could pretend to dislike or the opposite.

Ella Quinn

The particularly horrid room came to mind. As nonchalantly as possible, she took another sip of tea. "I especially liked the room with the striped and flowered wallpaper."

Alice hurriedly covered her mouth with a serviette.

"You cannot." The words seemed to burst out of Henrietta. "It is truly dreadful!"

When Harry looked at Madeline, his lips twitched. "You did an excellent job decorating."

She looked at her sister and his. "And leaving me just enough to do, but not too much."

"What I don't understand," Harry said, "is why keep it a secret? I mean, I understand why you wouldn't want to tell us ahead of time, but it was really fairly obvious someone who knew us well had had a hand in decorating the house." He raised his brows. "I suppose Grandmamma put you up to it."

"Go ahead and tell him the rest," Nate prodded.

Henrietta bit her bottom lip. "Grandmamma wanted to ensure you and Madeline not just liked the house but loved it. That gave me the idea of recruiting Alice."

That the Duchess of Bristol was involved did not surprise Madeline at all. "How long has this scheme been going on?"

"From what we understand," Alice said, "the duchess selected the house some time ago."

"Yes." Henrietta nodded, clearly warming to the story. "About the time you were elected to Parliament, Harry. She was impressed with the schoolroom at Merton House, which was based on what Grace did here."

"She did tell us the house was in good condition," Alice continued. "For example, the pink marble was already in place."

Madeline did not even want to think of the work that would have been needed to replace the marble. "The only structural addition was the schoolroom and nursery?"

"Indeed." Henrietta took up the tale again. "It was

mostly painting and papering and the like. We did move a wall or two."

"Except for the kitchen," Alice added. "Henrietta received advice from her cook."

That made sense. If Alice had done it here, Madeline would have found out. "Thank you. I must say, we were relieved that we found a house we both liked a great deal. And you are correct; I did not want a house that would be a project."

"I thank you as well." Harry grinned at them. "It has made our lives much easier."

Henrietta studied him for a moment and frowned. "Did you already know? What gave it away?"

"I had an inkling," he said. "Call it my suspicious mind. It was the schoolroom. I've had an opportunity to see a few of them, including ours. The only one I've seen with so much room and light was at Merton House, and Dotty told me she used Grace's idea."

"All's well that ends well." Nate leaned over and kissed Henrietta's cheek. "Now I can have my wife back."

She blushed. "The only problem now, is I have discovered that I enjoy decorating. I shall have to see about some changes at home."

Nate groaned as everyone else laughed. "I suppose a few changes can be made."

Madeline knew which fabric and furniture shops her family frequented, but she did not know the name of the decorator. She was trying to remember. Surely she had heard the name, when Matt said, "I suppose you want to start on the renovations immediately."

"Yes." What was his concern? "We would like to get it started before the wedding."

"Naturally." He sounded resigned. "Even though you are betrothed, I ask that you exercise discretion when entering and leaving the house. You do not want to become the latest *on-dit*."

He was right, of course. She and Harry did not want to be a topic of gossip. "We will have to think about how to be discreet."

Henrietta leaned toward Madeline. "When Dorie and Alex became betrothed, she entered his house from the mews. Something like that could work for you."

It could. But Madeline could not be seen wandering around the mews when she did not yet live on the street. "Harry." He gave a short nod. "It would be better for you to use the mews and for me to enter by the front door."

"Very well." He looked as if he was thinking about something. "I need to get the stables set up. That will give me the opportunity to do it."

"Excellent." Everything was proceeding nicely. "Grace, could you give me the name and direction of the decorator you used?"

Her sister-in-law smiled. "I shall do better than that. I will write to her and arrange a meeting. All I need from you is the day and time you wish to begin."

Madeline would have to make a list of everything that was needed, and some ideas about the rooms that needed furbishing. "As soon as possible after tomorrow. I should have made the lists by then."

Grace inclined her head. "I will attend to it after tea."

Nurse brought in the twins, and all talk of the new house ceased.

Gaia toddled to Harry and lifted her arms. "Up."

"Up, please," Grace prompted her daughter.

Gaia's blond brows puckered. "Up, peaze."

"Very good." He placed her on his lap. "Have you been having a good day?"

Her head bobbed up and down. "I play wit Posy."

Madeline glanced around. Where were the Danes?

"An now she sleep," Gaia said, putting a finger to her lips. "We mus be quiet."

Harry's green eyes sparkled with laughter. "It is important to be quiet when the dogs are sleeping."

Her head bobbed again, and Madeline's throat closed with tears of happiness. *He will make an excellent father.*

"What are our chances of having twins?" he whispered.

"They run in the Carpenter side of the family, but not in the Vivers side as far as I know." She thought of Dotty being shocked to be pregnant with twins. "Then again, sometimes they just happen."

Madeline was right about that. Twins were not easy to predict. Being around children made Harry want his own with Madeline. "We have a few hours until dinner. What do you wish to do?"

Her brows puckered slightly, much as her niece's had. "I would really like to go back to the house and start my lists. We must have everything from linens to china and silverware."

Good Lord. He hadn't even thought of all that. Well, possibly the linens. He had wondered if some were on the bed in their chamber. "Let's do that. I'll return to Merton House, fetch my groom, and meet you there. Just leave the door to the morning room unlocked."

She set her cup on the table. "I will walk you out."

He gave Gaia a kiss on the top of her head, put her down, and stood. "Grace, thank you for tea. I will see you later."

"Join us for dinner," she said.

He bowed. "With pleasure."

"I am going back to the house." Madeline rose.

"Take someone with you," her brother instructed.

"I will." She linked her arm with Harry's, and they strolled out of the parlor. "I will bring Finnegan. He can look at the stables as well."

And that brought up the question of who would be in

charge of the stables. "I suppose they can stake out the spaces for our horses." There were so many details to attend to, when all he wanted to do was make Madeline his in the most basic way possible. "We'll need a stable master."

"Umm." They reached the hall, and Roberts, her footman, was giving orders to a younger footman. "Oh, good. My bonnet and gloves are still here."

He bowed. "Will you need me, my lady?"

"Not at the moment. I do require Finnigan." He signaled to the younger servant. "I must tell you that Mr. Stern and I have found a house on Hill Street. Naturally, I would like you to be a part of our household, if you wish."

"There is nothing I'd like better, my lady."

Harry noticed the man didn't even smile. Was he training to be a butler? That would settle one of their issues. He'd mention it to her later.

"I will take you and Harper there tomorrow to inspect the house."

"As you wish, my lady." The footman bowed again.

She glanced at him. "Are you ready?"

"I am." Her footman opened the door, and they strolled to his carriage together. "I'll see you soon."

Madeline placed her hand on his cheek. "Yes."

Harry arrived at Merton House to find his groom gone on some errand.

"He'll be back soon, sir," the stable master said.

"It's fine. I'll wait. You didn't know I'd need him." After all, Gibbons couldn't sit around all day doing nothing. Harry might as well use the time to gain information. "I need to know something about stable masters. Lady Madeline and I are buying a house, and I'll need one." He didn't even have one for his estate in Bittleborough. Well, that wasn't quite true. But the one who was there wanted to retire.

The older man seemed to consider him. "Unless you have

a coaching master like we have, you'll want a man with knowledge of horses and carriages."

What he didn't know was whether either of their grooms had that experience, or even wanted to do the job. "How would I go about finding a stable master with the right experience?"

"I'll look 'round for you. You should probably ask the stable master at Worthington House too."

"Thank you." He'd do that when he was back at the house for dinner. Harry opened his pocket watch. How long had he been here?

He visited Willy and gave him an apple, then paced. He glanced at his watch again. Another fifteen minutes passed, and his groom had still not arrived. At this rate, he wouldn't have time to properly make love to Madeline.

"Sir." The stable master was clearly not happy Harry was still there. "Is there anything anyone else can do for you?"

He had to make a decision. Waiting here wasn't helping him. "Yes. Get my curricle ready, and if Gibbons hasn't returned by then, tell him to meet me at 19 Hill Street. He's to go around to the stable."

"Yes, sir." The stable master signaled to one of the men. "We'll have it for you in a few minutes."

It was a relief not to be waiting around. Why hadn't he thought of the idea sooner? Madeline was going to wonder what had happened to him.

As promised, the carriage was ready and brought out sooner than he'd expected. He climbed in and drove out of the mews onto South Audley Street, then over to South Street and behind Hill Street to the mews. It wasn't until then that he realized he didn't know which stable belonged to his house, nor did he know how the back of the house appeared.

Bloody hellhounds!

When he was about halfway down, he started looking at the stables. Only one seemed empty.

He stopped, and Finnigan came out. "I told her ladyship you'd be late. Ran into Gibbons when I was exercising one of the hacks. He'll be a right long time gettin' back."

"So I discovered." Harry climbed down. "How do they look to you?"

"Everythin's in good order. Just some cleaning up to do. I've started on that."

Harry wondered if . . . "Do you know anyone who'd be a good stable master here?"

The Irishman grinned. "Not me. My passion's the horses." He took off his cap and scratched his head. "There's an under stable master at Stanwood House. Good man with the carriages and cattle. He might want the job."

Harry would have to ask Stanwood if he minded. "Thank you. I take it her ladyship's in the house?"

"She is. Got her pocketbook with her. You'll find her somewhere."

"I'll let you get back to work." He started crossing over to the gate.

"You'll want this." Finnigan held up a key. "Weren't gonna leave the gate unlocked."

"Thank you again." Harry took the key and locked the gate again once he was in the garden.

Now to find Madeline.

CHAPTER THIRTY-THREE

Madeline was glad Finnigan had told her Harry would be delayed. Still, she wished he would arrive soon. She had already gone through the one room and made notes of everything that must be done. She went into the parlor next to their bedchamber and glanced out the window into the garden. *Harry.* Finally. Madeline started to open the window to call to him, then remembered that would only notify the neighbors they were at the house together.

She ran down the back stairs to the morning room just as he reached it and opened the door. "I am glad you are here."

He wrapped his arms around her. "So am I. It took me a while to become frustrated with waiting and just come here."

Reaching up, she kissed him. "I have finished the plans for the horrible room." He caressed her breasts and she almost melted on the spot. "Shall we go upstairs? I can explain how I want to change it."

"Is that what you truly want to do?" He swooped her up into his arms, and she wrapped her arms around his neck. Goodness, she had not been carried since she was a little girl. It felt good being in his arms. "There are other things I'd rather do." He headed toward the main staircase. "Stop me if you are not of a like mind."

"Not at all." The only reason she had not been bolder was because she was unsure about how to go about it. Charlotte had told her she had tried to seduce her husband but was too ignorant to do it properly.

Harry took the stairs two at a time. When they reached the door, she lifted the latch. "Our chamber." He carefully lowered her feet to the floor and his lips claimed hers. "I want to see."

Before Madeline knew it, her bodice sagged down. What was sauce for the goose and all that. She reached up and untied his cravat, hung it over the bed rail, then shrugged out of her sleeves. Her gown pooled around her feet and she stepped out of it. "I must put it over something."

"Leave it to me."

"You need to remove your vest." By the time she laid her gown over a chair, he'd divested himself of his vest and was lifting his shirt. She had not yet seen his chest or even touched it. "I want to do that."

He dropped his arms, and she took the bottom of his shirt, running her thumbs up from the top of his trousers over the broad planes of his chest, through the black curls, and over his dark rose nipples as he had done to her. When he groaned, she pressed her lips to the base of his throat before pushing the garment over his head. He was so warm and smelled so good. Clean, with a hint of lavender. What would happen if she tasted him? Slowly, she touched the tip of her tongue to the hollow at the base of his throat.

He groaned and threw the shirt onto the floor. "You are going to be the death of me." Harry untied her chemise, and stays, and pushed them and her petticoat down over her shoulders. "There they are." He plumped up her breasts, and his lips touched the tops. Heat pooled between her legs and the spot began to throb. He licked one nipple before taking it into his mouth, and her knees buckled. "I've got you."

Holding her, he applied himself to the other breast. Her breath came so quickly, she was almost panting. "Too many clothes." Suddenly the rest of her clothing fell to the floor. She unbuttoned his trousers, and his member sprang free into her hand. "Soft."

Harry groaned again. "We need to take off our footwear."

Why had she not thought of that before they started kissing? They broke away and she quickly removed her half boots while he took off his shoes. "Now what?"

"Now, my love, we go to bed." He lifted her up and gently placed her on the coverlet, then joined her. One by one he removed her hairpins, depositing them on the table beside the bed. Soon her hair was undone, and he spread it over the pillow. "I have dreamed of you like this. All your beautiful curls."

He caressed her body as he kissed her. Flames shot thought her until she thought her blood must be on fire and the pulsing between her legs was harder and harder. Then he touched her *there*, and his fingers entered her, and his tongue pressed on her mons, and everything exploded like a Catherine wheel. Sparks flew. Nothing ever felt so good. No wonder no one could describe it.

Harry rose over her. "Are you ready? This will hurt."

She nodded. She knew it would be uncomfortable. Her body wanted to tense at the coming invasion, but that would not help. She reached up and brought his mouth to hers. Their tongues tangled and the ache started between her legs again. Madeline gasped as a sharp pain pierced her.

"How are you?" He nuzzled her ear. "Shall I stop?"

"No. It is almost gone." He moved again, stretching her, but it no longer hurt. She followed her body's demand to thrust against him.

"Put your legs around me." Harry was as breathless as she was.

Ah, that was better. Pressure built and she shattered. "Harry."

"Madeline, my love." He pumped into her one last time before rolling to his side and pulling her with him, caressing her arm and kissing the top of her head. "That was a miracle. You are a miracle."

"I like being a miracle." She had never been happier. Being here with him, making love was perfect. "I love you."

"I love you too." Harry glanced down at Madeline as her breathing softened into sleep. How had he ever got so lucky as to find and win her love? Together, they could accomplish anything to which they set their minds. He tightened his arms around her. God, how he loved her. His father had been right. Sexual congress with a woman one loved was vastly different from with anyone else. It was lovemaking.

He glanced around the room. Someone had placed a clock on the fireplace mantel. They'd been here much longer than it seemed and, unfortunately, they could not remain. There was a screen that probably had a basin behind it, but he doubted anyone had had the forethought to fill it with water. How the devil would he clean her? His handkerchiefs were large, but she would go home smelling of him and sexual congress. He needed to get his handkerchief. But getting it entailed leaving her, and he wasn't ready to do that just yet.

Sometime later, her long, thick eyelashes fluttered and opened. "Did I fall asleep?"

"You did." Harry nuzzled her hair again. They'd have to pin that up. "We need to dress and go to Worthington House." He'd not say home. This was her home. *Their* home. "Stay here for a moment."

She propped herself up on her elbows, her lush breasts rose, and he stifled a groan. "We need to wash. Regrettably, we don't have any water."

"Yes, we do. I brought a basket." She pointed to the

corner of the room. "Right there. I brought water, some soap, a cloth, a hair comb, and food."

She wasn't only a miracle, she was amazing. "How did . . . . ? Your sisters."

Madeline grinned. "Not precisely. I knew it was a bit messy, and we would not have a basin already filled with water. I could not very well ask my maid and footman to accompany me." She lifted one shoulder in a Gallic shrug. "It was a practical idea."

He grabbed the basket, took it to the bed, and kissed her. "Imminently practical." If only they had more time. But they didn't. And she was probably sore. "I'll fill the basin."

"Give me my chemise first."

It hadn't occurred to him that Madeline might be shy being naked with him. He took it from the rail at the foot of the bed and handed it to her. "Does it bother you that I am naked?"

A smile grew on her rosy lips as she slowly pursued him. And his cock started to stiffen. He shouldn't have asked her that.

She donned her shift, threw her legs over the side of the bed, grabbed the cloth, soap, and water from the basket, then headed for the screen before glancing over her shoulder. "Not at all. You have a very fine body."

It wasn't too long before they were dressed, her hair was up in a simple knot, and they'd nibbled on the cheese, bread, and berries she'd brought. He carried the basket as they made their way to the hall. It was time to mention servants. "It seems Roberts has been training to be a butler. What would you think about hiring him for the position?"

Madeline grinned. "I think that is an excellent idea. I will ask Thorton what more Roberts needs to learn. He'll have less than two weeks to finish his training."

"Finnigan says there is an under stable master at Stanwood House that might want to work for us."

She raised her brows. "You are going to poach a servant from my brother?"

Needing to touch her again, Harry wrapped his arms around Madeline. "I was planning to ask him first."

"In that case, I think it is a wonderful idea." She started to open the door. "I almost forgot. I need Finnigan."

"I'll get him." Harry kissed her one more time before going to fetch the groom. He hadn't thought it was possible, but he loved her more now than before. Two weeks was going to feel like two years. Dear God, the church. "Do you want to go to St. George's before going back?"

"Yes. The Season is well underway, and the appointment must be made as soon as possible."

What was the best way to do this? "I'll find you as you are walking back and pick you up."

Madeline graced him with a broad smile. "What an excellent idea."

He reached the stables and told her groom what they were going to do. Finnigan nodded as he began to hitch Harry's horses to his curricle, then Finnigan's eyes narrowed slightly. Had Harry forgotten something? "I wonder if you could ask Lady Madeline if she might want to ask if Miss Parker would like to work here."

Ah. Harry had wondered if the groom had an attraction to the maid. "I will mention it to her."

Finnigan nodded and handed him the keys to the stable. "Thank you. I'll go to her ladyship now."

Harry locked the gate and the stable doors after the groom had gone. He assumed there were other sets, but he'd have to ensure there were. Now, to go fetch his bride.

CHAPTER THIRTY-FOUR

Madeline was taking her time strolling toward Berkely Square when Harry drove up beside her and stopped. "My lady. May I offer you a ride?"

She had a hard time not laughing. "Why, yes, you may. What a kind offer."

Harry's eyes twinkled as he came around and lifted her into his carriage. "We have just enough time to go to the church, speak with the rector, and get back for dinner."

She prayed they would be able to have their wedding on the date they wanted. There had been a great many weddings lately. "We had better go quickly."

"I'll need someone to walk the horses." He glanced at her groom. "Would you mind accompanying us?"

"Be happy to." Finnigan hopped onto the seat in the back, and Harry started the horses.

About five minutes later, he stopped next to a side door leading into the church, and Finnigan jumped down and ran around to the heads of the pair while Harry lifted her down.

Madeline tucked her hand into the crook of his arm. They strode to the door and knocked before opening it and stepping into the transept. Two of the clergymen were in conversation, and one of them saw them enter. "May I help you?"

Harry bowed. "We would like to reserve the church at ten o'clock in thirteen days."

The other man frowned and shook his head. "I am sorry to disappoint you, but the mornings are completely booked for the next three weeks."

"If you have a special license, we can reserve a time for you in the afternoon," the other clergyman said.

She glanced at Harry. "We have never had an afternoon ceremony." Mornings were so much nicer, especially if the weather grew warm. "If we have a special license, we may be married wherever we wish, may we not?"

"You may," the first clergyman said slowly. "What are you thinking?"

"That the garden might be perfect. If it rained, we could move it into the drawing room." There was only one other question. "Do you have someone who could come to Worthington House in Berkeley Square and perform a service in thirteen days in the morning?"

The younger clergyman smiled. "I thought you looked familiar. I have performed the ceremony for, dare I say, all your immediate family members." She wished she had paid more attention to who was conducting the services. He bowed. "I will make myself available and send a prayer for good weather."

"Thank you so much. That is very kind of you." And if fate was on their side, she would have a garden wedding. It would be the first one in the family.

"Ah well, I would not want to break my run." He smiled. "I look forward to seeing you and your family then."

Harry held out his hand. "Harry Stern is my name. This is Lady Madeline Vivers. Thank you so much."

"Stern? Did I not perform the service for your sister and Lord Merton?"

Harry grinned. "You probably did. She was residing with Lord and Lady Worthington at the time she wed."

The vicar nodded. "I shall wish you both happy."

"If you excuse us," the older man said, "we need to settle a few matters."

They had interrupted them. "Oh, of course. We will see you in just under two weeks." Madeline turned and led them out the side door. "That went well."

Finnigan brought over the curricle, and Harry lifted her in. Now that she knew the pleasure they could have together, she would have liked to go back to their house.

"It did." He picked up the ribbons as Finnigan climbed into the back. "I think a garden wedding is a wonderful idea. I'm glad you thought of it."

The carriage started forward. "Eleanor considered it." It might have been better for her if she had been wed in the garden. "I would rather take the chance of rain and having to move inside than wait three weeks or marry in the afternoon."

"I agree." Harry feathered the corner on to Conduit Street. "Three weeks is much too long."

Once again, they were of the same mind. "Will we be able to take a wedding trip?"

His lips pressed together, as if he was considering her question. "I'd like to. In fact, I would like to take you to Paris. Let me see if it can be arranged."

"If not now, perhaps later." She would be willing to wait for a few months if need be.

Harry glanced over at her and grinned. "I am definitely going to find a way to have you all to myself for a while after our wedding."

That was what Madeline wanted as well.

He pulled up in front of Worthington House. In the meantime, they might as well sort out their servant situation. "Shall we walk across the square and speak to Charlie if he is at home?"

Harry glanced at his pocket watch. "We might have to wait until after dinner."

"I shall send a message to him asking if we can meet." It was all she could do not to kiss him. They needed to be together again soon.

The front door opened, and Harry escorted her into the house.

Thorton bowed. "The family is in the large drawing room."

"That must mean everyone is here." Perhaps Charlie would be present as well.

Harry wouldn't be at all surprised if she was right. Thorton opened the door and, as expected, both their families had assembled, including Augusta, Phinn, Walter, and Charlie.

Augusta hugged Madeline. "I am so happy for you. I must make it a point of attending more family parties."

Phinn wished them happy.

Charlie slapped Harry's back. "Welcome to the family. I'm sorry I wasn't there for the announcement."

This was as good a time as any to see about hiring his servant away from him. "I understand you have an under stable master who is knowledgeable about horses and carriages. I'd like to offer him a position with us."

Charlie's brows drew together. "I'd like to keep him, but I am also aware that he is ready to be in charge of his own stables." He nodded, as if to himself. "Yes, offer him the position. We can go over after dinner if you'd like."

"I would. We have a very short time to have everything ready."

Harry breathed a sigh of relief. He now had two of the senior positions filled. He'd have to find out what other positions they could fill from their relatives' staffs. Madeline was speaking to her sisters and writing in her pocketbook.

Worthington strolled up to him. "It appears as if most of

your staff positions will be filled this evening. This is not something we've had to deal with before. But when Thorton told Grace you required a complete staff, she sent missives to our sisters and Dotty. They all came with names of servants who would be appropriate for your needs."

"It's better to have servants you know you can trust," Stanwood said. "As a Member of Parliament, you cannot afford to have servants who gossip."

Harry hadn't thought about it in quite that way, but Stanwood was correct. "Thank you. Both of you. I don't want to empty out your staffs."

Worthington barked a laugh. "You need not be concerned. Because of the charity Charlotte and Dotty began, we have more than enough servants. They are trained in our houses before finding other positions."

Harry remembered something Merton had said. "You and Merton search for former soldiers for your staffs?"

"We do," Worthington said. "I've made a list of grooms and footman. I expect him to do the same."

"Thank you." Harry was a little overwhelmed but grateful. Like the rest of them, he had been raised with servants who had been with them for years. He'd known they would assist him and Madeline where they could, but he had not imagined, could not have imagined, the amount of aid they were prepared to provide.

Thorton announced dinner, and Madeline meandered over to Harry, still looking at her pocketbook. When she reached him, she took his arm, and they led the others into the dining room.

He held a chair for her. "Have we filled all of our positions yet?"

"We are still in need of a cook, but Jacque has been tasked with finding someone. He has extensive connections."

"When will they start working for us?" He took the chair next to hers.

"In about a week." Madeline accepted a glass of wine from a footman. "Our housekeeper is coming from Louisa's house. She is currently the second housekeeper. Their housekeeper was to have wed and moved to a different area of the country, but she broke the betrothal and will remain." Madeline took a sip of wine. "She and I will have to make a list of linens we will require. Roberts and I will discuss the china and silver." She took a deep breath. "I had never thought what it would be like to start from scratch."

Harry took a larger drink of wine than she had. He didn't normally have to consider the costs of items. His needs were limited. But china, silver, and linens were expensive. "We will manage."

Madeline smiled at him. "We shall. Just think: We will be able to select patterns we like and not be left with what prior generations had."

He was positive his mother had purchased new china and silverware after she and Papa wed. They'd been in almost the same circumstances. He believed it was the china they still used. She hadn't liked the stuff in the manor house when they'd moved in. "How does one go about purchasing tableware?"

"There are stores and warehouses just like there are for fabrics and furniture. Grace is making up a list. We will start in the morning. The furniture, at least, will have to be made, unless we find pieces we like from orders that have been canceled."

He was dumfounded. "How do you even know all of this?"

Her smile broadened. She hadn't been raised to expect to have to furnish a home. "By listening to the conversations of other ladies. We are not the only ones to require new housewares, or who wish to replace what one has."

He was glad she knew what to do. He was decidedly ignorant. Then it struck him that she'd said the servants would be in place a week before the wedding. That meant he only had one week with her. How the devil did the others manage it?

CHAPTER THIRTY-FIVE

The following morning, Madeline was reading while waiting for Harry to return from procuring the special license. After which, they planned to take their personal servants to their new house.

"My lady," Harper said as she entered the bedchamber, "a note came for you."

Madeline put down her book, took the missive from her maid, and broke the seal.

My dearest Madeline,
    Please attend me today as soon as you are able.
                    Your loving mother.

That was odd. Usually Mama came to Worthington House. Madeline hoped there was nothing wrong. Had she heard about her betrothal? She should have gone to see her mother before this but was still trying to find a way to tell Mama about her and Harry. "Harper, I must go out. I'll wear my blue walking dress, and please notify Roberts."

"Yes, my lady."

In less than a half hour she was changed and on her way to her mother's house on South Audley Street.

The door opened as she approached, and the butler bowed. "Her ladyship is waiting for you, my lady."

"Is she well?" Madeline wanted to be prepared if her mother was ill.

"To the best of my knowledge, her ladyship is in excellent health."

If nothing was wrong, why had Mama only asked Madeline to come and not Theo as well? It was about Harry. That was the only thing it could be. Madeline's heart rose to her throat. "Thank you."

She was ushered into her mother's parlor. "Good morning, Mama." Madeline smiled and gave her mother a kiss on the cheek, then took a seat on the chair next to the walnut burl, kidney-shaped desk behind which her mother sat. "I am surprised you did not want Theo to accompany me."

Her mother sanded a letter and pushed it aside. "I had a conversation with Lady Greenly." Madeline almost groaned. She had managed to forget about that woman. "I was rather surprised to discover you had visited a village with him. It is, apparently, time that I discuss your attachment to Mr. Stern."

If Mama was going to attempt to interfere, one would think she would have done so well before Madeline and Harry had become betrothed. Then again, her mother might not know about the betrothal. She had not mentioned it. The question was whether she was better served by not approaching the matter directly. Yet that seemed to be the coward's way out. She took a breath and raised one brow. "What of it?"

Her mother seemed to stiffen. "I believe you could find a much more suitable match."

"Like you did with Papa?" No one talked about why Mama had married Madeline's father when she had been in love with Richard, Viscount Wolverton, her current husband. Yet she had the feeling her mother's first marriage had a great deal to do with this push for her daughters to wed for advantage.

Her mother smiled, and she relaxed. "I am glad you understand."

Although she had expected the response, disappointment in her mother washed over Madeline. She was not going to give up Harry for some idea her mother had that a gentleman with more rank would be a better husband. "I understand that is what you would prefer. And I must tell you that I tried to do what you wanted. But I could not. I have decided to wed the man I love now rather than wait almost twenty years to do it."

A pained look briefly crossed her mother's face before she looked away. "I was very happy with your father."

Somehow, Madeline did not believe her. Not only that, but had she not heard her say she was going to marry Harry? "In that case, I am glad that you found love twice. I would rather not chance it."

"My dear, I am sure Mr. Stern is a nice young gentleman, but the only thing he can look forward to is a baronetcy. Even though Augusta married a younger son, it appears as if their son will be the next marquis."

It was not as if Harry was doing nothing while waiting for his father to die. "Is that all you think is important? Mr. Stern is extremely well-connected, and he is starting his career in politics. As you know, one must have a certain financial well-being before becoming a Member of Parliament. He might not be the wealthiest man in England, but he is in no way poor."

Mama's lips tightened. "As to that. One must have a good name and reputation to do well in politics. I would be devastated to learn he did not."

Madeline's jaw clenched. She could not believe her mother had just threatened Harry's career. She would have to nip this in the bud at once. Madeline rose. "That was not wise. I suggest you rid yourself of any thoughts you might have of attempting to ruin Mr. Stern. I remind you that his uncle is the Duke of Bristol and his brother-in-law the Marquis of Merton. Not to mention the many other connections he has. I have nothing more to say to you on the matter. I assume you will receive an invitation to our wedding. Good day."

She turned and walked out the door. Roberts stood as she descended the stairs and silently followed her out to the pavement. Madeline needed to speak with either her brother or Grace immediately. But what could they do? Madeline could not be the reason Harry's career ended before it began. Should she give him up?

She walked as swiftly as was proper to Worthington House, and Thorton opened the door.

Madeline handed him her bonnet and gloves. "Are either his lordship or her ladyship at home?"

He gave the hat and gloves to Roberts. "Her ladyship is in her parlor."

Thank heavens. "Thank you."

A worry line creased his forehead. "Should I bring a tea tray?"

"Yes, please." The conversation might need tea, or something stronger.

She strode down the corridor to Grace's study and knocked.

"Come."

When Madeline entered, her sister-in-law was frowning at a letter. She waited until Grace glanced up. "Madeline, what do you need?"

She took a seat in front of Grace's desk, then indicated the letter. "Is something wrong?"

"Nothing that a little common sense would not solve." She set the letter down. "Tell me what it is you want."

"Mama asked me to call on her." Madeline took a breath.

"The long and short of it is that she does not want me to wed Harry. She actually threatened to ruin his reputation."

Grace rubbed her temples. "Why does she do these things? First Augusta and now you."

"I have no idea." Madeline shook her head. "I cannot allow her to put her plan in place."

"*We* will not allow it." Grace gave her a reassuring smile. "The gentlemen are at their luncheon. I will send a message to Dotty, asking if she can join us."

Grace dashed off a note and tugged the tasseled bell-pull, but Thorton had just opened the door with a tea tray. "This must go to Merton House as quickly as possible. Wait for an answer. And send a footman to Rothwell House. I would like Louisa to attend me as well."

"Yes, my lady."

Grace poured Madeline a cup of tea and made one for herself. She took a sip. Grace was right; tea did help steady one's nerves. "What are you going to do?"

"As much as I hate taking strong action against her, she must be stopped. That means, at the very least, someone must speak to Richard. She cannot be allowed to destroy a man's life because she wants you to marry a gentleman with greater rank."

Madeline picked up a ginger biscuit, then put it down. She was not at all sure of her stomach at the moment. "You would think having one daughter as a duchess would be enough."

"I do not pretend to understand her." Grace cradled her cup.

"I have to confess that after she threatened Harry, I was not at all kind to her." Madeline drained her cup and poured another. "I told her she was not being wise and left."

Frowning, Grace picked up a lemon tartlet, bit into it, and swallowed. "Any schemes she has must be stopped before they are begun."

Madeline remembered an event from a few years earlier. "Do you remember when Dotty was pregnant with the twins and ill-humored?" Grace nodded. "I wonder if it could be her pregnancy. She is, after all, not a young woman any longer."

The corners of Grace's lips rose. "I do not know. You have given me an idea. It would be no trouble at all to put it around that she might be moody due to her pregnancy."

Instead of a note being delivered, Dotty entered the parlor and lowered herself onto the other chair in front of Grace's desk. "Your message seemed urgent."

Thorton brought in another pot of tea and Dotty poured a cup.

"Patience is being difficult," Grace said.

"She does not want me to marry Harry," Madeline said. "She threatened his reputation, then I threatened her."

Dotty glanced at her. "I must say, you are having a much more eventful morning than I am. Do you have any ideas as to how to deal with her?"

"One." Madeline looked at Grace, then her future sister-in-law. "We shall put it about that her pregnancy is adversely affecting her behavior."

"I believe someone should speak with Richard," Grace said.

Dotty appeared to consider the ideas. "Merton would be happy to speak with him. I suppose Matt must, though, as he is Madeline's guardian. I believe we should bring Louisa into this as well. If she agrees to support the notion that her mother is being adversely affected by her condition, that will carry more weight than anything we say. Harry is my brother. Naturally, I would take his side."

Grace nodded. "I had not thought about that, but you are right." She took out two pieces of paper and wrote missives. "I have already sent for Louisa. We might as well bring Charlotte into this as well."

Madeline would have liked to have had Eleanor and Alice with her, but Eleanor was on her honeymoon and Alice had volunteered to go with Mr. and Mrs. Winters on an excursion to the Tower. Alice was toying with the idea of becoming a governess if she could not find a gentleman to wed.

Madeline's stomach grumbled. So much for being concerned about it. "May we have luncheon while we discuss this with everyone?"

"Dotty?" Grace said.

"Yes indeed. I am famished."

Grace tugged the bell-pull. When Thorton arrived, she handed him the other note. "The same as before. And tell Cook we would like luncheon served when Louisa and Lady Kenilworth arrive."

He bowed. "Yes, my lady. At once."

When the door closed, Dotty let out a peal of laughter. "If that were my butler, he would have been muttering something under his breath."

Merton's butler was famous in the family for his relative informality. Matt always said one gets the butler one needs. Madeline wondered what Roberts would be like. But first came the house. They only had two weeks to prepare it.

Not ten minutes later, Thorton announced that the Duchess of Rothwell and the Marchioness of Kenilworth had arrived. Dotty, Grace, and Madeline joined them in the family dining room, where a flurry of hugs and kisses ensued, as well as the information that Louisa had been at Charlotte's house, several houses away from Worthington House.

Once they were seated, Louisa said, "Your missive sounded urgent."

"It's Mama." Madeline almost groaned.

"Good Lord, not again?" Her sister's tone showed her exasperation. "Does she never learn?"

Madeline stared at Louisa. "Rothwell's a duke. To what could she have objected?"

Louisa's brows furrowed for a moment. "Oh, I had forgotten you would have been too young to know what happened. She objected to his father, his decision not to pay his father's debts, and his lack of funds."

"No one is safe," Madeline muttered, and told them about Mama's latest antics and the possible solutions they had discussed. "I wish I knew why she became this way."

Louisa swallowed the bit of the chicken and vegetable soup she had taken. "It is because of Papa." She went on to explain that their mother had been enamored by him at first, but then had become unhappy when he was never home. "It is my belief her mother convinced her an advantageous marriage was better than one based on emotions." She drank some of the chilled white wine that had been served. "She refused to admit her marriage to him was unhappy and focused on the status she gained from being his wife."

But what about her current marriage? "Even after she wed Richard?"

Louisa nodded. "She has been deluding herself for years. At this point, she is convinced she had a wonderful first marriage."

Madeline wanted to throw something. "That was arranged."

Her sister gave her a sympathetic look. "Indeed."

"Now that you know the why, we need to stop her from making a muddle of things," Charlotte said. "Louisa, I think blaming anything she says against Harry on her pregnancy is an excellent idea. What do you think?"

Louisa nodded. "I agree. I can easily put it about that she is having a difficult time and is slightly irrational."

"The first thing we should do is have Matt and Merton speak with Richard and tell him what she is doing, or planning to do," Dotty said.

"Except that he never interferes with her," Louisa pointed out.

Dotty shrugged. "In that case, we inform him what we will do to counteract anything she says."

"No," Charlotte interjected. "Not what we will do, what we have already done. We must be ahead of her. We start at the Huntingdons' ball this evening."

Matt strolled in, followed by Merton, Kenilworth, Rothwell, and Harry. Matt kissed Grace on the cheek and said, "What is going on?"

This time, Madeline did groan. "It's Mama."

In no time at all, Madeline, with the help of her sisters, explained what had happened and how they were going to combat her mother's plan to ruin Harry. The gentlemen had grabbed chairs and shuffled everyone around so that they were sitting next to their wives, and Harry was next to her.

He had been listening closely to the scheme. "We knew something like this could happen." He glanced at her. "I am not particularly comfortable with blaming her behavior on her pregnancy. The condition does not generally make women irrational."

"It does not, generally," Dotty said. "However, I can attest that it can make one tired and cranky."

Louisa shook her head. "Harry, I understand your objections, but this is the easiest way to counter anything she tries to do to harm you, and not harm her in the long run."

He crossed his arms across his chest. "Very well. How do we proceed?"

"I will send a message to Grandmamma," Dotty said. "She has a great deal of standing."

Madeline knew of one other lady who had standing and influence with her mother. "Lady Bellamny." Her sisters nodded. "Grace, can you write to her asking if she will receive us this afternoon?"

"I will invite her to tea. In the meantime, we need not

wait until this evening to begin our campaign. There are morning visits to make."

"I'll send a message to Wolverton asking him to meet with me today." Matt glanced at Harry. "I'd like you as well as Merton to be there when I speak to him."

Madeline did not think it would do any good, but it was worth the attempt. "What will you say to him?"

"I'll suggest that if Patience does not abandon her plan, he take her home."

Yet she could still write letters. Madeline appreciated her brother trying to stop Mama, but this was really something the ladies must resolve.

Grace placed her serviette on the table. "If everyone is finished, I suggest we get on with it. Louisa, Dotty, and Charlotte, the three of you should go together. Madeline will come with me."

Harry stood as she did and kissed her cheek. "Good luck."

She searched his face. There was no sign of distress, but there was a great deal of determination. "To you as well. I am afraid we will not be able to go to our house today."

"There will be tomorrow, and we have the rest of our lives."

They did. She would make sure of it.

CHAPTER THIRTY-SIX

When everyone rose from the dining table, Theo and Mary ran quietly across the corridor to a parlor. Theo shut the door and leaned against it. "They are right. She must be stopped."

Brows puckered, Mary paced the floor. "I do not like to see the family torn in this way."

"No." At least Theo knew why her mother behaved the way she did. "I wonder if she would listen to us."

"Louisa did not even suggest speaking to her," Mary pointed out.

"That's true. Still, there must be something we can do." Heavier footsteps sounded outside the door. "Matt and the others are probably going to his study."

"There is no place to listen to the conversation there," Mary said.

"No. But he told everyone what he would tell Richard." Theo cast around for an idea. Something that would stop the family from being at odds. "Madeline mentioned Lady Bellamny. Our sisters cannot meet with her until later, but there is nothing stopping us from visiting her before she goes out."

Mary's lips flattened. "If Thorton allows us to go."

Theo straightened and turned to open the door. "There is only one way to know. We must ask him."

"Wait." Mary held up her hand. "We are allowed to go for walks as long as we take footmen. It is a pretty day, and Upper Brook Street is not that far away." She raised her brows. "Are you sure you would not rather leave it to the others?"

"No. If we can make her see sense, it will be better than the whisper campaign. Mama will eventually discover who started it. I am afraid it will cause a rift that will be hard to heal."

Mary nodded. "In that case, we must change our shoes and get our hats and gloves."

As Mary predicted, Thorton only made them take footmen for their walk. He even gave them money for ices on the way home.

Lady Bellamny was leaving her house as they arrived. "My lady." Theo curtseyed. "We have a problem, and you are the only one who can help us."

Mary nodded and curtseyed as well. "You are."

Her ladyship studied them through narrowed black eyes, then glanced at her coachman. "Walk them for a few minutes." Then she looked back at Theo and Mary. "Come along and tell me what is happening. I received a note from Grace not long ago." Lady Bellamny took them to a small parlor and ordered glasses of lemonade. "You may speak."

As Theo related what her mother was planning and what her sisters were going to do to counter her mother's scheme, her ladyship frowned.

"Pure foolishness on your mother's part. She should know better. Yet I agree with your sisters; she would not listen to them. She will, however, listen to me. Finish your lemonade and come along. I need a reason to insert myself into this pickle."

Theo and Mary did as they were told and followed her ladyship to the carriage. The footmen climbed onto the back of the coach.

"Very clever of Worthington to have footmen accompany you instead of maids. Let us hope your mother has not yet left for morning visits."

When they arrived, Mary's footman went to the door and knocked. When the butler opened it, he stood back. "Lady Bellamny, Lady Theo Vivers, and Lady Mary Carpenter to see Lady Wolverton."

Theo's mother's butler bowed. "Her ladyship is awaiting her carriage, but I will show you in."

"That was lucky," Mary whispered.

Lady Bellamny inclined her head. "It was. Now, let us see what we can do to remedy this situation."

As they were shown into Mama's parlor, she came forward. "Almeria, to what do I owe this pleasure?" It was not until her ladyship moved to the side that Mama noticed Theo and Mary. "What are you girls doing here? I do not recall making plans with you." Her brows drew together. "What is this about?"

"Patience, please sit," Lady Bellamny said. "This might take a while. Although I hope it will not." She took a seat next to Mama.

Theo and Mary sat on the small couch across from them.

Lady Bellamny nodded once toward Theo. She took a breath. "Mama, we need to speak with you about Madeline and Harry Stern. What you propose to do is not right. She should be allowed to wed who she wishes as long as he is eligible and suitable for her." Mama's jaw dropped. "Your behavior will cause problems for the entire family because none of us support your plan, and we will not let you destroy our family."

"Theo," Mama sputtered. "You are much too young to

understand what is going on. I am only looking out for your
sister's future good."

Theo stared at her mother. What tripe! She opened her
mouth, but Lady Bellamny stayed her.

"Patience, Theo might be young, but I am not. The only
way you could ruin Mr. Stern is by spreading lies and innu-
endos. That, my dear, would only harm you in the end, when
the rest of the family counters them and shows you for a
fraud. You would also leave yourself open to a suit for
slander." Mama's head shot back as if she had been slapped.
"I know you do not want that."

Tears welled in her eyes. "I only want what is best for
Madeline."

Theo straightened her shoulders. "No. You want what
happened to you. Madeline *will* wed Harry. Your choice is
to still have your daughters or to lose them. If you try to hurt
Harry, none of us will ever speak to you again. Mama, you
have gone too far."

"But she could be a duchess. Salforth was going to offer
for her." She choked on her tears.

As much as Theo wanted to hug and comfort her mother,
she could not. "She does not care about being a duchess.
Aside from that, you did not like Rothwell either. His marriage to Louisa has turned out very well." Theo decided not
to mention Augusta wanting to attend university. "We want
you to still be a part of the family, but you will not be if you
continue your scheme."

Lady Bellamny nodded. "Patience, Theo is correct. Give
this up before you make a horrible mistake."

Mama glanced at Theo. "You would not abandon me. I
am your mother."

Theo bit her lip. This was much harder than she had
thought it would be. "I would, we all would. You cannot call
yourself our mother when you try to harm us."

Mama took out her handkerchief and blew her nose. "I am only doing what other mothers have done."

Lady Bellamny gave Theo a look of long suffering, then turned to her mother. "Patience, I cannot and will not support you in this. That is all I have to say." Her ladyship rose. "We will leave you to consider your actions."

Theo and Mary followed Lady Bellamny out of the parlor and to the coach. "What do you think she will do?"

The footmen helped them into the carriage. Lady Bellamny smoothed her skirts. "I pray she will choose the correct course. We shall see."

Theo hoped so too.

Mary put her hand over Theo's. "You have done all you could."

She had. As Lady Bellamny said, they would just have to wait.

Early that afternoon, Richard strolled into Patience's parlor as she was trying to dry her eyes. Yet the tears kept coming.

"My love, what is it?" He was with her in a second, holding her and rubbing her back. "What's happened to put you in such a state?" He touched her stomach. "Is it the baby?"

"No. Theo came to visit me, and she brought Lady Bellamny and Mary." A loud sob escaped her. "I tried to convince Madeline not to wed Harry Stern, and I might have threatened his reputation in the process." Patience blew her nose again.

Richard raised a brow. "Might have?"

"Very well." She wrung the wet handkerchief. "I did. I simply want her to marry well. That is what every mother wants. But Theo said they would never forgive me if I did anything to harm Mr. Stern, and Almeria said she would not support me if I said anything against him."

Richard sat down beside her and held her. "I have just come from Worthington House, where I met with Worthington, Merton, and Mr. Stern. Mr. Stern had his financials ready to show me. He is quite capable of supporting Madeline."

Did no one understand? "It is not only financial support. It is her status in Polite Society."

"My darling, you know as well as I do that as the grandson of a duke, Mr. Stern has a great deal of status if he chooses to wield it. Even on his father's side, his bloodlines are impeccable." He cupped her cheeks. "My darling, I understand why you married Worthington's father. But my question to you is, if I would have come back in time, would you have married him or me?"

How could Richard ask such a thing? "You. Of course I would have married you. I love you now and I loved you then."

He captured her gaze. "Despite your parents wanting you to make what was a better match in their eyes?"

"Yes. Yes. How can you doubt it?" *Oh my dear God.* "I am doing what they would have done if you had returned."

He kissed her and held her closer. "You are. But it is not too late to repair the damage. Write to Madeline and wish her happy."

Patience nodded against his cravat.

"I will also suggest that whoever Theo wishes to wed, as long as he is suitable, you do not object. Your daughters seem to have a gift for choosing the right husbands for themselves. And Worthington makes very sure no ineligible gentlemen can have access to them."

Patience nodded again. "Matt is a very good brother."

"And guardian," Richard added. He pulled out a handkerchief. "Use this and dry your eyes. You have a letter to write and fences to mend."

She took the handkerchief and dabbed her eyes. "You are very wise at times."

He barked a laugh. "Thank you, my love. I do have my moments."

"I hope you are correct, and it is not too late." She rose from the sofa, went to the writing table, and pulled out a piece of pressed paper. "I will have this sent straightaway. Although she is probably making morning visits."

"In that case, she'll receive it when she arrives home."

My darling Madeline,
I trust you have made the right decision in agreeing to wed Mr. Stern. I wish you and he very happy.

Know that I will always love you,
Mama

She sanded the paper and sealed it. "Will you take this to go out?"

"It would be my pleasure."

He started to walk to the door.

"Richard, I think I would like to leave Town after the wedding. The air is better in the country."

He nodded. "I agree. The country air will do you good."

Madeline and the others arrived at Worthington House in time for tea. She had been surprised not to have seen her mother at some point during the afternoon.

"My lady." Thorton held a letter in his hand. "This came for you while you were gone, and Mr. Stern left a message saying he would join you for tea."

"Thank you, Thorton." She took the missive, opened it, and almost dropped it.

"Madeline, what is it?" Louisa asked.

"It is from Mama. She has wished Harry and me happy."

"Really?" Louisa took the note. "I wonder what changed her mind."

Charlotte read the letter over Louisa's shoulder. "This is wonderful news. I must say, I am relieved we do not have to speak poorly of her."

Madeline agreed. Whatever made her come around, she was happy about it. "I am as well. I do wonder how this happened."

Grace and Dotty turned from removing their hats and gloves. Grace put an arm around Madeline. "Let us not look a gift horse in the mouth."

"Indeed," Dotty said. "All's well that ends well."

Theo and Mary descended the stairs. "What is going on?"

Louisa waved the letter. "Mama has accepted Madeline and Harry's marriage."

The two girls exchanged a look and grinned.

"That is wonderful," Theo said.

"I am so very happy for you," Mary added. "Can we go to tea now? I am starving."

They dashed down the corridor toward the morning room as a knock came on the door.

"My ladies, Lady Bellamny."

Madeline was glad they would no longer need her to speak with her mother. "Lady Bellamny, how are you?"

"Quite well, my dear." She peered at Madeline. "And you?"

"Oh, yes. We had a problem, but it has resolved itself."

"Good news indeed." Her ladyship inclined her head. "Lady Theo and Lady Mary, I trust your day has been successful as well."

Theo and Mary curtseyed and grinned. "It is everything we hoped," Theo said. "You are joining us for tea?"

Lady Bellamny had a satisfied look on her face. "I am, my dears. I certainly am."

Madeline exchanged glances with the rest of her sisters and Dotty, then lifted one shoulder in a light shrug. Whatever was going on between her younger sisters and Lady Bellamny was for them to know.

"My ladies," Thorton said, "tea will be served directly."

Grace looped her arm with Lady Bellamny's as they strolled toward the morning room, and the rest of them followed. "We are so pleased you could join us. We must tell you that Madeline and Harry Stern are betrothed. We could not be happier for them. This evening they will make their first appearance together."

"At the Huntingdon's Ball?" Lady Bellamny asked.

"Yes. After that, as you know, it is our custom to curtail most of our other events until after the wedding."

"I have often thought that wise of you. There is no reason to run yourselves ragged. Alice will benefit from a bit of a pause as well."

Madeline wanted that to be true. She would have to ask Alice. There was no hardship in attending a few less events than they normally did. Someone grabbed her arm and she stopped. "Alice! You are back. How was your excursion to the Tower?"

She pulled a face. "I have decided I would not make a good governess. I will have to find another profession."

"Or perhaps you will meet a gentleman you wish to wed. That reminds me. Do you mind that we will not attend many events until Harry and I wed? I could ask Grace not to cancel so many of them."

They turned into the morning room. "Not at all. Going out every evening becomes tiresome. I also want to see if Normanby will go out of his way to see me."

"Very well. We shall continue as planned." They went to the places on the sofa where they normally sat.

"Will you take a wedding trip?" Alice asked.

"We have not yet decided." Neither Madeline nor Harry

were sure they should leave Alice alone, as it were. Although with the rest of their family around, she would hardly be without company.

Just then, her brothers, brothers-in-law, and Harry joined them. They bowed to Lady Bellamny and scattered around the room to sit next to their wives.

Harry sat on the other side of Madeline. "You look happy."

She handed him the message from her mother. "You will be too."

After reading it, Harry closed his eyes and shook his head. "That's it? It's over? What happened?"

"Yes, yes, and I have no earthly idea." She slipped her hand in his. "We have decided to let sleeping dogs lie."

He glanced up. "Speaking of dogs." Posy made a direct line to him and put her head on his lap. "Yes, girl. I know you need to be stroked."

Madeline petted the Dane as well. "Were you able to purchase the license?"

"Yes. Another task accomplished. We are one step closer to being married."

CHAPTER THIRTY-SEVEN

Harry and his family had remained for dinner. Merton and Dotty returned home to change, but Thorton had arranged for Harry's valet to bring over his evening kit, and he was now dressing for the ball. He had never felt such a sense of relief in his entire life. Not even when he'd been accepted as a barrister or won the election for MP. He needed Madeline in his life as much as he needed to breathe. And this evening he would finally be able to show every gentleman in the *ton*, especially Salforth, that she was his, and every dance was his.

He finished the last lowering of his chin on his cravat.

"Excellent, sir. Excellent. A masterpiece, if you do not mind me saying so."

"Not at all." He was dressed in a black jacket and trousers this evening. His waistcoat was red, embroidered with silver-blue and emerald threads. "What do you think? The emerald tiepin or the sapphire?"

Burkham studied Harry's attire as if he was taking a fresh look at it. "A safe choice would be the sapphire, but I think tonight deserves the emerald."

"The emerald it is."

His valet fetched it from his jewelry box and affixed the pin to his cravat, then assisted Harry with his jacket.

The garment was snug but not tight. He glanced at the toilet table. "Damn it all! I forgot to give Madeline the ring, earrings, and necklace. It's probably too late now."

Burkham's jaw dropped for a brief moment. "This is all my fault. I should have reminded you, sir."

"Nonsense. I was the one who should have remembered. She is my betrothed. Drat."

His valet grabbed the box from the table and headed for the door. "Allow me to ascertain if it is truly too late for her to wear them."

Curious as to what Burkham would do, Harry followed the man out the door to the family corridor and a short way down it. His valet knocked on a door he could only assume was Madeline's. It opened. "Mrs. Harper, a dreadful oversight has been made. I completely forgot to inform Mr. Stern the jewelry for Lady Madeline had arrived." Burkham opened the box. "Will what she is wearing be suitable with these?"

"These" were a lapis and diamond ring, earring, and necklace set.

Madeline's lady's maid took the box. "They will be perfect. She is wearing yellow this evening." She turned toward the room and turned back again. "Is the ring in the way of a betrothal ring?"

Burkham's face fell. "I fear I do not know. I will ask Mr. Stern."

"Very well. You should take it in the event he wishes to present it to her himself."

"That is a very good idea, Mrs. Harper. I will do just that."

Harry rushed back to the bedchamber he'd been given and waited until his valet entered the room.

"Sir, is the ring the betrothal ring?"

That was a very good question. One for which Harry did not have an answer. He wanted Madeline to choose her own ring from the family collection. "Give it to me and I will allow her ladyship to decide."

"Very good, sir." He handed the ring to Harry and looked greatly relieved to have done so.

Who would have thought the question of jewelry would be so complicated? But Harry had a feeling Madeline would make it easy again. He glanced at the clock over the fireplace. "I must go. I cannot be late."

His valet nodded as Harry strolled out the door to the landing between the corridors to wait for his beloved. He knew enough of ladies to understand that a change in jewelry might necessitate a change in other ornaments.

He was surprised she arrived at the same time he did, wearing the jewelry. "Do you like them?"

She threw her arms around his neck, careful not to squash his cravat, and kissed him. "I do. Very much. They are old?"

"Yes, but don't ask me how old. I have no idea. Dotty might know."

She took his hand in hers. "Only because I am a curious person, I will ask her at some point."

"Wait a moment." He disengaged his hand and pulled out the ring. "This came with the set. Would you like it for a betrothal ring, or would you like to look over the family collection?"

She threw back her head, laughed, and held out her hand. "I love this ring. If I would have had one made, it would look like this one."

Mindful not to kneel, he took her left hand and slid it onto her finger. "My beloved, I would be honored if you would wear my ring."

"Oh, Harry." Her eyes misted, and even though he knew it was happy misting, he couldn't bear it if she cried.

"Madeline, my love. Let us join our families." He placed her hand on his arm. Twelve days. He willed the time to fly by. Especially the last week, when he wouldn't be able to be with her.

The ball was all he wanted it to be. Although his mother and possibly his father would have been disappointed in him for what they would see as pettiness in taking pleasure in Madeline standing up only with him. He and Madeline danced the first set. Then Harry kept Madeline's hand proprietarily on his arm. The next set was a waltz.

Bury was the first gentleman to approach her. "My lady, will you allow me this set?"

Madeline cut Harry a look. "Oh dear, I am sorry to disappoint you, but Mr. Stern has all my dances now. We are betrothed."

"Betrothed?" Bury's jaw dropped for a second. "Wonderful. That is wonderful. Please accept my condolences." He inclined his head. "Stern."

It was all Madeline could do not to break out into whoops. She covered her mouth with her hand while she struggled to get herself under control. She watched as he led Alice out. "He really does have a sense of humor."

Harry's lips were twitching as if he was struggling not to laugh out loud. "I have to say, that was what I would have expected from him in university."

Salforth strolled up to them and bowed to Madeline. "My lady, would you grant me a dance?"

Madeline wondered if she should feel sorry for him. Her mother had said he was planning to make an offer, but she was as certain as she could be that he did not love her. "I am sorry, your grace." She turned to Harry, then back to Salforth. "My betrothed has claimed all my sets this evening."

The duke stared at Harry as if he could not believe what she had said. "Betrothed?"

Harry inclined his head. "Indeed. Lady Madeline has made me the happiest of men."

Suddenly Salforth smiled. "In that case, I wish you very happy. Both of you."

How strange. She thought he would be at least a little upset. "That was unexpected."

Harry motioned in the direction of Eloisa Rutherford, who was standing with her family. "Perhaps he too was feeling pressured to wed where his mother wished."

Madeline had never considered that, but perhaps Harry was correct. She knew Eloisa felt something for the duke. "I hope he finds the wife who is right for him."

"As do I, my love."

He led her out for the set, and it amazed her that, after everything they had done, it was the same as it had always been. She was at home with him. "It was waltzing."

"What was waltzing?" he asked as they twirled.

Now she knew, and she reveled in that knowledge. "I always felt as if I belonged in your arms. I simply refused to acknowledge what I was feeling."

"Your mother was putting a great deal of pressure on you. Not directly, of course. I believe she knew that would set your back up against her. Nevertheless, it was there."

"It was. I spent the past several weeks wanting you and wanting to please her." Madeline gazed up at his emerald eyes. "I tried to do as she wished, but I love you."

"I was so afraid she would sway you." It wasn't until now that he understood how fearful he'd been.

"Harry, my love, as much as I tried, I had to follow my heart. It was the only thing I could do."

"Thank God." He pulled her closer as they twirled again. "I will never do anything to make you regret choosing me."

Madeline blinked away her tears of joy. She might never understand what made her mother change her mind, and it did not matter. She was just thankful she had.

* * *

The next morning, she glanced out the window to make sure it was not raining and made her ablutions. As usual, her maid came in with toast and hot chocolate. Today she and Harry would accomplish what yesterday they had not. "I must go to Madame Lisette's as soon as breakfast is finished. After that I want to take you and Roberts to the new house. Does that fit with your schedule?"

"Yes, my lady. I shall make myself ready." Harper fixed Madeline's hat on her head. "Will Mr. Stern's man come as well?"

"I believe so. I will ask him." She left her room and started down the stairs to the hall.

Harry was already waiting. He ascended the stairs and they met halfway. He held her hand as they descended. "Good morning."

"Good morning to you." They reached the hall, and she donned her gloves. "I have a fitting this morning; then I would like to take our personal servants to our house."

"I've already advised Burkham. When do you wish to show the house to the rest of the staff we have acquired?"

A footman opened the door, and they strolled to the pavement. "As soon as possible. I will have to meet with all of them first and formally hire them. Matt has employment contracts for each position that I will use."

Harry glanced around. "Where is Alice?"

"That is a good question. Perhaps she decided not to ride this morning." Alice might have decided to give them time alone.

Harry helped her mount Rose, and as soon as he was on Willy, they trotted toward the Park. They were preparing to leave when she spotted Alice, Henrietta, Dorie, and Georgie galloping to the Serpentine. Madeline was glad her sister was not alone. They should have considered what to do if they wed one by one.

"We should go." Harry turned Willy around and Rose followed.

"We are going to have a busy two weeks."

"Eleven days," he countered.

Madeline couldn't hide her grin. "Yes. Eleven days."

The days flew by like birds migrating south. They had visited warehouses, met with the decorator and a gardener. Soon their house was starting to look like a home. It had been a pleasant surprise that they had been able to make time to make love until the week before the wedding, when they had no time alone at all. Generally, the staff took different days as their half days, but Madeline decided to surprise Harry, and two days before the wedding, she gave everyone the same half day off.

They met in the morning room, and he pulled her into his arms and kissed her. "This is going to be the longest two days of my life."

"Maybe not. I have a surprise for you." She led him by the hand to their bedroom. "I gave the staff a half day off."

"Did you?" Passion, love, and lust warred in his green eyes.

"I did. What do you think we can do, being all alone as we are?" Madeline turned, and she was in his arms again, and in less time than she thought was possible, her bodice sagged and he was toeing off his shoes.

"Oh, I believe we can think of several things to occupy our time." He moved her toward the bed.

Madeline shrugged out of her gown, petticoat, chemise, and stays. "I was hoping you would say that."

She woke when the clock struck two thirty to find him propped up on his arm, gazing down at her. "Have you been awake long?"

"Not really. I just wanted to watch you while you slept." He twisted himself to take something from the bedside table. "This message came while you were sleeping. Eleanor and Montagu have returned."

"That is wonderful. When are we all getting together?"

"In about a half an hour."

Madeline bolted from the bed. "And you let me sleep?"

"Harper and Burkham are here to ensure we are on time."

Heat filled Madeline's face. "Oh, dear."

Harry stood. "We are betrothed and almost married. Did you think they didn't know what we have been doing?"

"I suppose I should have realized Harper did when I returned so often with my hair dressed differently than when I went out."

"They've been bringing our clothing and other items over so that all will be ready." He pulled on his shirt, trousers, and shoes. "I'll use my dressing room."

As much as Madeline was still embarrassed, she tugged the bell-pull, and seconds later Harper entered the room.

"We'll have you dressed in no time, my lady."

Harper was as good as her word. Madeline was ready to leave shortly before three.

When they arrived at Worthington House, they found not only Eleanor and her husband but Sir Henry and Lady Stern and the Duchess of Bristol. Harry shot her a rueful look. Next time he would know to wake her up earlier.

CHAPTER THIRTY-EIGHT

The day of Madeline's wedding to Harry dawned bright and sunny. She sent up a prayer of thanks for the weather. Much brighter than it usually was when she awoke. Rolling over, she was shocked that the clock said it was already eight o'clock. She never slept so late. On the other hand, with Harry's family—even his uncle, the Duke of Bristol had stopped by for a few minutes—and hers helping set up the garden, then gathering for dinner, yesterday had been extremely busy. Remembering the way the duchess sat on a chair and attempted to direct everyone made Madeline smile. She covered her mouth as she yawned and almost talked herself into going back to sleep when the door to her dressing room opened.

"My lady, you must rise and dress. Breakfast is being served," Harper said as she bustled around the room, laying out garments.

Madeline hurried to the washbasin, made her ablutions, and threw on the chemise hanging over the screen. Harper helped her with the stays, petticoat, and day dress before fixing her hair in a low knot.

Not bothering with stockings, Madeline shoved her feet into a pair of slippers and hurried downstairs. There had been so many large gatherings at breakfast lately, the table seemed strangely empty. "Good morning."

Grace and Alice returned Madeline's greeting. Mary and Theo mumbled around their food; Matt inclined his head. Her nephew and niece swallowed at the same time and returned Madeline's greeting. A pot of tea and a rack of toast was set before her. It was not until then that it struck her this would be the last morning she would break her fast with everyone at the table unless she and Harry visited for breakfast. She finally understood exactly what Eleanor had felt. And what would it be like for Alice to be all alone for the rest of the Season? Perhaps she and Harry should remain in Town to help her sister.

A footman came around. "Shirred eggs, my lady?"

"Yes, please." She also selected ham and some strawberries. "The weather appears to be perfect for the wedding."

Grace set down her cup. "It does. I have been told it will hold until at least tomorrow." Her lips flattened. "I received a note from Richard. Patience is not feeling well. She is insisting she will attend the ceremony, but he is equally determined to take her to the country directly afterward."

"I hope it is nothing serious." At least she wanted to be here for the wedding.

"I do as well." Grace nodded. "It is likely that she has fagged herself to death with everything going on this Season."

"She has been going around a great deal." More than Madeline had seen her mother do in a long time. "I will wish her well when she arrives."

Grace glanced at the fireplace. "You must hurry."

Madeline glanced at the clock. It was almost nine. Where was the time going? Thank goodness her dresser had insisted she wash her hair yesterday. There would not have been time for it today. She hurried through her breakfast and rose. "I will see you all later."

By the time she returned upstairs, Harper had a bath ready. "I should have awoken earlier."

"You needed your sleep. It wouldn't do to have dark circles under your eyes on your wedding day."

"You have a point. I am well-rested." Although Madeline wanted to, she did not linger in the fragrant water. Her maid handed her a towel that had been warmed. A few minutes later, she was seated at her toilet table having her hair arranged. Dotty had sent over sapphire-tipped hairpins as something new.

A knock came on the door, and Grace, Alice, Eleanor, and Elizabeth entered.

"It is time to begin the formalities," Grace said. "You have something new. Now it is time for something old."

Augusta rushed into the room. "Sorry I am late." She held out a satin bag. "As you might have guessed. This is something old. I found them during our travels."

Madeline took the pouch, opened it, and removed two gold bracelets studded with lapis stones. "They are beautiful! Where did you find them?"

"In Spain. They really do the most beautiful goldwork. The bracelets date back to the sixteenth century."

Tears sprang to Madeline's eyes, but she blinked them back.

Alice held out a box covered in velvet. "This is something blue."

Madeline opened it to find a single sapphire pendant hung on a gold chain and the earrings to match. "How lovely, but how . . ."

"They are from Grace and me," Alice responded.

Elizabeth held out a handkerchief. "This has blue flowers. I made this myself. I think I am improving."

Madeline took it, making a point to inspect the work. "You *have* improved. Thank you so much."

Eleanor held out a watch fashioned into a bracelet. "And

this is borrowed. I need it back straight after the service. I shall be lost without it."

Madeline laughed. "I know you would be. Thank you so much for offering it."

A sharp knock sounded on the door, and Matt said, "Madeline, it is time to go. Harry is waiting."

"I am coming." Thank goodness it was only downstairs.

Louisa opened the door and entered. "You cannot forget your headdress."

Because Madeline was marrying in the garden, she had not given it any thought at all. She stood still as her sister placed a ring of flowers on her hair, then turned her to look in the mirror.

"Oh! It is beautiful."

Louisa smiled. "Charlotte and I racked our brains trying to come up with something that would fit the day."

"Now," Matt said sternly. "We must all go."

"Yes, sir." She took his arm as the others descended ahead of them.

"I wish I would have thought of this," he said. "I was as nervous as a cat waiting for Grace."

"Perhaps it will become a tradition in our families." This had to be much easier than shepherding all the children to church and back.

"We shall see."

They strolled through the house, through the morning room, and out the door. In front of an arch that had been erected and decorated with flowers stood Harry, looking more handsome than he ever had before. His eyes lit as he glanced her way.

Harry was wondering what was taking Madeline so long when his brother-in-law nudged him. "She's here."

He couldn't believe how much more beautiful she seemed

this morning. The sun glinted off her hair as she approached. "She is exquisite."

Merton chuckled. "We all seem to say the same thing when we see our brides."

Her turquoise gown floated around her and hugged her breasts. He'd never seen that color gown before.

She and Worthington stopped before the rector, and Harry took his place next to her. He'd seen enough weddings to know he had to wait until Worthington released her.

Finally, the clergyman said, "Who gives this woman to this man?"

"I do." Worthington placed her hand in Harry's. "Take care of her."

With his life, Harry vowed. When Madeline faced him, she had a smile on her lips that threatened to turn him into porridge, and everything went straight out of his head. Thankfully, all he had to do was repeat the vows. The strength in her voice when she said hers gladdened him, and he was able to do the same. Finally, they were pronounced man and wife, and a cheer went up from their families. Even the dogs joined in.

Madeline laughed. "I am so happy we had our wedding here."

He put his arm around her waist. "I am too. This is perfect. The noise, the children, and the dogs. Perfect."

They walked up the aisle formed by the chairs and received everyone's greetings. There was still the wedding breakfast to get through, but they wouldn't remain long. He and Montagu had come up with the perfect plan for the honeymoon.

Shortly after they cut the cake, Harry drew Madeline aside. "As you know, we have not made any definite honeymoon plans. Montagu thought you and Eleanor would like to remain close to Town in the event Alice needs you or weds.

He has a place a few hours away near the sea in Kent. Would you like to spend time there with them?"

Heedless of the other guests, she threw her arms around his neck. "I love that idea. It is the perfect solution."

"We'll take two vehicles. My uncle gave us a traveling coach as a wedding gift."

"How thoughtful of him." She sounded shocked.

"He has his moments." He kissed her lightly. "Shall we go? We'll spend the night at our house and head to Kent in the morning."

Madeline smiled broadly. "Our house. How nice that sounds."

Epilogue

Stern Manor, Mid-February 1822

Harry's butler, Roberts, knocked on the door to his study, opened it, and bowed. "They have arrived, sir."

That was early. Harry hadn't expected them for another two or three days. "I'll go out now. Tell her ladyship."

"Yes, sir."

He donned the loose jacket he wore in the country and strode to the front door to welcome his in-laws.

Grace, Louisa, and Augusta smiled as he entered the hall.

"Harry." Grace held out her hands and took his. "Your mother and father are a few minutes behind us. Rothwell and Phinn have come to lend their support as well." She unpinned her hat and handed it to Roberts. "Now, where is Madeline and how is she doing?"

"I am doing very well." Madeline entered the hall from the opposite corridor and went straight to Grace and hugged her. "We received a letter from Eleanor telling us how you routed the doctor. You will not have to worry about that here. We have an excellent midwife who the doctor concedes is more experienced at birthing babies than he is."

Holding her at arm's length, Grace looked at Madeline. "You look well."

She looked as if she was going to go into labor at any second.

"Thank you. I was advised to remain active but not to tire myself. I believe that has helped to make me feel better." She touched her hand to her stomach. "He or she is quite active, but fortunately, not at night."

"I wish Alexandria had been so considerate," Louisa said as she hugged Madeline as well.

"Phinn swears Anthony kept him up kicking all night, but I did not feel a thing."

"It was true." Phinn strolled into the hall holding their son, who was starting to fuss. "I think he wants his mama."

Augusta glanced at Madeline. "Is there—"

"Yes, of course. Roberts will show you to your chambers. You can join us in the morning room when you have finished."

The ladies followed him up the stairs. Once they had turned the corner corridor, Madeline placed her hand on her back and closed her eyes.

Harry wondered if he should be concerned about that. "Does your back hurt?"

"A little." She grimaced. "It started this morning, and no matter what position I am in, the pain will not go away."

If the midwife was not scheduled to examine Madeline today, he'd call for her. "Is Mrs. Heatherfield coming today?"

"She is. I expect her in about an hour."

"Good. She'll be able to tell us how to ease the pain."

Madeline leaned against him and sighed. "I know I am not due for another week, and that first babies are often late, but I do wish it would come earlier."

"I do as well." He slipped his arm around her waist and led her to the morning room. "I know you don't like to hear it, but for me, will you sit for a while?"

"Sitting makes it worse."

"Then just lean against me." He rubbed her back, and

they stood together as bags and trunks were carried in along with an odd-looking chair.

"The birthing chair," Madeline said, as if she could read his mind.

"Ah. I've heard about it."

They were still standing there when Grace came down the stairs and gave Madeline a narrow-eyed look. "Is your back hurting?"

She looked at her sister-in-law with surprise. "Yes. How did you know?"

"An experienced guess." Grace moved behind Madeline. "When did it start?"

"Early this morning." She frowned. "Why?"

"Is it your lower back, and do the pains become more intense at times?"

"Yes, and yes." Madeline sounded irritated. "Why?"

"I want your midwife to confirm my opinion, but, my dear, I believe you are experiencing back labor."

Harry closed his eyes and sent a prayer it had arrived early.

"But why should I be any different from everyone else?" He held her closer.

Grace smiled gently. "You are not different. Patience once told me that she had back labor with Theo. If I am correct, you have been in labor for several hours now." She glanced at Harry. "Perhaps it is time to call the midwife."

"I'll go, sir, my lady," one of their newer footmen said as he ran out of the house, only to come straight back. "She's here. The midwife."

"Excellent timing," Grace said.

Mrs. Heatherfield strode through the door. "What is this I heard about you being in labor, my lady?"

Madeline indicated Grace. "My sister thinks I am having back labor."

The midwife gave a no-nonsense nod. "Intense pains in

the lower back that increase slightly every once in a while, and it's occurring more frequently?"

"Yes." Madeline's lips pressed together.

"Your sister is correct." She looked around the hall, which seemed to be filling with people. "Can one of you take my bag up to the birthing room?" A maid took the bag. "Her ladyship will also need small portions of food and drink."

"I'll tell Cook," Roberts said.

Mrs. Heatherfield glanced at Madeline. "Sitting will not help you because it causes the baby's head to press against your spine. The best thing you can do is walk and lean against a wall or"—she grinned—"your husband."

Mama appeared at the open door as Louisa and Augusta descended the stairs. "Well, it seems I arrived just in time."

"The maid rushing past us said Madeline is in labor?" Louisa said.

"Back labor," Grace confirmed. "We all need to be ready."

"Well said, my lady," the midwife concurred. "We'll have a better idea after I examine her."

Madeline let out a loud groan, and her gown became damp.

"It seems this baby is ready to be born," Mrs. Heatherfield said. "My lady, I suggest we remove to the area of your chambers."

"So much for tea," Madeline joked as Harry supported her up the stairs.

"I'm sure you can have a few sips." He'd read all he could about labor and delivery, but there was nothing about this situation. Consequently, he felt rather helpless.

After the examination, Mrs. Heatherfield glanced up. "The babe is coming."

Harry got Madeline into the chair just as she let out a loud groan. "Hold on to me, sweetheart." Even though he knew what to expect, when she squeezed his hand, he was surprised she didn't break it.

"Push, my lady," the midwife said. "We're almost there."

Madeline took a breath and gritted her teeth. Her stomach moved as she bore down.

"Perfect." Mrs. Heatherfield smiled as she held up the baby. "You have a fine little girl."

Tears pricked Harry's eyes as Grace took the babe and cleaned her. They had a daughter. He waited until the after-birth was pronounced whole before he gave into relief. Madeline and his daughter were alive and well.

"I suppose someone had better tell Papa and the others."

"I'll do it," Augusta said.

"Wait until we learn the name," Grace said.

Madeline changed into a clean nightgown, and Harry helped her into bed before giving her their daughter. The baby started to root, and Grace showed Madeline how to nurse the child.

Once they were settled, he glanced at his wife. "Shall I tell them or will you?"

"You may."

He turned to the others in the room. "She is Nicol Olivia Isabell."

"That is lovely." Louisa blinked rapidly.

Madeline smiled. "Thank you." She looked up at Grace. "I am very glad you arrived in time."

"We are as well."

AUTHOR'S NOTES

The 1869 Debtors Act finally brought an end to debtors' prisons in the UK.

In the early 1830s, as Parliament became more preoccupied generally with the exploitation of child labor, the Chimney Sweeps Act was passed in 1834, outlawing the apprenticing of any child below the age of ten. Furthermore, no child was to be actually engaged in cleaning chimneys under the age of fourteen.

The Society for the Protection of Cruelty to Children (later the NSPCC) was at the forefront of improvements to child protection in late-nineteenth-century England. It played a key role in the campaign for legislation known as the Children's Charter—more formally, the 1889 Prevention of Cruelty to, and Protection of, Children Act.

It was not until 1870 that most rights of married women were codified in the Married Women's Property Act. It was amended in 1882 to give married women all the rights of single women.

Members of the House of Commons and eligible voters had to meet certain financial requirements, as well as be male and a member of the Church of England.

The death of King George III triggered a parliamentary election. However, it was rare that the members would change because of the many rotten boroughs, and once an MP was elected they normally remained until they choose to leave office.

I do hope you loved Madeline and Harry's story. If you'd like to know more about my books, please visit www.ellaquinnauthor.com. You will find all my social media links and my newsletter sign-up.

Ella

Visit our website at
KensingtonBooks.com
to sign up for our newsletters, read
more from your favorite authors, see
books by series, view reading group
guides, and more!

Become a Part of Our
Between the Chapters Book Club
Community and Join the Conversation

Betweenthechapters.net

Submit your book review for a chance to win exclusive
Between the Chapters swag you can't get anywhere else!
https://www.kensingtonbooks.com/pages/review/